Also by T. J. MacGregor

From Pinnacle Books

KILL TIME

T. J. MacGregor

PINNACLE BOOKS
Kensington Publishing Corp.
www.kensingtonbooks.com

PINNACLE BOOKS are published by

Kensington Publishing Corp.
850 Third Avenue
New York, NY 10022

All Kensington titles, imprints, and distributed lines are available at special quantity discounts for bulk purchases for sales promotions, premiums, fund-raising, educational, or institutional use. Special book excerpts or customized printings can also be created to fit specific needs. For details, write or phone the office of the Kensington special sales manager: Kensington Publishing Corp., 850 Third Avenue, New York, NY 10022, attn: Special Sales Department; phone 1-800-221-2647.

ISBN-13: 978-0-7860-1832-1
ISBN-10: 0-7860-1832-1

First printing: October 2007

10 9 8 7 6 5 4 3 2 1

Printed in the United States of America

This one is for Kate Duffy,
the best editor in this time
—or in any other

ACKNOWLEDGMENTS

Rob and Megan are my anchors, my first readers, the ones who make everything possible. So thanks, you two, for always being there for me.

I'd also like to thank Cheryl Kravetz; Nancy and Joe McMoneagle for creating such magic at the Old Fenimore Inn; Julie Thacker Scully, for reading the manuscript when it mattered; and Nancy Pickard, the rarest of friends, who has listened, advised, believed, been there.

Nora McKee

Blue River, Massachusetts
Friday, October 27

It may be said with a degree of assurance
that not everything that meets the eye is as it
appears.
—Rod Serling

1

Her marriage had begun on the rebound and now it would end over a Caesar salad. It wasn't how Nora McKee had envisioned her life five years ago when she and Jake had stood barefoot on Marconi Beach and traded vows and rings. But there you had it.

She pushed her way through the lunch crowd of tourists that spread through downtown Blue River like some sort of colorful, toxic spill. They were everywhere, these tourists, as ubiquitous as gods. They bolstered the local coffers and the town probably would die without them. But they were in her way, flooding the sidewalk and side streets, illegally parking wherever there was space, their numbers so great that the good tables at the Lighthouse Pub would be gone before she arrived. And it wasn't even noon yet.

Maybe that was just as well. She could forgo lunch with Jake altogether and just drive home, move her stuff out of the apartment, and leave him a note. *I'm outta here*. An appealing possibility, but that was his MO, not hers.

Quite often during their marriage, he had accused her of being too confrontational, too blunt, too in-your-face. But when she countered that he was duplicitous, deceptive, and avoided any discussion about feelings, he invariably stormed out of the room. So there was something very right about a restaurant as the punctuation at the end of their marriage, a public place where neither of them was likely to shout or to leave in a huff of self-righteousness.

She squeezed the bridge of her nose and struggled to shake off the feeling that she stood at the edge of some wide, steep abyss from which she would be required to leap, with her eyes shut, acting on nothing more than faith that she would land safely at the bottom. A Carlos Castaneda moment. Sure. Like she had whatever that took.

What does your life lack?

Thirty minutes ago, she had assigned this topic as an essay to her senior psych class. The lack, she had told them, couldn't be a material thing like money, a new car, the dream job, the dean's list. The lack had to be emotional, even spiritual. The irony was that her initial personal response to this question was material. *My life lacks tenure, health insurance, better pay*. But her bottom-line response, the deeper issue, the only one that counted, was that for twenty-three years, her life had lacked *closure*. And today she would begin to reverse that pattern by telling Jake she intended to file for divorce.

They didn't have kids or own joint property, just two cars and personal belongings. Divide the goods, one or the other would file, and that would be it.

Nora picked up her pace. The light breeze coming in off the ocean blew strands of her black hair across her eyes. It had an autumn bite to it, this breeze. She buttoned up her blazer and dug her hands in the pockets, glad she'd worn it and slacks. She wondered if, forevermore, she would associate these clothes with the end of her marriage. Wondered if, when she was eighty, she would conjure up these mental snapshots of herself moving through the crowd in a brown and black speckled wool jacket, a soft pumpkin-colored blouse, in dark slacks, her purse slung over her shoulder, lapis lazuli earrings swinging at the side of her face like miniature pendulums. Would she see it all as a bird's-eye view, the Lighthouse Pub at the end of the block, the lighthouse itself rising in the distance, a monolith of simpler times?

Jake had suggested the pub for lunch. Yet, he rarely suggested lunch away from campus and she didn't have any idea why he'd done so today. Maybe *he* intended to tell *her* that he wanted a divorce. She could almost see it, Jake leaning across the table, his handsome face skewed with his earnest intentions. *I think we both would be happier if we separated, Nora.*

That she could be so lucky.

"Hey, lady, what an amazing body you've got," said a husky voice behind her. Jake trotted up alongside her and hooked his arm through hers, grinning like a two-year-old who thought he'd done something clever. He bussed her on the cheek.

As if the last several months of problems hadn't happened. Jake, the great pretender. "I thought you'd be in the restaurant already," she said.

"Couldn't find a parking spot. I had to park along the river. Looks like Autumn Fest has begun already." He referred to a tradition that had begun in the fall of 1695, a celebration of a newly enacted law that made witch trials illegal. It had grown out of the execution that winter of several people accused of witchcraft, the darkest period of Blue River's past, an era about which she taught in her advanced psych courses. The festival drew tourists from all over the Northeast.

"People have been arriving all week," she pointed out.

"They ought to give residents one side of every street for parking. And herd tourists into the municipal lots. And why didn't the college just cancel classes yesterday for the rest of the week? I had more absentees today than I've had on any single day this year."

"Yeah, me, too."

She taught two classes on Wednesdays and Fridays, an introductory psych course for freshmen and a course on Jungian theory for juniors and seniors. Both classes were practically empty today. Except for her courses on the witch trials in Salem in 1692 and in Blue River in 1695, her classes rarely were well attended. She wasn't as popular an instructor as Jake. As the maverick chairman of the English department at Blue River College, his classes were unconventional, his grading system too easy, yet he made language and literature an intriguing adventure. In fact, the adventure was so intriguing for some of the sweet young things in his classes that it had broken the marriage irreparably.

"We may not get a table, you know," she remarked.

"I called from campus and made a reservation."

"What's the occasion?"

"No occasion." He flashed that impish smile and combed his fingers back through his hair, a boyish gesture that made him seem younger than his forty-three years.

But Jake had never looked his age and maybe that was part of the problem. He had a compact, sinewy body honed over decades as a runner, a quick, winning smile that made you feel you were special just because he had noticed you, and a full head of salt-and-pepper hair. He moved and spoke with the practiced impatience of a salesman pressed to make the day's quota and did it all with such charm that it had taken her years to accept that it was mostly smoke and mirrors.

People who knew them well—and there weren't many—remarked that they were like the sun and the moon. His hair was light and curly, hers was straight and dark. He was blue eyed, her eyes were the dark of freshly poured asphalt. But deeper than that, he was sociable, the life of any party, and she was very much a loner.

"We should go away this weekend," he said, which had nothing at all to do with their table reservation or anything else.

"We can't afford to go anywhere, Jake." *Divorce is expensive.* Why couldn't she just say it? Now, immediately, get it over with. "We can't afford this lunch, either."

"I found some cheap airfares south."

As if she hadn't spoken. *I want a divorce, Jake.* The words, perched at the tip of her tongue, tumbled into the air. "Jake, I want . . ."

She suddenly collided with a tall cop and immediately realized he wasn't just a cop. He wore a uniform the color of rich, bitter chocolate that identified him as a fed with the Department of Freedom and Security—*Freeze,* to the ordinary guy on the street. She murmured an apology, but his gaze locked with hers—strange, dark, intense eyes that scared her. Even though she was six feet tall, he made her feel like a midget.

"Watch where you're going," he snapped.

Then they were past him, Nora nearly tripping over her own feet to put even more distance between them. The sight of him brought back all the horrifying memories of that evening twenty-three years ago, when she was ten. An ordinary evening on Valentine's Day, the TV news on in the background, her mother opening her gifts, bits of colorful wrapping paper strewn across the table like fallen stars. And suddenly, two Freeze officers, a man and a woman, burst in with a warrant for her mother's arrest—supposedly for funding terrorist groups—and hauled her off into the winter darkness.

Just like that, her mother was gone. Nora never saw her again.

Her father had hired attorneys, private investigators, people with connections. He'd had the money to do it. But within several years, his money had run out, he was forced to sell the house, the catering business, everything that had represented stability to her. Her brother, Tyler, had been in college when it had happened. He'd dropped out of school and worked for a year to finance his education. Eventually, his life and her father's had moved on. Her dad met another woman and married her when Nora was fourteen, pushing her into the land of fairy tales—wicked stepmother, nightmarish teen years, all the rest of it.

At least there had been no wicked stepsisters. She was grateful for that. But a part of her had gotten stuck back there in that winter evening more than two decades ago. She still didn't know what had happened to her mother, where she was, or the real reason for her arrest. Open-ended. No closure.

The only time she and her father had discussed it at any length, Nora was home from college for Christmas and demanded to know everything he knew about it. *It's like she fell off the face of the goddamn earth, Dad. I need more than that.*

Shadows seized his face; he looked utterly miserable. *I've told you all I know,* he'd whispered. *I pushed and searched for answers and got nowhere. Four years, Nora, and by then I'd lost everything and I was tired.*

Tired. Nope, sorry, *tired* didn't cut it.

It was like the stories of the disappeared in South America, parents and grandparents who vanished in the middle of the night and were never heard from again. Dissidents. Undesirables. Hauled off to torture chambers.

"Stop thinking like that," Jake said suddenly.

"Like what?"

"About your mom. It was a long time ago."

"And that means it's not worth thinking about?"

"I'm just saying to let it go, Nora. It's been twenty-three years."

"I can't. You can't just let something like that go."

"You have to."

"Don't tell me what I *have* to do, Jake," she snapped.

He started to say something, but by then the hostess was leading them to their table out on the balcony. The waitress came over shortly afterward, a chirpy little thing who was all smiles and dimples, with curves in the right places. Jake turned on the charm, the distinguished professor asking the sweet young thing for her opinion on the wines, everything in his body language suggesting that he found her attractive, desirable. Had he been like this when they'd met? She couldn't remember, probably because back then *she* had been the sweet young thing. Months ago, such a display would have humiliated Nora, left her feeling that she was somehow at fault, flawed. Now it just irritated her, increased her restlessness, her urgency to end the relationship.

Nora already knew what she wanted and ordered the Caesar salad. Jake said he hadn't made up his mind yet and seemed annoyed that Nora had violated etiquette protocol by ordering before they'd gotten their wine.

As soon as the woman hurried off, Nora leaned toward him. "Is that how it starts with your students, Jake? Seemingly harmless flirtations?"

A flush swept up his neck and through his face. "Jesus, Nora, you're so fixated on the past."

This was how he fought back, by turning things around, making it seem that *she* was the problem, that *she* had the issues. "Look, Jake. I've been thinking things over and I . . ."

"I'm resigning," he interrupted. "That means I can withdraw my pension contributions."

Resigning? That was why he'd asked her to meet him for lunch? What she felt apparently showed in her expression because he rushed on, not giving her an opportunity to respond.

"They've been after me. For a year or longer."

Here we go again. For months now, Jake had been convinced that he was being watched, followed, that his online activities were being tracked. At first, she'd thought he was going through a midlife crisis or, worse, that he was bipolar. Eventually she got tired of listening to his paranoid litany and fired back with the obvious questions. *Who* was following him? Watching him? Tracking his online activities? *Who* would give a damn about a college professor?

The shadow government. A cabal. A brotherhood. Call it what you want. They may be the same people who arrested your mother.

And right then, she'd shut down. Her mother, like the disappeared in South America, hadn't disappeared because of some insidious conspiracy. It was the system—corrupt, cruel, wrapped in secrecy. Jake sounded like one of those Internet fruitcakes whose conspiracy blogs choked up the information highway—Roswell, UFOs, end times, the assassinations of JFK, RFK, MLK. Nearly every conspiracy seemed to share her bottom line—lack of closure due to secrecy, misinformation or not enough information, or flat-out lies. When she'd compared him to the conspiracy nuts, Jake had distanced himself from her, had found solace elsewhere, and had stopped talking about it.

"C'mon, Jake, we went through all this months ago."

"It got worse. I just stopped mentioning it. I think our phone is tapped, too."

The chirpy waitress returned with their wine and glasses, and asked Jake if he would like to taste it first. "No," he said curtly, all his charm gone. "I'd like the lobster bisque."

The bisque. With that and the wine, their lunch tab was soaring. Well, guess what? Instead of them splitting the tab as they often did, he could pay. The waitress quickly set the wine bottle and glasses on the table and left.

"Our home phone is tapped?" Nora asked.

"Yes. And maybe the work phones, too. They don't like me, Nora. They don't like *what* I teach, *how* I teach."

"Who? The shadow government?"

"Them and the other department heads and the chancellor."

"Right. That's why you have tenure."

"Tenure may be a big part of it." Whispering again, he leaned in closer to her. "Why should they pay my salary when they can hire someone new for half the price? If they fire me, I lose my pension. I can appeal the firing, but during the appeal process I don't get paid and I don't have access to my pension. But if I resign, I get everything in the pension plus a month's wages."

Me, me, me. It was all about Jake. It always had been all about Jake. She had no idea what she'd ever seen in him.

No, that wasn't correct. She knew exactly what she had seen in him—whispered sweet nothings on a windblown beach, a charm that she had mistaken for the genuine person, a man who had said and done all the right things at a time in her life when she was vulnerable. She'd been in her late twenties, still licking her wounds over a relationship that had gone south. She, too, was at fault. But five years of trying to make this work was long enough. "Frankly, I don't give a shit what you do. I'm filing for divorce, Jake. I'll move my things out as soon as I find my own place."

She couldn't tell if he was stunned, shocked, or simply incredulous that *she* would want to divorce *him*. "But . . . I . . . I thought we were doing better, Nora."

"Better than *what*? Better than when you were screwing the cute chiquita in your junior English class? We haven't slept together in months, we don't really have a relationship anymore, so let's just end the charade and call it quits, Jake."

His jaw tightened. "You're doing this because I'm resigning."

"Excuse me, but I'm doing this because fidelity is a foreign concept for you and I'm tired of pretending."

"My God, Nora, I can't believe you're . . ."

The sudden shriek of tires against the pavement interrupted them. She glanced quickly toward the street, but the dozens of customers waiting along the patio wall for seats blocked her view. Then two Freeze officers marched onto the patio as though they owned the restaurant, the man moving with a macho swagger, the woman a few brisk steps ahead of him. Waiters and waitresses hurriedly stepped aside, customers slid their chairs out of the way, Nora's body went stiff, her eyes flashed dry, a pulse beat at her throat.

Like when they took Mom.

The male officer was the same guy with whom she had collided on the street and he looked much taller now, at least six feet four, with thick, muscular arms. She stole a look at Jake, to see if he recognized the man as well, but he was huddled in on himself, as if he hoped to vanish, his eyes glued to the menu, hands gripping it. He looked terrified.

The feds moved slowly and deliberately among the tables, scanning the faces around them. The woman wasn't close enough for Nora to read the name and numbers on the shoulder of her jacket, but she could clearly see the identifying information on the man's jacket: *T6747, Agent Ryan Curtis, DFS,* for Department of Freedom and Security. For the briefest moment, his eyes caught Nora's, then darted to Jake.

"Mr. McKee?" the fed said. "Professor Jake McKee?"

Distantly, the sounds of traffic punctuated the silence that now gripped the balcony. Everyone watched them.

"Mr. McKee?" the fed repeated.

Jake suddenly shot to his feet, his chair crashed to the floor, and he grabbed the edge of the table, overturning it. The bottle of wine, ice, glasses, silverware, plates, everything crashed to the floor. Bedlam erupted on the balcony, the two feds lunged for Jake, but he was gone, racing between tables, knocking over empty chairs, leaving an obstacle course behind him. Then he leaped over the low wall that separated the patio from the street and the feds took off after him.

Nora jumped up and tried to shove her way through the crowd that had gathered like a flock of vultures circling roadkill. She finally found an opening, vaulted the wall, and followed them.

Her shoes pounded the sidewalk, her breath exploded from her mouth. Despite the chill in the air, sweat poured down the sides of her face. Young, she thought, but not in very good shape, not like Jake, who ripped a ragged path through the shoppers and tourists on the other side of the street. Pedestrians scrambled out of Jake's way as soon as they saw the Freeze officers, as if the chocolate-colored uniforms were an archetype synonymous with bogeymen, then gawked or turned away, pretending they hadn't seen anything.

Nora raced after the feds and Jake. As the tall guy—*Curtis, Agent Ryan Curtis, T6747, remember that name, those numbers*—closed in on Jake, she spotted a possible escape route off to the left. But she didn't think that Jake saw it. Adrenaline poured through her; she drew on reserves she didn't know she had and sprinted toward Jake and the fed. A heartbeat after the bastard tackled Jake, Nora slammed into him from behind, knocking him forward. His arms flew out to break his fall, his knees struck the sidewalk, she could hear it, bone smacking concrete.

Nora grasped Jake by the shoulders, tried to pull him up. "*C'mon, Jake, get up, run, fast . . .*"

Blood streamed from the corner of his mouth, his eyes looked dazed. "*Leave*," he said hoarsely. "While you can. Glove compartment. Leather case. Parked five blocks south."

The female fed—*Agent Katherine Sargent, T7960*—shoved Nora roughly to the side and swung, punching Jake in the face. He fell back, grunting with pain, blood pouring from his nose, and the woman handcuffed him. Nora scrambled to her feet, shocked that the street had become her parents' living room twenty-three years ago, as though her life were caught within a loop that played and replayed, endlessly. But she was an adult now, not afraid to demand answers.

"Where's your warrant?" she shouted. "What're you charging him with?"

"Section fourteen, code three," Curtis barked, waving a document that he pulled from his jacket pocket. "Now back off, Mrs. McKee, before I arrest you for assaulting a federal officer and interfering with an arrest."

"What's section fourteen, code three? What's that mean in plain English? I have a right to know that, to know what the charge against him is."

He looked—bored? Pissed off? "You don't have any rights, ma'am. And since you're guilty by association, my advice it to go home and call your attorney."

Guilty by association? "Where're you taking him?"

"Call your attorney."

He pushed past her, but Nora shouted, "Hey, you jerk, that isn't good enough." She grabbed his arm. "I'm entitled to an answer."

He wrenched free and spun around, his face seized up with a kind of primal rage, as if no one had challenged his authority before now. He stabbed his index finger so close to her face that she leaned back, breathless, terrified.

"I'll say this only once, Mrs. McKee. If you touch me again, if you continue to interfere, I'll charge you with assault and handcuff you and haul your ass off this street and out of this town and you won't be able to help your husband."

With that, Agent Ryan Curtis, T6747, turned away and pushed Jake into a car that had pulled up to the curb. He slammed the back door and slid into the passenger seat. As the car sped away, Nora just stood there, powerless, arms clutched against her body, tears coursing down her cheeks, an image burned into her mind of Jake's bloody face pressed against the window as he mouthed, *Run.*

2

When Nora finally moved, the Freeze car was gone and it was as though nothing unusual had happened here. Life had gone on. Tourists wandered in and out of the shops, the restaurant balcony looked normal, with customers seated again, eating, chatting. Cars drove on through the intersection, the lighthouse still stood. The only signs that anything had occurred were the curious glances from some of the people nearby and the stuff on the sidewalk that had spilled from Jake's pockets. Loose change, keys, a pen, and a small key ring with a compass on the end. A gift from her, last Christmas, before she knew about his nasty little secret with the student. Engraved on the back of it was: *So you'll always find your way. Luv u, N.*

One more sham of their marriage, she thought, choking back a sob. She scooped everything off the sidewalk and hurried up the street just to get away from there. *I'm so sorry I didn't believe you, Jake.*

Yeah, *sorry* and a quarter couldn't help either of them now. But if she had believed him, listened to him, maybe he wouldn't have sought solace elsewhere. Then again, it probably wouldn't have changed a thing. After all, the sweet young

thing in his English class hadn't been the first. She was just
the first one Nora had found out about.

She walked faster; her mind raced, thoughts slamming
into each other like bumper cars. What the hell should she
do first? She needed a plan, a list, something. Even though
she wanted to divorce him, she couldn't abandon him, not
like this, not now. Besides, on a purely selfish level, she refused to be denied closure again.

Find Jake's car, that was first. *Parked five blocks south.
Along the river.* And she was supposed to look for the leather
case in the glove compartment. She didn't have any clue
what leather case he was talking about. As far as she knew,
his glove compartment held peanut butter crackers, sticks of
gum, music CDs, and the little notebook where he meticu-
lously recorded his gas mileage. Never mind any of that. She
would look. She would drive his car back to the apartment,
then ride her bike downtown to retrieve her own car.

And then she would call a lawyer. Or she would do that
first.

Except that they didn't have a lawyer. The only time either of them had ever needed legal advice, they had gone to
the college attorney. That was years ago and she didn't know
if he was even still there. Regardless, would the college attorney handle a case like this? What was section fourteen,
code three? *What just happened?*

Why was your mother arrested, Nora? Jake's question,
months ago. The echo of his voice haunted her, pushed her
forward faster, faster, until she was nearly running up the street.
Once she was away from the prying stares of cowardly,
bloodthirsty bystanders—*who turned away, pretending nothing had happened*—the sob lodged in her throat suddenly
burst from her, an ugly, raw sound.

She sucked at the cold air. Sucked again. The sobs died at
the tip of her tongue. She started to shake and clutched her
arms against her. She was on the river road, moving fast across
the cool, damp grass, stumbling now and then, her jacket un-
buttoned, flapping like a flag in the breeze. The river after

which the town was named meandered through the autumn light, gulls pinwheeling above it. She frantically searched both sides of the road for Jake's boxy silver car.

Alex Kincaid—college librarian, Jake's closest friend, her ex-lover—had designed it, built it, a hybrid that he'd given to them as a wedding gift. There were nearly a thousand of them on the roads now; they didn't look like any other car, so how come she couldn't find it? *Five blocks south. Along the river.* How far along the river? A mile? Two miles?

Nora called Kincaid's cell and when she heard strains of John Lennon's "Imagine," she disconnected and tried the library. The reference librarian who answered said that Kincaid was on vacation, that she hadn't seen him in three days. "Did he leave a forwarding number?" Nora asked.

"No, he didn't, Dr. McKee. I figure he's tending to his car business."

Right. His car business. As though building and manufacturing hybrids was like changing oil and tires. The administration gave Kincaid a lot of latitude because he was the college golden boy now, the inventor of the AK Hybrid, good advertising for Blue River. But now she wondered if his absence was connected to Jake's arrest. Maybe Kincaid had been hauled off, too. No possibility seemed too strange, too over the top.

Nora thanked the woman and punched out Kincaid's home number. No answering machine, just the incessant ringing. Frustrated, she tried his cell again and when the music came on, she waited for voice mail to kick in.

"*Hola, amigos.* I'm in the midst of *A Hundred Years of Solitude* and can't take your call right now. I'd appreciate it if you left a positive message. Thanks."

A Hundred Years of Solitude. The book title he mentioned in his answering machine greeting was never random. It reflected his mood, his state of mind, so it was obvious he wanted to be left alone. After they had split up six years ago, the books in his greeting had ranged from *War and Peace* to *The Great Gatsby.* So at the beep, she said, "Nick and Nora

Charles, *The Thin Man*. It's urgent. Call me as soon as you can."

She waited another moment, hoping he would pick up. When he didn't, she disconnected from the call and walked faster.

Nora finally spotted Jake's car parked under a tree on the river side of the road and walked quickly toward it, struggling to shake the images of Jake, running for his life.

Section fourteen, code three.

You don't have any rights, ma'am.

Shadow government.

. . . guilty by association . . .

Run.

When she was inside the car, sitting in the seat where Jake sat every morning, she flexed her fingers against the cold, hard steering wheel, fighting back a rising panic. She breathed in the scent of the seats, the dashboard, as though the car were still brand new, right out of Kincaid's warehouse. And behind these smells were those of crackers in the glove compartment, of Jake's aftershave. She forced herself to think of Jake in this car, fiddling as he always did with the radio buttons, changing from one station to another, a habit that drove her nuts when she was in the car with him. Or he switched from one CD to another, searching for the music to fit his mood. Or he chattered away on his cell.

To his honeys . . .

"Focus," she hissed, and unlocked the glove compartment.

There, buried under the crackers and the CDs and his usual inventory of stuff, was a small leather case she'd never seen before. Frowning, Nora removed it, unzipped it. A bunch of music CDs. She started slipping the CDs out of their slots and behind the fifth one she found a note. Nora smoothed it open against her thigh.

Trust no one but Alex and Pham. J

That was it? When had he tucked this note in here? And why Kincaid and Pham, the owner of Pham's Fresh Market here in town and an old friend? Why them? Why would they know what she did not?

Had Pham been arrested, too?

A dark car moved up the street toward her. *Freeze?*

Nora quickly dropped sideways across the passenger seat, her mouth dry, the leather case pressed against her chest. *Go past me, please. Just keep driving.* Her cell chirped. Terrified that it could be heard outside the car, she held it against her chest, muffling the sound. When it finally stopped ringing, she put it on vibrate and checked the number. Diana Pierce, her buddy from grad school, her maid of honor, a psychologist now working out of her home for one of the major advertising companies in Boston. Had she heard about Jake's arrest already? But why would it be on the news at all?

Several cars drove past, oppressively close. She counted to ten, then raised up slowly and spotted the Freeze car in the side mirror, moving slowly up the street. If they were looking for Jake's car, the license plate wouldn't be visible unless they made a U-turn. But wouldn't they know he drove an AK Hybrid? Maybe not. Just because he was arrested didn't mean the people looking for his car knew what kind of car he drove.

Nora opened the passenger door and slithered out, keeping her body low. She swung her legs around; her shoes touched the ground. She straightened up, locked the doors, slipped the leather case into her shoulder bag, and moved quickly across the street and into the nearest neighborhood. Her phone vibrated several times. Diana again, then her boss. Should she call Pham? And what would she say? *Hey, Pham, Jake got arrested and he seems to think you know something about it.*

But that wasn't what the note had said. Pham and Kincaid could be trusted. No one else.

Trusted with *what*?

Kincaid and Pham were *his* friends, Diana was *her* friend.

No, that wasn't the full story. Kincaid was the rebound part of the equation in her marriage. But in her life now, that didn't count. He was Jake's friend and she and Kincaid merely had "history."

Wrong, wrong. She and Kincaid had nothing. In the five years she and Jake had been married, their contact with him as a couple had been sporadic, rare, and only when he had a woman at his side, so they were a foursome. Double dates. Uncomfortable for her, for Kincaid, she always had felt that. She, Jake, and Kincaid were not the *tres amigos.* They were not like the people in *The Big Chill*, sharing spouses with best friends. They never had that kind of comfort zone. They never had a comfort zone at all.

Nora pressed the speed dial for Diana's number; she picked up on the second ring. "Hey, Nora, wow, girl, have you been on my mind today."

"On your mind how?" This was an important nuance for two psychologists who shared an admiration for Carl Jung.

"Well, last night I dreamed about you. See, I've been teaching a class in the adult ed program about dream recall and lucid dreaming and I've been using some of the pointers . . ."

"I'm in trouble," Nora blurted, gripping her cell harder. "Jake's in trouble, he was arrested. They wouldn't give me any information. They . . . they just took him, hauled him off . . ."

"Christ, I *knew* it. I *knew* something had happened. I'm leaving for Blue River as soon as we get off the phone," Diana said.

"No. No, don't do that. I don't know what's going on. I need to decide what I'm doing first. I'll call you. Or e-mail you."

"Is this, like, Jake's shadow-government shit?"

"Yes." Nora lowered her voice. "But I'm beginning to think it isn't shit, that he was on to something."

"Call the college attorney, Nora. Get legal counsel. Call Tyler. And call me back as soon as you know anything. I mean it. If you don't call me back, I'm coming down there."

"I'll be in touch."

She disconnected. Call this person, that person, call the president, call God.

The chilly breeze stirred the fallen leaves on the sidewalk. Birds fluttered upward from the colorful trees, their perfect songs urging her to believe it had all been a mistake.

Mr. McKee? Professor Jake McKee? How the hell could that be a mistake?

When she reached the corner, she saw a tow truck driving away, pulling Jake's car behind it, hauling it off. No mistake.

Nora waited until it disappeared, then hastened toward downtown, where she'd left her Beetle. It was wedged between a pair of pickup trucks on Hawthorne Street. Before she went over to it, she glanced quickly around, looking for Freeze officers, unmarked cars. She didn't see anything or anyone unusual, and moments later, slid behind the steering wheel.

Campus or home?

Word probably had gotten around by now; the campus was a rumor mill, and the rumors would be swirling. She didn't want to be seen there. She didn't think she could tolerate the curious stares, the questions. She would call the campus from home, get the name and extension for the current college attorney that employees were allowed to hire.

Armed with a plan, as pathetic as it was, she sped away from downtown.

Their apartment building stood on the north side of Blue River, on the outskirts of town, in an upscale neighborhood that surpassed where either of them had lived when they were single. The air here smelled of trees, water, solace. And never mind that the trees and the water were scarce, that the solace—at least at the moment—was nonexistent.

Had Freeze come here first, looking for him?

Probably not. It was a Friday, a workday, they would know he was teaching. But how did they know where he was having lunch?

I think our phone is tapped . . . maybe the work phones, too.

Jake had called her from his office around ten, suggested lunch at the Lighthouse. And he had called from his *office* phone, not his cell, to *her* office phone rather than her cell.

She sped through the complex, past the four buildings that formed a half-moon around a small body of water. She scanned the other side of it, where oaks and maples were dressed out in full autumn colors, and looked for unmarked cars. Cops. The sight of a dark brown uniform. There weren't many trees, maybe not even enough of them to qualify as a thicket, and she didn't spot anyone lurking around in the shadows. Didn't see any unmarked cars, either.

She screeched into their parking spot at the back of the complex, grabbed her purse, slid out, and loped toward the back door of their apartment, second building from the right, first floor. The moment she slipped inside the tiny utility room with the stacked washer and dryer, and shut the door behind her, the familiar air embraced her. She stood with her back pressed against the cool metal door, her mind coughing up images of Jake shooting to his feet, running, crashing to the ground. She slid down the length of the door, the heels of her hands pressed against her eyes.

Cries, shrieks, and wails clawed at her throat. But nothing came out of her mouth. She needed to function, to stand, make calls, pack a bag, something, anything. But she couldn't seem to move. It was as if the force of gravity held her against the door, butt hard on the floor, legs pulled up against her chest. She pressed her forehead against her knees.

She suddenly remembered that in those first terrible moments after the Freeze officers had taken her mother away, she and her father had stood there, frozen in time and space like figures in a faded photo. And then a noise had escaped him and he slapped his hands over his mouth and turned to her, his eyes wide and panicked. *What're we supposed to do now?* he'd asked.

Yeah. What?

She finally forced herself to stand, to punch out Kincaid's cell number again, and now even his voice mail didn't come on. "Shit, shit." *Calls, make the calls. Attorney, boss, brother, Pham, in that order.* Then she would pack a bag and drive out of town toward—where? Where the hell was she supposed to go?

Even more to the point, why should *she* flee? She hadn't done anything wrong. All she had wanted from that lunch was the first step toward closure to the marriage. Instead, here she was, panicked, cornered.

You're guilty by association. Yeah? Since when? Had the Constitution collapsed overnight?

For you, it collapsed twenty-three years ago.

On her way through the kitchen, Nora tore off her jacket, dropped it on a chair, and hurried into the bathroom. Faucet on. Pipes clattering. She thrust her hands under the rushing stream of cold water and splashed it repeatedly against her face. She finally turned off the faucet, groped blindly for a towel, pressed it to her face.

The fresh, clean scent of it calmed her, the smell of open meadows, summer, earth, simple pleasures. When she finally let the towel drop away from her face, she didn't recognize the woman who looked back at her. Gone was any semblance of her mother's dark, startling beauty. She saw, instead, the hardened bitterness and terror that had claimed her father's face during the years after her mother was taken. Her dark eyes seemed washed out, faded, afflicted with some sort of soul fatigue. Her disheveled black hair, pulled back from her face this morning and held with a clip, now dropped to her shoulders in a tangled mess. She looked like one of the homeless women she often saw on her route to work, the panhandlers with knotted hair, desperate faces, broken lives.

Her clothes felt soiled. She stripped off the blazer, the sweater, her slacks, left them on the bathroom floor, and made a beeline for the bedroom. Jeans, a blouse, a pullover sweater, fresh socks. She realized she needed to sit for a minute, think things through, breathe.

She returned to the kitchen, forced herself to sit down at the breakfast table, to collect herself so that she could speak clearly, rationally, and wouldn't sound like a nutcase. But her thoughts had scattered like startled birds, the arrests of her mother and Jake all mixed up in her head, the past crashing over into the present, one wave after another. She shot to her feet, paced, rehearsing what she could say, getting it straight, exactly as it had happened. She felt like a criminal trying to hammer out an alibi that would stand up under scrutiny.

Nora called an assistant professor in the math department with whom she often ate lunch. She wasn't in, but the department secretary gave her the name and extension for the college attorney, the same man she and Jake had used years ago. Good. This would make it easier, right? That would give her an edge, wouldn't it? Even if he didn't remember her and Jake, she could attach a face to his name.

Nora thanked the woman, but even as she was calling the attorney's number, a part of her analyzed the secretary's voice—did she know about Jake's arrest? Had the word gotten around campus yet? She imagined them, all the secretaries and clerks and other professors, gossiping, whispering. *Hey, did you hear about Dr. McKee, arrested outside the Lighthouse Pub? Hey, did you hear about. . . .* As though her life were a reality show, exposed, obvious, a travesty. These people were probably the same ones who had whispered about Jake's indiscretions. *Dr. McKee's screwing one of his students.*

She reached an automated menu and navigated her way through it until she reached a live person, a male paralegal. As soon as she identified herself as an employee of the college, he put her through to the man himself.

"Hi, Dr. McKee. What can I do for you?" Hank Barrow's gruff troll's voice belied his friendly tone, as if he'd spoken to her yesterday.

"My husband needs legal counsel. He was arrested this morning."

"Your husband . . . that would be . . . ?"

"Jake McKee."

"English department," he said.

Did he remember them or had he heard the rumors already or did he just have faculty facts at his fingertips? She could see those fingertips, tapping and tapping at computer keys or walking through some old-fashioned Rolodex. Plump fingers, with defined joints. For some reason, she remembered this about Barrow. "Yes, that's right."

"Was he arrested by Blue River police?"

Did he actually know or was he just doing his attorney thing, digging for facts? *Stop analyzing.* "No, two officers from the Department of Freedom and Security."

"The charge?"

"Section fourteen, code three. I don't know what that means in English."

"I see."

She detested the way he said it, his voice flat, resigned. "What's that mean?"

"It means that I probably can't help you, Dr. McKee. Section fourteen falls under the terrorist laws. Code three refers specifically to terrorist computer crimes against the United States."

"What?" Jake, a terrorist? And a computer terrorist? She nearly laughed. Would have, except the tightness in her throat made it difficult to even form words. "That's absurd. He's chairman of the English department, for God's sakes. How does that make him a terrorist?"

"Look, I'm sure there's been a mistake. Identity theft is so widespread now that what happened to your husband isn't all that extraordinary these days, Dr. McKee. Have you noticed any unusual charges on your credit cards? Unusual e-mails or phone charges for calls you didn't make?"

She couldn't remember anything off hand, unless she counted Jake's paranoia—*They've been after me*—and a few cell calls from the sweet young thing. "Possibly, yes, I'd have to give that some thought. But yes, it's possible."

"Did the arresting officers give their names?" he asked.

"No, I saw their names—Ryan Curtis, T sixty-seven forty-seven, and Katherine Sargent, T seventy-nine sixty."

"That's a start. And the arrest happened downtown?"

"Outside the Lighthouse Pub, shortly after noon today."

"I'm going to make some calls and see what I can find out, Dr. McKee. In the meantime, I'd like you to go through your records—phone bills, credit card bills, your husband's e-mails. . . . Flag anything questionable. But please understand, once the Department of Freedom and Security enters the picture, it's much more difficult for me get information. I'll see what can I do."

"Suppose you can't find out anything? What do I do then?"

"I can refer you to an attorney here in town. But that's going to be extremely expensive, so let me work on this first. I'll get back to you this afternoon. Can I get you at this number?"

"Or my cell phone." She gave it to him. "Thank you, Mr. Barrow. I appreciate it."

When they disconnected, she sat there with her fists pressed into her eyes, her head spinning. *Terrorist, a computer terrorist.* Jake was no computer whiz, that was Kincaid's domain. Computers and cars. Jake could barely keep his antivirus software up to date.

She went into his office, hit the wall switch. When they had moved in here, this room had been a postscript, a windowless pantry. They had expanded it by knocking down the wall between it and the breakfast nook and now it was large enough to accommodate a desk, his computer, files, a bookcase.

His desk was as neat and organized as usual. His work area was the only part of his life that was so scrupulously tidy. A couple of yellow Post-it notes were stuck to the lower edge of the flat-screen monitor, a short grocery list, a reminder to grade research papers by November 1. She pulled out his chair, sat down, turned on his computer.

The computer hummed to life, the monitor came on—but the screen was gray, blank. Nora checked its connection to the computer box. It wasn't loose. So had the computer crashed?

Or was the monitor just dead? The system had been working fine this morning. Jake had been in here, checking e-mail, before breakfast.

From the supply closet, she brought out a second monitor, the bulky and heavy seventeen-inch that the flat-screen had replaced. She hooked it up to the computer box, turned the system on again.

Gray screen.

"For chrissakes." She turned everything off again.

Dust bunnies on the motherboard? A loose screw? She opened the top desk drawer, plucked out a screwdriver, removed the screws at the back of the computer, and lifted off the shell.

The motherboard was gone.

3

She stared at the empty space where the motherboard had been, her brain refusing to connect it with anything that made sense. Kincaid removed motherboards from his computers all the time, especially when he was tinkering with his cars, but he had the knowledge to do that, the expertise, he was wired that way. Jake wasn't.

Why would Jake remove the motherboard? If it had anything on it that might be incriminating, wouldn't it make more sense to copy the information onto memory sticks and then simply reformat the hard drive? He usually carried a memory stick in his briefcase, which probably was still in his office on campus, and kept another here at home. But where at home?

She jerked open the top right side drawer—and frowned. Wrong, something was very wrong here. This drawer looked like a kid had dumped everything out, then put it back together again without realizing it should bear the signature of a neat freak. Pads of paper lay at odd angles, the paper clip container rested on its side, clips spilling out, pencils and pens bunched together every which way.

Nora checked the other three drawers. Same story. All wrong.

They *had* been here. Had come while she and Jake were at lunch. *Came for the goddamn motherboard.*

A chill sliced up her spine.

What's this mean?

She pushed to her feet and turned slowly, her gaze darting around the office, checking for anything else that looked wrong. She ran her hands over her slacks and backed out the doorway, the chill now stabbing into her chest cavity.

What else had they taken?

It didn't matter that she was now nearly as paranoid as Jake had been. She knew it was true, knew they had come here, into her home. She checked the windows in the kitchen, the utility room doors, the windows in the bedroom, looking for obvious signs of forced entry. She didn't find anything, but as Freeze officers, they wouldn't have to break into the apartment. They would just go to the main office, flash their badges and their warrant, and the manager would let them in.

That was how it worked. Privacy was just an illusion.

She needed to know if anything else was missing, but like what? They weren't looking for a TV or a DVD player or her mother's china. They weren't street thieves. A motherboard contained information. So did Jake's PDA. That was in his briefcase, in his desk on campus, or he'd been carrying it and his cell phone when he'd been arrested. She guessed they had gone through his office already, so she couldn't do anything about that. But what about his files?

The only hard files he kept related to his classes. And she already knew the file drawer had been searched and that she wouldn't be able to recognize whether or not something was missing.

She ran into the bedroom, her resolve to slow down now forgotten, and snatched a suitcase off the closet shelf, tossing it on the bed. She couldn't stay here. She felt violated, threatened. She already had been told she was guilty by association, so what was to prevent Freeze from barging in here and hauling her away? *Like mom, like Jake. A family curse.* She would check into a hotel somewhere, wait for Barrow's call, for Kincaid's call. She would drive over to Pham's market. Or she could drive to Boston and stay with Diana for the weekend. She just couldn't stay here.

As she hastily packed, she wondered which phone she should use to call her brother. Land or cell? Was either one safe? *Is anything safe when you've gone down the rabbit's hole?*

Nora finally settled on her land phone and punched out Tyler's number. Her brother was smart, grounded, a businessman who knew a lot of people. His computer business had military and other government contracts. He had a legal department, money, resources that she didn't. He would be able to recommend an attorney if Barrow couldn't help her. Even more to the point, he would recognize the parallels between what had happened to their mother and Jake's arrest and would offer insights that she just didn't have right now.

He answered on the second ring, his voice hushed, urgent. "Jesus, Nora," he breathed. "I was just going to call you. Let me call you back on a secure line. I'll call your cell."

A secure line, like a spy. "Yes, all right. Hurry. It's important."

She went into the bathroom, her cell tucked in the pocket of her slacks, and swept up shampoo, makeup, a razor, hair dryer, anything and everything that she might need. Her cell pealed before she reached her suitcase and when she answered it, she felt an absurd gratitude for her cell phone. Just the sound of her brother's voice mitigated her fear.

"This line should scramble things enough so if anyone's eavesdropping, they won't hear anything except gibberish. Are you okay?"

"No. Jake . . ."

"I know. I just saw it on the news. It's happening again, Nora. It's a repeat of what happened with Mom. Have you found a lawyer?"

She gave him her two cents on Barrow. "I don't know if he'll be able to do anything or not."

"If you're still in your apartment, pack up and get out. Come here. With Freeze involved, you're a suspicious person just because you're Jake's wife. That's how it was with Dad. We'll figure out what to do and find an attorney who can actually help Jake."

"I'm in the midst of packing now. But I don't want to barge in on you and your wife."

"We're separated. Things have been shitty for a long time and I finally called it quits. I'm staying in a condo over on Falmouth Beach. Write down the address and the number for this secure line. Got a pencil?"

"Shoot." At least Tyler had the beginnings of closure, she thought, and scribbled the info on a piece of paper. "If they're after me, why didn't they just arrest me when they took Jake?"

"Maybe they think you can lead them to Alex."

"They're looking for Alex?"

"That's my guess. Right after I saw the news piece about Jake, I got a weird e-mail from Alex. He's calling himself Nick Charles. I don't know what the hell *that's* about."

I do. It meant he'd gotten her message. "What'd the e-mail say?"

"He's spooked and obviously had heard about Jake. He said I should call you and tell you to come to the Cape and asked if I could spare a car. He'll be in touch with both of us through e-mail and says that Pham has information for you. You should follow whatever instructions Pham gives you. Once you have Alex's secure e-mail address, you're supposed to contact both of us so we're all on the same page here."

"Okay. Can you call Diana? Tell her the plan? She was the first person I spoke to after it happened."

"You bet. Look, if you're delayed getting here, call me on the secure line. When we get off the phone, I'm going to set up a secure e-mail account for you through my computer, so we can communicate without using phones."

He gave her more details and she scribbled again. "The motherboard in Jake's computer is gone, Tyler."

"Those fucks," he breathed.

"Why wouldn't they just transfer everything on his hard drive to memory sticks?"

"Because it's faster and they get everything. They can explore at their leisure. Did you look for signs for a break-in?"

"They're with Freeze. They don't have to break in."

"Nora, they're saying Jake's a suspected terrorist. Is it true? Do you know anything about it?"

"They said mom was funding subversives," she shot back. "Was *that* true?"

"No. No, of course not." His voice softened. "Did Jake piss off someone? Cheat on his taxes? Is he involved in anything illegal?"

"He's just screwing some students," she blurted.

"Aw, shit. I'm sorry, Nora."

"Don't be. At lunch, I'd just told him I wanted a divorce when the Freeze guys arrived."

Silence—not long, not more than a breath or two, but enough so that she knew her brother was taking it all in, absorbing it. Information junkie, that was Tyler.

"We'll wade through this, okay?" he said finally. "And one other thing. Alex says a sure way to find out if you're under suspicion is to use your ATM card. If you get a message that your funds are overdrawn or that you should contact your bank, then Freeze has put a hold on your account."

How did Kincaid know that? Was it some stray bit of information he'd come across in the college library? Or was it from personal experience? "I'll check it out. I'll be there later this evening. I'll contact you when I'm thirty minutes out."

"Be careful."

As soon as they disconnected, Nora tossed more clothes into her suitcase, then tore everything out and whittled the contents to whatever would fit in her backpack. She desperately wanted to believe Jake was just a nice guy who had made bad choices, but rage swept through her with shocking swiftness. He was not a nice guy. He was an opportunist. The fact that she had remained in this marriage for five years was a damning indictment of her own flaws. She grabbed their wedding photo off her bureau and hurled it across the room. It crashed into the wall, the glass shattering.

"You bastard," she muttered.

Aside from Jake's sexual indiscretions, he had kept secrets that had compromised her and thrust her into this position. Now she would have to flee like some sort of criminal because of what she didn't know.

She left the shattered photo where it lay, slid the empty suitcase under the bed, and shoved other items into her large backpack. Her laptop was small, the PDA the size of her hand, but just the same, she had to remove several pairs of shoes and one change of clothes for everything to fit. She hurried back into the kitchen, checked her wallet.

Her cash was pitifully low. Two twenties, a ten, some ones. The ATM would be her last stop. *If you get a message that your funds are overdrawn . . .*

Then she would be in really deep shit. But maybe that wouldn't happen at all. It was possible they'd wanted nothing more than Jake and his hard drive. Another possibility: Tyler was right that Freeze was looking for Kincaid as well and perhaps hoping that she would lead them to him. But a third possibility was that Kincaid had been the real target. Since Freeze hadn't been able to find him, they had nabbed his buddy as bait, figured Kincaid would hear about it and would get in touch with the buddy's wife and she would lead them to Kincaid.

Perverted, maybe brilliant, and not necessarily true.

Right now, she didn't know what was true. She went back into the bedroom and combed through bureaus, gathering up spare change and looking for any other bills that might have been tucked away. She managed to scrounge up another twenty bucks.

She scribbled a note to the postman to hold their mail, then hastened outside into the late afternoon light, her pack slung over her shoulder. As she dropped the pack in the passenger seat, her cell chirped, an incoming text message. Was it safe to open it? If her cell was monitored, could they also read her text messages? She didn't know. Kincaid swore that the encryption he'd put on her and Jake's cells couldn't be intercepted by anyone, anywhere, but why should she believe anything that Kincaid had ever told her?

The text message was from Pham. Nora opened it.

Nora, let's talk. I have information you need.

Pham

She messaged him that she was on her way.

Before she reached her bank, she finally got a call back from Hank Barrow. He apologized for not calling sooner, then got right to the point. "It was very tough getting any information at all, Dr. McKee. The official charge against your husband is for crashing Pentagon computers. That definitely falls under section fourteen."

Jake, crashing Pentagon computers. And her mother, funding subversives. Here it was again, a family curse. She felt like she was trapped inside some sort of weird mathematic equation that functioned according to laws no one had discovered yet. "And where's he being held?"

"I couldn't get that information."

"How's this possible? They at least have to tell us where he's being held."

"I'm afraid they don't have to tell us anything. As a terrorist suspect, he falls under a whole other set of laws. I'm not even sure at this point if he's entitled to legal counsel."

Or perhaps what Barrow was really saying was that he didn't want to be involved.

Stricken, Nora swerved to the side of the road. "Excuse me, Mr. Barrow, but we're not living in a Kafka novel here.

There has to be some legal recourse. They can't just lock him up and throw away the key."

"Look, I'm in complete agreement with you, Dr. McKee, and all I can offer you is personal advice. If this had happened to my wife, I would retain counsel that has experience with this kind of thing. I would start bombarding my congressman and senator with e-mails and calls. I would go to the press. Let me give you the name of the attorney I mentioned earlier. He's local and has experience with situations like this."

That was it? He would pass her off to another attorney? And suppose this new attorney couldn't do anything for her? She added the information to the same sheet on which she'd scribbled everything Tyler had given her, tucked it down inside her wallet. Then she sat there, staring through the windshield at the gathering dusk. The last of the afternoon light was hidden behind a strange cloud that now looked like the bleeding knuckles of a god.

The press. Her dad had gone to the press, she remembered, and it hadn't helped her mother's cause. But in the twenty-three years since then, the Internet had been born and now flourished. If all else failed, she would put up a blog about what had happened to Jake and ask to hear from anyone else who had similar experiences. Then when she had enough stories, she could go to the press. But that could take days, weeks, months. She couldn't wait that long. She needed answers and direction now.

Nora pulled back onto the road and a few minutes later, stopped in front of the drive-through ATM. *Test the theory.* From her wallet, she slipped out two ATM cards—the one for her and Jake's joint checking account and another for the money market account she'd started with the small inheritance she'd gotten after her dad had died. It was under her maiden name, Walrave. It had about eight grand in it and she used it only for emergencies—a root canal last year, an unexpected tax bill, the rare doctor's visit. This situation definitely qualified as an emergency.

She slid her ATM into the slot first, went through the menu. The maximum she could withdraw a day was $1,000. She pressed that button and bills slid out.

Maybe Kincaid was wrong. She removed the bills, grateful for the cash, and slid the second ATM card into the slot. She went through the same process, pressed the button for the daily maximum withdrawal of $500—and got a message:

> This account is frozen.
> Please see the bank for details.

Not too subtle. Nora snatched the card out before the machine could swallow it again. Apparently the hold had been placed on McKee, not on Walrave. So it was Jake they wanted, Jake they were after. How much would an attorney cost? Her father had spent tens of thousands of dollars and that was more than two decades ago. No telling what it would cost her now. Fifty grand? A hundred? She and Jake didn't have that kind of money.

Take it minute to minute, hour to hour, day to day. She couldn't think beyond the next twenty-four hours. Who was she kidding? Right now, she couldn't think beyond getting to the market to talk to Pham.

Pham's Fresh Market loomed across an entire city block, a mammoth concrete structure festooned with art and graffiti by local artists. The property alone was worth millions and every few years the Blue River City Council broached a proposition for seizing the property under the laws of eminent domain so it could be turned over to private developers. But because the market was responsible for a third of the city's tourist revenue, the proposition died before it ever reached a vote. And so here it stayed, Nora thought, a city landmark that sold everything from ant farms to zit zappers.

The grocery store, located a third of the way through the

complex, was huge, the aisles packed with products from every corner of the globe. The prices were competitive, at least 15 to 20 percent below what was charged at the two smaller grocery stores in town. Instead of forking over five bucks for a cantaloupe at Roger's Corner Store, you could get one here for three and change. This was due to the owner's tireless bargaining with his suppliers. Pham Cong Khai had learned the hard way, as a teen scrambling to survive in war-torn Saigon. He'd brought those lessons with him to the States when he'd fled Southeast Asia in 1971.

Nora wandered around the store for fifteen minutes, her heavy pack over her shoulder because she was too uneasy to leave it in the car, and searched for Pham. Finally, one of his three sons spotted her, waved, and gestured for her to head down the far aisle. As she did so, Pham came toward her from the opposite direction, driving an electric cart loaded up with boxes. He wore a Pham Market cap and the trademark blue shirt with a Vietnamese symbol on the pocket that meant, *Welcome*. Jake, a loyal customer of the market for twenty years, had taught Pham's three grandsons English—for free, away from the college—which had made both him and Nora honorary members of Pham's extended family. He smiled at her, his small, wizened face crinkling like crepe paper.

"Nora, Nora." Pham spoke in a soft, deliberate voice, and got out of the cart. "I'm so pleased to see you, that you could come."

As if he had invited her to a party. He pressed his palms together and bowed his head slightly.

"I'm delighted to see you, too, Pham." She lowered her voice. "Thank you so much for the text message."

"I fear I should not have called you." He glanced around warily, frowning. "Let's talk privately." He touched the small of her back and they moved farther down the aisle. In a soft, hushed voice, he continued. "Two men came here a few minutes ago with pictures of you and Alex. That's where I was. My son made sure they did not see you as you came in."

"What men? Freeze officers?"

"No uniforms. But I think they're Freeze. They're still here. Come, you can see them from here." He led her to the end of the next aisle, peeked out, then gestured for her to do the same.

A blond man stood near the front door, paging through a magazine, glancing up now and then to scan the crowd. His companion, with an intricate tattoo that covered most of his neck, stood in the checkout line. They looked like Blue River townies, but that was probably the point. No one paid much attention to townies. Nora stepped back. "Alex was here?"

"Yes." He touched her arm, urging her down the last aisle, the electric cart forgotten. "Down here. Let's talk in the back." Pham hurried toward the last aisle, making a beeline for the double doors that led to the rear of the market. Shelves of bottled water rose on one side of them, bins of vegetables rose on the other. "Alex was here early yesterday, Nora. He left town. He's scared. He asked me to give you this."

He reached into the pocket of his blue shirt, brought out a small envelope, handed it to her. Nora dropped it into her bag. "I don't understand what's going on, Pham." Her voice cracked, then broke. For seconds, she nearly choked on her own rising panic. "They say . . . Jake crashed Pentagon computers. They say . . ."

"Lies, all lies," he hissed. "You listen to me, to your own heart. Jake knows a lot of things, but not that. Someone wants him gone. Disappeared." He snapped his fingers.

Someone's watching me. Following me. Shadow government. "Disappeared? What's that mean? Disappeared to where?"

"Nora, Nora. *Disappeared.* Like your mother."

Hauled off to where?

Pham pushed through double doors and they moved swiftly through the kitchen, where members of Pham's large family worked noisily, fixing sushi and stews, sandwiches and salads for the market deli. No one seemed to notice them. Smells assaulted her, of salt and sea, field and stream.

He stopped at an electric cart with a basket attached to the front that was heaped high with Pham Market caps and shirts. He grabbed a cap, a shirt, and thrust them at her. "Put these on."

She tugged the cap down low, poked her arms through the sleeves of the shirt. "Disappeared to where, Pham?" she prodded.

But he turned away, chattering in Vietnamese to a young man who carried a stack of wrapped foods for the deli display. The young man immediately set the stack on the nearest counter and hurried over to one of the doors that opened into the store. He peered out, spun around, barked something in Vietnamese. Pham snapped back a reply and gestured madly at the cart from which he'd taken the cap and shirt. The young man ran over to it, leaped behind the wheel, and drove it to the door, blocking it, then threw the dead bolt.

"Hurry. They're coming." Pham grabbed her hand and they ran toward the rear door, Nora stumbling along, scared. Another employee was already holding it open, motioning for them to hurry up. "Take the blue wagon, second space from the garbage bin. There're supplies inside. Go to Wood's Hole. Alex will be coming on the ferry from the Vineyard." Pham pressed keys into her hand. "He'll meet you there. Follow the directions in the envelope."

Her heart slammed against her ribs, her mouth went bone dry again, it was happening too fast. "Pham, please, what does *disappeared* mean? Tell me what it *really* means. Where have they taken Jake? Do you know?"

They were outside now, on the concrete stoop that faced the parking lot. Pham gripped both of her hands, kept glancing over his shoulder, then back at her. She could hear shouts coming now from the kitchen—in English, Vietnamese.

"Disappeared." He snapped his fingers again, very close to her face. "Poof, gone. Internet. Freeze. Travelers. Mariah

Jones. Read the urban legends, Nora. Read the directions from Alex. Go now, fast. Go." And he suddenly released her hands and pushed her forward.

She half-stumbled, half-ran down the steps, and saw the blue wagon just where he said it would be, near the garbage bin. She threw open the door, scrambled inside, jammed the key into the ignition. Her hands shook, the strap of her pack slipped off her shoulder and down her arm, her body headed into meltdown.

Nora struggled to drive slowly out of the lot, but her head roared and shrieked. She looked frantically around for the exit, spotted it, then floored the accelerator and the car took off, tires screaming against the pavement.

In the side mirror, she saw the blond-haired man and his tattooed companion racing down the steps. Nora swerved out onto the road and they vanished from sight.

The longer she drove, the louder her body complained. She desperately needed to sleep, her bladder ached, her stomach kept cramping with hunger. She hadn't eaten anything since breakfast at seven this morning. But fear kept her going, up and down rural back roads, winding in and out of woods that might as well have been the forest primeval.

Nora had been driving for hours, but had no idea where she was. Jake's compass said she was headed south, though, in the general direction of Cape Cod, and that was good enough for her. She was pretty sure she had lost Surfer Boy and Tattoo Man, yet felt that if she stopped, they somehow would catch up to her, find her, haul her in.

No closure. Again.

She should call Tyler, let him know she wouldn't make it tonight, but the Freeze guys she'd lost might triangulate her location if she used her cell. Tyler would figure it out. Best to keep the cell off.

She turned onto yet another rural road, passed two open gas stations, but didn't dare stop. She still had a little more than half a tank. How could that be? She'd been driving for—what? Three hours? Four? The tank, which hadn't been full to begin with, should've been scraping empty. It suddenly seemed likely that the wagon had an AK Hybrid engine. It made sense. Pham was as close to Kincaid as he was to Jake. But why?

She didn't know. And it wasn't enough to say that Pham liked Kincaid because he was Jake's buddy. There had to be something more, something she didn't know about, something about the good ole boys' club.

This private men's group, this good ole boys' club, was apparently privy to all sorts of information she didn't have. She felt like she'd been living under a rock the last five years.

As she crossed through yet another wooded area, she spotted a dirt road that led into pines. On impulse, she swerved onto it and bounced her way through the trees. The road ended at a fence in a thicket of pines, bare oaks. End of the line. She was too exhausted to drive another hundred feet.

She turned off the wagon, the headlights. The engine clicked, punctuating the immense silence. The blackness closed around her like a tight, hard fist. Nora locked the doors and crawled in between the seats to the back of the wagon. She turned on the inside light and surveyed the supplies Pham had provided.

He had prepared a basket filled with fresh fruits and vegetables, a container of coffee, cans of tuna fish, soups, fresh rolls, half a dozen eggs, a box of Kleenex, two flashlights with extra batteries, blankets, a pillow, a down sleeping bag, a case of bottled water, a box of kitchen matches, even some camping equipment. Emergency supplies and then some. He might be a member of the good ole boys' club, she thought, but she was deeply grateful for his thoughtfulness. Maybe she should have been married to Pham.

Nora skinned a banana and wolfed it down. She really had to pee, but sure didn't relish the thought of getting out of the car in the dark. She would never make it to morning, though, so she tested one of Pham's flashlights, helped herself to some Kleenex, unlocked the door. When her feet touched the ground, a kind of shudder went through her. After being in the car for so long, it felt strange to stretch her legs, to feel the solidity of the ground beneath her. The temperature had plunged and the cold bit through her heavy sweater and jeans. She scurried a little distance from the wagon, unzipped her jeans and squatted. The indignity of it all, she thought.

As she stood again, the hairs on the back of her neck rose, and she sensed she was being watched. She stepped back closer to the wagon, shone the flashlight around. The beam impaled a pair of eyes, watching her from between the trees.

Wolf? Please don't be a wolf, please, please.

The eyes vanished. Nora kept stepping back, moving the flashlight from side to side until she saw the animal's eyes again. Closer this time, brighter, glowing chunks of amber. If she spun and ran for the car, would she make it inside before the wolf got to her?

How fast can a hungry wolf run?

Faster than you.

She kept moving back, back, stirring up fallen leaves, nearly tripping over rocks, branches, her own feet. The flashlight's beam danced through the dark, an erratic firefly. And then she stumbled and fell back and landed so hard on her butt that she lost her grip on the flashlight. Air rushed from her lungs. Gasping for breath, she frantically slapped the ground for the flashlight—as much for the light as for a weapon. Just as her hand closed over it, the wolf shot toward her, a blur of speed and fur, an absence of color.

Nora propelled herself backward, the heels of her shoes digging into the leaves, against the hard ground, and then scrambled to her feet. A heartbeat later, the animal landed less than a foot from her.

Not a wolf. A dog. Reddish gold fur. A retriever, a golden retriever. It stared at her, teeth bared, but it wasn't growling. That was a good sign, right?

It wore a collar with a tag; its ribs showed beneath its thick coat.

"I . . . I thought you were a wolf," she said softly.

Her hushed voice, the fact that she made no sudden moves, apparently told the dog that she wasn't a threat. Its tail wagged—slowly, reluctantly. Nora saw that the dog was a female. She sank to her knees and held out her hand, palm exposed. "I won't hurt you. I don't have dog food, but I've got tuna. You like tuna?"

The dog cocked her head, those amber eyes studying Nora, then finally came toward her, tail wagging enthusiastically, nose working the air. She sniffed at Nora's outstretched hand— her tongue and breath as warm as toast—and finally allowed Nora to touch her, stroke her. The contact with another living thing softened something inside of her, she could feel it, almost as if her tissues, organs, and bones turned into something else, something pliable. Tears burned the corners of her eyes.

"Okay, I admit it. Deep down, I'm a mush head." She shone her flashlight on the dog's collar and read the tag: MY NAME IS SUNNY JESSIE, I BELONG TO SMITH COLLEGE. Under this was a phone number and an area code she didn't recognize. Smith was in Northampton and she knew that area code was 413, so did this refer to some other Smith College?

"Tuna, Sunny? Or do you go by Jessie? Or both?" she asked, and turned toward the wagon, the dog trailing her— friendly but wary, cautious, holding back.

Nora opened the side door and invited the dog to climb into the wagon. She sniffed, checking things out, then lifted her front legs, climbed into the back, and settled near the case of water. Nora climbed in after her, locked the doors, turned on the overhead light, both flashlights, and opened up the camping gear, several cans of tuna, water. She shared what she had with the dog, then made beds for both of them with the blankets and the sleeping bag. She had to move some of the supplies into the front seats, but when they were finally comfortable, Sunny curled up and went to sleep. Nora took off her shoes and rested her stocking feet against the dog's warm fur and got out her laptop and the envelope from Kincaid that Pham had given her.

It held both a compact flash card, for a PDA, and a CD. She booted up her laptop, noticed that she wasn't getting a wireless signal, no surprise, she was in the middle of nowhere. She popped the CD into her laptop, clicked on the only file, *Nora*.

> Forgive all the cloak & dagger stuff, but we can't be too careful. I have good reason to believe I'm the one they're looking for, Nora. But I got tipped off and split town before they could move in, so they arrested Jake, perhaps believing that he would be able to tell them where I am. Or maybe they took him in the hopes that you would turn to me for help and inadvertently lead them to me. I'll explain more when I see you.

> Call Tyler if you haven't spoken to him already. Memorize the e-mail address listed below, then reformat the CD.

> Alex

That was it? Other than the fact that he was tipped off by someone—who? And what had he done?—he still hadn't told her anything. Why should she meet Kincaid at Wood's Hole? Why couldn't he just tell her what really was going on? Right now, *she* was the one at risk, *she* was the one hiding out in a woods, huddled under a blanket in the back of a wagon, with a stray she had befriended.

Six years ago, at the height of their affair, Nora's PC had crashed and she had gone over to Kincaid's to finish a research paper on his computer. He was out of town, visiting his folks, and she knew where he kept the key and had let herself into the house. While working on his computer, she'd run across a file called *peoplesfriend*. She clicked it and a password window had popped up. Yet, none of his other files were password coded.

She didn't think much about it until several weeks later when she had stopped by Kincaid's warehouse after an evening class and found him fast asleep on the couch, his laptop on his desk, booted up and running. There, on the screen, was an e-mail from *peoplesfriend* that had arrived just moments earlier.

From the tone, Nora knew immediately knew the writer was female. Even though there was nothing sexual about the e-mail, it was flirtatious, chatty, and it was obvious that she and Kincaid had been communicating for some time. They seemed to have a mutual interest in alternative fuels, cars, and other scientific stuff that was way over Nora's head. She clicked back up through the column of e-mails and found another half dozen that had been received that evening.

As she was glancing through them, Kincaid woke up. *Why're you reading my e-mail?* She could still hear his voice, hear it echoing down through the years, quiet but edgy, soft but dangerous.

And she could still hear her own response, her voice accusatory. *Who is she?*

A colleague.

Bullshit, Alex. Just tell me the truth, okay? That's all I'm asking.

I can't, he snapped, and marched over to the laptop and shut it down. *I can't.*

If you're not involved with her, then why can't you talk about it? Why're you keeping it a secret?

It's not what you think.

Then what the hell is it? Why can't you tell me?

I can't. I just can't.

If she had to pinpoint the moment when their relationship had begun to collapse, that was it. To this day, she still didn't have any idea who this woman was, where she lived, the extent of her relationship with Kincaid, why he couldn't tell her the truth, nothing. But in her heart, now, in retrospect, she didn't believe Kincaid had been sleeping with her; he wasn't the type, he wasn't like Jake.

And yet, here she was, a fugitive who had been brought to this place and moment by the impenetrable secrets of a man whom she had loved passionately and another man whom she had married. *Forget it.*

She memorized the e-mail address, reformatted the CD and the flash card. She turned off the laptop, set it in the passenger seat, slapped a pillow down next to the dog, jerked the blanket up over her body, and turned off the overhead light, the flashlights. *Forget it.* She was going back to Blue River to play by the rules.

Oh? The rules saved your mother?

She slipped her cell phone out of her jacket pocket. A quick check, for messages. She turned the cell on, saw that she had a signal, and went into her voice mail, hoping for a message from Jake, that he somehow had escaped, that he was hiding out, or from Kincaid, telling her that for all these years she had been married to Jake, he had loved her.

Yeah, right. Laughable.

But the messages were from Tyler, Diana, her boss, the attorney. She clicked the last one, from Barrow. He had called the attorney whose name he had given her and he'd said he would take the case. The price? Eight grand down, five hundred an hour after that. Sure.

She sent a text message to Tyler's secure e-mail address, then fluffed up the pillow, crawled into the sleeping bag. She rolled onto her side and put her arm around Sunny. Tomorrow she would decide what to do. After she had slept. Tomorrow, tomorrow, she thought, and buried her face in Sunny's fur, inhaling the dog scents, the smells of wilderness. She choked back sobs, then finally released all of it and wept for what she had lost, didn't understand, didn't know, and for what she would face tomorrow and the next day. The lack of closure in her life had become her battle cry.

The Travelers

Cedar Key, Florida

Ultimately, solving the problem of warp drive,
time machines, and quantum gravity may
involve solving the "theory of everything."
—Michio Kaku

4

October 28

The twin-engine Cessna touched down on the Cedar Key runway shortly after midnight. Ryan Curtis and Kat Sargent waited nearby in an electric cart to pick up the passenger. Neither of them spoke, but they had long since passed the point of discomfort in their silences, Curtis thought.

Her lightweight leather jacket was buttoned up against the cool breeze that blew in off the Gulf and across the salt marshes. She'd let her ebony hair down and it spilled in wild curls over her shoulders and halfway down her back. He felt like running his fingers through it, but knew if he did, they would abandon the VIP in the Cessna and simply drive off in the electric cart, go to his place, fall into bed, and screw their brains out.

"Couldn't they find some other lackeys to pick him up?" Kat griped. "I mean, I don't recall ever seeing chauffeur in our job description."

"We'll have the next two days off."

"Unless they want Jake McKee disappeared tomorrow morning."

"I don't think the Council will move that quickly."

She looked over at him and in the backwash of the runway lights, her blue eyes seemed fathomless, inviting him to dive in. "We don't know that for sure. We never know anything for sure. I'm so fed up with trying to plan anything when nothing is certain."

They'd had this conversation a million times in the two years they'd been lovers and his response had become a joke between them. "Free health care, great pay, exciting travel, opportunities for advancement, and each other. Those are the certainties."

"C'mon, Ryan, you know what I'm talking about." She watched the Cessna as the engine died and the propellers went still.

"Yeah, yeah. We sold our souls when we signed up, we're like indentured servants, we have no say in anything that matters and . . ."

"Okay." She pressed her hand over his mouth. "You made your point. I sound like a broken record."

Her hand smelled good, of soap and a light perfume. He kissed the heel of her palm. "I can't wait to jump your bones."

"Ditto."

Late this afternoon, they had delivered McKee to the authorities here on the island. Believing their job was done until the Council ruled on the charges against McKee, they had gone back to Kat's condo and collapsed. But half an hour ago, Curtis's boss, Ian Rodriguez, had called and asked them to pick up the VIP whose plane had just landed. They were supposed to take him out to Snake Island, where McKee was being held. So here they were, obedient and reliable employees who made so much money and enjoyed so many benefits that the lack of overtime pay, the inconvenient hours, and unreasonable requests weren't supposed to be issues.

For Kat, it was all an issue because of the lack of personal freedom. She had come from a comfortable, secure childhood in the Northeast, where she had done pretty much whatever she wanted to do and never worried about money. She and her older sister had attended private schools and Kat had gone on to Princeton, majored in American Lit, and was in graduate school when she'd been recruited. She had joined for the adventure.

By contrast, Curtis had grown up in a two-bedroom house in South Miami, the oldest of three boys. His father drove for an airport limo service, his mother cleaned homes in upscale neighborhoods, and on Sundays the family worked together, selling junk at the huge outdoor flea market in Fort Lauderdale. The only reason he had gone to college at all was because he was the oldest—and, therefore, the best hope. But it wasn't as if his parents had stashed away money for his college education. Curtis had won scholarships and taken out loans to attend the University of Florida, where he had majored in political science.

When he got out of graduate school, he married a woman he was crazy about, but was nearly a hundred grand in debt and his prospects looked about as bleak as a Charles Dickens novel. Within several months, he'd landed a job at a private high school in Broward County and his wife had found a job as a preschool teacher. Half of what they made went to the repayment of college loans, they didn't make enough to afford health insurance, and could hardly pay their utility and phone bills. But they had each other and big dreams.

For the next three years, they struggled to make everything work, yet nothing had worked. They had sunk deeper into debt, he had grown progressively more bitter, and he and his wife argued all the time about money. Then he had gotten sick, some undiagnosed ailment that had put him in the hospital for a week.

His debt had risen by fifty grand because he had no health insurance.

He was released with half a dozen prescription medicines and dire warnings about how he might relapse at any time from this mysterious malaise. But the medicine was costing them a third of their monthly income, so Curtis quit taking all of it, started running, meditating, and became a vegetarian. He used the summer hiatus to look for a new job. Within several months, he was running in local marathons, was healthier than he'd ever been, but couldn't get out from under his crushing debt. Despite his wife's objections, he finally declared bankruptcy.

Just before the start of the new school year, a man he'd gotten to know through the marathons had offered him a job in a special ops program with the Department of Freedom and Security. Ian Rodriguez spelled out the extraordinary benefits that came with the job, but warned that in return, Curtis would be signing away some of his most basic freedoms. When Curtis had pressed him for details, Rodriguez simply handed him a card and told him to report to Cedar Key on Monday for a month of testing, for which he would be paid handsomely.

If you pass the testing phase, then you'll start training, Rodriguez had told him.

If. So many things in Curtis's life had hinged on IFs. *If* he got scholarships and loans, he would go to college. *If* his wife had moved to Cedar Key, perhaps they would still be together. *If* he hadn't declared bankruptcy, *if* he'd had health insurance, *if, if if.* But the rigorous testing to which he was subjected was like no other *if* he had ever experienced. It wasn't a matter of *if* he could pass the tests—medical, psychological, physical, mental, emotional, intuitive—but how badly he might fail.

His group of twenty—evenly divided between men and women—lost six people at the end of the first week, three at the end of the second, three at the end of the third week. By the end of the fourth week, only eight people remained. Of these, only five signed the confidentiality agreement required to be admitted into the year-long training program and within the first two months only three of the original group remained.

During the four-week testing period, he had lived on Cedar Key during the week and had gone home on weekends. By the time he had passed the tests and begun training, his marriage was unraveling faster than a spool of thread. His wife didn't understand why he couldn't talk about his job, she refused to move to Cedar Key, their sex life fell apart, and within several months she filed for divorce.

So yes, the inconveniences and unreasonable requests were issues for him and yes, he and Kat were like indentured servants. But when he recalled the position he'd been in seven years ago, bankrupt and without prospects, the inconveniences and demands ceased to matter.

Kat slapped the back of her hand against his thigh. "C'mon, the senator's coming down the steps. We'd better get over there and pick him up. If he walks three yards, he might keel over from a heart attack. I mean, what do you figure he weighs, anyway?"

Probably around two-fifty, Curtis guessed, and he didn't have the frame to support all the weight. Senator Joe Aiken looked like Humpty-Dumpty, bald head and all. But he was also one of the wealthiest and most powerful senators on the Hill, responsible for Freeze's funding and, therefore, for the massive part of that budget that went to SPOT—Special Projects Operation Temporal. Only Aiken and one other senator—and about two hundred employees—knew that SPOT was something other than the dog in the Dick and Jane books.

Both Curtis and Kat got out of the cart to greet Aiken and although he shook their hands, it was readily apparent that he didn't like doing it. Curtis wondered if he suffered from a fear of germs or if this was something that happened to politicians after they'd been in the game as long as Aiken had, twenty years and counting. All that campaigning, all those barbecues and reception lines.

"May I take your briefcase, sir?" Curtis asked. "And your bag?"

"The bag, thank you, Mr. Curtis."

Now he added bellhop to his job description. He slung the bag over his shoulder. "How was your flight, sir?"

"Tedious." He got into the cart's passenger seat and Kat climbed into the back with his bag. "I understand you two brought in Professor McKee?"

"Yes, sir," Kat said, and passed him a bottle of cold water that she'd pulled from the cooler on the floor in back.

"Thanks." He unscrewed the top and guzzled down about half of it. "That's mighty good. And where's the professor now?"

"In a holding cell," Curtis replied. "We'll take you over there."

"And where is that, exactly?"

Curtis stabbed his thumb out into the dark. "Snake Island. It's about three miles from here. The tide is high now, so we'll go over by boat."

"And what's the status on McKee's wife?"

"I haven't heard, Senator." Curtis turned the cart toward the marina, where the boat was tied up. "We just got called back to work thirty minutes ago. You'll have to ask Mr. Rodriguez. He's already over on the island."

"I understand McKee resisted."

"And his wife gave us some trouble," Curtis added. "The techs are going through McKee's motherboard, but so far they haven't found anything useful. And nothing of any use was found in his car."

"Did McKee give you any idea where Alex Kincaid is?"

"He claims he doesn't know," Kat replied. "Says he hasn't seen him in three days, which is about the time we think Kincaid went on the run. His apartment had been cleaned out."

"Everything?"

"Except for his phone," Kat said. "And that service wasn't turned off."

"Now *that's* disturbing. Was he tipped off?"

"It would seem so," Kat replied. "But we don't have any confirmation and have no idea where his tip would have come from. We've been very discreet."

"But perhaps not discreet enough. The arrest created quite a stir in Blue River."

Aiken obviously wasn't happy with any of this and if Aiken wasn't happy, Rodriguez wouldn't be either. And when Ian

Rodriguez wasn't happy, neither was Lydia Fenmore. And since they mentored him and Kat, Curtis could just imagine what the fallout would be for them. He tried to smooth things over a bit.

"Would you like to stop by our cafeteria first for a bite to eat, Senator? To freshen up?"

"Perhaps afterward. Right now, I just want to get to this island."

Apparently food wasn't the way to soften Aiken. Curtis pulled into the dimly lit marina and stopped at the end of the dock. Half a dozen boats of various sizes were tied up, but he put the senator's bag into the smallest and fastest vessel.

Aiken balked. "We're going in *that*?"

"Uh, yes, sir. It's fast and can get through the salt marshes even when the tide is fairly low. It's only three miles."

"I can't swim," he said.

"We have life jackets." Kat touched his arm and turned on her charm.

Curtis marveled at how, within moments, she transformed Aiken from a gloomy, moody fat man into a guy marginally more personable. He actually laughed at one point, his jowls shaking, and Curtis wondered what she'd said to him.

Among their peers, Kat's charm—like her good looks—was practically legendary. Not a single one of the other Travelers disliked her, the twenty recruits in training thought she was cool, and the opinion of Kat among all twenty mentors was unanimous, that she had enormous potential. Rodriguez liked her well enough, a good thing since he was SPOT's director, and Lydia Fenmore, her mentor and the assistant director, was crazy about her. Her only detractors were among the five Council members, two old male farts who thought her penchant for tight, flashy clothing was suggestive and that her methods were sometimes too unconventional. Whatever that meant.

She obviously had a new fan in Aiken, which wouldn't hurt her standing among the Council members.

As the boat neared Snake Island, a pair of dolphins suddenly appeared, arcing through the cold moonlight, the noise rushing from their blowholes echoing eerily through the dark. Curtis cut the engine way back and Aiken sat up straighter, watching with fascination as the dolphins escorted them to the island. They cut away before the water got too shallow and Aiken sat there grinning, nodding to himself.

"Spectacular," he exclaimed as he heaved his massive body out of the boat and onto the dock. He unfastened the life jacket and tossed it back into the boat. "I don't think I've ever seen dolphins that close up."

Kat told him about how she had gone swimming with dolphins in Hawaii and in Key Largo. She described it in such beautiful detail that Curtis thought the senator might be ready to jump overboard and learn to swim the old-fashioned way—*do it or sink*.

While Kat walked with Aiken toward the main building, Curtis tied up the boat.

He hated Snake Island—the name, the untamed wildness of the place, its abject ugliness. It was one of thirteen islands that comprised the Cedar Key National Wildlife Refuge and hadn't been open to the public for the last fifteen years, since SPOT had taken it over.

Other than the few improvements SPOT had made, the island hadn't changed that much since the 1800s, when Cedar Key and the neighboring islands had been covered in cedar trees that had provided the pencil factories with endless supplies of wood. The crowning glory for Snake Key had occurred in 1880, when a yellow fever epidemic had plunged the island into quarantine. That curse had pretty much endured for more than a century now. To Curtis, Snake Island was the government's version of Devil's Island, a perfect prison.

They followed the dock and then the elevated walkway toward the one-story building, painted green to blend into the surrounding cypress trees. Three security lights burned from the corners and front of the building, illuminating the walkway. It kept the critters away. Just once, he shone his flashlight over the walkway railing, impaling a slithering dark brown mass six feet below. Cottonmouths. Also known as water moccasins, they were a pit viper as venomous as the copperhead, with heat-sensing organs that allowed them to locate warm-blooded prey. One of them leaped several feet out of the water, its jaws gaping wide, and the beam of his flashlight exposed the inside of its mouth with the puffy white lining after which the species was named.

Curtis wrenched back, his mouth flashing dry, his heart slamming into double time. He hurried up the walkway after Kat and Aiken and called Rodriguez's cell. He answered immediately. "I heard the boat. I'll buzz you into the building."

"He wants to see McKee ASAP."

"He's awake and ready."

The electricity on the island came from solar panels and two propane-powered generator systems that, like the walkway, were elevated and covered in enough concrete to shield the worst of their noise. But as they neared the front door, Curtis could hear them, a steady clatter that made him want to grind his teeth.

The front doors clicked and Rodriguez opened them, smiling. "Joe, it's great to see you."

Rodriguez, Cuban to his core, gave Aiken an *abrazo*, a bear hug, then quickly motioned them into the lobby, as though untold dangers lurked outside. Something other than the cottonmouths, Curtis thought.

Lydia Fenmore waited just inside, her plump moon face straining against what Curtis guessed was lack of sleep and anxiety that something would go wrong during Aiken's visit. She seemed to be perpetually braced against worst-case scenarios—their funding yanked, some horrible flaw revealed in the program, no telling. Curtis never thought of her as Lydia. She was simply Fenmore, the embodiment of SPOT bureaucracy and, because she was the first recruit back in 1974, its greatest repository of knowledge about the program.

"Joe," she gushed. "How nice to see you."

"You're looking well, Lydia." Aiken gave her a quick hug. "These late hours must agree with you."

Curtis and Kat exchanged a glance and she rolled her eyes too quickly for anyone else to catch it. So much bullshit, he thought, stifling a smile. Kat fell into step beside him and they followed the three big shots through the building.

From this angle, they looked like an odd trio. Rodriguez, with his thinning gray hair, was as tall and thin as bamboo. Fenmore was shorter but muscular, with a long braid that bounced against her spine. She had turned fifty this year, which made her a decade younger than Rodriguez and ten years plus younger than Aiken. The senator was the roly-poly man, and already wheezing from the short walk. A carnival circus act, Curtis thought.

"We won't be getting out of here for hours," Kat whispered. "Aiken wants us present when he's talking to McKee."

"He said that?"

"Yeah."

Shit, Curtis thought. Wasn't it enough that they'd had McKee and Kincaid under surveillance for nearly a year? That they'd brought McKee in safely? That they'd accumulated enough evidence for the Council to sentence him? Now they were supposed to stick around while Aiken questioned him? Why? And why was Aiken *really* here? In Curtis's six years with SPOT, this was only the second time Aiken had been to the Cedar Key facility, at least that Curtis knew of, and the first time Curtis had met him.

Rodriguez opened the door to the Council chamber and they all filed inside. No windows, no decoration on the concrete walls, no clock, just a front and rear exit. To Curtis, it felt like a death chamber.

The table where the Council members sat, empty now, was set up at the front of the room, on an elevated platform, with another dozen tables in the chamber for spectators. One table held a colorful buffet and Rodriguez, with a grand sweep of his arm, invited them all to help themselves. Once they were settled, he said, "Professor McKee will be brought in shortly. Lydia and I want to bring you up to speed first, Joe."

"Where's Alex Kincaid?" Aiken dipped his spoon into a bowl of fruit salad.

"We, uh, don't know, Joe." Fenmore tapped a couple of keys on her laptop. "And we still don't have any word on it. Our original plan was to bring him and McKee in together, but Kincaid disappeared three days ago."

"Yes, I know that." Aiken made an impatient gesture. "Ms. Sargent filled me in. So you decided to bring in Jake McKee alone rather than risk having him vanish as well."

"We're pretty sure Nora McKee will lead us to Kincaid," Rodriguez added.

"And she is where?"

Fenmore looked extremely nervous now, Curtis thought, and was surprised at how satisfying it was to see her squirm. "We, uh, had two Freeze officers following her in Blue River, but she gave them the slip and escaped."

"And now she is where?" Aiken asked, pinning Fenmore with his icy eyes.

"We don't know."

"Marvelous. And she created quite a scene when McKee was arrested. The media was all over it."

"And by tomorrow, it'll be a forgotten story," Rodriguez said. "We believe she's headed toward Cape Cod, where her brother lives.'"

"We need to do a lot better than this, Ian. I'm not blaming your Travelers, they did the job they were supposed to do," he added quickly, with a warm glance at Kat. "But your methods stink. McKee should have been arrested at home, Kincaid should have been brought in a week ago. And if your intention all along was to get the McKee woman to lead you to Kincaid, then your strategy should have been more focused. In other words, it seems to me there should have been better planning and stronger communication between you and the arresting officers."

Rodriguez and Fenmore looked stunned by the senator's

indictment of their methods, their protocol, their *process,* as Rodriguez constantly referred to it. Curtis suddenly felt vindicated. He and Kat had done their jobs, all right, at least in the senator's eyes, and right now, his eyes were the only ones that mattered.

"I was never quite clear on why we were supposed to bring in Kincaid," Kat said.

"You weren't *told?*" Aiken looked shocked.

"We never are." Curtis struggled to ignore the dagger looks that Rodriguez and Fenmore hurled his way. "That's part of protocol."

"Now just a goddamn minute, Ryan," burst Rodriguez. "You're told enough so that you can do the job, so . . ."

"Shut up, Ian," Aiken barked, and gave Curtis and Kat his full attention. "Just so that you're fully informed, Mr. Curtis, the government wants the AK Hybrid. The best minds in the industry have worked on this engine for months and can't figure out how it works. The technology is light years ahead of anything we know. That's probably why he doesn't have a patent. No one else can build these things. We've approached Kincaid several times through an intermediary, offering to buy him out, but he has refused every offer. So we need him to explain the construction of the engine to use. We need his blueprints."

"The government wants the blueprints so it can go into the auto-building business?" Fenmore asked with a laugh. "That's the silliest damn thing I've heard yet. The car is a piece of junk. It doesn't go faster than sixty, you can fit maybe three small people inside of it, and the American consumer is *not* going to embrace it. They haven't so far."

"Only because Kincaid has produced barely a thousand of them," Aiken told her. "And Lydia, you haven't done your homework. Kincaid's Hybrid gets between two and three hundred miles a gallon. And once we have the blueprints, we can have five to six million of these cars on the road within two years and do it without *outsourcing* jobs. It will begin to sever our dependence on foreign oil."

Interesting, Curtis thought. The last he'd heard, Senator Aiken was in bed with the oil company lobbyists, who probably hoped to buy out the hybrid so they could kill it.

"But we're not here to discuss the hybrid," Aiken went on. "Just tell me, Mr. Curtis, how the protocol works in SPOT. A Traveler is given an assignment. Then what?"

Rodriguez butted in before Curtis could reply. "He or she carries out the assignment."

"I didn't ask you, Ian." Aiken didn't even bother glancing at Rodriguez; his eyes remained pinned on Curtis. "Mr. Curtis?"

Didn't Aiken realize he was putting him on the spot? "We, uh . . ."

The senator sat forward, his eyes skewed with earnestness. "If you don't feel comfortable speaking freely in front of Ian and Lydia, Mr. Curtis, then I can ask them to leave the room for a few minutes."

"You know how this organization is run, Joe," Rodriguez snapped.

"I have vague outlines, erratic reports, incomplete information."

"We're not trying to hide anything," Fenmore piped up. Quickly.

Curtis nearly laughed aloud. The entire organization was shrouded in secrecy, everything about it was hidden. But he wasn't sure how much he should say.

"Go on, Ryan," Rodriguez said. "Answer the goddamn question."

"When we're, uh, given an assignment, we're told that the person is under suspicion for something—terrorist activities, antiwar protests, animal-rights activism, whatever. Our job is to begin surveillance of the individual and gather supportive evidence of the suspected activities that can be presented to the Council, so they can pass judgment and then a sentence."

"And what were you told about Jake McKee and Alex Kincaid?"

"Just that they were wanted for subversive activities and that McKee had crashed Pentagon computers."

Aiken nodded, leaned forward, his salad forgotten. "Then allow *me* to bring all of *you* up to speed. Our economy is in meltdown. The country is so far in debt now to foreign nations that if they all called in the loans at once, the country would sink faster than the *Titanic*. Freeze is facing a massive cutback in funding, which will impact SPOT."

Uh-oh. Curtis caught the stench of incipient unemployment in this conversation, and judging from the look on Kat's face, she sensed the same thing. No wonder Rodriguez and Fenmore didn't want them in the room.

"Joe, our policy and budget issues are discussed only among the director, assistant director, and Council members." Rodriguez sounded royally pissed now, and Curtis wasn't surprised when he said, "Ryan and Kat, if you could please leave the room."

"They stay," Aiken snapped. "I'm not finished yet and they're going to be involved and need to hear the bottom line. Your outfit is facing a funding shortfall of . . ."

"Excuse me, but as director of this organization, *I* decide how policies are implemented." Rodriguez's testy tone cut the tension like a knife through jelly. "*I* decide . . ."

Aiken exploded with laughter, the flaps of his double chin jiggling, then slammed his fist down so hard against the table that plates and glasses and silverware shuddered. Rodriguez and Fenmore wrenched back, Curtis and Kat exchanged a glance. "Taxes pay your salary, Ian." His pudgy finger slid through the air, pointing at Fenmore. "And yours. And yours and yours." He pointed at Curtis and Kat. "And mine. *Taxes fund a time travel operation that doesn't exist officially. The ultimate black ops.*"

Silence. All eyes on Aiken now. He leaned forward, his jowls jiggling, and laced his pudgy fingers together. In a calmer voice, he went on. "I understand how easy it is, Ian, for you and Lydia to believe you're king and queen of this operation. Tucked away down here, with almost no oversight whatsoever. But the facts are simple. The Freeze budget is being cut way back, which means your budget is going to be pummeled. There's going to be a shortfall of at least a hundred million."

"They can't do that," Fenmore burst out. "SPOT is essential to national security, it's . . ."

"Save the rhetoric for the pubs, Lydia," Aiken snapped. "The figure I just gave you is only an estimate. It could end up being twice that. The way I see it, there are several ways to mitigate the damage. Stopgap measures, until we come up with something better." His plump index finger popped up. "One, massive employee cutbacks and drastic cuts in pay and services. I don't particularly like that option. Two . . ." His middle finger came up. "We tap into the Pentagon budget. They would love to utilize SPOT's technology. But we all know they eventually would seize control. I don't like this option, either."

Bad enough, Curtis thought, that they'd become chauffeurs and bellhops. But he couldn't see himself and Kat saluting generals and living under military law. "That option sucks," Curtis muttered.

Rodriguez and Fenmore gave him a dirty look, making it clear that he wasn't allowed to speak, that he shouldn't even be here. It pissed him off and tempted him to bring up the major problems they'd had in the past eight months with the biochip that made the entire program possible. The forty Travelers were normally chipped every sixty days, but now it was necessary to do it every month because the failure rate of the chips was increasing. In September, three Travelers had gotten stranded in the past; another two had gotten stranded this month. They'd all been retrieved, but it cost a lot of time and money to do it.

The accelerated failure rate meant that production of the biochips had increased beyond the five hundred that were usually made annually. Another huge expense that the senator didn't know about, Curtis thought, and not necessarily a good solution since no one knew why the chips were failing. But neither Rodriguez nor Fenmore chose to enlighten Aiken about any of this.

"The third option," Aiken went on, "is private funding."

"*Corporate* funding?" Rodriguez asked, obviously appalled. "Forget it."

"*Private* funding, Ian. Not corporate. Ten to twenty individuals with the financial resources to pay for a trip to the era of their choice, within reason, of course. If the price is set at around ten million, that would raise between one hundred and two hundred million for SPOT within a few months. It would buy us time."

"Out of the question," Rodriguez snapped. "You'd have billionaires wanting to witness the JFK assassination."

"Or the crucifixion of Christ," Fenmore added.

"Or the big bang," Kat said.

"And that's just for starters," Rodriguez spat. "Look, Ian, for thirty years, SPOT has managed to exist under the radar by adhering to the policies and regulations that Mariah Jones and her original group established. We still don't know enough about the repercussions of time travel to start sending multimillionaires into the past for goddamn vacations. And even vetting these people for security doesn't guarantee they won't talk about it at some point in the future. A cocktail party, too many drinks, who the hell knows what these people might blurt out?"

Aiken folded his pudgy hands together, as if he believed his response required not only patience, but also prayer, the intervention of some higher power. "I understand your concerns, Ian. And I've given all of this a great deal of thought. The participants must be recommended by someone we know personally or by another participant. Only experienced Travelers—like Mr. Curtis and Ms. Sargent—would be assigned to these journeys. These individuals would also provide valuable input for the program. You could debrief them afterward, run medical tests on them, psychological tests, whatever would help expand your knowledge. And if any of them gave the Travelers a problem, the participants would be disappeared to the Jurassic era, somewhere so far back they wouldn't be a threat. Bottom line, we'd have *cash*." Aiken leaned forward, his face set. "And without that influx of cash, this whole program folds in about ten days."

"Ten days?" Fenmore whispered.

Sweet Christ, Curtis thought. Kat was right. There were no guarantees, nothing was certain. "It sounds as if you have candidates, Senator," said Curtis, noticing that neither Rodriguez nor Fenmore gave him dirty looks now. They were too shocked by that timetable. *Ten days.*

"I have twelve possible candidates so far, men and women whom I know personally. These are people who would pay fifteen or twenty million just for time on the international space station. We'd be offering them something so far beyond that it's almost incomprehensible."

"I just can't buy this." Rodriguez shook his head vehemently, like a father so exasperated by a two-year-old that he didn't know whether to scream or hit the kid. "We're talking about private citizens knowing that we possess the means for time travel, that we've spent the last thirty years disappearing criminals, undesirables, and dissidents into the past. Good God."

"They don't have to know about that part of it," Aiken said. "As far as the time travel part. . . ." He shrugged. "These people want a totally unique experience and we'd be giving it to them."

"Absurd," Fenmore snapped. "The whole thing is just too absurd to even consider."

"We're talking about one to two hundred million in cash, Lydia." Then he reached into his back pocket, brought out his wallet, and removed a slip of paper than he passed to Rodriguez. "That's a deposit slip for SPOT's Cayman account. Twenty million was deposited this morning by your first two candidates."

The reality seemed to hit Rodriguez all at once. He looked as if he'd been kicked in the balls, Curtis thought.

"Christ almighty," Rodriguez muttered. "And who are they?"

"My wife and me," Aiken replied. "And Mr. Curtis and Ms. Sargent will accompany us. Now bring in McKee."

5

Handcuffed and shackled, Jake McKee shuffled into the chamber in a navy blue jumpsuit that marked him as the accused. Curtis noticed that he moved with the wariness of the hunted, the abused, shoulders hunched, eyes narrowed, startled, darting here and there. He needed a shower and a shave and looked confused, as most of them did when they entered this room.

The guard pushed him down into the chair for the accused, just below the Council table, and spun the chair around so that McKee faced Curtis and the others. "You two again," McKee muttered, glaring at Curtis and Kat.

He sounded congested, probably due to his bruised, swollen nose, from Kat's punch. His right cheek was the color of plums. "We have some questions to ask you, Professor McKee." Curtis got to his feet and walked over to where McKee sat. "The quicker you answer them, the faster you're outta here."

"Ever heard of habeas corpus?" he spat. "I've been imprisoned unlawfully and I have the right to be brought in front of a court so that can be determined. This isn't a goddamn court. It's a travesty, a tribunal. And I'm entitled to an attorney. Until I get one, I'm not answering any questions."

Not as confused as he looked, Curtis thought, and spelled it out for him. "As a suspected terrorist, you checked your rights at the door."

"A terrorist." He laughed, a sharp, ugly sound. "For teaching English literature to college students?"

"For crashing and hacking into Pentagon computers."

"I did? I did that? When? How? I can barely load software into my computer."

"Where's Alex Kincaid?"

"How should I know?

"Did he move, Mr. McKee? Did he flee? Where'd he go?"

"You speak English, so I'm assuming you understand it. *I. Don't. Know.*"

Curtis kept hammering away at him and tried, as he often did, not to think about how he and Kat had selected evidence to support the charges against McKee. But that was their job, right? "You're his closest friend. You should know."

"Really?"

"Where's your wife?"

"How the hell should I know? I haven't seen her since you and your friend hauled me off the street in Blue River."

"Actually, she's on the run, Mr. McKee, and your buddy Kincaid has been in touch with her and as soon as they connect, we'll bring them both in."

"She'll outwit you pricks any day of the week."

"When was the last time you spoke to Kincaid?"

"*You* were watching us, *you* had our phones tapped, *you* were tracking our online shit. *You* tell *me.*" He was deeply agitated now, sitting forward, eyes spitting fire.

"If you're not guilty of anything, why did you run from the restaurant?"

The question threw him—his features tightened, his mouth twitched, he quickly lowered his eyes to his cuffed hands. After a moment, he spoke in a sharp, menacing voice. "Because I know all about you people." McKee raised his eyes again, glaring first at Curtis, then lifting his shackled hands and pointing his finger at each of the others. "You're the same people who arrested my mother-in-law twenty-three years ago, hauled her off and made her disappear."

Huh? His mother-in-law? Nora McKee's mother? Disappeared? If that was true, wasn't it something he and Kat should have been told? Curtis felt like marching over to Rodriguez and demanding an explanation. But that would make him look confrontational or foolish or weak. Best to move forward. "Your mother-in-law. That would be who, exactly?"

"Elizabeth Griffin Walrave. She was arrested on February 14, 1983. For funding subversives. I mean, c'mon, she and her husband owned a catering business." He stabbed his finger at Aiken, hissing with menace. "And you . . . you're the worst of the lot. You're Senator Aiken. I've seen you on TV, the man who supposedly upholds civil rights, whose votes come down on the sides of the individual rather than on the side of government or corporations . . . what bullshit." His voice had steadily increased in volume and now he was shouting. "You swore to uphold the Constitution. More bullshit. You're sitting in on this tribunal. You're murderers, all of you . . ."

McKee's tirade ended abruptly, his head snapped back, his eyes rolled upward in their sockets, and a low, horrifying noise spilled from his mouth. His body shook violently, spittle frothed in the corners of his mouth, the shackles rattled noisily. Curtis realized that someone—Rodriguez, it had to be him—had signaled the guard to electrify the chair, that the charge raced through the metal shackles attached to the underside of the armrests.

Curtis threw himself at the guard, knocking him back into the wall, and the device that triggered the charge skittered across the floor. He swept it up, left the guard stammering, marched over to the table where the others sat in a stunned silence, and slammed the device down in front of Rodriguez.

"Don't you *dare* torture someone I'm questioning, Ian. Indulge your sadism on your own time."

Color raced up Rodriguez's neck and into his face, his dark eyes bulged in their sockets, and he shot to his feet. "You're *way* out of line, Ryan. I'm the director of this organization and *I* call the shots here, not *you*."

And Curtis suddenly saw Rodriguez for what he was—not an adopted father or a benevolent mentor, as Rodriguez had led him to believe when they were fellow marathon runners. Hell, Rodriguez wasn't even a concerned boss. He was just one more petty tyrant who bestowed blessings on the faithful and retribution on those who questioned his authority. "Go pound sand."

"For chrissakes," Kat muttered, and got up with a bottle of water in one hand, a napkin in the other. "Now he's not going to be in any shape to answer questions." She hurried to McKee, doubled over at the table, his limbs twitching like those of a splayed frog. She soaked the napkin with water and held it against the back of McKee's neck.

"It's not torture," Rodriguez spat, glancing at Aiken and the others. "It ends their tirades, forces them to understand the rules, the *process*."

But his argument sounded weak, feeble, cowardly, and Curtis knew that even Aiken recognized it. "Ian, you sound like a redneck trying to justify why he beat his dog with a baseball bat," Aiken said. "Go get some fresh air. We're done here. Ms. Sargent, is he okay?" He heaved his body to his feet.

"I think so. But I'm not a doctor."

McKee groaned and tried to lift his head. His skin was as white as Wonder Bread; a pulse throbbed at his temple. "He looks like crap," Curtis said.

"You," Aiken said to the guard. "Take the accused back to holding and get someone over from medical to check him out."

"Yes, sir."

Aiken went over to Kat and McKee, the two of them conferring in hushed voices. Fenmore hadn't moved, Rodriguez looked like he was on the verge of a stroke or a massive coronary, and Curtis just stood there, struggling against a tsunami of exhaustion. Rodriguez brought his fingers just under his eyes, then pointed at Curtis. *I'm watching you.* Like a bad spy movie, Curtis thought, and returned a gesture much more universal: his third finger shot up.

The ride back in the boat was tense; no one spoke. The wind had a nip to it. The temperature had dropped into the upper forties, Curtis guessed. The tide was starting to go out, too, with islands of wet sand visible now, shimmering in the moonlight like beached dolphins or whales.

Curtis had heard about the electric chair in the chamber, but until the moment when he'd seen McKee's head snap back, seen him frothing at the mouth like a rabid dog, it had been an abstraction, one more rumor in a mill of endless rumors. His knee-jerk reaction probably would land him in counseling or could result in a suspension. Or, worse, it might get him fired.

But when you were fired from SPOT, you didn't go home again. You were sent to rehab and it wasn't just your ordinary drug and alcohol rehab. This place was specifically for recruits who washed out of training, for Travelers who broke the rules and didn't adhere to the *process.* It would mean amnesic drugs, intense brainwashing, electroshock treatments. He knew. He knew because one of the recruits during his training—a bright young woman from the northwest—had challenged their instructor, Lydia Fenmore, about some of the time-travel theories.

Are you saying that it's forbidden to change anything in the past or that the past is static? the recruit had asked.

It's forbidden, Lydia had replied. *We simply have no way of knowing for sure how our actions in the past change the present.*

But doesn't our very presence there and the fact that we're disappearing people into the past, change it?

Everyone in the class, of course, including Curtis, had wondered the same thing. But until that moment, no one had the guts to ask. They were all too afraid of calling attention to themselves.

We take every precaution, Fenmore had said, her tone sharp, irritated. *We've found that the first twenty-four to forty-eight hours are critical. After that, time seems to accommodate our presence. But the bottom line, until we learn differently, is that a butterfly flapping its wings in Brazil may set off a tornado in Texas. Do you understand what that means?*

And the recruit, who apparently knew more than Fenmore had anticipated, had replied that Edward Lorentz was talking about weather when he made his discovery about the butterfly effect. *Isn't time flexible enough to accommodate such changes by creating a new timeline?*

Fenmore, he remembered, had frowned, peered at the recruit over the rim of her glasses, as if really seeing her for the first time, and right then, Curtis had known that she had been tagged as undesirable. *As far as we know, there is just one timeline, from past to present to future. And until we discover otherwise, we act accordingly, never taking undue risks when we travel into the past.*

If there's one timeline, then why can't we go into the future? the recruit had persisted.

At that point, Fenmore had gotten flustered. *We don't know why,* she replied, and shortly afterward, the recruit had failed to show up in class. When Curtis asked about her, he was told she was dismissed from the program. Several weeks later, during an intense period of training in a long and difficult year, he'd gotten a call from the banished recruit, her voice hushed, urgent. She claimed she was in a supply closet, she'd stolen a cell phone, they were killing her, electroshock, drugs, wiping her memories clean, help her, dear God, he had to help her. She thought she was somewhere in Santa Barbara, California, swore she would find out the exact address, the name of the facility, but he'd never heard from her again.

From her, Curtis had learned that the secret to making it through training and beyond was to agree with everything. *Nod, smile, follow the rules, be a good dog, bark when they tell you to bark, roll over and play dead.*

He'd sure blown it tonight.

During his first year as a Traveler, he had gotten the name of the facility in Santa Barbara and had gone there to track down the woman. Posing as a distant cousin, he had learned that she died in the facility. Complications from diabetes, that was the official cause of death. He hadn't believed it for a second.

So he knew the repercussions. He knew that when you signed up, when you entered training, there was no turning back. You sold out, just as Kat had said. You became an indentured servant, forever in their debt, and if you screwed up, as he had tonight, you paid. One way or another, you paid. The only question now was how severe that payment would be.

In fact, when he thought about it, Travelers fell into two distinct groups. Either they were like Kat, inordinately adventurous, free-spirited individuals who could adhere to rules only as long as the game fed their sense of adventure, or they were like him, people whose emotional or material deprivations earlier in life kept them in the game because of the security that SPOT offered.

Curtis brought the boat into the marina. Kat helped the senator out and Rodriguez and Fenmore followed. Kat collected the life jackets and passed them to Curtis, who returned them to the storage bin on the dock. While Rodriguez and Fenmore talked with the others, Curtis puttered around, stalling for time in the hopes that Rodriguez and Fenmore would leave. He didn't want to deal with Rodriguez again tonight. But as he was tying up the boat, Rodriguez came over to him, face drawn, voice thick with nuance.

"Joe is staying for a few days, Ryan. Over at the condos. Building C, apartment three. Can you and Kat drop him off?"

"Sure." He waited for Rodriguez to ream him from one end of the universe to the other, to remind him of the rules, the protocol, the goddamn process. But nothing happened and Curtis wondered if Rodriguez was waiting for him to bark, roll over, play dead, or beg for forgiveness. He finally said, "Will you be needing us tomorrow morning?"

"I doubt it. At the earliest, the Council won't meet about McKee until tomorrow afternoon. I'll talk to him once more, but I think he's useless to us, except as bait. We'll have to find Kincaid on our own. But I'll call you. Make sure the senator is comfortable, Ryan." He paused, eyes fixed on the ground. "Accommodate him, show him what we do here. Not a full-fledged transition, just a taste of it." He raised his gaze and there, in the dim light of the marina, the expression on his face reminded Curtis of the way his old man had looked the day he'd left for college eighteen years ago— aware that some delicate balance of power had shifted. "But watch him closely. And Ryan . . ." His voice dropped. "I would appreciate it if you don't mention the problems we've been having with the chips."

No wonder he'd gotten a reprieve. Since Aiken had tapped him and Kat as "experienced Travelers" and requested them as the guides for his own excursions, he and Kat now fell under a protected status, like an endangered species. So the unstated contract was that if Curtis would keep the chip business to himself, Rodriguez would overlook his insubordination in the chamber. Yeah, okay, he could play this stupid game.

"When should Kat and I take him back?" Curtis asked.

"The sooner the better. Once he's tasted the possibilities, he'll leave, sell the program to his investors, and we can schedule a full-scale transition later."

Rodriguez hastened off with Fenmore, got into an electric cart, and the two of them headed toward downtown and home.

It was common knowledge that Rodriguez and Fenmore had been lovers way back when Fenmore had recruited Rodriguez in 1980. But they subsequently had married other Travelers, as Travelers were encouraged to do because it kept the divorce rate down, and had started families. They'd had six kids between them, all of them grown now. When their spouses had died a decade ago, several months apart, they had moved in together, into a loft downtown. Good thing for them both, Curtis thought. A partner who was also in SPOT lessened the loneliness of the job.

Curtis hurried over to the electric cart where Kat and Aiken waited for him and headed up Airport Road. He and Kat, like some of the other Travelers, owned condos at the Old Fenimore Mill at the other end of the island, where the senator would be staying. Curtis also owned a place between Cedar Key and Gainesville, an old Florida house with jalousie windows and terrazzo floors, set in the midst of tremendous banyan trees on five acres of riverfront property. It was where he and Kat lived their real lives together when they weren't on call or working. No one within SPOT knew about it.

He hung a right at the end of Airport Road and took Palmetto Drive toward town. Deserted at this hour of the night, the road curved along the Gulf, which looked like a flat black sheet in the moonlight. The houses on the other side of the road had stood here for years, throwbacks to the 1950s, when Cedar Key had been primarily a fishing village. Now tourism was the island's lifeblood.

It suddenly struck him that he was attracted to islands, that they spoke to him in the same way that certain works of art spoke to art collectors. He and Kat often visited islands in their free time and more often than not, those visits involved other eras. The Dominican Republic during Columbus's time, the Hebrides in the 1940s, Easter Island before its giant statues were erected, the Galapagos at the time of Darwin's journey.

During many excursions together, they had gone to Aruba in their own time and stayed at Waverunner, a charming spot built on the grounds of an old coconut plantation where they had a one-bedroom apartment and plenty of privacy. He sometimes thought that Aruba would be an ideal location for SPOT. It was larger than Cedar Key, embraced foreigners and foreign investment, and had just enough of an international flavor to keep life interesting.

"I'm curious," Aiken said suddenly. "Why did you choose such a public location in which to arrest McKee?"

"We were told it should be public," Curtis replied.

"By Ian?"

"And Lydia," Kate added. "They think it's a good thing for the public to be reminded every so often about how ubiquitous Freeze is."

Aiken shook his head, but Curtis had no idea what it meant. A kind of pensiveness entered the senator's demeanor at this point—not gloomy, like earlier, just thoughtful, as if he were turning certain details over and over in his mind, examining everything from various angles. When he finally spoke again, the cart was humming through the silent downtown, past shops and restaurants long since closed up for the night.

"And Mr. Curtis, you seemed surprised about Nora McKee's mother."

"Yes, sir. It was the first I'd heard about it."

"Christ, that's sloppy. What's the point of keeping that information from you? That's got to change. If we're going to open the program to investors, a number of details have to change. Mrs. McKee must've been—what? Eight? Ten?"

"If it happened twenty-three years ago, then she was ten."

"That's got to be traumatic for a kid. It's going to affect how she reacts. It may make her extremely difficult to track."

Curtis thought of Nora McKee's reaction when she had bumped into him on the street, on her way to meet her husband for lunch. No wonder she'd looked as if she had seen a ghost. Just the sight of his uniform might have triggered the memory of her mother's disappearance. "I think it already has, Senator."

"You didn't know about Nora McKee's mother?" Kat asked Aiken.

"No. In 1983, I had been in the Senate for just two years. My old man was the contact person for SPOT. Mariah Jones was still the director. The program was eight years old and there were only a handful of Travelers. So I'm guessing

Lydia and Ian or Lydia and her husband disappeared Nora's mother."

"Where did they take her?" Curtis asked.

"I have no idea. The record-keeping in SPOT is deplorable. Or, at any rate, I never see the records and the monthly reports are, at best, sketchy. You know, Ian talks about how certain protocols and procedures have been in place since Mariah was director, but the truth is that everything was evolving back then. Even Mariah's biochip wasn't what it is now."

Oh yeah, Curtis thought. Back then, the biochip worked. Now it was so flawed it had become a Traveler joke, laughed about in the cafeteria, whispered about when one of their own got stranded, a new fact of life that hadn't been addressed in a satisfactory way by anyone.

"Did either of you ever meet her?" Aiken asked.

"She was gone before either of us ever started here," Curtis replied.

"Fascinating woman. Brilliant. Back in the late sixties, she was one of the few black women on the faculty at Smith College. That was when she created the biochip, as a cure for insomnia. Did you know that?"

"They don't teach that in training," Kat said. "You're just spilling secrets right and left here, Senator."

He laughed at that, at the idea of himself as an information subversive. "All things you need to know. Should have known all along."

"How could she have created the biochip in 1968?" Curtis asked. "That sort of technology didn't exist back then."

"Oh, I think it's fairly obvious that she went back to 1968 from this time and created the chip with twenty-first century technology."

"What really happened to Mariah?" Curtis had wanted to ask this question ever since he had heard about the history of SPOT during training. Mariah Jones, creator of the biochip, the first director of SPOT, the woman who had put everything in place thirty years ago.

"What do they teach you in training?"

"That she just didn't come to work one morning," Kat replied. "The official version is that in the early nineties, she died during a transition, her chip malfunctioned or her body rejected it and she was stranded in the past or died back there. But speculation among Travelers runs the gamut—from she was murdered during a power grab to she disappeared herself."

"I suspect the latter," Aiken replied. "By the early nineties, the number of Travelers had grown to twenty, a Council had been established, there were job descriptions for the director, the assistant director, the mentors, the Travelers, the med techs, the computer techs, the damn janitor. SPOT was mired in bureaucracy."

"Like it is now," Curtis remarked.

"It's worse now. But even back then, it was pretty bad, and Mariah hated bureaucracy. Not long before she vanished, she told me she felt she'd created a monster." Then he quickly changed the subject. "Look, I'm in the midst of writing a report for Ian and Lydia about how their beloved *process* is going to change. Because if it doesn't change, the entire program will fold."

"Would you like a taste of what a transition is?" Curtis asked. "So that you can really flesh out your report?" Pandering. A part of him was pandering to Rodriguez, to the father figure he had been since he'd offered Curtis a job. But another part of him really wanted Aiken to understand what they did.

"I'd love it. In fact, that was my next question. How soon can we do it?"

"That depends on where you want to go." Kat leaned forward between them, her voice soft, conspiratorial. "And for how long."

"This excursion would be just long enough so that I can convincingly describe the experience to other investors. Once I know what it's like, I'll choose a destination for my wife and me."

"The most accurate transitions occur to places we've been to already," Curtis explained. "Sometimes, these transitions are replays, where we return to the time and location of a recent event to scrutinize what we could have done differently. We're observers. Other times, the transitions are to places we've visited frequently. It's why each of us has at least one particular date and location in the past to which we're so emotionally attached or that's so intimately familiar that we can transition there without even thinking about it. We also have one special date and location in the present that we can transition to if we're injured. We've been to those places so often they've created a groove in the chip's memory." Or the soul's memory, he thought. The word you chose depended on your opinion of what the chip really was. "Otherwise, the further back in time we go, the more preparation we need in terms of clothing, provisions, and so on."

"What are your special locations?" Aiken asked.

Kat, a true Deadhead, a fan who had followed the Grateful Dead from city to city, concert to concert, for a dozen years, had picked her special location with the band in mind: August 16, 1969, at Max Yasgur's six-hundred-acre dairy farm in upstate New York. Otherwise known as Woodstock. On the night of the sixteenth, the Dead had played. Kat had been there numerous times, but never for the entire extravaganza, one of her dreams. Curtis's location was Madison Square Garden on November 28, 1974, John Lennon's last concert. The problem with his location was that he tended to get lost in the music and the nostalgia.

The point in this time to which he and Kat returned if they were injured during a transition was the medical building here on Cedar Key, on a night when Dr. Berlin, the primary physician for all Travelers, was working. But their place as a couple, the place no one knew about, was The Waverunner in Aruba.

Aiken's question, addressed to both of them, disturbed Curtis and he knew that Kat felt the same way. To a Traveler, this particular question was the equivalent of a stranger asking you about the intimate details of your sex life. A breach of etiquette.

"Joe, if we told you that," Kat said with her usual charm, "then our locations wouldn't be special anymore."

"Time travel propriety." He sounded amused. "Is it possible to return to Blue River and McKee's arrest? I'd like to see what actually happened."

"Sure. We can do that," Curtis replied, relieved he hadn't pressed them about their special locations.

"It won't create any kind of paradox? Since you and Ms. Sargent—from, uh, yesterday, will already be there?"

"Not as long as we just observe," Kat replied. "And please, Senator, call us Ryan and Kat, all right? This Mr. and Ms. stuff is so, like, yesterday."

He laughed. "Ryan and Kat it is. So where do we leave from?" He sounded like an eager kid who just couldn't wait to get on with it.

"From anywhere," Curtis and Kat said simultaneously.

6

Bones & Nails, a local biker bar fives miles from Cedar Key, wasn't Lydia Fenmore's favorite spot. But it served its purpose.

Tucked away under towering oaks draped in veils of Spanish moss, the bar was where she and Rodriguez met with members of the Council when they didn't want to be seen by any of the other SPOT employees. Tonight, they had taken their usual booth in the back room, far enough from the jukebox so they weren't blasted with music, but close enough to it so they wouldn't be overheard by people at any of the other booths. Not that those people, the drunken stragglers of an office party and some pool players gathered around the pool table, would be listening.

She could smoke here, which was about the only positive thing the place had going for it. In fact, the entire bar was smoke filled. The owner, a smoker himself, didn't bother enforcing the Florida Clean Air Act.

"So where is she?" Rodriguez glanced anxiously at his watch, sipped his beer, and kept eyeing the door that adjoined the front room, the bar area. "Didn't you say she'd meet us here in twenty minutes?"

"You know Simone. She's always fuzzy on time," Lydia replied.

"Call her again, Lydia."

"*You* call her." Lydia slid her cell over to him. "She can't stand me."

"She's not nuts about me, either."

"Bullshit. She wouldn't be the senior Council member if you hadn't nominated her to the Council all those years ago. She owes you. She knows it."

Rodriguez gave her an irritated look, picked up her cell, and punched out Simone White's number. Lydia slid out of the booth and went over to the bar. Adam Bradley, the aging biker who owned the bar, was perched on a stool, sipping his tequila and watching an old Clint Eastwood movie on the wide-screen TV. His gray, thinning ponytail trailed over his right shoulder, an emblem of bygone years, and every line on his interesting face held a story.

There, that erratic thread that ran the length of his left cheek: that was the end of his second marriage, when his wacko wife sliced him. And across his forehead ran the worry lines created by his oldest daughter, a druggie somewhere in the Northeast whom he heard from whenever she needed money. When he smiled, the dimple at the corner of his mouth was actually the scar from a stick that pierced the skin when he was a kid. She knew all this because years ago, during her marriage, she and Bradley used to get together in his apartment above this bar and go at it.

At the time, Lydia had been filling in on the Council for a member who had passed on, and she'd hated it. Bradley had been her R & R, a diversion from her responsibilities at SPOT and to her husband and two young daughters. In the vernacular of the fifties, an era for which she had no great fondness, she had been a slut—and loved every moment of it.

But then, fidelity had been an issue in her family for as long as she remembered. She had grown up on a military base in California, an insular world that succumbed to the freewheeling sexual revolution of the sixties in ways that everyone knew about but no one discussed in polite company. Spouse-swapping was her parents' favorite weekend pastime, so by the time Lydia was ten or eleven, she never knew for sure who she would find in her parents' bed on a Saturday or Sunday morning.

Her parents' marriage fell apart when she was thirteen and she and her mother moved to San Francisco, the heart of the peace, love, and antiwar movement. Her mother, a nurse by training, found work easily enough, and got involved with violent antiwar groups like the SDS. By 1972, her mother had been implicated in several bombings of government buildings and was being sought by the police. She returned Lydia to her father and went underground.

Her father, who had remarried, didn't want Lydia around and sent her off to boarding school. Lydia hated it—the rules, the restrictions, people always telling her what to do and when to do it. She ran away after several months and ended up in a military base school in Virginia, where her father was then stationed. And there, in her senior year, she met Mariah Jones, the woman who had changed the course of Lydia's life.

Mariah had come to the base with Joe Aiken's old man, a longtime senator who had sold several of his colleagues on the extraordinary possibilities of the biochip. She was scouting for her first recruits for the time-travel program and Lydia's test scores and background had caught her attention. Mariah and Aiken Senior had talked to Lydia for an hour, plying her with the oddest questions about her life. And when they were done, Mariah handed her a card. *Call me as soon as you graduate. I have a job for you. With the government. We need someone who isn't afraid to think outside the box.*

The day after she got her diploma, she was flown to Cedar Key. Within three months, there were three more recruits, two young men and a woman. Before the year was out, Lydia was sleeping with both of the men. Maybe it was a genetic thing, she thought, embedded in her DNA.

"Fill me up, will you, Adam?" She pushed her empty glass across the bar.

"Dark or light this time?" he asked.

"Dark." Very dark.

He put her empty glass in a sink, brought out a new glass, drew dark ale from a spigot, set it in front of her. "Haven't seen you around for a while. How've you been?"

"Oh, you know. Same ole shit."

He shrugged, eyes wandering from her to Clint Eastwood up there on the screen and then to Rodriguez and back again. A full circuit. "Ian looks like crap," he murmured. "That means the job is in crisis mode, huh?"

"Yeah, you can say that."

Bradley knew she worked for Freeze, in some sort of highly classified capacity, but didn't have a clue about SPOT. However, he knew a lot of the rest of her history—marriage, kids, her off again, on again relationship with Rodriguez, even some of her early history, Mom gone, Dad remarried, life on the military bases. Pillow talk. But all that was history half a dozen years in the past. Now, they mostly traded information, the bulk of it generic—but some of it personal.

Last year, for instance, she had warned him that the IRS was combing through his deductions and two years ago she had found his name on a SPOT "suspect" list—and had deleted it. He knew that he owed her and when he had information, he passed it along.

"Thought you should know, Lydia, there was a guy from D.C. in here tonight, asking questions about you and Ian."

D.C. meant a politician. "Describe him."

"Don't have to. It was Rick Lazier. I voted for the fuck, then he screwed every voter in the state when he weighed in for drilling for oil off the Florida coast."

Lazier? He was Aiken's counterpart, the only other member of Congress who knew about SPOT. Young—younger than her and Rodriguez and Aiken, at any rate—and ambitious. "What'd he want?"

"A seven and seven."

"Besides that."

Bradley looked amused. "Oh, you know, he was just fishing."

"For?"

"I don't know. You tell me. A senator comes in here, asking about you and Ian . . . well, I gotta wonder, Lydia. Maybe you're involved in something other than Freeze, huh?"

"Yeah, maybe we are, Adam. And I'm watching your back. If it hadn't been for me, the IRS would've billed you for, hmm, maybe another fifteen grand in taxes. You watching my back, amigo?"

"Bet your ass." He sipped from his glass of whatever. "I told Lazier you were a class act and that if he really wanted to do something for the people in Florida, he should get rid of those pricks at FEMA, that all over the state we got more blue tarp roofs than real roofs and where were the FEMA trailers, anyway? Hurricanes that done that damage was two years back. Hello, anyone listening? Not him. He took his drink and wandered off." Bradley laughed. "Dumb shit."

The rear door opened, the emergency door, but no alarms sounded. A burst of cold air rushed in, preceding Simone White's grand entrance. The senior member of the Council looked like an aging pinup babe for some biker Web site, that leather jacket, those leather boots, her helmet tucked under her arm. Her long, curly, chestnut hair fell to her shoulders, a cascade that she tended to with the same precision that she applied to everything else in her life. *Anal* didn't begin to describe her.

"Shit, bitch woman is back," Bradley murmured, and poured two fingers of his best scotch into a glass. "Give her this, on the house. It'll loosen her up. And hey, just curious. How come you and bitch woman wear those sticks around your necks?"

Lydia quickly tucked her memory stick inside her shirt. "Secret club, Adam." She winked, picked up her dark ale and the scotch for Simone and went over to the table. She scooted in beside Rodriguez, pushed Simone's drink across the table. "Adam says it's on the house, Simone."

"Really." She laughed, tilted the shot glass to her mouth, and downed it in seconds flat. Then she slid the glass back toward Lydia. "I need another. You two get me out here at one in the morning, I definitely need more than one of these."

"By the way, Adam noticed that we both wear memory sticks around our necks," Lydia said. "Better tuck yours away."

"Observant sucker," Simone remarked and glanced at Rodriguez.

"Mine never shows," he said.

Simone snickered. "Wear it where the sun don't shine, Ian. Shit, I love it."

Rodriguez grinned, Lydia rolled her eyes and signaled Bradley for another shot for Simone.

"So?" Simone asked.

"We've got a big problem," Rodriguez said, and reiterated everything that had happened that evening.

Simone listened closely. She had spent fifteen years on the Court of Appeals in Atlanta and for her listening was an art. Nothing escaped her; no detail was too small. She had started out as a Traveler fifteen years ago, had become a mentor after three years, and landed on the Council two years later, when Rodriguez, as director, had nominated her to fill a vacancy. Now, as the senior member of the Council, she was part of their private power cabal.

"For years, Joe Aiken does his job, gets our funding, and leaves us alone," Simone observed. "Now, suddenly he shows up here, insinuating himself like a nightmare. Ten days until SPOT folds because of lack of funding?" She laughed. "Give me a break. There's something else going on here."

"Yeah, it's an election year," Rodriguez said.

"C'mon, Ian, we've gone through election years before and it hasn't made a dent in our budget."

"The country's debt has never been quite like this," Rodriguez said. "We're basically owned by foreign nationals and are borrowing against our grandchildren's futures. The United States is a credit card company's wet dream."

"How eloquent, Ian."

Her voice dripped with sarcasm, but Rodriguez just shrugged. "You want a turning point? That's it. The piggy bank is busted."

Simone leaned forward, hands folded together on the surface of the table. "Okay, and on a more personal level, it sounds like Ryan has become a liability. No surprise there. I mean, no offense, Ian, I know how fond you are of him and no one can dispute his talent as a Traveler. But he's never been a team player. *Never.*"

"You don't have to be a team player to become a Traveler," Lydia reminded her. "We're strengthened by independent thinkers, Simone."

Simone turned her gaze on Lydia, eyes like ice. "There's a very fine line between an independent thinking Traveler and one who has gone rogue."

"Ryan hasn't gone rogue," Rodriguez said quickly. "He got pissed off that I used electroshock on McKee."

"Excuse me, Ian. But you're not only his mentor, you're the director of SPOT. Ryan Curtis is your underling, okay? He has no right to challenge that relationship in a place like the Council chamber. We have *laws, protocols, etiquette,* and every recruit learns them. As a mentor, you can't get too close to your charges."

Lydia felt the air around Rodriguez tighten. "Don't presume to tell me my job, Simone."

She sat back, smiling slightly, resigned, properly chastised, her hands patting the air. "Whatever. Regardless, the bottom line to us is the same. What the hell are the three of us going to do if SPOT folds?"

"If we embrace Joe Aiken's idea, we won't fold," Rodriguez said with more conviction than Lydia felt at the moment.

Bradley delivered Simone's scotch to the table. She ignored him and leaned forward, her beautiful hands folded around her glass. "Guess what, guys. I'm not going to babysit rich WASPs on a time tour of the Holy Land. I don't care how much money it's going to bring in. You tell Joe to fucking forget it."

"No one tells Joe to forget it," Lydia said. "His check for twenty million—for him and his wife—is already in the SPOT coffers. They're our first private Travelers."

Simone sat back, frowning, drumming her fingers against her shot glass. "You know what this is really about, don't you? Joe and Rick Lazier are going to assume control of SPOT. They'll create an oversight committee that we'll have to answer to. They'll control every facet of what we do—from the money we spend, to the sentences the Council imposes, to how recruits are trained, to the eras where Travelers will be permitted to go. We can't allow that to happen."

"We don't have a choice," Rodriguez said. "We need two billion a year to operate. Three or four would be better, but we've been doing it on two. To raise that kind of money privately, we'd have to sign up two hundred people a year, for ten million each." He shook his head. "We need the senators on our side, Simone."

She gave an exaggerated sigh. "Oh, Ian, your lack of imagination sometimes appalls me. Since Joe has paid already, we give him what he wants and he recruits a few more millionaires and we raise fifty or a hundred million or so. In the meantime, I'll touch base with some of my contacts on the hill and we'll find a couple of senators who're willing to play the game our way."

"And what about Joe and Rick?" Lydia asked.

"We eventually disappear them permanently and then perhaps do the same to whoever else he's recruited."

"I don't like it," Rodriguez said. "But it might work. It would depend on who we tap."

Simone named three senators with whom she had working relationships—which meant that she had arranged for the disappearances of people in their lives who were troublemakers—and for the next several minutes, she and Rodriguez debated the pros and cons. Lydia listened and mulled things over as she finished the last of her dark ale.

"Excuse me, but we're all overlooking something really important," Lydia finally said. "SPOT is the glue that holds the power elite together in this country. Without us, dissidents, subversives, undesirables, and your usual intellectual liberals are running around creating chaos. Without us, serial killers and rapists would be eating up valuable tax dollars doing their lifetime sentences in prisons. *We* . . . the three of us, our forty Travelers, our twenty mentors . . . are the experts in this technology. *We* know better than anyone how it works, what its limitations are. Instead of letting politicians like Joe and Rick call the shots, let's turn the tables on them by becoming private contractors."

Rodriguez and Simone just looked at her as if neither of them had ever heard the phrase before. "I'm not following you," Rodriguez said.

"Ian, it's a no-brainer," Lydia said excitedly. "We charge them *per disappearance*. A flat rate. You want a dissident disappeared? A serial rapist? A subversive? Fine, but each one will cost you. And if they don't want to play that way, we'll threaten to engage foreign governments. Believe me, they'll do the math and figure out the ramifications and realize they've had a very easy time of it the last thirty years. They'll play. And in return, we become autonomous, no longer folded into Freeze. Our Travelers won't be wasting valuable time on surveillance and arrests, but will be doing what they're trained to do."

"It would take some major reshuffling," Rodriguez said.

"To say the least," Simone scoffed. "Right now, the accused come to us through Freeze. But if SPOT is autonomous, where do we get people to disappear?"

"They'd still come to us through Freeze. But now the government has to pay per person. It'll limit or maybe even eliminate some of the favors we do—you know, the dickhead in the Pentagon who wants his mistress gone, the CEO who wants the company competition squashed."

"When do we present this to Joe?" Rodriguez asked.

"As soon as a few of his millionaires have paid for their excursion into the past."

"So, in a sense, we hold him and Rick hostage to our proposal," Simone said, smiling now, nodding.

"Exactly," Lydia replied.

"I love it," Simone said, and signaled Bradley for another round of drinks.

"Hold on," Rodriguez said. "There's a problem we need to address. The chips. I don't think we can send any of Joe's investors back until Dr. Berlin and his staff have corrected the problem. It's one thing when Travelers get stuck in the past. They're trained to know what to do. It would be quite another for one of Joe's investors to get stuck."

"None of the investors will be chipped, Ian," Simone pointed out. "It's not like we're just going to turn them loose on their own. They'll each be accompanied by a Traveler. And every Traveler now carries a spare chip. So there's no problem."

"I agree with Simone," Lydia said.

Rodriguez looked miffed. "Excuse me, ladies, but you're missing the goddamn point. We don't know why the chips are malfunctioning. They can malfunction after an hour, a day, ten days, three weeks, there's no pattern. And suppose a spare malfunctions before the Traveler and the investor get back here? Then what? Right now, we've got three Travelers, a mentor, and a recruit who are missing. We've sent back a small search team, but we don't know yet where the hell they are."

"So when investors are sent out, the Travelers accompanying them are carrying *several* extra chips," Simone said, impatience thick in her voice.

"We don't have the chips to spare, Simone. In fact, let me do the math for you."

He grabbed a napkin, plucked a pen out of his shirt pocket, and scribbled a bunch of figures. Lydia rolled her eyes at Simone, making it abundantly clear that she thought Rodriguez was making a big stink over nothing. Simone concurred with a nod. But when Rodriguez turned the napkin around so they could both see the columns of figures, Lydia frowned, suddenly uncertain.

"I must be reading these figures wrong," she said.

"I'm afraid not," Rodriguez said. "As you both know, the frequency with which anyone in SPOT is chipped depends on how many transitions they make. Some years back, we came up with the optimum number for each group, which determines how many chips are produced annually. Five hundred a year." He circled that number, then his pen dropped to the next figure. "Our forty Travelers are chipped six times a year for a total of two hundred and forty chips."

"We can do the math, Ian," Simone said dryly. "Just get to the bottom line."

"I'm spelling it out for you, Simone. Another sixty chips are used annually by our twenty recruits, who are chipped three times a year. Since you and I, Lydia, as the director and assistant director, rarely transition, we're chipped just twice a year. Four chips. So we're up to three hundred and four chips. The other eighteen mentors are chipped six times a year, for a total of a hundred and eight chips. So, already, we're up to four hundred and twelve."

"Then every year, we have eighty-eight chips left over," Lydia said. "And since we never use them all, the number is cumulative from year to year. We must have a stockpile of several hundred."

"We've been chipping Travelers monthly as a precaution and every Traveler has at least one spare during transitions. So our reserve has been depleted since April and at the moment, we have exactly forty-one chips left, roughly a month's supply. And that's about to go down by one, because my body rejected my chip last night."

In her haste to find a solution, Lydia's thoughts tripped over each other like kids converging on a piñata that had resisted all the swings. "But without chips, there're no investors, no SPOT, nothing."

"Yeah," Rodriguez said dryly. "It's called unemployment."

Simone blew up. "How the hell has it gotten to this point, Ian? You're the goddamn director, you're supposed to stay on top of this stuff, you're . . ."

"I *am* on top of it," He snapped. "Russ Berlin and his people are working twenty-four/seven to find out what's wrong with the chips. But none of us are magicians, Simone."

"Jesus," she whispered. "So what do we do?"

"We need the money the investors will bring in," Lydia said quickly. "And we just don't tell them about the chips and hope for the best. Right, Ian?"

"At the moment, I don't see that we have any other choice," he replied.

7

Due to the vastly fluctuating tides and the propensity for flooding, the dozen buildings that comprised the Old Fenimore Mill were raised up on ten-foot concrete pilings that were at least two feet thick. The vast spaces beneath the buildings served as parking areas for cars, boats, trailers, and RVs and lacked lighting. Good thing, too, Curtis thought, what with the three of them lurking around out here at 1:30 in the morning.

He, Kat, and Aiken made their way single file along a dirt path that sloped down to the shore of the moonlit bay. On either side of them, the tall reeds and grasses rustled and whispered in the chilly breeze. Night sounds rose and fell around them, nature's cacophony.

Curtis had a small pack slung over his shoulder. Like Kat, he wore street clothes instead of a uniform, and a heavy jacket that held his two cell phones, cash, a wallet.

When they reached the edge of the bay, they stopped, Aiken between them. "What do I have to do?" the senator asked.

"Nothing." Kat hooked her arm through his. "Just follow our directions. What's our mnemonic this time, Ryan?"

"How about *wart*?"

"Wart?" Aiken laughed.

"The W in *we*, the AR in *are*, and the T stands for *there*," Curtis replied.

"See," Kat explained, "when you replay an event that's happened already, it's sometimes tough to remember that you've transitioned. So as soon as one of us remembers it, we call out the mnemonic to the other. That's one of the reasons they have us travel in pairs. And we've used *wart* successfully in the past."

"We're targeting the moments right after McKee made a break for it," Curtis said.

"You can be that precise?" Aiken asked.

Odd, Curtis thought, that Aiken supposedly had been in charge of this program for years, but didn't seem to have any idea about what was involved. "When it's a replay. Otherwise, it can be tricky. It takes practice. Didn't anyone ever spell out how this works, Senator?"

"In vague terms. Never forget that Lydia and Ian have a vested interest in keeping me very much in the dark."

Curtis filed the remark in the back of his mind. "Kat, you have your backup cell?"

"Check. Do you?"

"Right pocket."

"Why backup cell phones?" Aiken asked.

"In case we get separated," Kat explained. "We can't call each other on our regular cells because our yesterday selves would answer. Okay, Joe, say *wart* to yourself a couple of times. *Wart*, *wart*, like that, rhythmic. Have you ever been to Blue River?"

"Drove through once."

"Okay, never mind. We'll do the visualizing for you. We'll both be touching you. There has to be physical contact to transition someone who isn't chipped. Now just shut your eyes, breathe deeply through your left nostril, and exhale through your right. Like this."

While they practiced their alternate nostril breathing, Curtis grasped Aiken's wrist, shut his eyes. His senses immediately heightened in anticipation of the transition. He could taste the salt in the air, hear fish jumping in the water just beyond them, feel Aiken's pulse beneath his fingers. His imagination stirred to life, conjuring up images of downtown Blue River, the Lighthouse Pub, the shops across the street from it. The rich, wet scent of the air here reminded him of the air in Blue River. He easily summoned the chatter and movement of tourists on the street yesterday, could see the block of colorful shops where he'd tackled McKee.

As the past whispered to the present, the biochip in his pineal gland calculated probability fields in his brain at the speed of light. He *reached* for Blue River yesterday, *reached* for that street, those moments, *reached* until he felt as though he were a kid, spinning wildly beneath a glorious, sun-struck sky, the world spinning with him. Then white noise burst inside his head, his inner eyes went blind, and he felt as if he were swept up inside a furious wind, like Dorothy headed for Oz.

Curtis stood outside a store in Blue River, shoppers moving around him, his shadow a dark blob against the sidewalk, the cold air nipping at the back of his neck. He felt sort of nauseated and light-headed and wondered if he was coming down with the flu.

He noticed that the air possessed a strange, indescribable quality, as though it were made of something corporeal, soft, like fabric. And everyone around him seemed to be moving in a weird slow motion, people in a dream. Even the passing cars moved like snails, relative to his own speed.

He knew he was forgetting something, but had no idea what it might be.

A ruckus broke out in a restaurant patio across the street and a man tore away from the crowd, obviously panicked, yet he, too, appeared to move in slow motion, his legs practically frozen in what appeared to be a flat-out run. A man and a woman in dark brown uniforms chased him; they looked like they were moving through thick syrup. Then Curtis recognized himself in that dark uniform and the realization crashed over him. This was Blue River, yesterday. A replay.

He frantically searched the crowd for Kat and Aiken and spotted them outside the Lighthouse Pub, watching with other bystanders as the drama unfolded—the pursuit of Jake McKee. Curtis groped in his jacket pocket for the backup cell phone and tried to get out of the way as McKee veered toward his side of the street. But Curtis stumbled over something behind him and, arms pinwheeling madly for balance, fell back into the wall and lost his grip on the cell. A tall, stunning black woman in tight jeans, a blue pullover sweater, and a heavy denim jacket swept it up.

"Very clever. A backup cell for the mnemonic." She pocketed the cell. "I'll have to remember that."

Shocked, Curtis stammered, "Who . . . who the hell are you? And that's my phone you just took."

"Did you like the flowerpot trick?" She gestured at the large ceramic pot over which he'd tripped. "In about twenty seconds, your yesterday self is going to trip over it and the punch that Kat intends for McKee will glance off your shoulder. Consider it your wake-up call. If you move the pot, then on that timeline you end up in the Quang Ngai Province, 1968, and take a bullet to the chest that kills you. I really don't want that to happen because out of all the idiots in the kingdom of Ian and Lydia, you and Kat have the most promise."

"Holy shit," he breathed. "You're . . ."

"Mariah Jones. It's a real pleasure to meet you, Ryan."

"But you're . . ."

"Dead?" She laughed. "Hardly. Very much alive and not at all pleased with the way these schmucks are running things."

Despite his astonishment, Curtis's mind raced, calculating the years, the passage of time. Mariah Jones was in her early fifties when she'd disappeared in 1991, so in 2006 she would be in her late sixties. Yet, the woman in front of him looked no older than thirty-five. How the hell could that be?

His puzzlement apparently showed in his expression, because Mariah smiled. "Yeah, I know. It all gets pretty confusing. I should look older. A lot older. Well, it's not Botox or plastic surgery, I can tell you that. I've got plenty of theories about it, but no easy answers. In fact, easy answers about any of this are in short supply these days. That's the real tragedy."

Then she tossed him the cell phone and just as he caught it, it rang. Kat, breathing hard, shouted, *"Wart, Ryan, wart, and get out of there."*

He turned abruptly, shocked to discover that Mariah Jones was gone, and broke into a run. He loped around the corner, away from yesterday's drama, and ducked into the doorway of a shop. He squeezed his eyes shut, steadied his breathing, and drew Cedar Key around him like a cloak. Seconds later, the white noise exploded in his skull and he transitioned.

His knees sank into the damp grass, he fell forward onto his hands. His head spun, his stomach heaved, his muscles and tendons felt as if they were strung too tightly to his bones. His arms trembled, then collapsed beneath his weight; the soft grass caught his head. He had the presence of mind to keep his eyes squeezed shut until the fluid in his inner ears stopped moving, until his equilibrium stabilized. He finally turned his head to the right and the grass against his cheek felt as cool as a mother's hand.

He lay there, breathing in the sweetness of the grass, the salt of the air, but his head shrieked, his mind struggled against the incomprehensible. *Mariah Jones is alive and well.* Sounds finally began to penetrate his miasma—his own heavy breathing, night noises from the tall reeds in front of him, something splashing in the water nearby. And then he heard Kat, calling to him.

Curtis staggered to his feet and glanced around through the parking area under the buildings. He didn't see her, but heard her voice again. It wasn't loud, but in the absence of other human sounds it echoed and clattered like a ghost in chains. He moved toward the water, through the reeds, wondering when the moon had set, where his flashlight was, whether he even had packed it.

He sloshed through the water, grateful that the tide was receding. When the reeds ended, he saw the beam of her flashlight about half a mile offshore. She and Aiken appeared to be stranded on a mound of sand that had appeared as the tide ebbed. In between them and the shore was a large pool of water. It couldn't be very deep, they probably could wade across it. But he remembered that Aiken couldn't swim.

He pulled his cell from his jacket pocket, his regular cell, and punched in the speed dial for Kat's cell. It rang several times before she answered it.

"You didn't answer when I called." Her voice hushed, anxious. "Jesus, I . . . I thought something had happened, that you didn't get back."

"I was out of it. Are you both okay?'

"Physically, yeah, we're fine. But he's freaking, Ryan. He's terrified of drowning. I don't think the water's too deep, but I can't convince him to wade into it. Can you find a dinghy fast?"

"Sure, in the hidden wireless connection."

He could almost hear her smile at that. It referred to a love letter she'd left in a hidden file on his computer after their one big blowout a year ago; the phrase meant that neither of them would ever abandon or desert the other.

"Hurry," she said.

"I'm on my way."

He disconnected, shrugged off his jacket, set the cell on top of it. He tore off his shoes, his jeans, then put his shoes back on just in case the bottom of the pool was littered with broken oyster shells, a common occurrence here. He scooped up the cell, headed into the water. Thirty yards offshore, the bottom dropped away and he had to swim, the cell phone clamped between his teeth.

Half a mile wasn't all that far, not in the summer, when the sun was out. But it was dark, cold, and the transition and all the other events tonight had drained him. His calf muscles started to cramp; the chill of the water seeped through him. Now and then he paused, treading water, his feet seeking purchase. But the water was deeper than he'd thought, even at an ebbing tide.

Curtis glued his eyes to the glow of Kat's flashlight and it kept him going, drawing him forward, moth to flame. By the time he reached the mound of sand, shudders swept through him, his teeth chattered; he didn't know if he had it in him to swim back, hauling a man who weighed two-fifty. But Aiken wasn't just any man. He was the senator who would determine the future of SPOT and, therefore, the man who would determine the future for him and Kat.

Kat shed her jacket and wrapped it around Curtis's shoulders. She removed the cell from his mouth, urged him to sit up, to sip from a bottle of water and nibble from a high-energy bar. She figured his blood sugar was low due to the replay. Probably true, he thought, and bit into the bar. The nut shit got stuck in his teeth, but he gobbled the sucker down and after a few minutes began to feel almost human again.

"So how was your transition, Joe?" he finally managed to ask.

Aiken, kneeling in the wet sand, hands pressed against his thighs, regarded Curtis with the rapturous expression of a man who had experienced an epiphany. "Incredibly liberating. But you are one crazy bastard, Ryan, swimming out here. Maybe we should just wait out the tide and I'll walk back."

"Sir, with all due respect, that's going to take at least another four hours and I need to sleep and get warm before then. Besides, the gators start creeping in before the tide's completely out."

That was bullshit. Even though gators were sometimes found in salt marshes, they had no fondness for briny water and, as far as he knew, hadn't been found on Cedar Key for years. The biggest threat was the water moccasins that called Snake Key home. But it did the trick.

"Gators." He slapped his wet hands against his even wetter thighs and laughed again. "Well, shit, let's get moving. If you're up to it," he added quickly.

"We'll both do it," Kat said.

It was easier going back, with Aiken between them, his arms slung around their shoulders. Kat reminded him to let the water support him and not to drag his legs. He listened, did what she told him, and they somehow made it to shore, crawled through the reeds, into the grass, and finally surrendered to exhaustion.

Lifetimes passed. The solar system collapsed and was reborn.

Aiken moved first, rolling onto his back, arms flung out at his sides, a kid primed for spotting animals in the formations of clouds. Except there were no clouds. No moon, either. Just the faint light of the stars remained. "It was real." He breathed the words. "We were *there*. But everything moved like molasses. Is that normal?"

"No," Curtis replied.

"It's never happened before," Kat added. "Never. Not during a normal transition, not during a replay. Never."

"And then it got weird," Aiken said. "I knew what had happened, but Kat didn't. By the time she did, your yesterday self had seen her and she was afraid it was going to create some sort of paradox, so she called you. I thought I saw you, Ryan, the present you, on the other side of the street."

"I tripped," Curtis said. "I tripped over something that wasn't there in the original event. I was about to call Kat, to give her the mnemonic, but I tripped and lost the cell. This . . . black woman grabbed it and . . ." The rest of the story tumbled out, every last detail of what Mariah Jones had said to him. The act of saying it aloud, of sharing it not only with Kat but with this man he barely knew, solidified the details in his own mind. It had happened. It was real.

In the moments immediately after Curtis finished talking, no one spoke. Or moved. Curtis began to wonder if his karma was to be permanently impaled against the patch of cool grass, just outside the condo where he lived, with the woman he loved and a U.S. senator who wasn't like any politician he'd ever met.

"Describe her," Aiken said finally. "Repeat exactly what she said to you."

Curtis did.

"Christ," Aiken murmured. "It was her. It was definitely Mariah. The last time I saw her, she warned me about kingdoms. She said, and I quote, 'Ian and Lydia will create a kingdom from my invention. They'll corrupt everything. You just watch, Joe. You watch. History will prove me right.' Two days later, she was gone." He sat up, rubbed his hands over his face. "I need to sleep."

Yeah, Curtis thought, rising up on his elbows. Ditto twice.

"Tell me again what she said about the timeline," Aiken said.

"That if I moved the pot I tripped over . . . which was supposed to be my wake-up call . . . I would end up in the Quang Ngai Province, 1968, and take a bullet to the chest that would kill me."

"Quang Ngai Province, 1968," he repeated softly, hands dropping to his thighs. "That can only be one thing. My Lai. The Council will sentence McKee to My Lai. Are you willing to take him there, Ryan?"

Curtis had figured out that much, too, and wrapped his arms around his knees, hugging them to his chest. "No way."

"I am not going to My Lai." Kat sprang to her feet and reached out to help Aiken to his feet. "That's a suicide mission."

"You can refuse the assignment," Aiken said. "You have that right."

"Oh, yeah," Kat said. "We get to do that twice in our entire tenure with SPOT without getting a black mark against our record. I've already done it once."

"It's not an option for me," Curtis said. They stumbled along like a trio of drunks, weaving past the parked cars and boats beneath the buildings, headed toward Aiken's condo. "I've done it twice. They would send me back to training." Or worse. Rodriguez would fire him or send him to the rehab unit. "Look, it's possible that Mariah is wrong. I mean, the Council isn't ruling on McKee until late this afternoon. How can she already know how they'll rule?"

"Probably the same way she knew where you would be, Ryan," Aiken replied. "Since she's apparently alive and knows details about time travel that we don't, I think it's safe to assume she's aware of some of the choices that are being made."

"It could be a trick," Kat said. "She may want us to think she's a god, but she isn't. She may be using us just to get back at Ian and Lydia."

"That wouldn't surprise me," Aiken said. "I think we have to play this one by ear. I'm going back to D.C. later today to get the ball rolling on the funding. But I want one of you to call me when you hear about McKee. If the Council *does* sentence him to My Lai, then we really need to rethink our strategy because it means that Mariah is up to something. Has either of you met Senator Rick Lazier?"

Curtis and Kat shook their heads. Lazier was the other senator who knew about SPOT. He was younger than Aiken by probably two decades, had served twelve years in the Senate, and was one of the progressives around whom speculation swirled about a possible presidential run in two years. "Does he know you came here?" Kat asked.

"It was his idea. He feels that SPOT needs more oversight and after what I've seen, I agree with him. Right now, as you know, suspects are referred to SPOT through the Department of Freedom and Security. A large number of these referrals are the result of personal grudges, vendettas, trumped-up charges. A CEO doesn't like the coverage he's getting in the media, so he calls his buddy over at the Pentagon, who calls his buddy in Freeze, and suddenly, the journalist is indicted on trumped-up charges and disappears down the rabbit hole. Or a teacher takes on religion or politics in the classroom, gets fired, makes a big stink on the Internet so that the blogs create a mass grassroots movement in the teacher's defense, and suddenly, the teacher vanishes. Guilt or innocence is never an issue. Once the person enters the system, he has no attorney, no rights, no way to defend himself."

Sort of like Travelers who fell from grace, Curtis thought. "Like what happened to Nora McKee's mother."

"Yes."

Curtis waited for details, elaboration. But Aiken said nothing more about it. "So the system has worked like this for thirty years?"

"No, that's another fallacy you learn in training. Things were much different when Mariah was director. She managed the organization on a tight budget, was scrupulous in her choice of employees, knew what the hell she was doing. Rick ran an audit on SPOT's budget. The waste is inconceivable and part of it is because Ian, Lydia, and the Council members act like they're Olympians. That will change once we privatize the funding. The entire hierarchy of SPOT will change. Rick and I will appoint a committee that will have oversight."

That might be worse, Curtis thought.

"Power is never surrendered so easily," Kat remarked.

Aiken's smile smacked of sadness, remorse, resignation. "I didn't say it would be simple or easy." They reached the stairs to his condo. He asked for paper and a pen. Curtis fished both out of his pack and Aiken scribbled down several numbers and an e-mail address. "I'm the only person who answers at these numbers or the e-mail address. Day or night."

With that, he started up the stairs, moving slowly, leaving a trail of water behind him.

* * *

Curtis bolted upright, his heart hammering, breath exploding from his mouth, as if he had been running in a dream he didn't remember. He sat there, listening hard. The first twittering of birds outside, the distant chug of a boat, Kat's soft, even breathing. That was it.

The quilt had slipped off her shoulder, exposing the pale, graceful curve where arm met shoulder. In the milky light that spilled through the slats of the wooden blinds, her skin looked surreal, like something in a painting. Curtis brought his mouth to her beautiful shoulder and ran it up to the curve of her neck. She stirred and rolled over, her arms urging him against her, and he slipped under the covers again.

They made love and always, for him, it was like the first time, a secret, languid exploration of an unknown country. Silken ravines, the tautness of muscle, hidden caves of such intense pleasure that for a long time, the night's events were driven so far from his consciousness it was as if they hadn't happened. But afterward, it all rushed back, and as they lay there, he said, "If Mariah is right, then you didn't punch McKee, you hit my shoulder instead. Do you have any memory of that?"

She was quiet for a moment. "I don't seem to. But would I?"

"I don't know. But my shoulder aches and it didn't earlier in the evening. This was the first time I've done a replay where something in the past got changed. But if McKee doesn't have a busted nose or a cheek that's black and blue, then it would be definite proof that something in the present was changed as a result of our actions in a replay. Right?"

She lifted up on an elbow. The watch face she wore around her neck swung like a pendulum. She gazed down at him, her tangled hair falling along the right side of her face, a dark, exotic veil that covered one breast and left the other exposed. He brought his mouth to the nipple, tongue sliding around it, and she slid her fingers through his hair and whispered, "If you start that again, Ryan, we'll never get over to Snake Island to check out your theory."

"You want to go? Really? Or are you just humoring me?"

She rolled away from him, kicked her legs up in the air, and vaulted over the side. "Let's take my dinghy."

When they pushed off from the reeds fifteen minutes later, a pearl light streaked across the eastern sky and flocks of gulls rose, shrieking, from a spot just up the shore. Fog hugged the water, drifting like spun sugar halfway up the tallest reeds. They would be back long before Rodriguez or Fenmore got to work, he thought, and that could only be a good thing. Even though Travelers weren't expressly forbidden from visiting the accused in holding, it was discouraged. But then, not too many Travelers wanted to visit someone they'd brought in. They knew they would be seeing the person again soon enough for the disappearance and there was usually some guilt about it.

They came in to their earlier spot, when they'd brought Aiken over here. Curtis pulled the dinghy onto the beach, disturbed by the tight, eerie silence that covered the island, by the fog that swirled across the beach and up into the trees. It all looked like special effects for a movie.

Since the main building was sealed up for the night, they followed the path around to the back, where the vegetation was thicker, the trees leaning in toward each other, completely shrouding the path. It made Curtis nervous; you never knew where the snakes might be hiding. He kept glancing up and walked faster. He didn't hear the backup electric generator, which meant that only the propane generator was on, keeping the holding building secure, lit, its temperature regulated.

The holding area was a low, ugly concrete structure without windows. It had three dozen cells and a small kitchen and bunk area for the guards, two for each eight-hour shift, 24/7. Curtis knocked on the main door and when it opened, he was relieved that the guard wasn't the one he'd tackled earlier, during McKee's proceedings in The Chamber. This guy had headphones hooked around his neck, an iPod clipped to his belt, and held a mug of coffee. The ID clipped to his jacket pocket read: ART QUINTELLO, SNAKE ISLAND SECURITY.

"Morning," he said. "What can I do for you?"

"We're here to see Jake McKee."

"ID, please."

They handed over their ID and Quintello, a muscular man in his early forties, ran each card through a handheld device, then opened the door wider. "C'mon in." He returned their ID and they accompanied him into the staff kitchen. Snug, warm, comfortable. The table in the middle held magazines and some paperback books. A TV on the counter was tuned to early morning satellite news, the volume on low. He offered them coffee and Danishes.

"Coffee's fine," Curtis said. "Where's your partner?"

"He called in sick. It's not a problem, though, with just one in holding. Things seem to be slowing down lately," he remarked.

Due to the malfunctioning chips, Curtis thought.

"So where're you moving him to?" Quintello asked.

"What?" Curtis replied.

"McKee. I just got word an hour ago that he's being moved. That's why you're here, right?"

"Uh, no," Curtis said. "We just wanted to talk to him. Who called about the transfer?"

"Mr. Rodriguez. A few minutes later, I got a call from Simone White."

"Is that usual?" Kat asked.

"Yes, ma'am. The calls for transfer always come in pairs—either from the director or assistant director and from a Council member, usually Ms. White."

In the six years Curtis had worked here, he hadn't known, until just now, how this part of the transfer for transition functioned. Rodriguez and Fenmore kept it that way, of course, compartmentalizing everything so that only the top dogs knew how every piece of SPOT worked. But, bottom line, Rodriguez had told him McKee wouldn't be sentenced until this afternoon and that, apparently, was just one more lie.

"Well, we'll be quick," Curtis assured him, and wondered when Rodriguez was going to call him and tell him McKee was ready to be disappeared. Or maybe he had called someone else, his new favorite son, whoever that might be. "We just need to clarify some details."

"If you could leave your weapons on the table, I'll take you back."

"Too early for weapons," Kat quipped. "We didn't bring any. Okay to take our cells in there?"

"Sure."

Quintello unlocked the cell block door and in they went. Curtis felt as if he were entering the belly of a concrete and metal beast—cold, dimly lit. The jazz that played softly through the ceiling speakers made the place seem only slightly less gloomy.

All the cell doors stood open—except one, and that was where Quintello stopped. "McKee has already eaten, showered, and dressed. He's pretty hyped up, but hasn't been violent or aggressive, at least not since I came on duty a couple of hours ago. I'll leave the cell door open, but the block door will be locked and I'll be just inside, waiting for you. And by the way, the surveillance cams are on."

"That's fine," Curtis said. "Did anyone from medical come by here last night?"

"Yeah, it was in the log."

"What'd the doc say?"

"They don't write that in the log. They just check in and out." He unlocked the small metal door through which food was passed, and slid it open. "Mr. McKee, you have visitors. Please sit on the bunk where I can see you. . . . Thank you. You need the lights to be brighter, Mr. Curtis?"

"The light's fine," McKee said.

Curtis stabbed his thumb in the air, indicating that *he* wanted the lights brighter. Quintello nodded, unlocked the door, and Curtis and Kat stepped inside.

McKee sat on the bunk, wearing jeans, a sweater, sneakers. The light in here was too dim for Curtis to see McKee's face clearly.

"Haven't you harassed me enough?" McKee grumbled.

"We just want to ask you a couple of questions," Curtis said.

"Yeah, like am I guilty and where's Alex and where's my wife and then you'll zap me again, right?"

The recessed ceiling lights suddenly brightened. A ripple of shock went through Curtis. No busted nose, no swollen cheek, no creeping dark blue bruise on his face, no sign at all that McKee had been punched.

"Jesus," Kat whispered.

McKee frowned. "What is it? What's wrong with you two?"

Curtis had trouble finding his voice. If McKee hadn't been punched, then the flowerpot over which he'd stumbled, the flowerpot that Mariah Jones had placed in his path, had changed not only the past, but *this* timeline. It had changed it in an immediately verifiable, tangible, physical way. It meant that everything they had been taught in training about the nature of time was a lie.

"Do you recall my partner punching you when you were arrested?" Curtis finally asked.

"I remember you tripping over something, then leaping up and wrestling me to the sidewalk. I . . ." He abruptly stopped, his frown deepening, then he rubbed his fist against his temple, as if to put pressure against a stab of pain. "Shit, what's going on?" Alarm sharpened his voice. "I . . . I seem to have two sets of memories, and in one of them . . . she punches me." His head snapped up. "But that's impossible, it's . . ." He shook his head, as if to clear it. "Where're they transferring me to? What's . . ."

"We'll answer your questions, Mr. McKee," Kat assured him. "But first tell us more about what you remember from the events in Blue River."

"There isn't anything else, okay?" Agitated now. "It's like remembering a vivid dream that's already fading away. That's all I can tell you. Now where the hell are they taking me and what . . ."

The cell door slammed open, clattering and clanging as it struck the wall, the noise echoing loudly through the corridor. Then the air turned the consistency of Elmer's glue and Curtis struggled through it like a worm inching across a continent. He knew what was happening and tried to transition, but couldn't. He shouted at Kat and his words stretched on forever, a long, elastic garble of vowels and consonants. Kat turned but it took so long, her motions were so hideously slow, that Mariah Jones eliminated her as a threat before Kat even knew what hit her. Then Mariah kneed Curtis in the balls, slammed the heel of her hand against the back of his neck, and his knees buckled. He didn't crash to the floor. He dropped against it, light as a feather. The slowed time buffered his fall, but it didn't buffer the pain. His skull and balls exploded with agony.

"So sorry, Ryan," she said, and handcuffed him to a metal ring on the edge of McKee's bunk.

He knew why she did it. He couldn't transition if he were restrained. He couldn't pursue her. All he could do was watch. McKee freaked out and lunged for the open cell door, but because the time distortion had affected him as well, Mariah brought him down with the ease of a cat nabbing a baby bird. She jabbed a needle into his neck and he lay there, twitching, drooling, and more helpless than Curtis. Conscious, but seemingly paralyzed.

Mariah knelt between them, one hand on McKee's back, the other on Kat's, and looked straight at Curtis. He struggled to keep his head raised, so that he could meet her gaze. "Don't take her," he pleaded. "Please. Don't do this."

"It's got to be this way, Ryan. Now My Lai will be a nonissue for you. There's only so much I can change alone."

Curtis tried to grab her, but the cuff snapped him back and nearly tore his hand off at the wrist.

"Now listen very closely," Mariah said. "I suspect that

Rodriguez and Fenmore urged the Council to confer by phone about McKee's sentence. Can you imagine that? No formal meeting. Just a goddamn phone conference. And what the hell did McKee do that was against the law?"

"He crashed Pentagon computers."

"You have proof of that? Absolute irrefutable proof?"

No, he didn't. He shook his head.

"Exactly. But that doesn't matter because the college chancellor wanted McKee gone, so she reported him to Freeze for subversive activities and SPOT took it from there. Once that happened, I saw how I might be able to use McKee to bring down SPOT. I have to rewire the past. It's a long shot, but I have to try. I can't allow Rodriguez, Fenmore, and the rest of these thugs to destroy what I built. So if I succeed, SPOT as you know it dies and a new SPOT is born."

"With *you* in control," he spat.

"That's right. And no Senate oversight committee, no King Rodriguez and Queen Fenmore, no government budgets."

"Even a new improved SPOT will need money to function."

Mariah's laugh seemed to echo inside this strangely languid time bubble. "Money is easy to come by when you can bounce around in time, Ryan. You rob a bank in 1958 and rob another in 1972 . . . who's to know? How will they catch you? Regardless, my much smaller group of Travelers will have their base of operation in the past somewhere and will work to avert the catastrophic future that's going to annihilate the planet in the next six years unless something changes. And one of those changes involves bringing back people SPOT has disappeared who have the knowledge, expertise, insights, that would put the planet on a much more positive path."

Keep her talking. Buy Kat time. "Like who? Inventors? Scientists? Politicians? CEOs? Who?"

"Ordinary people also make contributions. People like Elizabeth Walrave, for instance."

What? What the hell was she talking about? "Nora McKee's mother?"

She nodded. "Unfortunately, I don't know where they took her or some of the other people we need. But before this is all over, I will."

Curtis started to say something, but suddenly Mariah was behind him and he felt a cold, sharp stinging sensation in his neck. He realized she'd injected him with whatever had rendered Kat and McKee to twitching, drooling babies. He could feel the drug burning its way through his carotid artery, spreading like fire through his veins. He could no longer hold up his head.

"I want you to know Joe Aiken is a decent enough guy, Ryan. But he's a politician. Be sure to tell him he won't get Kincaid's hybrid. He's in bed with the oil people and they just want to squash it. On one timeline he becomes your strong ally; on another, he becomes one of *them*. Every possibility is equally probable now. I'm just trying to stack the odds in my favor."

"You don't . . . need Kat to do that," he whispered, and hated that he sounded as though he were groveling, pleading, begging. But he *was* groveling and she knew it.

This elicited an odd, almost sad smile from her. "Yes," she said softly. "I *do* need her."

Blackness claimed his peripheral vision. He managed to keep his eyes open long enough to see Mariah, McKee, and Kat disappear. Then the drug she'd injected into his neck took him away.

8

Curtis's hearing woke up first, recording clicks, hums, beeps. Then his sense of smell stirred to life, bringing in the stink of disinfectants, cleansers, medicine. But it was the rush of memories, bright and vivid and horrifying, the knowledge and certainty that Kat was really gone, that Mariah Jones had disappeared her, that snapped his eyes open.

He stared at the round, ugly clock on the opposite wall. It was noon. He and Kat had left on the dinghy around 6:30 this morning. And he was now in medical.

His right arm was secured to an IV board, the drip on, and his left ankle was cuffed to the bed, a precaution so that he wouldn't transition. That meant they'd left his chip in, probably because they didn't know yet what drug Mariah had given him or because he was unconscious. Or both. It was also possible they intended to send him off to find Mariah when he recovered and rather than give him a new chip, they had opted to let him keep the one he'd gotten three days ago. But if that were true, then it lent credence to the rumors that the supply of chips was running low.

Bottom line? His reasoning might be as flawed as the chips were now. It could be that they intended to remove his chip before he was released from medical. That would be his punishment for defying Rodriguez last night, for going to holding with Kat, for commiserating with Aiken, for all of the above or none of the above, who the hell knew? But the chip was the only way he could find Kat. They would have to kill him before they removed it.

With his free left hand, he unfastened his right arm from the IV board, peeled the tape away from the needle stuck in his arm, and slipped it out. He sat up, leaned forward, and pulled the sheet back from his left foot. *Bastards*. It was similar to the shackle they'd put on McKee, heavy duty, with double locks. Who had the keys? Rodriguez? Fenmore? Or the head of security? He was no Houdini. He needed the keys to escape. Or his pick, that beautiful handy little pick that had gotten him into and out of spots worse than this.

He glanced around, hoping to see his pack. The small one he'd taken to Snake Island was probably still in the staff kitchen. His pick was in the larger bag that he used for transitions and it was in his bedroom closet. The only items he saw that belonged to him were his clothes, hanging in the closet, and his shoes, side by side, on the closet floor.

Curtis rolled to his right, opened the drawer to the nightstand. Nothing useful. He eyed the hanging IV needle, still dripping fluid. Would it work? Maybe. It was sharp, made of stainless steel, but wasn't very long. What the hell. It was worth a try.

He turned off the drip, removed the needle from the IV tube, wiped it on the sheets. He squeezed it between his thumb and index finger, leaned forward again. He turned the leg cuff with his left hand, so he could see the locks, then stretched a little farther, his hamstrings screaming, and slid the needle into the first lock.

He worked the needle hard, begging it not to snap, and grinned when he heard the telling click. *I'm so outta here, Ian, you prick*.

Just as he stuck the needle into the second lock, he heard voices in the hall, close, maybe just outside the door. *Shit,*

shit, hurry. Curtis yanked the sheet back over himself and stuck the needle in the side of the mattress, so that he could find it easily again. He tucked the IV tube under the sheet and hoped that whoever came in wouldn't notice that the drip was turned off.

The door creaked as it opened. He quickly shut his eyes.

". . . surveillance cameras in the cell block didn't work. That's a major lapse in security, Ian, and Art Quintello's ass should be fired."

Simone White, senior member of the Council, sounded enraged. But then, she usually did.

"They worked," Rodriguez said. "They just went haywire—the images blurred, no sound, just static."

"And what would cause that?"

"A time distortion," said Fenmore. "It doesn't happen often now, but in the early days it happened a lot. Mariah claimed it was an anomaly that we just had to live with."

"She apparently perfected it," White snapped. "She must be able to do this at will. None of our Travelers have reported anything like this. So does that mean her chips can do this and ours can't?"

"We, uh, don't know," Fenmore replied. "We didn't even know she was still alive until this whole thing happened."

Someone kicked the side of the bed, then White said, "And just look at golden boy here, sleeping like a prince. It's been more than five hours. Why hasn't he come around yet?"

"The docs said it could be as long as twelve hours," Rodriguez replied. "He apparently got a much larger dose than Art did."

"Yeah, and when he comes to and remembers his babe was disappeared by Mariah Jones, he's going to transition and that'll be it, Ian."

"For chrissake," Fenmore hissed. "Calm down, Simone. We're all on edge, okay? This is a whole new battle for us. And Ryan can't transition. His leg is cuffed."

Someone threw back the sheet, exposing his shackled

ankle. Curtis caught the whiff of perfume and figured it was Simone White.

White: "Maybe he's faking it."

Rodriguez: "Not with you practically shouting in his ear. The only questions we should be asking ourselves right now is what does Mariah want?"

Fenmore: "This was her declaration of war. She's pissed at the way we're running things and has thrown a huge monkey wrench into the works. She's made us look like a bunch of incompetent fools in front of the senator."

Someone walked across the room. From the rhythm of the footfalls, Curtis thought it was White. When she spoke, he was sure of it, her voice came from the other side of his bed, near the window. "So what options do we have?"

Rodriguez: "Find the bitch and bring her back."

Fenmore: "Ryan's the best Traveler we've got now. Can you convince him to do it, Ian?"

White: "*Convince* him? It's his job. It's his goddamn assignment. If he refuses, that's it. He's out."

Rodriguez: "Yeah, he is. But you don't threaten Travelers, Simone. You compromise, cajole, bargain, but never threaten. The sooner you learn that, the better off we'll all be. And right now, we're short on Travelers. Four, including Kat, are missing. We sent a dozen on vacation to cut back on chip usage, three others are out sick because their bodies rejected the chips. Eleven are on assignment. That leaves ten—and most of them are newbies."

All of this was news to Curtis.

Fenmore: "What about Hank Vachinski? He's inexperienced, but he's got promise. One of us could go back with him, Ian."

Rodriguez: "Vachinski is an arrogant fool."

A cell rang, reminding Curtis that he didn't even have his phone.

Rodriguez announced, "It's Aiken again."

"He hasn't left yet?" Fenmore asked.

"He probably wants to talk to Curtis first," Rodriguez explained.

White snapped, "Tell him we'll call when the golden boy is awake."

Footsteps, headed away from him, toward the door. Curtis heard Rodriguez answer his cell, heard Fenmore greet someone in the hall. The door whispered shut, but he still didn't open his eyes. He sensed that Fenmore or White or both of them had stayed behind, but didn't know for sure until he caught the scent of perfume.

"Ryan, Ryan," White said softly. "Such an innocent, handsome face. It's a face that fools people. Julie told me that before she went off to rehab." She folded back the sheet, exposing his left foot again. "Remember Julie?"

Aw, shit. Simone's daughter.

"She was your partner for a year and you sold her down the river. She warned me that your only loyalty was to yourself."

Something sharp and cool trailed along the sole of his foot. His toes begged to twitch, to curl, his foot screamed to jerk away. But he held his leg steady, his toes still, and kept his breathing soft and even.

"She warned me that you had no loyalty to our organization, to the work we do here, that all you did in your private time together was complain. Is that what goes on between you and Kat? She's probably better off wherever Mariah took her. That way you can never betray her the way you did my Jules. That way she'll never end up in a rehab unit, like my Jules did. You lied about Jules, Ryan. She hadn't set up a life in the past, she wasn't going rogue. She wouldn't have done that to me."

Then she leaned in close to him, her perfume a cloud that enveloped him, swallowed him, and whispered, "So this is for Jules, you son of a bitch." She jammed the sharp, metal object up through the sole of his foot, right into the center of the arch, where the skin and nerves were the most tender, and twisted it hard.

Curtis had steeled himself against pain, but not against agony, not against the explosion of searing white heat that tore straight up through his foot and radiated through his ankle, calf, his entire leg. He bolted upward, swinging his fists, decked her on the jaw, grabbed her by the head, and slammed it against his knee. She dropped like a fly, without ever uttering a moan.

Shaking, his foot shrieking with pain, he struggled not to make a sound, and acted quickly. He turned his shackled ankle so that he could see what she'd done and nearly puked. Cuticle scissors, slightly open, so that both blades were buried to the handle in the center of his foot. He took one long, shuddering breath, pulled, and nearly passed out.

Move, you don't have much time.

He slapped the scissors against the sheet, cleaning off the blood, then stuck one of the blades into the second lock, twisted hard twice, and it clicked. He pulled his injured foot free, blood dripping all over the sheets now, tore the case from the pillow, ripped it with scissors and then with his teeth. He stood, favoring his left foot, unable to put his full weight on it, and removed the shackle from the railing.

White was still alive, so he grabbed her arms and pulled her into the bathroom. He turned her on her side, cuffed her ankle to the leg of the sink, then gagged her with a strip of cloth from the pillowcase. He tied her hands behind her back with the second strip.

He made one more trip into the room to get his clothes, limped back into the bathroom, locked the door, and dropped to his knees, unable to stand anymore. He yanked a towel off the rack, ran it under hot water, and pressed it to the bottom of his foot, wiping away the blood.

But as soon as he wiped the blood away, more blood oozed out. He pressed the towel against his foot, pressed hard, panic bubbling up inside of him. *Think, think, what do they do for you when you step on a nail?* Tetanus shot, that was the only thing that came to mind. He'd had a tetanus shot, had every inoculation on the books and then some. He needed to get the hell out of here and the obvious exit was a transition. He wasn't sure that he could do it, but if he could, where should he go?

He needed to treat his foot, stop the bleeding. He needed clothes, his large pack, provisions, before he could head into the past to find Kat. And he needed a lot of information on Mariah Jones—*real* information, not the shit he'd been fed in training—so that he could try to narrow down the possibilities of where she might have taken Kat.

Someone had said he'd been out for five hours. So he could transition an hour or two back, to his house—*the place where Kat and I live our real lives.* He nearly choked on the memory. He had his large pack there, provisions, antibiotics, everything he needed and, best of all, no one in SPOT knew about the house. He and Kat had been careful about that, perhaps unconsciously anticipating a day when they would need an escape hatch.

But would this create a paradox? In training, they'd drummed into you that two versions of yourself could not exist on the same timeline. One version would be annihilated. But from what Mariah had said to him in the holding area and from what he'd learned from seeing McKee again indicated that it was just one more deception, another lie to keep Travelers in the dark about the true power of the chip and the genuine nature of time.

Replays supposedly had different rules—they were like giant holograms, phantom images the brain coughed up, and yet, you still couldn't change any details because that might create a paradox. Or so they'd been taught. But in the replay he and Kat had done with Aiken, Mariah had changed certain details that had impacted the present—specifically that McKee wasn't injured now. No paradox. Events simply had changed to reflect what had happened.

Lies, lies, he had been surrounded by lies for the last seven years. He'd been living a goddamn lie and the longer he remained in an organization so corrupt and heinous, the more corrupt he became. Even if he hadn't knocked out Simone White, even if Kat hadn't been taken, he would have to leave.

White stirred, moaned, her eyes fluttered open. She and Curtis stared at each other. She looked bad, blood smeared across her forehead, her jaw turning black and blue. But her eyes remained the same, dark and cold, analyzing, scheming. "Just to set the record straight, Simone, your lovely Jules begged me to go rogue with her. She planned on rendering my chip inoperable so I couldn't get back. That's why I turned her in."

Noises, on the other side of the door. White heard them, too, and her muffled shouts echoed in the tiny bathroom. Curtis had just run out of time.

The blood in the room told most of the story and the dead-bolted bathroom door told the rest. Lydia Fenmore already knew what they would find when the maintenance guy finally got the lock off—Simone bound, gagged, possibly injured, and Curtis gone.

But when the door opened and she saw Simone, Lydia realized that her injuries didn't account for the blood that stained the sheets and smeared the floor in front of the closet. Curtis had to be hurt. Good. That would make it difficult for him to transition back very far—a few hours at the most. Even though Curtis was a gifted Traveler, talented in ways that most were not, he couldn't defy the body's own wisdom. When you were hurt and bleeding, your body rallied to your defense and your immune system attacked everything that it construed as an invader. And since the chip was definitely an invader, it would be rejected. Lydia guessed that Curtis had transitioned to his condo and that finding him would be a matter of waiting an hour or two in his living room.

Within moments, Simone was lying on the other bed, a nurse and a doctor tending to her injuries. Lydia and Rodriguez stayed with her, listening to her chopped-up version of what had happened, that she had slipped back into the room because she believed Curtis was faking it, that he was actually awake, and he had attacked her and somehow freed himself from the cuff.

Her story didn't ring entirely true, but that was okay. There had been bad blood between them ever since Curtis had ratted on Simone's daughter, his partner before Kat, who had broken the cardinal rule: she had set up a life in the past and was preparing to go rogue. But everyone around here had a gripe against someone. Shit happened in an organization as incestuous as this one.

"Well?" Rodriguez said as soon as they were in the hall. "What do you think?"

"That Simone did something to him, trying to force him to reveal that he wasn't unconscious, and Ryan retaliated.'"

"She must have done something pretty bad for him to do what he did."

"Why do you always defend him? Last night he humiliated you in front of Aiken and now this."

"I'm not defending him. I'm explaining why he defended himself. I mean, let's face it, Lydia. Simone's a vindictive bitch and because of whatever she did to Ryan, we've got a huge fiasco on our hands."

One more fiasco in a string of fiascos. "It may not be that huge. He won't be able to transition very far back. He's hurt, bleeding. If anything, his body will reject the chip and we'll find him in his condo in a little while. Or he'll be in Kat's condo, smelling her clothes or something."

Rodriguez gave her one of those looks that often preceded an argument. But instead of saying anything, he brought out his cell and assigned Travelers to Curtis's condo and to Kat's. "They'll cover until we relieve them," he said as they stepped onto the elevator.

She was pretty sure she knew what that meant, but she wanted to hear him say it. "So you're getting re-chipped and I'm getting a new one?"

"We're facing extinction, Lydia. You have a better idea?"

"Not at the moment."

Her anticipation at having a specific assignment thrilled her. It had been three years since her last assignment and that had been with Kat, when she was in training, a disappearance to the Crusades. Before that, there had been several small disappearances as an observer for recruits. Her last disappearance as a Traveler had happened eleven years ago, when she and her husband had disappeared three generations of dissidents—grandparents, parents, and two kids—to Iceland during the Viking era. That was a biggie. It was also the last disappearance they had done together before a cerebral hemorrhage had taken him in minutes, in the middle of the night, as he had lain beside her.

During the dark days immediately afterward, Lydia had tried to figure out where in the past she could go to circumvent her husband's death. She had driven herself half crazy in the process, transitioning back six months, a year, ten, fifteen. In the end, she had realized that Mariah's rule about death was true: once you died, that was it. Death couldn't be tricked, cajoled, or changed. One way or another, you died on the appointed date. It was as if your soul was imprinted with the date of death as soon as you were born.

Mariah had been gone four years by then; Rodriguez had been voted in as director and had asked her to be assistant director. She had debated it for weeks, not sure that she wanted to work that closely with him again. He was still married and she, as a widow, felt too vulnerable around him, because of their past history. She, after all, had recruited him when they were both single and lovers. But even more important was that the assistant director, like the director, were involved in relatively few transitions, mostly as observers or in emergencies. To shut the door on her life as a Traveler was almost inconceivable to her.

Ultimately, she'd realized that when her husband had died, she had lost her enthusiasm for exploration of the past, that the present held the greatest promise. So she had become assistant director, responsible for the training of new recruits, for mentoring at least one of them, and for filling in for the director and the Council members if and when the occasion arose.

Not long afterward, Rodriguez's wife had died of cancer and within a year, they were living together, the king and queen of SPOT. And until this very moment, she hadn't understood how much she had missed the ability to move back through time whenever she wanted, the challenge of tailoring herself to fit the mores and culture of certain eras, the sheer pleasure of the exploration itself.

Rodriguez grasped her hand and held it tightly until the doors opened on the first floor, the main area for the medical building. "Are you sure?" he asked.

The question couldn't be answered with a simple yes or no. It was more layered and complex than that and encompassed all the years they had known each other, in the many roles they had played in each other's lives. "I am *not* going the way of the dodo bird and the raptor."

"I was hoping you'd say that," he whispered, and brought her hand to his mouth, kissing it.

The procedure itself was quick, painless. The chip, injected through the sinus cavity, migrated to the appropriate spot in the brain and dug in, like a parasite or a virus. It released an enzyme that hastened the decay of the old chip, so that within a few hours the old chip would be completely dissolved, absorbed by her body.

Triggering a chip, activating it, lay in training—vigorous visualization techniques, learning the language of your own body and psyche, immersing yourself in the details of particular eras, developing rituals that spoke to you. Sometimes, when she was teaching recruits, she felt that the training was just bullshit, that the real power lay in the chip itself. Other times, it struck her that they were all lab rats, scrambling to reach the food, the treat, the prize at the end of the maze.

During their time in recovery, Dr. Russ Berlin sat with them. He was a quiet, thoughtful man with black, curly hair who wore contacts that seemed to keep his eyes perpetually large and startled. Mariah had recruited him in 1982, when they had met at the Monroe Institute in Virginia, to head the medical and research department. At the time, Berlin was a pediatric oncologist in Baltimore.

Lydia realized that she knew almost nothing about his personal life, other than the fact he had been married and divorced and had lost his young son to leukemia years ago. There had been rumors that he and Mariah had been lovers. She didn't know if it was true. The only thing that mattered about Berlin was that he knew as much or more about the biochip as Mariah did. He was the gatekeeper of the technology. So when he gave the rundown on how serious the situation with the chips had become, she listened closely.

"With your chips and the spares you'll be given, our reserve is now down to about thirty-six. Production has fallen to twenty a month. We . . ."

"Why has production fallen?" Rodriguez asked.

"These chips aren't motherboards, Ian. We don't make them on assembly lines. We need biological material that's free of disease, that's O positive blood type, that takes to the gel in which the chip is frozen. It's complicated by the fact that we don't know yet why the chips are being rejected. Ideally, I'd like you both to wait at least twenty-four hours before you transition. We've found that with the flawed chips, experienced Travelers who make it past the first day or two without rejection can usually make it about a month. And part of what makes you experienced is not straining for a particular era and location, not making numerous transitions in a very short period of time, and having a place in mind that you can transition to effortlessly. Do you both have that location?"

They nodded. In the old days, her safe spot in the past had been a lake in upstate New York where she had vacationed as a kid. That would do. Her safe location in this time, in the event that she was injured, was medical today, whatever date it happened to be. She didn't have any idea what Rodriguez's locations were, but suspected that he, like her, would fall back on what had worked before.

"Excellent," Berlin said, shutting his notebook. "So, please, wait twenty-four hours. After that, the odds are about eighty percent in your favor that you'll do just fine for about five weeks."

"And if our bodies reject these chips before we get back?" Lydia asked.

"Use the spares, but understand there are no guarantees."

What he was really saying, of course, was that once a primary chip failed, it was likely that a spare would fail, too, and quickly, and they would be stuck in the past. They wouldn't get home again.

9

Curtis had targeted the river side of the house, so that he could approach from the back, where he was less likely to be seen by passing neighbors or anyone else who might be driving through the neighborhood. Even though he had transitioned back three hours, before the shit with Simone White had hit the fan, it was possible that the house wasn't the secret he and Kat had thought and that the property was under surveillance. So he hobbled, hunkered over, between the hedge and the side of the house, every step so painful that by the time he reached the corner of the building, air hissed through his gritted teeth.

Everything in the front yard looked undisturbed—the shadows of the trees indicating that it was early morning, leaves rustling in a cool breeze, the garage door shut, a newspaper in the driveway. There would be mail in the box, he thought, but he would get it later. Right now, he had to get inside the house and tend to his foot before he fell over.

He entered through the rear porch door, shedding his clothes as he limped into the bedroom he and Kat shared. The impossibility of the task ahead struck him then, and a shudder of uncertainty and near panic seized him. How the hell was he supposed to find Kat with the entire spectrum of history to explore?

Curtis stood under the hot spray until he couldn't bear the throbbing ache in his foot any longer. He rifled through the med supplies in the linen closet, picking out the items he needed, then sat down on the toilet lid and blotted his foot dry. It had stopped bleeding, but was now bruised, hot, beginning to swell. He soaked it in Betadine first, then spread antibiotic salve across the arch and wrapped it in gauze. Travelers were always well supplied with antibiotics and over the years he had stashed away enough drugs to treat everything short of radiation sickness. For the infection that now raged through his foot, he chose the five-day Zapper, as he and Kat called it, and swallowed one of the giant pills. He followed it with a couple of Advil.

He still couldn't walk very well and doubted if he could get a regular shoe on his left foot. So he resorted to heavy socks and a pair of soft moccasins. He repacked his bag, included a nine millimeter with half a dozen clips, a prepaid cell phone with two backup batteries, and his PDA. It held a one-gig memory card, large enough to accommodate any files he would download.

What about cash and ID? Thanks to his rampant fear of being poor, to the bitter memories of bankruptcy, he always carried about five grand in the pack, money from the present, and had plenty of cash in the house from a number of historical eras and decades in history. But since he didn't know where he was going yet, era-appropriate cash and ID would be the last items to add.

He carried everything into his office and while his laptop and PC were booting up, went into the kitchen to fix himself something to eat. When he had lived here alone in the years before he had met Kat, the fridge usually looked like Mother Hubbard's cupboard. But Kat claimed that a full fridge made her feel secure, so this one was always full. Curtis made a huge omelet, using up most of the fresh vegetables in the bin, started a pot of strong Cuban coffee, polished off the organic OJ. He then returned to his office to eat.

To determine his target, he desperately needed biographical information on Mariah Jones with a chronology of her life—the real info, not the lies and disinformation he'd been told. He recalled that Aiken had said that in the late sixties, she had taught at Smith, where her early experimentation with the chip had begun as a cure for insomnia. So he started there.

The Smith link about Mariah was sketchy. It focused primarily on the fact that she was the first black female professor at the college and had made significant research contributions to the study of insomnia, for which she sought a cure, just as Aiken had said. In 1970, she was booted off the faculty for her experimentation with human subjects, something Aiken hadn't mentioned and that Curtis hadn't known.

In 1998, one of Mariah's former students, Kim Runyon, a professor at Harvard, won the Nobel Prize for her discoveries in some obscure facet of botany. She credited Mariah as the instructor who had awakened her passion for botany and research. He clicked on Kim Runyon's name and discovered that in 1968, at the age of fifteen, she had won a full scholarship to Smith and studied under Mariah Jones. As a result, her mother, Dee, had left a lucrative career in the California film industry, where she worked with legendary Rod Serling, and moved to Northampton with her.

The most frequent mention of Mariah Jones occurred on the conspiracy blogs, many of which he and Kat had explored over the past several months. In SPOT's decades of existence, information had leaked out here and there, as it had with Roswell and other government cover-ups, and there was just enough of it to keep the conspiracies alive and well.

The connect-the-dots information ranged from the patently absurd to the astonishingly accurate. There wasn't much biographical info in the blogs, but he downloaded a lot of it just the same and transferred the data to his PDA and then to his laptop. He decided to bring his laptop and use the PDA as backup. Another redundant safety feature.

Every biographical sketch he found on Mariah had a different date of birth for her: 1923, 1933, 1942, even 1913. If, as they'd been taught, Mariah was in her late fifties when she left SPOT in 1991, then that meant she was now in her seventies and had been born around 1923. If she was born in 1913, then she would be in her early nineties. The 1942 date seemed the most likely. That would put her in her early sixties now. So why did she look thirty-five? Did constant transitions impact the aging mechanism in some way? During the replay, even Mariah had remarked that there were no easy answers.

During the second hour of his search, he started to feel pressured for time. If Rodriguez, Fenmore, White, or one of the other top dogs knew about this house, then they could be here within a few hours and he still didn't know what time period to target. So he made a concentrated search for the specifics of Mariah's research. When did the human experimentation begin? Who were her test subjects? He hoped the information would yield a precise chronology.

When his prepaid cell suddenly rang, it startled him. Who knew this number? Kat, of course. And his mother and one of his brothers. Then the caller's information appeared in the window. Aiken, D.C. suburbs.

Had he given the senator this number? He didn't think so, but perhaps Kat had. He answered the call, but didn't say anything.

"Hello? Ryan? Kat?"

It was Aiken, all right. "It's Ryan."

"What the hell is going on?"

That depends on what time zone you're in, Senator. He glanced at his desk clock. It was 11:07 A.M. So yes, the senator had heard about the fiasco over on Snake Island and, according to his frame of reference, Curtis was supposed to be unconscious, in medical.

"It was Mariah," Curtis said. "And just so you know, Joe,

I've transitioned back several hours. And since you don't know yet what happens in medical, I'm going to tell you." And he did.

"Sweet Christ," Aiken whispered when he finished. "Now that you've told me, what should I do?"

"You call Ian around twelve twenty or so. He leaves the room to take the call, Lydia goes with him, Simone stays behind. That gives me the break I need, so it's important that you make that call, okay?"

"Right. Of course. I will. What else? What're you going to do? How're you going to find Kat and McKee?"

The entire conversation was surreal for Curtis; he couldn't imagine what a mindfuck it was for Aiken, especially when he got to the part about Mariah's message for him. "I'm quoting, Joe. She said, *'He's a decent enough guy, but he's a politician. Be sure to tell him he won't get Kincaid's hybrid. He's in bed with the oil people and they just want to squash it. On one timeline, he becomes your strong ally; on another timeline, he becomes one of them.'*"

Curtis stopped there and hoped that Aiken would comment on his relationship with the oil industry. When he didn't, he was glad he hadn't divulged Mariah's supposed plan. If nothing else, his years here had taught him that it was wisest to hold back some information. Always.

"What can I do for you?" Aiken asked. "What do you need to find them?"

"Give me dates, Joe. I need specific dates about Mariah's life. Or the names of her friends, peers, that kind of thing."

"You know about Dee and Kim Runyon?" he asked.

"About Kim. Her Nobel and all."

"Right. After leaving Hollywood, Dee worked at a local bookstore in Northampton and she and Mariah became good friends. I mean, this was the late sixties, Ryan. There just weren't that many black women in an academic town like Northampton."

Curtis locked all this information away in the metal filing cabinet in his head. "What else?"

"Okay, let me think. In the fall of 1967, Mariah started the experiments on humans that eventually resulted in her expulsion from the faculty. I met her in April, through my dad, when he was still in the Senate. We were in a restaurant in D.C., I can see what she was wearing, what she looked like. She said she was celebrating the one-month anniversary of a major breakthrough on human experimentation with the chip. So, March 1968 was important. By the time she was kicked off the faculty two years later, she'd discovered the by-product of her insomnia cure and went to my old man to see if the government was interested. She needed funding, a facility. That's how it all started."

"Who was her first subject for the insomnia cure?"

"Besides herself? I don't know."

"Do you have any idea where she was living?"

"A suburban neighborhood in Northampton. She had her own house. I remember that was a point of pride for her. You might check property records."

"What else?"

"Dee and her daughter lived in an apartment on Green Street in Northampton, near the campus."

"What did Dee do in Hollywood?"

"She worked with Bari Serrano Ovis, or maybe it was Bari Ovis Serrano, I'm not sure. Bari was pretty well known for her time, wrote for a lot of the TV shows back then—*I Spy, Mission Impossible, Twilight Zone.* Her old man, Charlie Ovis, was a renowned producer who worked with Rod Serling on a lot of shows, including *Twilight Zone.* If I remember correctly, Ovis, Serling, and Bari worked on a pilot in the late sixties that became a big hit. I think it was called *Connections.* Maybe that will lead to some other information, Ryan."

"You've given me a lot to work with here, Joe. I appreciate it."

"Go find them, Ryan. Mariah, Kat, even McKee, that poor bastard."

Curtis didn't consider McKee a "poor bastard." If anything, he was getting exactly what he deserved. Then again, some of the people he and Kat had disappeared might say the same thing about him.

I'm just trying to stack the odds in my favor.

You don't need Kat to do that.

Yes, I do need her.

His conversation with Mariah haunted him. "You realize I'm now considered a rogue agent, Joe. That means if I'm caught, I'm out." *And worse.*

"You're not rogue. I'm giving you the orders to find Mariah and her two hostages and to do whatever you need to do to accomplish this. From this point forward, Ian will no longer have the sole power of Traveler assignments. It will be going through me and a committee."

He didn't particularly like the sound of that. "I'll be in touch."

Connections. Curtis had a vague memory of the TV show, a time-travel adventure story in which people from the twenty-second century had traveled to the sixties to inter-breed with the locals because nearly all humans in the future were sterile and humanity was dying out. The few episodes he'd seen in reruns hadn't impressed him in the least, but his parents, he remembered, had been regular viewers. His mom and dad used to sit down together for an hour a week to indulge in one of their few common interests.

Curtis googled Bari Serrano Ovis and started clicking on links. The Internet Movie Database had the most extensive information on Serrano, a vivacious-looking redhead who had broken into the business because of her father and his friendship with Rod Serling. She was legendary among fans of *The Twilight Zone,* still in reruns after forty years, but her crowning achievement was as cocreator of *Connections.* IMDB described it:

> The time-travel adventure series was the highest rated show in 1970, when it debuted, with more than 40 million viewers, which in today's numbers

would run around 80 million. It topped the Nielson charts during its six-year run. In retrospect, it's astonishing that Serrano described cell phones, personal computers, laptops, PDAs, and the Internet with such uncanny accuracy before any of these items existed.

In the spring of 1968, while Serrano was staying at her childhood home in Utica, New York, she was implicated in a car theft when she and two unidentified people fled a local bar. Shortly afterward, Serrano disappeared. Even now, nearly 40 years later, her disappearance is the subject of endless speculation and conspiracies.

It's known that she was working on the pilot script before she disappeared on March 7, 1968, when a home she and her father owned in Old Forge, New York, burned to the ground. Her remains were never found, but police eventually declared she had died in that fire.

Her father, Charles Ovis, says that he and Rod Serling used Serrano's extensive notes to write the subsequent episodes. However, fans adamantly believe that no one but Serrano could have written these episodes—and this is the point where it all turns weird.

One theory is that the shady organization that lay at the heart of the TV series actually existed and that Serrano was forced into hiding because of what she knew (pilot). Another theory is that the two people with whom she fled the bar were from the future about which she wrote so vividly (episode 2) and that they all took refuge in some other time.

What's curious about all of it is that several years ago, a photo of Serrano and her close friends, novelist Ken Kesey and music icon Jerry Garcia, surfaced

on the Internet. The third man in the photo is
unidentified, but the most avid conspiracy theorists
believe he's not only the source of Serrano's inspira-
tion, but is, in fact, from the very future she wrote
about **(photo)**.

Whatever the truth, Bari Serrano's disappearance
remains an enigma that has endured to the present
day.

Curtis clicked on the link to the photo—and nearly fell
out of his chair. *Impossible*. He enlarged the picture and just
sat there staring, wrestling with the implications, the complexities, the *connections*. He was bearded, his hair was lighter,
longer, he wore glasses. But it was him, all right. Jake McKee.

Mariah had disappeared McKee to the late sixties.

He started to send the article and photo as an attached file
to Aiken, but then decided to keep this piece of information
to himself for now. He clicked on the summary for the pilot
episode:

When Jim Danforth is arrested for crimes he didn't
commit and subsequently disappears, his wife, Eva,
is plunged into a search that leads her into the heart
of a shadow government that holds the secret of
time travel. She discovers that dissidents and "undesirables" are disappeared into the past by a unit
of specially trained Travelers and that the shadow
government uses this ability for its own nefarious
agenda. On the run for her life, she must figure out
where in time her husband has been taken and how
to get him back.

"Holy Christ," he whispered. This summary bore no resemblance at all to his memory of the show.

He clicked on the synopsis for the second episode.

Eva Danforth, with the help of her brother, George,
meets up with Jim's close friend, Kevin Richardson,

who is also being sought by the time travel unit. But they are ambushed by director Sanchez and his group and escape into the past only because a time distortion occurs. Eva and George are separated from Kevin during the transition.

Meanwhile, Sanchez has an even larger problem— his best Traveler has gone rogue, threatening the very existence of the unit.

It was like discovering that the people you thought were your parents were actually alien hybrids. Did this mean that if he clicked on the summary for the last episode he would discover that he never found Kat? That he died? That she had died? How did this happen? How could his memories of the show be so radically different from what was written here?

Somehow, somewhere, reality had changed. Was it because Mariah had disappeared McKee to the late sixties and he had hooked up with Bari Serrano? It was the only conclusion that made sense.

He downloaded every episode summary onto his laptop, then his PDA. He started to e-mail Aiken the link to the site, but changed his mind. Not yet, he thought. He checked sites for Utica, New York, and for Northampton and downloaded maps and photos that would make it easier for him to target a specific destination and to get around once he was there.

Which place first?

He wasn't sure yet.

He copied all his important PC files onto a memory stick, then onto his laptop. Just in case someone knew about this house, he took additional precautions—he removed the motherboard from the PC and hid it in a compartment in the attic, where he kept his various IDs and stash of money. His cash for the sixties amounted to only several thousand, but it would have to do.

He decided that his target date would be around March 1,

1968. He would focus on both Northampton and Utica and let the chip calculate the most auspicious destination. This technique was something he and Kat had developed on their own, through experimentation, and they usually had luck with it.

He hoisted his pack onto his back and although it was heavier than he liked, the Advil had kicked in and he could put some weight on his foot now. As he walked through the house, making sure that the doors and windows were locked, that the light timers were on, he felt a stab of deep regret, disappointment, even shame, that he'd spent six years of his life—seven if he counted his training—in an organization as morally depraved as SPOT. Maybe Mariah's plan for SPOT was the right thing to do, the right way to proceed. But it didn't excuse her disappearing Kat.

Yes, I do need her.

He didn't give a damn what happened to Rodriguez, Fenmore, White, and the rest of the Council members. He didn't really care what happened to SPOT. But once he found Kat, he intended to somehow make amends for the lives he had shattered by disappearing those people whose only crimes were that they had pissed off a boss or spoken out against the government.

Curtis let himself out the through the porch door and limped down toward the big banyan near the river where he often transitioned. It was just past two now, the air still and pleasantly warm, but the anxiety and apprehension he'd felt upon fleeing the medical building hugged him like a shadow. He sat down under the tree, got out the photos and maps, and studied them.

He was so engrossed in what he was doing that the sound of an approaching car nearly didn't register. And when it did, he sank down low in the grass, grateful that the trunk of the grand old tree hid him from view.

Sure enough, two Freeze officers skulked along the side of

the house, weapons drawn. *Not such a secret house,* he thought, and shut his eyes, drawing the past around him. The telltale static burst to life inside his skull, he felt a brief and disorienting equilibrium, and then he transitioned.

Cape Cod & After

Our Society is run by insane people for insane
objectives.
—John Lennon

Reality is that which, when you stop believing
in it, doesn't go away.
—Philip K. Dick

10

As the sun sank behind the trees, Nora pulled out of her safe haven with the dog in the passenger seat, her bags re-packed, and her courage faltering. She kept checking the mirrors to see if anyone was following her. But the two-lane road, empty of cars, angled back through the mirror like a long, sun-struck ribbon to nowhere.

When she had awakened early this morning, after a solid five or six hours of sleep, her mind had been much clearer. She had decided she would meet Kincaid, but on her terms, tonight, when it was safer to travel and she'd had time to think about things. She had texted him and her brother about her plans and got immediate responses from both of them. Kincaid asked for them to meet him at Wood's Hole, said he would arrive sometime after dusk this evening, and would wait near the terminal for them. Tyler told them to look for a white camper truck and asked Nora to call him when she was thirty minutes out.

Off and on throughout the day, she'd been able to browse the Internet with her cell phone and had checked for stories about Jake's arrest. By this morning, the local Blue River paper carried the story—no surprise, scandal connected to the college always sold papers—and so did the large daily in Boston. The article was short, but included photos of both her and Jake. By afternoon, that story had been picked up by Reuters, then by Google news, and each time she checked, it had spread like a virus to some other site.

It wasn't that she and Jake were so fascinating, at least not outside the scandal-hungry confines of Blue River. But the charges against Jake—crashing Pentagon computers— were compelling. And the Department of Freedom and Security had issued APBs on both her and Kincaid, describing them as "armed and dangerous." Three faculty members, in other words, had bitten the dust, and she was sure she eventually would find articles on the college Web site about "terrorists in our midst."

So with her photo plastered across the Internet, her first task would be to change her appearance in some way. She couldn't do much about her height, but she would cut and dye her hair as soon as she could buy the supplies and find a place to do it. Within an hour, she spotted a small shopping center and a gas station and turned into the station first.

The idea of entering a well-lit building made her uneasy. Security cameras, crowds, she might be recognized. She desperately wanted to use her ATM card or a credit card so that she wouldn't have to go inside to pay. But she suspected her account had been flagged by now and Freeze would be looking for any activity on it in order to determine her location. She dug a baseball cap out of her pack, tugged it on, and tucked her hair up inside of it. It hardly qualified as a disguise, but was better than nothing.

When Nora entered the building, she kept her head turned away from the security cameras. The clerk was watching a small TV, barely looked at her, and she was in and out in less than three minutes. A gallon of diesel filled her tank. Considering the distance she'd driven, this miracle of Kincaid's hybrid had never struck her as more personal.

Her luck didn't take the edge off her paranoia. She now appreciated how awful these past months must have been for

Jake as he struggled to keep his worst fears—and his secrets, she reminded herself—from her. Even though she sympathized, it didn't change her feelings about their marriage.

She drove into the shopping center, aware that the next stop could be trickier. The center was crowded and featured all the usual neighborhood stops. In addition to a drugstore, she saw a supermarket, liquor store, video store, used bookshop, two restaurants, and a lot of people coming and going. But maybe that would work to her advantage. She would be just one more person in a crowd.

She pulled into the closest parking space she found, removed three twenties from her stash, and gave Sunny a pat on the head. "I'll be back in a jiffy. I promise. Guard the car."

Like so many drugstores, this one attempted to stock something for everyone—groceries to incidentals, drugs to school supplies. Nora bought dog food and treats, more soup and tuna, writing essentials, a memory stick, hair ties and scissors. In the hair product aisle, she selected a color that would turn her black hair to a light brown. Blond would be better, but it would take longer.

The line at the register was long, just one clerk on duty and, no doubt, three others off on break. The woman at the front of the line used her ATM card; the machine wouldn't take it, so she tried a credit card and it didn't work, either. She finally threw up her hands and left her merchandise on the counter.

C'mon, c'mon, hurry.

The next person in line, a man, had to swipe his ATM card a couple of times before it took. He had a lot of stuff and the woman at the register bagged it slowly, chatting the entire time with another clerk. Nora glanced at the wall clock. She'd been in here twenty minutes.

By the time she finally set her basket on the counter, she could barely muster a polite smile. Bubbles of panic surged in her throat. Maybe she imagined it, but it seemed that the clerk gave her a second, furtive glance, the sort of look reserved for people whose face you remembered from some-

where—*like maybe the Boston paper or an Internet site?*—
but which you couldn't place. She rang up Nora's purchases,
ran her special marker over the twenties, making sure they
were real, and was interrupted by several calls.

During the second call, the clerk turned so that her back
was to Nora and the growing line of impatient customers behind her, and whispered into the phone. It could be her boyfriend, her mother, a friend with whom she was trading gossip.
But Nora was now too paranoid to believe any of those possibilities.

"Keep the change," she murmured, and scooped up her
purchases before the woman had turned around. The instant
she passed through the door, Nora broke into a run and loped
across the parking lot.

"Hey, hold on," someone shouted behind her. "You forgot
your change."

Nora looked back. Two security guys galloped through
the glow of street lamps and across the parking lot like mustang studs, one with a handheld radio to his mouth, the other
with a cell pressed to his ear, both of them armed. The bubble of panic in her throat burst, adrenaline flooded through
her, and she tore toward her car, moving like the wind.

Fortunately, she hadn't locked the car and didn't have to
waste time fiddling with her keys. She threw her purchases
onto the floor in front of the passenger seat, startling Sunny,
scrambled behind the steering wheel, jammed her key in the
ignition. She screeched out of the space and shot for the
closest exit.

The men opened fire, but she was too far away by then.
Within seconds, she careened onto the road. She wouldn't
outrun anyone in this car; the engine's top speed was around
seventy. But it handled so smoothly that when she made a
sharp turn, she didn't have to slow down much. She kept
turning, right and left and left again, working her way deeper
and deeper into the labyrinth of a rural countryside. She
sped past slumbering old farmhouses, winter fields where

horses huddled for warmth, places the twenty-first century hadn't reached.

A chopper approached at one point, sweeping the area, and Nora stopped under a tree, in front of a farmhouse, killed the headlights, and waited for it to move on. Silently begged for it to fly on past. Even when it did, she waited a while longer. Twenty or thirty minutes later, she was in open countryside dotted with family-run businesses. No choppers overhead, no cops behind her. She swung into a gas station that looked like the last outpost of civilization. Two of the four pumps were broken, the building screamed for fresh paint, the windows hadn't been washed in decades.

Nora parked at the side of the building, next to a green Dumpster. No one was around, and the restroom door stood open. She dropped the scissors into her purse, slipped her PDA and cell phone into her jacket pockets, and she and Sunny got out. A brisk, chilly wind blew across the open field at the side of the building. She took a reading on Jake's compass; she was still headed south, toward the Cape.

While Sunny bounded out into the field, Nora went into the restroom. Dingy didn't describe it. No telling what horrors grew in those darkened corners, in the mold under the sink, the filth encrusted around the faucet. The mirror, small and tarnished, was positioned on the wall for someone much shorter than she was. When she bent her knees slightly, she could see enough of herself to butcher her hair. Where to start?

She ran her fingers through the left side, holding her hair out from her head, and snipped. There went a childhood memory, of her mother combing her hair when she was four or five, marveling at how beautiful and soft it was. A snip at the right excised another memory, an old one, of Alex Kincaid's fingers sliding through her hair as they made love. And now a snip from the back and there went the memory of her first braid, her first date, her prom.

When her hair was halfway up her neck, her distress col-

lapsed into rage at Jake for excluding her, for keeping secrets that had put their lives at risk, for screwing his young,
pretty student, and at Kincaid for commiserating with Jake
and knowing more than she did about what had happened
and why. The good ole boys, it always came back to that.
Most of all, though, she blamed herself for being so oblivious, so caught up in her classes, her professional life, *herself.*

When she was done, her neck felt exposed, vulnerable,
cold, and she resembled a teen having a really bad hair day.
But she doubted if even her brother would recognize her.
When she glanced down at the carpet of black hairs at her
feet, she felt enraged all over again. She kicked the door shut
and hurried back outside.

Sunny was sitting by the car, waiting for her with such
openness and trust that Nora wrapped her arms around the
dog's neck, buried her face in that cool, soft fur. Tears stung
the backs of her eyes. Grief, loneliness, abject terror: yes,
yes, all of these. But in her world, as small as it had become,
redemption lay in the truth, whatever it might be and wherever it might lead.

She opened one of the cans of dog food and dished some
into a bowl for Sunny, put it in the backseat, and coaxed her
back into the car. Sunny wolfed down the food, some water,
then returned to her spot in the passenger seat.

Her cell jingled, a text message from Tyler, asking how
far away she was. Nora wasn't sure where she was and replied
she would text him when she had a fix on her location. She
asked if Kincaid was with him. Tyler said he and Diana had
just pulled into the lot at the Wood's Hole terminal and were
going to look around for Kincaid now. He added that Diana
had suggested a destination in the Berkshires where they
would be safe.

The Berkshires. That would be the cottage in the middle
of nowhere that her grandparents used a couple of weeks a
year. Nora had been there just once, before she'd met Jake,

and it was so remote, so buried in obscure geography, that even Freeze wouldn't be able to find them.

After that, she drove like a bat from hell. She took periodic readings on Jake's compass, glanced at the map, and forty minutes later reached the parking lot of the Wood's Hole terminal. It was close to nine p.m.

She cruised through the lot, searching for a white camper truck, and saw only one, a battered heap that looked as though it wouldn't make it five miles, much less into the Berkshires. It was parked well away from any of the lampposts, so if she could find a parking space close enough, she wouldn't have to walk under any lights. She was starting to feel like a vampire, as if bright lights or the sun might vaporize her.

Nora circled the lot, found a spot several rows over, pulled in. "Okay, girl, we're getting out and I need to you to stay close to me."

Sunny wagged her tail and barked, as if she'd understood every word. Hell, maybe she did. Nora wondered what twist of destiny had brought this dog into her life and what, if anything, it meant in the broader scheme of things. Whatever the truth, she was grateful for the companionship.

The air here was colder, a damp, penetrating chill. She zipped up her jacket and hoisted the pack onto her back. She had added some of the supplies that Pham had provided and the damn pack was now so heavy it felt like a huge, mutant growth on her back. Thirty-three years old, she thought, and her life had been reduced to this, traveling around like some college backpacker in Europe.

When she reached the camper, she found it empty and locked. She set her belongings on the ground and stood against the side door, rubbing her sore shoulders. Should she go inside to look for them? Forget it. No more crowded, well-lit buildings.

Then she spotted them, Tyler and Diana emerging from the terminal building, into the bright lights around the entrance. He had a bottle of water tucked under his arm, was peeling the wrapper from a candy bar, and looked very much like their dad had when he was about Tyler's age, as handsome as a movie star. All that beautiful dark hair, the lean physique, the chiseled features. Diana, petite and bundled up in a thick jacket, was studying a brochure, maybe a ferry schedule, and as she turned, the wind caught her curly blond hair and whipped it across her face.

Nora stuck her thumb and index finger into the corners of her mouth and let out a long, piercing whistle, just as Tyler had taught her to do when she was a kid. His head snapped up, seeking the source of the whistle. She waved wildly, started toward him. He saw her, looked right at her, but seemed momentarily confused. Her hair, she thought. Tyler didn't recognize her with short hair. But he knew the whistle and broke into a run, Diana racing alongside him.

They wrapped their arms around her at the same time, the three of them hugging with the abandon of kids at a birthday party. For Nora, it was one of those Zen moments that would be forever burned in memory. Then they all started talking at once, Sunny barked, and Nora introduced her. Both Tyler and Diana made a big fuss about the dog, which Sunny shamelessly ate up. They piled into the camper, Tyler turned on the engine and the heat, and they huddled together as if around a campfire, talking fast, catching up.

"We've waited through two ferries from the Vineyard," Tyler said. "I've e-mailed Alex repeatedly, but haven't gotten any answers. If he's not on the ferry that's due in a few minutes, I think we should e-mail him again and if he doesn't reply, we'll head to the Berkshires and set up some other rendezvous."

"That sounds like a plan," Nora agreed. "I just hope I haven't put the two of you at risk."

"Not me," Diana said. "I wasn't followed. I came down last night and stayed in a fleabag, then met Tyler at a coffee shop this morning. But his ex got visited by thugs last night. They were looking for him."

"Oh, Tyler, I'm so sorry." Nora squeezed his shoulder. "What happened?"

"I went over to the house and talked to them. They wanted to know where you were, had I heard from you, gotten any calls, e-mails . . . the usual intimidating shit." He grinned. "I'm a good liar, Nora. I had plenty of practice in my marriage. And I also took one of our company attorneys with me. They weren't prepared for that."

"Were they Freeze?" she asked.

"Absolutely." He described them.

"Tattoo Man and Surfer Boy. They pursued me when I fled Blue River."

"Look, this would've happened sooner or later just because of Mom. You and I are on a watch list because of her arrest all those years ago."

"A watch list? Is that like a no-fly list or something?"

"Similar. I just learned about it a couple of months ago. We'd submitted a bid for a government contract and even though we came in well under our competitors, we didn't get it. The well-connected guy who advised me to make the bid, a client we've done a lot of business with in the past, told me later, in confidence, that we lost the bid because my name showed up on a federal watch list. Anyone on that list is denied the kind of security clearance we needed. When I pressed him for more information, he asked if anyone in my family or among my close circle of friends had been arrested for subversive activities. Or if anyone had disappeared."

Disappeared. The same word Pham had used. "Did you tell him about Mom?"

"Sure. I've got nothing to hide from this guy. My company has done contract work for the military, for the Pentagon, the FBI, NASA, and this was the first I'd heard about any *watch list*. He said the job was for some sort of black ops unit within Freeze."

"I always figured that Freeze was just one big, bloated black ops outfit," Nora said.

"No, no, no." Diana shook her head. "I recently got into this with one of my clients, at a cocktail party. Freeze is in charge of national security, period. They employ nearly two hundred thousand people, are responsible for security at our borders, ports, nuclear and chemical plants, for the aviation industry, and they investigate all incidents of possible terrorism or suspected terrorists within our borders. That's their official description. But there are black ops hidden in this budget."

"Yeah," Tyler agreed. "That's basically correct. Apparently this special security my contact was talking about is a black ops outfit that's folded into Freeze, but operates with hardly any oversight. These specially trained men and women do the real dirty work."

"Oh, you mean, like set off bombs and kill people and then blame it on terrorist groups in other countries?" Nora remarked.

"No. They do the disappearances."

"And what's that mean, exactly? What does it mean to be *disappeared*? Did he say?"

Tyler sounded irritated now, as if her lack of knowledge or her questions or both indicated a serious gap in her understanding of how the world worked. "I'm assuming he meant what it means in other countries, Nora. People are arrested and vanish into secret prisons or they're killed."

If that was true, then she hoped her mother was dead. Death would be preferable to being confined to a secret prison for twenty-three years. But whenever she thought about her mother, that smaller self reaching out to her across time and space, Nora felt she was still alive. Alive, like Jake.

But alive where?

A horn blew, a long, mournful sound that echoed through the darkness, a signal that the incoming ferry from Martha's Vineyard was approaching. "Alex better be on it," Tyler said. "I'll wait for him on the dock and . . ."

Sunny started to growl, a low rumbling noise deep in the

back of her throat, then leaped up and clawed frantically at the closed window, snarling and barking. Nora whipped around in her seat, certain the dog had sensed something that the rest of them had missed. Just then, an SUV screeched to a stop behind the truck, blocking them in, the doors flew open, and Tattoo Man and Surfer Boy leaped out, guns drawn.

Tyler shouted, *"Get down, both of you!"*

He slammed the truck into reverse, gunned the accelerator, and crashed into the SUV, crumpling the front fender, shoving it back a hundred yards and jarring Nora's body to the bone. The two men jumped out of the way and Tyler, a man now possessed, slammed the truck into reverse again, hit the SUV once more, and spun the wheel to the right, edging out of the space.

The men opened fire and bullets struck the side of the truck. Nora grabbed a blanket off the floor, threw herself over Sunny, and jerked the blanket over them. Seconds later, the side window shattered and glass showered over them. Then Tyler lurched for the exit and something in the back of the truck banged against the pavement. Probably the rear fender.

Nora snapped upright, shaking off the blanket so the glass fell away from her and Sunny. Just when she thought they were free, everything around them collapsed into a languorous slow motion. The cars headed into the parking lot moved like slugs. The flag on the pole that had flapped in the wind earlier had gone limp. The air looked and felt thick, heavy, weighted.

"What the . . ." Tyler stopped the truck and they all scrambled out.

There, beneath the magnificent sweep of moonlit sky, the entire area resembled a still life. Tattoo Man and Surfer Boy, frozen in crouches, clutching their weapons. Cars immobilized. People who had dived for cover when they'd heard the gunshots looked like wax figures in a museum, some with their bodies still in midair, arms thrust outward, others huddled on the ground, arms covering their heads. Two cops stood just outside the terminal building, weapons drawn, legs frozen in midstride. Cars on the ferry's ramp no longer moved, people on the decks looked like life-size dolls.

"What *is* this?" Diana whispered.

"Time has stopped," Tyler whispered back.

"But it's only stopped for them," Nora said. "We still move normally. It's like we're on different time frequencies."

"My watch stopped," Tyler said.

"Mine, too," echoed Diana.

Nora glanced at her own watch: the hands had frozen at 9:27.

As they approached Tattoo Man and Surfer Boy, she saw the horizontal column of their bullets, suspended in the air like tiny fish trapped in transparent ice. Nora carefully plucked a bullet out of the air, stared at it, pocketed it, then slammed the palm of her hand along the entire column. It collapsed like a row of dominoes and dropped at the same rate she was moving, the bullets clicking like castanets as they struck the pavement.

The three of them stopped in front of the two Freeze officers. "Ugly suckers," Tyler remarked.

"Bastards, shooting out your window," Diana said, and worked Tattoo Man's fingers off his gun and relieved him of it.

Tyler did the same with Surfer Boy and both of them tucked the weapons into their jacket pockets. "You know how to shoot those?" Nora asked.

"Nope," they replied simultaneously, glanced at each other, and laughed softly, conspiratorially, and Nora sensed there was some sort of chemistry happening between them. Maybe weirdness did that to you. Maybe when you experienced something this strange, this over the top, this *outrageous*, it bonded you forever.

Nora went through the men's pockets, took their wallets, their extra ammo, two more guns, knives, and dropped everything but a knife on the pavement. She hurried over to the battered SUV and, like a psycho in some awful horror movie, slashed all four tires.

"We really need to get out of here," Tyler said. "We don't know what this phenomenon is, what's causing it, how long it's going to last . . ."

"There's Alex." Diana stabbed her finger wildly toward the dock and the motionless cars on the ferry's ramp.

Nora turned. The sight of him, illuminated by the nicotine-colored glow of the parking lot lights, seized her viscerally. He weaved between the cars frozen on the ramp, six feet two and moving with the practiced grace of a man who had absolute control over his own body. That was the result of yoga, tai chi, martial arts, she thought, as if Kincaid were forever seeking some complicated mind/body fusion. He waved his arms like a pedestrian trying to flag down a cab and Nora waved back, mimicking his opposing arm movements.

"Nora," her brother said urgently. "We're going to bring the camper around."

She nodded without looking at Tyler, the sight of Kincaid pulling her like a moth to flame, and started toward the ramp, toward him, her heart screaming, *No, yes, no, yes, no, yesno-yesnoyes,* as though she were a teenage girl plucking petals from a flower. *Love me or love me not? Love him or love him not?*

Yesnoyesnoyes . . .

In the moments it took to reach him, she drank in every detail—that he looked disheveled, his jeans as wrinkled as his gray pullover sweater, his dark hair windblown, his jaw unshaven. Disguise or the result of being on the run for three days? Or both? And now he was close enough for her to see his face—a broad forehead, dangerous dark eyes, a magnificent bone structure that hinted at a forbidden bloodline somewhere back in his genetic history, the union of an Olympian goddess and a mortal Celtic king.

Mythic, she thought, that was how Kincaid looked.

And then he stopped, she stopped, and they just stared at

each other. Here, with everything around them motionless, frozen in time and space, their past both bound them and separated them. This was the first time in five years that they had been alone together and neither of them seemed to have any idea how to act, what to say, how to *be*.

"Your hair," he said finally. "I like it."

Nora nervously combed her fingers through it. "My face is all over the Internet. I had to do something. What the hell is going on, Alex?"

A frown jutted down between his brows and he rubbed the back of his hand across his mouth. "I think it fits *The Maltese Falcon* better than *The Thin Man*."

This indirect acknowledgment that he had gotten her message didn't answer her question, but she understood what he meant. "So you and Jake stole something? That's why Freeze is looking for you? Why Jake was arrested?"

"I'm not a goddamn thief, Nora."

"Hey, you're the one who referred to *The Maltese Falcon*." She threw her arms out at her sides, a gesture that encompassed the motionless world around them. "So what is *this*?"

"Some sort of time distortion. I don't know how long it'll last. But we'd better get out of here before it breaks wide open. Where's Tyler?"

"Getting the car."

"C'mon," he said, and grabbed her hand.

They hurried past people and cars as still as statues, making their way toward the camper, which was now headed toward them. Nora was so acutely aware of the shape of his hand, of the warmth of his palm, the shapes of his fingers, that for a few moments she forgot that she had intended to grill him, to demand answers. Then the camper screeched to a stop in front of them and they scrambled into the backseat with the dog.

Tyler took off, swerving around the still-life people and cars, past Tattoo Man and Surfer Boy and their fallen bullets. "Thanks for doing this, Tyler," Kincaid said.

"We want answers, Alex, and we want them now," Tyler snapped.

Kincaid leaned forward. "I know. Hold on, just hold on. Let's get out of here first. Go to the parking garage outside Falmouth. My car's there. I think it's best if we split up, Tyler. You and Diana and your dog, Nora and me."

"The dog's with me," Nora said quickly. "And that's not the answer we want to hear, Kincaid."

"Hey, it's not that fucking *simple*. How long has the distortion been going on? Any idea?"

"None," Tyler replied. "The dashboard clock stopped, our watches don't work . . ."

"It feels like it's lasted for hours," Diana said. "But it's probably been, I don't know, maybe twenty minutes."

"What's causing it?" Nora asked.

"Me," Kincaid replied.

"How?"

As he explained, it struck Nora that he'd waited a long time to break his silence and confide in someone. A decade or so ago, when he was in the midst of struggling with the design for his hybrid car, he found a package in his mailbox that contained a blueprint that had all the missing pieces he hadn't been able to put together. "It wasn't postmarked, so someone had left it there."

"Was there a note? An address?" Diana asked.

"Just an e-mail address that I was supposed to write to if I had any questions. Well, I had plenty of questions, so I started up a correspondence with this person. Over the years, as the Internet evolved, I realized the person was a woman. Her knowledge of engineering, cars, alternative fuels, zero point energy . . . it was staggering. Our exchange was irregular, but friendly."

"Who was she?" Tyler asked.

"I knew her as, uh, peoplesfriend at yahoo dot com."

He glanced quickly at Nora, whose incredulity felt like the weight of excessive gravity, pressing her back against the seat, squeezing her vocal cords, burning her eyes. Even if she were able to speak just then, she wouldn't know what to say. And in those first few awful moments, that night five years ago rushed back at her.

Who is she?

A colleague.

Bullshit, Alex. Just tell me the truth, okay? That's all I'm asking.

I can't.

Her expression apparently revealed what she was thinking and Kincaid's eyes darted away from her face to his hands, to the back of Tyler's head, to Diana, now turning around in the passenger seat.

"What were her motives for sending you the blueprint?" Diana asked. "Did she want a cut of the profits?"

"What profits? Up until six or seven months ago, anything I made off these cars went back into research and development. She claimed that her only motive was to see the car become a reality. I figured she was part of a dissident group because she changed her e-mail address every couple of months, then changed it every few weeks, then every couple of days.

"Anyway, some shit happened several months ago," Kincaid went on. "Jake and I were supposed to, uh, sell a couple of hybrids to a group. I didn't feel comfortable about these people. I already knew we were being followed, watched, that our phones were tapped, that we were under heavy-duty surveillance. I developed insomnia, and I'm talking full-blown. I would go for thirty-six hours without sleep, crash for four hours, go forty-eight awake. I mentioned it to peoplesfriend. She said that she, as a former insomniac, had a possible solution; it had worked for her and her friend, Bari. I was desperate at that point and said I was interested. So a couple of days later, there's a package on my doorstep."

Nora's hands shot up. "Wait a minute. Back up. Just back the fuck up. Why would Jake be involved in this at all? You make the hybrids, not him."

"Let him finish the story, Nora," Tyler said.

"I'm in this goddamn mess because of Jake. I want to know what's going on."

"I'm trying to tell you what the hell's going on," Kincaid said sharply. "And the bottom line is that you don't know anything about the man you spent the last five years with."

Nora started laughing. "No kidding. I don't need *you* to tell me that, Kincaid."

"Just go on, Alex," urged Diana. "What was in the package?"

Disgusted with all of them, Nora turned her head toward the window, struggling to untangle her emotions. But Jake aside, she kept coming back to the secret of *peoplesfriend,* the secret that had ended her relationship with Kincaid. The secret he was now telling, years after the fact.

"Six syringes, directions about how I should use them, and the research behind the theory about why this treatment would either mitigate or cure my insomnia. The treatment would begin working within a few hours, but there was a possibility my body would reject it. If that happened, I was to wait for at least forty-eight hours, then use one of the other syringes. She was just starting her human trials with this treatment and it wasn't approved by the FDA, so she would understand if I didn't want to participate. I used the first syringe that night. And I slept for fifteen hours straight."

"So it's an injection?" Tyler asked.

"No, it's some sort of biochip I shot up into my sinus cavity and it migrates to the appropriate place in my brain."

"Jesus God, Alex," Nora exclaimed. "Some e-mail person you've never met, who could be a nutcase, sends you a syringe and tells you to inject it up into your nose and you *do* it? That's insane."

"But it licked my insomnia. It's a form of nanotechnology, that's the only thing I've figured out. Very sophisticated, very effective, and with some, uh, side effects that started a few months ago. I . . ."

"Your time distortion thing just ended," Tyler interrupted. "We've got a line of cop cars on our asses. We'll never make it to the garage and out again before they catch up to us. Can you do it again? The time thing?"

"Do it *again*?" He emitted a sharp, strained laugh. "I told you, I don't even know how I did it the first time. Keep driving, man, fast, open it up."

The urgency in his voice frightened Nora.

"Diana," Tyler snapped. "Get out those weapons. We may need them."

The camper tore past the parking garage and half a mile later, Tyler took an abrupt right turn, then a left, two more rights, never slowing, never faltering, the fender clattering and banging until it finally fell off. No one spoke; the air turned brittle with silence. Nora finally asked where they were going.

"I've got another car nearby," Tyler replied.

Within minutes, they were inside a storage compound, no one around, just the incessant glow of the bright security lights exposing them like an anomaly in an X-ray. The shriek of sirens filled the air around them, as if the cops were approaching from all sides, Nora thought, and knew the choppers would arrive any moment.

Tyler stopped at the end of the second row, in front of the last storage unit, pressed the button on a garage door opener attached to the visor, and the door started up. "Here's where we switch cars," he said, and drove inside.

The headlights washed across stacked furniture, boxes, a mattress, bed frame, the detritus of Tyler's failed marriage. As the door clattered shut behind them, Nora threw open the camper's side door and the dog leaped out. Nora and Kincaid scrambled out behind her. Tyler hurried over to a blue Mustang, opened the lid of the trunk. "Let's put all our stuff in here."

Kincaid stood close to the front of the camper, pale, sort of swaying on his feet, like a man in trance. Nora, frowning, said, "Alex? Are you okay?"

"I feel kind of . . . sick," he murmured, then blood started streaming from his nostrils—not just a trickle, not an ooze, but a rushing current, as if someone had turned on a spigot inside his nose. His hands flew to his nose to stem the flow, then he suddenly pitched forward.

Nora caught him. His dead weight caused her to stumble back. She tripped over Sunny, crashed into the boxes against the wall, and landed on the mattress with her arms still around Kincaid, who was groaning, struggling to get up. Tyler, Diana, and Sunny rushed over and Nora flung her arm over the dog's back for leverage, to push to her feet. But before she could get up, before she could even roll Kincaid to the side, a terrible crushing pressure filled her head, a field of white exploded across her vision, static burst inside her skull, and the dog emitted a shrieking howl.

The last thing she thing she heard were the echoes of Diana screaming, *"Tyler, they're gone, Nora, Alex, and the dog . . . just disappeared . . ."*

11

The gray gloom of the predawn sky stretched like an empty canvas across the picture window in the conference room. Lydia Fenmore stared at it, waiting hopefully for that first streak of gold light, for the sight of a gull or pelican soaring across it, for some sign that the sun actually would rise, that the rhythmic cycle of day and night would continue, that life would return to normal.

But nothing was normal on three hours of sleep, no coffee, no breakfast, and with everything apparently collapsing at the same time.

She and Rodriguez had gotten here an hour ago, shortly after Joe Aiken and his younger sidekick, Senator Rick Lazier, had arrived to view the security feed from the Wood's Hole terminal. They kept pausing the feed and barking questions at her and Rodriguez as though they were on the witness stand.

What's that? Why're all the bullets on the ground? This distortion is the same thing that happened in McKee's cell and it can't happen unless you're chipped, so who's got the chip? Nora? Her brother? Her best friend? Kincaid? Or is this Mariah's work again? Who? Who? Who?

Like a game of Clue, she thought. Who did it and where? "Of course it's Mariah's work," Lydia snapped. "None of the people in that group have access to chips and none of them ever knew Mariah. She interfered here just like she did on Snake Island."

"When McKee and Kat Sargent disappeared, there were two witnesses and a security tape," Aiken said. "Where's your proof, Lydia?"

His voice, authoritative but quiet, made her feel as if he had shouted at her. She even flinched. Then a swell of anger swept through her. Who did this fat schmuck think he was, anyway? He showed up here unannounced yesterday with his bad budget news, his new plan, his ultimatums, and now he was demanding proof?

"Excuse me, Joe. But the security tapes of McKee's cell don't show much of anything and one of the witnesses to what happened—Ryan Curtis—is now a rogue agent."

"Curtis's description of what he saw matches that of the security guard's. Both descriptions fit Mariah Jones," Aiken said. "These security tapes from Wood's Hole don't have anything on them that tie this incident to Mariah."

She nearly exploded and Rodriguez, sensing her rage, intervened.

"The proof is right here." He opened his briefcase, brought out a Baggie with red hairs in it, and slapped it down on the table. "This arrived by special courier earlier this morning. The Freeze officers in Wood's Hole removed this fur from the seat of the truck that was found in the storage unit and from the wagon Nora McKee was driving. DNA tests match it to a dog that was chipped in 1975, in one of the early animal experiments conducted with the biochip. The dog was a golden retriever that belonged to Mariah Jones. The results of the test are in here." He dropped a folder on the table. "How much more proof do you need?"

"So the dog would be—what? Forty years old?" Lazier asked with a smug smile. "Clearly impossible."

You prick, she thought. "The DNA was an exact match. So it's obviously not only possible, it's the same goddamn dog."

"And how would you explain this?" Lazier asked.

She quickly sized up Lazier. He smelled of money. She could see it in the way he dressed, hear it in his voice, and it was written all over his handsome, appealing face, that aging preppie look that invariably seemed to be good genes, but was born of financial ease. And in her experience, preppie politicians generally thought they knew more than they actually did and it was this intellectual arrogance that irritated her so deeply.

"It's an anomaly," she replied. "That's the only explanation I have. The retriever was the only dog we ever chipped. A year after she was chipped, in 1976, she escaped from the lab. She was two years old. We don't know what happened to her. Mariah figured the dog had died somewhere in the past. What we do know is that it's likely Nora was the only person to drive the wagon from the time she left Blue River to when she showed up in the terminal lot. So Mariah must have contacted her at some point during that time and had the dog with her."

Lydia didn't believe for a second that Mariah had contacted Nora McKee or was helping her in any way. But the argument supported her contention that Mariah was behind the events in Wood's Hole.

"That doesn't answer my question," Lazier pressed on. "Is the chip known to extend the lives of Travelers?"

"Not that we know of. But if you're bouncing around in time, like this dog apparently has been doing, there's no telling what it does to the brain. Maybe it disables the aging mechanism. Maybe it's an earlier version of the dog. Maybe it's the dog's twin. We don't know. We don't have all the answers."

Lazier, obviously frustrated, sat back and shook his head.

"Joe, we can't have investors shelling out millions unless we're able to make some guarantees."

And honey, once we have things back on track, you'll be paying us per disappearance, she thought.

"And I can't get Congress to allocate the funds we need without bringing some of our colleagues into the circle and informing them about what this program is," Aiken said.

Rodriguez exploded with laughter. "Oh, sure, Joe. That's going to work. Once ten members of Congress are told, the news will move across the Hill at the speed of light and suddenly, the entire Congress and their staff know, the White House finds out about it, the Pentagon, the spy agencies. It'll be the best *un*kept secret around. And once the word is out, several things will happen."

Aiken rolled his eyes, as though he found the entire discourse unbearably tedious. "Spare us the worst-case scenario, Ian,"

Rodriguez's voice boomed with anger now. "For twenty-five years, Joe, you've been sitting up there in the Senate doing your job in the greater scheme of things and letting us do our jobs. Then suddenly you meddle and just look at everything's that gone wrong. So allow me to spell it out for you.

"We'll be inundated with requests to disappear spouses, lovers, the causes of scandals and ruined careers. Or the Pentagon will turn the technology into a weapon. Or SPOT will become a government tourist agency, with people buying tickets to witness the assassination of JFK, the crucifixion of Christ, the bombing of Hiroshima, the attack on Pearl Harbor. Or some whistleblower will leak the news to the press, to bloggers, and suddenly, taxpayers know about it. People sue the government through the Freedom of Information Act to find out if their spouses and children, parents and grandparents are on the list of those who have been disappeared. Meanwhile, skeptics and debunkers will claim it's all a lie. And you can be sure that Congress won't spend another tax dollar on SPOT."

"You're really exaggerating this whole thing," Aiken scoffed. "The . . ."

"And *you* aren't getting the picture." The sharp edge in Lydia's voice silenced the senators and they looked at her as though she were an alien who had dropped, suddenly, into their midst. "Once foreign governments know, all of them will scramble to get their hands on the technology. So we have to cut deals. Venezuela gets let in on the action in return for all the oil we can consume. Instead of further enriching a bunch of guys in sheets and turbans parading around in their Porsches and private jets, we've got macho men and drug lords zipping around in their Porsche and private jets. Then China, of course, makes vague threats about war if we don't give them the technology. We have to give into them because they can afford to lose twenty or thirty or fifty million soldiers and not even blink. And that's just for starters. Pretty soon, they're so many people hopping through time that the fabric of space-time itself starts to unravel. Or we nuke each other and those of us who can, leap into the past to save ourselves, to . . ."

"We've got the picture," Lazier said quietly.

He and Aiken looked deeply shaken. It was obvious that neither of them had thought through the vast complexities that were involved. "This organization is *regulated*," Lydia said. "Without regulations, it descends into chaos. Yes, mistakes have been made, favors have been done, innocent people have been disappeared. But our successes far outweigh our failures. The crime rate has declined steadily, the . . ."

". . . the rich are richer, the poor are poorer, and the powerful are more powerful than at any other time in history." Lazier didn't bother disguising his scorn. "For some of us, life is heaven, for the rest of us, life is hell. How is that a solution?"

"*Your* life is hell, senator?" Rodriguez laughed. "Or *yours*, Joe?"

Aiken looked pissed now, she thought. And although Lazier was more dangerous because he was more ambitious, Aiken might be the only thing that stood between SPOT's survival and its extinction.

"We're not talking about *us,* Ian." Aiken shoved the Baggie back across the table. "We're talking about the people who pay our salaries, who put us in office. We're talking about doing what's *right.*"

Idealism. Music to her ears. It was lovely to know that some people still clung to their ideals, believed in them, worshipped them. But ideals rarely held up against reality. "That's very nice, Joe. But, bottom line, these are the same people who believe anything if they hear it often enough. Your life is good, crime is down, things are under control, the economy is great, your borders are secure, you are safe in our hands. But this works only if your secrets are kept secret. And when there's secrecy and fear, manipulation of mass thinking is much easier. Mariah is the real enemy here. Not me, not Ian, not SPOT."

"So what's her motive for interfering?" Lazier asked.

"She doesn't like the way things are being run," Rodriguez said. "For her, it's a big chess game. She threatens from many different angles, so that we're running in a thousand different directions, and then she ambushes us when our guard is down. SPOT collapses or its existence is made public, people go to jail, the technology is lost, or she seizes control. No telling. Any of these possibilities spells disaster for SPOT. For the country. For all of us sitting at this table."

Aiken sat back, rubbing his eyes. "One more thing. That wagon Mrs. McKee was driving. It was registered to the Pham Market in Blue River. What's the story on that?"

Rodriguez replied, "The owner lent it to her. He said she told him she was having car trouble. He was questioned, but he didn't seem to know anything else."

Aiken nodded, then pushed his chair away from the table, and got to his feet. He replenished his mug of coffee. "Anyone else need a refill?"

Coffee signaled that it was time to reconnoiter, she thought. The cafeteria had sent over a breakfast buffet, so they helped themselves to scrambled eggs and bacon, fresh fruits, pastries, cereals. Lydia just wanted to lay down and sleep for about five days. But she forced herself to eat, drink, be *sociable*—and kept thinking about Kat, McKee, and where Mariah might have taken them, and about Curtis, that bastard traitor. But if they could pinpoint Curtis's location in time, they could find him.

Whenever a recruit was chipped and inoculated, he or she received an RFID as well, a radio frequency identification tag, a microchip smaller than a grain of sand injected just under the skin in the forearm. A spy tag. No recruit was ever told about it; that would defeat its purpose.

In the United States, companies like Gillette and Levi Strauss were testing RFID tags on their products. Several major retailers here and in the United Kingdom were installing "smart shelves" in their stores that were networked with RFID readers. She suspected the technology eventually would be embraced by other retailers and chains, perhaps as a means of cutting back on theft. Law enforcement salivated at the thought of cradle-to-grave surveillance. Privacy advocates hated the whole notion and envisioned a society in which people's spending habits, likes and dislikes, would be tracked through what they bought, wore, ate. Sort of like the world Philip K. Dick had written about in *The Minority Report,* she thought.

But within several years, RFIDs would be embedded in all U.S. passports and, perhaps, eventually, even into currency. The ultimate tracking device.

The RFID tag didn't have batteries or any other power source of its own. Instead, it listened for a radio query and used the power from that signal to transmit its unique code. For a Traveler, that code was the number assigned during recruitment. Curtis's was T6747.

SPOT had improved on the technology so that RFID tags could now be read from several miles away. Recently, this had been enormously helpful in retrieving Travelers who had gotten stranded in the past because their chips had failed.

But it was also invaluable in keeping track of a Traveler's private life. It was how she and Rodriguez had known about Curtis's little love nest on the river.

She didn't divulge any of this to the senators. Their plan to take over SPOT would never work precisely because they lacked this kind of vital information, the intrinsic details. Let them think what they wanted.

Rodriguez suddenly excused himself and went into an adjoining office and shut the door. Aiken and Lazier whispered and commiserated on the other side of the room, returned to their laptops to finish watching the security feed, whispered some more. Lydia felt alone and isolated; her eyes burned from lack of sleep, and she kept touching the side of her nose, feeling a certain tenderness there, where the chip had gone in. Had that happened in the early years? She couldn't recall. Did the tenderness mean her body was rejecting the chip? *And where's Ian?* What the hell was he doing back there, anyway?

"Could you get Ian back out here, Lydia?" Aiken asked. "We need to finish this discussion."

"Sure."

But the office was empty, the door to the adjoining bathroom shut. She knocked. "Ian, you okay?"

A muffled response.

"Ian?" When she opened the door, the bottom dropped out of her stomach. He was on his knees in front of the toilet, holding a towel to his nose, his head tilted back, the toilet bowl filled with vomit and blood. "Aw, shit." She yanked a towel from the rack, soaked it in cold water, and pressed it to the back of his neck. "Talk to me, Ian. Tell me this isn't what I think it is."

"My body's rejecting the chip. The second one in three days."

His eyes were wide, panicked, scared—and that scared her. "That's ridiculous. You're exhausted, you haven't eaten . . ."

"I can feel the fucking thing moving in my sinus." Then he dropped the towel and held his head up straight and blood

poured from his right nostril, a torrent that splashed into the toilet bowl, suffusing the air with an odor like menstrual blood.

She nearly gagged—*nopleaseanythingbutthis*—and yanked another towel from the rack, soaked it, wrung it out, and held it hard against his nose. "Keep pressure on it, Ian, and tilt your head back again."

He knocked her hand away and gripped the sides of the toilet bowl, coughing, the blood still streaming, and the chip plopped into the toilet.

It looked like a very small metal tick, its body bloated, as though it had been engorging on blood. Its hideous exterior had sharp, protruding spines and twitched as it struggled to turn over, to right itself, as if it were alive. In all her years here, she had never seen the actual chip. Her hands flew to her face, pressed against the sides of her nose. *It's inside of me, that's inside my brain.*

After a few moments, it lost the struggle and went still, floating in the blood and the puke, a deflated tick. She quickly flushed the toilet and helped Rodriguez sit back, then to stretch out on the floor, on his side, so that he wouldn't drown in his own blood if his torn, raw sinuses kept bleeding. She grabbed more towels from the linen closet, folded them, slipped them under his head to elevate it, and under his cheek.

"Christ, Christ," he murmured.

"Just stay right here. Don't move around. Let the bleeding stop. I'll deal with the senators. I'll tell them you ate something that disagreed with you."

"Right." He sounded breathless, was sweating profusely.

Was he having a heart attack? Going into shock? What? "Does your arm hurt? Do you have chest pain? C'mon, let me help you on the couch in the office. Then I'm calling Dr. Berlin."

"I'm *not* having a heart attack, okay? Go deal with Aiken and Lazier. Get rid of them. If Berlin sees me like this, he'll want to remove *your* chip. One of us has got to be able to transition, Lydia. Don't call him. I'm fine."

And still she hesitated, her fingers feathering across his temple, his cheek, and lingering at his neck. His pulse was fast, but not erratic. "Stay put," she whispered, and brushed her mouth against his temple.

Her body felt strange as she left the bathroom, limbs as pliable as warm, newly blown glass. She desperately wanted to stay with Rodriguez, but if she stayed too long, the senators would become more suspicious than they already were. *We're losing this round, Ian.*

In the conference room, everything seemed to have changed. A soft, pearly light now spilled into the room and suffused the sky, ribbons of gold and orange woven through it. Aiken paced back and forth in front of the window, a cell pressed to his ear, his voice quiet, urgent. Lazier typed furiously on his laptop. Something had happened in her absence, she thought, something that had sent the senators into a frenzy of activity.

"How's Ian?" Lazier asked, glancing up from the laptop.

"Sick to his stomach. He thinks he ate something that disagreed with him. I need to get him home, so can we wrap things up?"

"This won't take long." Aiken hurried back to the table, cell clutched in his hand, eyes pinched with worry.

"It's already taken more than two hours, Joe. And there was no reason to lie to us about where you were going when you left here yesterday."

The vitriol in her voice surprised her and elicited a sharp, piercing look from Aiken. "It was just a change in plans. Rick had decided to join me here, so I rented a car and drove into Gainesville to pick him up. But since we're on the subject of lies, you and Ian are guilty of a lie of omission. I had to hear about the events on Cape Cod from the TV news."

"We were going to call you later on today."

Aiken made a dismissive gesture. "Whatever. Ask your questions, Rick."

Yeah, fire away, Rick old buddy, old friend. And he did.

"In thirty-some-odd years, SPOT has disappeared—what? How many thousands of people?"

"I'd have to look up the exact figure, but it's between fifteen to twenty thousand." Officially. But the unofficial rate—favors, vendettas, mistakes, blackmail—was well beyond that. Lazier didn't have to know it.

"How many were disappeared between 1975 and 1990?"

"I'll have to check."

"An estimate, Lydia," Aiken said irritably.

"Hey, I don't keep these figures in my head, okay?" she shot back. "We disappeared fewer people in the early days. Maybe ten thousand over the first fifteen years."

"The size of a small town." Lazier nodded. "And as far as we know, these ten thousand haven't changed the present in any discernible way. Isn't that correct?"

Most of them probably had died, she thought. Contemporary Jane and John Does in the Western world, accustomed to their lattes and high-speed DSL, their PDAs and laptops and gas-guzzling cars, their nice homes with electricity and running water and indoor bathrooms, learned the true meaning of culture shock when they were disappeared. Maybe those who survived somehow found each other and banded together in the equivalent of expatriate communities. But even the survivors would be so busy surviving and trying to build lives for themselves that they presented almost no threat at all to the present.

This present. *Her* present. SPOT's present.

But she didn't say any of this. "Here's where the regulations come in, Senator. First, the disappeared are rendered infertile. Women are injected with a subcutaneous time-release birth control hormone that lasts indefinitely. Men receive an injection that kills nearly all their sperm. So that even if they survive in the past, they can't have children. That eliminates the threat of descendants affecting the present in some way. Second, they are disappeared too far back to make a difference, at least by our calculations." She wasn't sure where he was going with these questions and that troubled her. "Why're you asking?"

"We're trying to calculate the odds here," Aiken said.

"Of?"

"How the program would be impacted if Mariah Jones is eliminated in 1968, when she was just starting her human trials with the chip."

A dreadful coldness seeped through her. "*Kill* her? Is that what you're saying?"

"Well, yes." Lazier's mouth pursed, as if it offended him to hear the word rather than its sanitized counterpart.

"But . . . we don't have any idea of how that would impact this program."

"You just said yourself that ten thousand people disappeared into the past long enough ago to have made an impact on our present haven't changed the present at all," Aiken pointed out. "So, using that same logic, killing Mariah in 1968 won't change a damn thing here in the present. We'll still have the technology, SPOT will still exist, but Mariah won't be screwing things up for us."

Stunned that he had turned the statistics around in this way, she sat there, her mind racing. "No, you're wrong, Joe. Really. All these years, we've operated on the premise that there's just one timeline, from past to present to future . . ."

"C'mon," Aiken said with a sharp, cutting laugh. "If that were true, Lydia, the sheer numbers of all the disappeared— ten thousand, fifty thousand, a hundred thousand, whatever the *true* figure—would have changed something in our present. And since you claim that nothing has changed, I think it's safe for us to assume that new timelines are created constantly. And if Mariah is killed, then on this timeline"—he rapped his knuckles hard against the table—"we're free of her interference and SPOT's existence won't be threatened."

"You can't be sure that what you're saying is true," she argued.

"There's some scientific evidence that it is true," said Lazier.

Okay, she knew where this was going. The Many Worlds Theory. Or string theory. She had read the theories, entertained the myriad possibilities, been confronted by bright recruits who chafed at the idea of a singular timeline. Maybe there were multiple timelines. Maybe at this very moment one of her parallel selves had married Rodriguez way back in the beginning and they had lived happily ever after. Or some other parallel self hadn't married anyone, hadn't had children, had never gotten involved in SPOT. The longer you played with the idea, the more possibilities you could imagine.

"I'm aware of the multiverse theory, Senator."

"Good. Then we can talk about the various possibilities. In one probability—one universe, if you will—the technology never existed. In another, it's public knowledge, in yet another it's become the property of a government tourist industry, and in yet another . . ."

"And on and on, ad infinitum. And next, you'll be telling me you're a quantum physics expert," she said with a laugh.

"Actually, I have a doctorate in theoretical physics."

Her laughed died, her smirk shrank, she felt like crawling under a rock.

"That's one of the reasons I selected him to be a partner in all this," Aiken explained.

They were both staring at her, studying her as though she were an interesting, mutant insect. She felt compelled to say something. "So where are you leading with all this information? To a certainty? Or to just another theory?"

"Here's the certainty." The extra flaps of skin at Aiken's throat trembled now; his voice crackled with intensity. "You and Ian are right that Mariah is the enemy. She's out to obliterate us." Then he turned his laptop around so that she could read the e-mail on his screen:

From: peoplesfriend@yahoo.com

To: jaiken@earthlink.net

Hi, Joe. Here are my thoughts and I'll try to keep them brief. You're a busy man and are about to get even busier.

When I left Spot in 1991, I had hoped that the core group—Ian, Lydia, and several members of the Council—would be able to help the organization evolve and become a more positive force in national and world affairs. I hoped that you and your advisors or colleagues would act in an oversight capacity, guiding Spot toward that end. Instead, the entire organization is a sham for controlling people, a platform for power.

Between 1975 and 1991, when I was director, there were 7,504 disappearances; 85 percent of these were legitimate. In other words, incontrovertible criminal evidence. If disappearances continued at about the same rate between my departure and 2006, then the total would be around 15,000. But I have evidence that the figure is much higher than that, Joe, and I suspect that many of them aren't even on the books. They were due to favors, vendettas, grudges, the means to winning elections, to overthrowing governments this country doesn't like . . . well, you know how it goes.

I've tried to rectify some of these horrors, to make amends for the lives that were destroyed and to appease my own conscience. But an army of one can do only so much. I'm left with just a single option.

You have 48 hours to shut down Spot—i.e., by Halloween 2006, at midnight. If you haven't shut it down, then I will do it for you by releasing the attached information to every major media and

Internet source. To qualify as a shutdown, the following must happen:

1) Disappearances cease immediately.
2) The Council must be disbanded.
3) All employees take paid leave until further notice.
4) The Cedar Key facility and the Snake Key holding area must be locked up, shut down, and completely vacated.
5) The production of chips stops.

In the event that you think you can beat me at my own game by sending back a gang of Travelers to assassinate me, I urge you to reconsider. The chip is my invention, I know more about how it works than anyone else in Spot, and I have been moving around in time long enough to have strongholds you don't know about.

Mariah Jones

Lydia knew immediately that the e-mail was genuine. Only Mariah would write SPOT as just another capitalized word, like the dog in the Dick and Jane books. She felt that if she clicked on the Word logo in the attached file box she would be opening a Pandora's box. But she couldn't appear weak or indecisive right now, so she clicked it.

A chill bit into the base of her spine and raced upward. *We are so fucked.* Mariah had outlined the essential details of the program—its genesis, its evolution, its corruption—and she had named names. And then she had done the unthinkable, listed the names of 50,000 of the disappeared and the approximate dates these people had vanished. It meant that Mariah had hacked into their computers, lifting information from here, there, everywhere, and done it right under their noses. But because many of the names of the disappeared and none of the locations and eras to which people had been taken weren't kept on computers, because there were deliberate errors, Mariah didn't have the full information. Somehow, though, that didn't make Lydia feel any better.

"When did you get this?" she asked.

"When you were in the bathroom," Aiken said.

She rubbed her fists into her eyes, her mind hurling up horrifying images of what would happen if the information was released—and the most vivid image was of herself and Rodriguez locked up or executed. Then her hands dropped into her lap, fingers pulling at each other, knuckles cracking.

"We aren't even going to discuss what would happen if this information is released." Lazier, preppie quantum physics whiz, spoke quietly but passionately, the feverish glint in his eyes oddly compelling. "Right now, anything is possible. Anything. I'm betting that Mariah knows that." He slid an object across the table, a paper box made of envelopes that had been taped together. "Inside the box is a cat that's been kept in there for days without food or water. Maybe it's even been zapped with radiation. Or maybe it's been gassed. Is the cat alive or dead? We won't know until we open the box, so both outcomes are possible. Both are *waves of probability*, to use the physics term. But once we open the box, one wave collapses into particles and becomes what we experience."

"Schrödinger's cat," Lydia said.

"Exactly. So what do we want to find when we open this box?"

He asked it as though it were a question on a final exam. "That the cat is dead."

The ensuing silence seemed total, like an eclipse of the sun. Then she became aware of the tick of the wall clock, the shriek of some lonesome gull outside, the chug of the first boat motor out in the salt marshes, as some fishermen headed out to conquer the seas.

Aiken broke the spell. "I spoke to Ryan Curtis before he disappeared. I told him to go back to 1968 and find Mariah, Ms. Sargent, and McKee."

"You *what?*" Horrified that he had intervened like this,

she could no longer contain her anger. "You had no god-damn right to do that. He assaulted a member of the Council and . . ."

"Get used to it, Lydia," Aiken barked. "You and Ian and the Council no longer run this organization all by your-selves. From now on, it's a group effort. And just so we don't have any further misunderstandings, let me spell out a few things. We don't want the design to Kincaid's car so that we can mass-produce it; we want to bury the design. That alone is worth billions in profits to the oil companies and we, of course, will take a nice percentage of those profits, which will fund SPOT for many years to come. And it would free us completely from government oversight."

This man was sly and much brighter than he looked. "What else?"

"Curtis was going rogue regardless to find Ms. Sargent. To find her, he'll have to track down Mariah. I figured it was best to make him think I was in his court. I even gave him his target date and location, making it easier for you and Ian—or another Traveler, if Ian is too sick to make the trip—to find Curtis. Find Curtis and you find Mariah, Ms. Sargent, and perhaps McKee as well. Then you eliminate the lot of them."

Her anger bled away and the brilliance of what Aiken had done suddenly cast him in a whole new light.

"So what do you think?" Lazier's cool preppie eyes scru-tinized her.

"*Tempus fugit*, gentlemen," as her military father used to say. "When do we leave and where and when are we going?"

Light Chasers

Truth is something you stumble into when you
think you've gone someplace else.
—Jerry Garcia

Belief is nearly the whole of the Universe,
whether based on truth or not.
—Kurt Vonnegut

12

One moment Nora was in Tyler's storage unit on the Cape and then she was on her knees, gulping at the bitterly cold air, her eyes sweeping across the long, thin shadows that sliced up the mounds of snow around her. Off to her right, a snowplow trundled noisily along a city road and she stared at it, struggling to place it into a context that made sense.

But she couldn't find any connection between one location and the other, one event and the next. It was as if she had fallen asleep in between two moments and awakened inside a dream. Except that she was not dreaming. The cold left her breathless, the air had a remarkably clean, unfettered scent to it, and she no longer smelled the sea. Her most recent memory was of darkness, yet the shadows told her it was late afternoon, crawling toward dusk.

What the hell just happened?

Her confusion collapsed into alarm and then outright panic. Nora scrambled forward on her hands and knees, away from the road, the cars, down a gradual slope until she couldn't see the road anymore. She rocked back onto her heels, aware that her pack felt considerably lighter. She tore it off, unzipped a side pocket, pulled out Jake's compass. The needle spun wildly. She thrust her hand into the side pocket again, brought out her cell and PDA; neither of them had a signal.

Still in a crouch, she turned and saw more snow. The bare trees just in front of her seemed to huddle closely together, as if for warmth.

Not in Kansas anymore, Dorothy.

Where are the others?

She dug her hand into a nearby pile of snow, nibbled at it, barely quenching her enormous thirst, and rubbed the rest over her face. She got shakily to her feet, still clutching her PDA and cell, her jeans scraped and dirty and wet at the knees, her joints popping, a dull throb between her eyes. She made her way down the slope, through the barren trees, and stopped. There, stretched out in front of her like a scene from a movie, was a cemetery, gravestones like huge packs of chewing gum standing on end, mausoleums like small houses.

I'm dead. Nora had read the literature on near-death experiences; her courses dealt with the possibilities. She didn't know if she personally believed that consciousness survived, but the benchmarks were familiar to her. The bright light. The tunnel. Friendly voices, familiar people, a sense of peace. She wasn't experiencing any of that. Besides, if she was dead, what had killed her? She remembered grabbing Kincaid as he had stumbled forward, the two of them falling back into boxes—and then a crippling pressure had seized her skull. An aneurysm? A stroke? And if this was death, an afterlife hallucination, why did she feel cold? Thirsty? Hungry? Scared shitless?

Because you aren't dead. Something else had happened. Something worse. *What's worse than death?* She had no idea, but knew she was about to find out.

She moved forward, her legs stiff, as if they had been hollowed out and filled with sludge. She zipped up her jacket against the biting cold, blew into her hands to warm them, wondered where her gloves were. She checked her cell and PDA again, but neither of them had a signal yet. She whistled the way Tyler had taught her years ago, the long, piercing sound echoing across the gravestones, the mausoleums, through the leafless branches. The only thing she heard in return was the whisper of the cold, bitter breeze.

Tyler, they're gone, Nora, Alex, and the dog . . . just disappeared. . . . She clearly remembered Diana shouting this. But what did it mean? Disappeared to where? How?

Disappeared . . . poof . . . gone. Pham's words, disturbing, haunting. She had grown to despise the word *disappeared.*

Off to her right, beyond a column of more barren trees, stood a parking area, deserted now. On the other side of it rose a tall, wire mesh fence with barbs along the top. And past that lay a wide road where the plow moved like some prehistoric beast, a hospital on the other side of it. None of this looked familiar.

Nora whistled again and Sunny suddenly loped out from behind a mausoleum and raced toward her, barking frantically. Even someone as inexperienced in dog talk as she was recognized a cry of alarm. Nora raced toward her, ducked under the gnarled branches, and rounded the corner of a mausoleum.

Kincaid was sprawled on the ground, his head turned to one side, blood smeared across his mouth and cheeks. There was so much blood that she couldn't tell if fresh blood still ran from his nostrils. But he was breathing and when she felt his neck for a pulse, was relieved to find that it was strong, steady. His pack had slipped off his shoulder and lay next to him, a bulging heap of canvas.

"Hey, Kincaid, c'mon, wake up." She shook him gently several times, then reached into her pack for a bottle of water—and realized the bottles she'd taken from Pham's supplies were gone. They must have tumbled out when she and Kincaid had fallen back against the boxes. Fallen out with her gloves, most of her spare clothes, her extra pair of shoes. No wonder the pack felt so much lighter. So she scooped up snow, rubbed it between her hands, and let the bits and pieces rain down over Kincaid's face, where it began to melt and to roll down the sides of his neck.

"Jesus, that's cold." He heaved himself to a sitting position, running his hands down over his chin and neck, brushing the snow off the front of his bloodstained sweater. "It looks like I hemorrhaged."

"That's how it looked to me when it was happening. Blood was pouring out of your nose. Where the hell are we, Alex? What happened?"

"I remember . . . feeling sick, nauseated, like I was going to throw up or pass out and . . . and then I remember falling forward." He reached for his pack, grasped the strap of his pack, pulled it toward him. His hands shook as he unzipped it and brought out a bottle of water, a shirt, a sweatshirt. He poured water onto the shirt and rubbed it over his face, wiping off the dried blood. Nora stared at the bottle of water, suddenly aware that her thirst had reached such an extreme that she simply had to drink some of that water. Now. Immediately.

So as Kincaid rubbed the damp shirt over his face with one hand, she took the bottle of water out of his other hand and tipped it to her mouth, gulping down so much of it that she felt it sloshing around inside of her, one wave after another crashing against the beach of her stomach lining. When she finally lowered her arm, hand still clutching the bottle, Kincaid had replaced his bloodstained sweater with a heavy sweatshirt. Color was returning to his face.

"Can I have some of that?" he asked. "It's the only bottle of water I had in my pack. I bought it on the ferry."

"Only if you tell me what the hell just happened. I don't recall snow or driving or walking to a cemetery. Help me out here, Alex."

He glared at her as though she were an intriguing but unknown specimen of insect that had fallen inexplicably into the same space that he inhabited—and took the bottle out of her hand. "That's fucked up, withholding water from someone who needs it because you want answers to an unanswerable question." And he drank, finishing off the contents.

Nora scrambled to her feet, suddenly livid. "*You're* the

one who's fucked up. Not me. *Peoplesfriend?* I mean, c'mon, that was the secret you couldn't tell me. Remember that? Remember the night in your warehouse? That was the end of us, of you and me, and back there in Wood's Hole, you were spilling all of it. But that night in your warehouse, you kept telling me you couldn't say what it was about. I remember every goddamn word of that conversation, Alex. You want me to repeat it?"

She had been backing away from him as she spoke, as she shouted, as she dredged up those terrible memories from that night, that discovery. And with every word, his expression tightened, shifted, became something else. The dog started to whine, bark, whimper, to pace back and forth between them.

Nora stumbled over a mound of snow—*snow, where the hell did the snow come from? Where am I? What is this place, what's going on?*—and her legs gave way and down she went, knees smacking the cold, unforgiving ground, arms and hands flopping against the snow.

And suddenly Kincaid was beside her, hands pressing gently against the sides of her face, forcing her to look at him, to see him, to acknowledge him. His dark eyes, thick with everything she rejected—risk, heartbreak—seized hers, held them, and then he kissed her.

His mouth: the skin cold but yielding. His tongue slipped between her lips, familiar yet strange, both a homecoming and an exploration. She didn't know what it meant, didn't care what it meant, wanted more of it. Nora dropped back into the snow and he collapsed on top of her, his fingers sliding upward through her hair, his mouth everywhere and nowhere in particular, and suddenly she was back in his house in Blue River, back six years, before Jake, before her marriage, before everything had fallen apart for her and Kincaid.

His mouth slipped to her throat, he murmured something, and she abruptly pushed him away. "Stop. Please. Just stop. What're we doing?"

He rocked back, away from her, his expression confused, a deep frown pushing his eyes closer together. He rubbed his hands against his thighs, his palms making a scraping sound against the denim of his jeans, his gaze holding hers. "I'm . . . I'm sorry. I didn't mean . . . no, fuck, that's a lie. I've been wanting to do it ever since you stormed out of the warehouse that night."

Now he tells her? More than five years after the fact? Nora rubbed again at her pounding temple, certain she was losing her mind. Something inexplicably strange had happened and instead of dealing with it, defining it, they were circling the unsettled issues in their relationship. Then again, even unsettled personal issues were more comforting than a complete unknown. She got to her feet, slung her pack over her shoulder, her mouth still burning from the kiss, a phantom sensation.

Kincaid stood, too, and looked slowly around, his frown deepening. "I know this place, Nora." Whispering now. "It's the Burrstone Road Cemetery. We're in Utica, New York." His expression was that of a man who had just learned that he held a winning lottery ticket. "St. Luke's Hospital is over there." He pointed off to his left. "Down that road a ways is a watering hole called Rummy's. C'mon, we need wheels, I've got to hotwire a car."

Sunny leaped up, ready to go, to follow them, but Nora patted the air, shaking her head. It was too much to absorb all at once—Jake's arrest, Freeze pursuing her, the time distortion in Wood's Hole, Kincaid kissing her, confessing he'd wanted to do it for years, and now this, whatever *this* was. "Hold on, Alex, just hold on. Wood's Hole is more than three hundred miles from here. You take the New York State Thruway. I don't remember being on any thruway, I don't even remember being in a car, just explain what's happening."

"I don't know if I can explain it. But I'll try, okay? Let's walk."

"To steal a car."

"Yes. But first I want to show you something."

"It's bad enough that Freeze is after us. Now we're going on a crime spree?"

"Believe me, right now, Freeze is the least of our problems and it'll take me twenty seconds to hotwire a car. But I have to show you something first, Nora. It'll help explain what's going on."

"It's related to that thing in your nose, right?"

"Technically, it's in my brain. My body was trying to reject it. That's happened before. The first time I got a really bad nosebleed and the . . . the chip fell out and I got sick. The second time, I just had the nosebleed."

"How do you know it's still in there?"

"It is." No equivocation.

"Did Jake know about this . . . this chip?"

"No one knew. Three days before Jake's arrest, I got an e-mail from peoplesfriend, telling me to put my stuff in storage and get out of town. So I cleaned out my place and took off for the Vineyard."

"So all these years you never even met this peoplesfriend?"

"Never."

Sweet Christ. It meant everything that had happened since that night in the warehouse could have been avoided. If she had known the truth about peoplesfriend, that Kincaid not only hadn't slept with her but had never even met her, their relationship might have continued. Instead, she ended up marrying a man who *had* betrayed her, who *had* been unfaithful. The irony, the horrible irony, she thought. Years gone, lost.

Kincaid apparently sensed what was going through her head. "I shouldn't have kept any of it a secret from you, Nora."

"You're goddamn right." How quick and eager she was to blame him, to rub it in, to force him to see what it had been like from where she had stood that night. But instead of contrition, he reacted with anger.

"Hey, you're to blame, too, you know," he snapped. "You

immediately thought the worst of me, didn't trust me, and basically trampled all over the relationship and then hurried off and got involved with Jake. And married the bastard."

Was that what she'd done? Was it? Was that how he remembered it? *Is that how it happened?* "I don't feel like talking about it right now," she shot back.

They walked on, the silence tense and thick between them, the cold working its way through her jacket, into her bones. Nora finally broke the silence. "Why would you leave town just because someone you've never met tells you to? Why would you stick a syringe up your nose because she tells you to?"

"Because she'd been right about everything else—the hybrid, my insomnia, tips on stocks . . ."

"She's psychic? Is that it?"

"I don't know what the hell she is."

"Does she have a name?"

"MJ, that's what she told me to call her."

"Does . . ." She stopped herself. Some part of her apparently believed that if she had more information, more pieces of whatever puzzle, she would find the answer not only to what had happened in the past, but to what was happening now. But even more questions wouldn't help now. "Forget it. I could keep asking questions from now until next week and I still wouldn't understand any of this." *I still don't understand why you kissed me, but please do it again.*

"You will. I promise."

They made their way through the cemetery, to the gate. It was padlocked, but Kincaid pulled a small, lightweight hammer from his pack and smacked it several times until it popped open.

"Is this, like, a Boy Scout thing or something? Having a hammer with you?" she asked.

"Be prepared. Boy Scout motto."

"I thought that was the Girl Scout motto."

"Hell, maybe it's the Brownies motto. I bought it on the

Vineyard. With some other tools. I thought it might come in handy."

He removed the padlock, swung the gate open enough for them to squeeze through, shut it behind them. They appeared to be in a residential neighborhood, the lighting so dim the shadows seemed as deep as graves. Piles of snow hugged the curbs. Cars, all of them old, lined either side of the road. Lights glowed in windows like Halloween pumpkins. Smoke spiraled from chimneys, the smell of it sweetening the cold air.

They walked several blocks to the end of the neighborhood and stopped in front of a neighborhood grocery store, a mom-and-pop operation. "What I want to show you is in here, Nora." Kincaid opened the door for her.

"We'll be right back, Sunny. You stay," she said, and the dog sat down, resigned to the wait.

The air inside was deliciously warm, fragrant with incense. The crowded aisles seemed to contain a little of everything—from shawls to socks, canned goods to fresh fruit, homemade breads to pastries. She wasn't sure at which point it struck her that something was very wrong with this place. Maybe it was the sight of the peace symbols hanging on colorful strings from the ceiling. Or the young woman at the counter with her long straight hair, her jeans and peasant blouse, beads strung around her neck, a throwback to the sixties who was smoking a cigarette and reading Herman Hesse's *Demian*. To her left sat an old-fashioned register, a genuine artifact of the nondigital age.

"Hey," the hippie girl said, glancing up. "Can I help you two with something?"

"Two cans of dog food, a can opener, a jar of peanut butter, and a loaf of bread."

"Sure thing."

Hippie girl set her book facedown on the counter, slipped off of her stool, went over to a shelf on her right. Nora stared at the large calendar on the wall that the woman's body had been blocking. It read: *Thursday, February 29, 1968.*

Talk about being stuck in the past, Nora thought.

"That'll be ninety-two cents, sir," hippie girl said, setting the items he'd requested into a paper bag. "And I'm tossing in some dog treats for your beautiful pooch outside there on the sidewalk."

"Thanks. She'll love them. Here you go." Kincaid handed her the change.

What? How was that possible? At home, cans of dog food were at least a buck apiece, peanut butter was probably twice that, and no telling what a manual can opener cost. Then Nora realized the obvious, that it was all a clever retail gimmick—the young woman's clothing, the cheap prices, the sixties relic cash register, even the calendar on the wall.

"Excuse me." Nora gestured toward the calendar. "Something's wrong with that date."

Hippie girl glanced back, laughed, and flipped through the pages on the calendar. "I just can't get into the habit of doing this every day. I mean, if it's a weekend, who cares? There we go."

Sunday, March 3, 1968. Nora smiled. "That's a clever sales gimmick."

Hippie girl frowned slightly. "I'm not sure what you mean."

"I mean," Nora started, but Kincaid touched her arm.

"The calendar's real, Nora," he said softly.

"Sure."

"Ma'am," Kincaid said to the hippie girl. "Were you born around 1947 or eight?"

She looked pleased. "Actually, I was born in 1944. I'm twenty-four."

Ohmyholygod. She's serious. He's serious. Blood rushed out of Nora's face, her throat closed up, she grabbed onto the edge of the counter to steady herself.

"Shit, oh shit, are you okay?"

Hippie girl's voice echoed and seemed to reach Nora as if from a great distance. She couldn't pull air into her lungs, blackness seeped like thick syrup into the corners of her vision, her head spun, she doubled over at the waist. Blood rushed into her head, the blackness ebbed. As she sucked greedily at the air, someone slid a chair under her and Nora fell back into it, unable to connect any dots now.

The woman—*genuine hippie, Nora, real hippie, not a clever gimmick, it explains all the old cars outside, the cheap prices*— handed her a glass of cold water and Nora sipped. *I am drinking water thirty-eight years in the past.*

"Better?" hippie girl asked anxiously.

"Yes, thanks." She just wanted to get out of here.

"She slipped outside, on a patch of ice." Kincaid talked fast, like some slick salesman. "Hit her head. She should be in the ER, but insisted she was okay."

"Well, St. Luke's ER is always crowded with kids from the college. You sure don't want to go there."

They went on like that for a few minutes, Kincaid piling one fiction on top of another while Nora's thoughts raced around like rats chasing their own tails.

"Listen," Nora said finally. "This is going to sound like a weird question. Maybe that knock on the head gave me amnesia or something. But who's president now?"

The woman made a face. "Tricky Dick."

"Uh, yeah, okay. That's what I thought." Martin Luther King would be assassinated next month, Robert Kennedy would be assassinated in June. *Dear God.* She managed a small, embarrassed laugh. "I guess my memory's okay."

"Can I get you anything else? Something to eat? Soup? Coffee?"

"No, I'm fine, really. Thank you very much for your help."

She had trouble getting up from the chair, as though the shock had damaged her nerves. Kincaid grabbed the bag of groceries, grasped her hand, pulled her to her feet, and they left the store, neither of them speaking. Half a block later, Nora couldn't stand it anymore. *"Time travel?"* She could barely spit out the words. *"Fucking time travel? Is that what it's all about, Kincaid? Is that what this thing in your nose really does?"*

"Nora, c'mon, lower your voice." His hands came up, as if to ward off a blow. "We don't want to attract any attention."

Nora swept past him, unable to listen to his explanations, his rationales, his excuses, his bullshit. Sunny loped after her and Kincaid caught up with her a moment later. "Nora, hold on, at least hear me out."

"Hear you out. Right. Sure. You *knew* this. All along you *knew* it. Jesus, Alex, you could've just told me in an e-mail. Or when we were in the car with Tyler and Diana. Or even back there in the cemetery. Why does everything with you have to be so buried in bullshit?"

Blood rushed into his face. "Get real," he shot back, his voice razor sharp. "If I'd told you, you wouldn't have believed me about this any more than you would have believed me about peoplesfriend that night in the warehouse. Back there in the cemetery, if I'd come out and said, 'Hey, Nora, we're in 1968,' you would've written me off as a complete nutcase. You had to see the evidence for yourself."

She hated to admit it, but it was true, all true. "But I didn't stick one of those gizmos up my nose. How come Sunny and I ended up here, too?"

"I don't know. Maybe because you were holding on to me and touching the dog. This happened to me only once before and I was alone and . . . and afterward, I wasn't sure what the hell had happened."

"When was this?"

"Four or five weeks ago, right after classes started. I was in my office on campus, paging through a library book called *Hippies,* filled with photos and text about the hippie culture and the sixties. And I remember thinking how cool it would've been to be a part of it. And then suddenly, I'm in that same cemetery, it's snowing, and I'm in jeans and a long-sleeve shirt, with my wallet in my back pocket and sneakers on my feet. I got out of the cemetery and ended up in a thrift store downtown and traded my watch for a sweatshirt. Then I just started walking, trying to figure out what had happened. I eventually walked into that same grocery store and saw the wall calendar. It was February 1967."

She was afraid to ask the next question. "How . . . do we get back, Alex?"

"I don't know."

The darkness suddenly felt much colder. "How did you get back when it happened before?"

"I had met this woman at Rummy's, that bar I mentioned. We spent a couple hours talking, eating, sharing a pitcher of beer, smoking a joint. I was hoping she'd take me back to her place. I didn't have anywhere to go, I didn't know anyone, it was snowing like a son of a bitch, and I couldn't risk using the money in my wallet, the bills were too different from the money now. Then we finally got around to introducing ourselves. Her name was Bari."

"Bari," Nora repeated. "That's the name of MJ's other human subject."

"Yeah. That was the first thing that occurred to me. It's not a real common name. Anyway, she went off to the restroom and I sat there, mulling over the name, wondering what the odds were, if there was a connection. She had a wad of cash stuck under her glass and I . . . I took fifty bucks, figuring it would be enough to get me a bed and food for the night. And then suddenly—" he snapped his fingers—"just like that, I'm in my office again. I'm stoned, my clothes reek of smoke, Mick Jagger is still shrieking in my ears, and I'm clutching a twenty and three tens. I was gone maybe two minutes in real time. I left work right after that and as soon as I got home, I shot off an e-mail to MJ, telling her what had happened, demanding to know if this was a side effect of her goddamn insomnia cure. Weeks passed. I didn't hear anything from her until she sent me the e-mail telling me to get out of Blue River."

Nora tried to absorb all this and Kincaid apparently took her silence as disbelief. "Here, look at this." He brought out his wallet and removed bills. "I kept the cash. So I'd know I wasn't delusional, that it really happened. And look how different these bills are from ours, Nora."

They paused under a streetlight and Nora studied the bills, marveling at the differences in color, complexity. She handed them back to him. At least they wouldn't starve. They would be able to get a motel room, buy a few clothes; the money would provide an edge, however small.

"What about the time thing back at Wood's Hole? Has anything like that happened before?"

"It happened briefly on the ferry over to the Vineyard. I didn't have any idea what was going on. It ended as suddenly as it began."

"So you don't have any conscious control over it?"

"Not that I know of. But it's not like I've experimented with it."

Nora blew into her hands, trying to warm them. She was so cold now she could barely feel her feet. And Sunny was shivering. "We need to find a car," she said. "We can't just keep walking around."

"Down here." He tilted his head left. "This street is dark."

"How far will fifty bucks take us?"

"A lot farther than it does at home." He touched her arm. "Listen, Nora," and he took her hand and she loved how it felt, like in those early days when they held hands just because they needed to touch each other. "Here's my theory. I want you to hear this. I want your feedback. I know how it's going to sound. But I think this woman, MJ, manipulated me, used me for some agenda of her own, and I think that Bari is part of it and now you and Jake are part of it. Shit, maybe even Sunny here is part of it. I don't know. Right now, nothing is too over the top."

She sure didn't have any argument with that last part. "Go on."

He paused, released her hand, passed her the bag of groceries, and tugged on the handle of a car door along the dark street in yet another residential neighborhood. The door was locked. They moved on, and he took her hand again. "After that first time, I did some massive research on insomnia and possible cures and came across something that set off all my alarms. In the late sixties, there was a biology professor at Smith named Mariah Jones who supposedly found a cure for insomnia."

That name again. Pham had mentioned it to her first. "Your MJ?" Nora asked.

"I think so." He rushed on, eager to explain what he'd discovered. She remembered this excitement from the early days of their relationship, when he was describing some fine point about the hybrid or alternative fuels or even about some book he had ordered for the college library. His massive intellect had attracted her right from the start. "She was the only black female professor at Smith at the time. She mentored this science prodigy, a black teen who, in 1998, won a Nobel in botany. Kim Runyon. Now, this is where it gets really interesting. Kim's mother, Dee, worked in the film industry in California, with Rod Serling and a guy named Charlie Ovis. Charlie had a daughter in the biz, too, a scriptwriter who wrote under her mother's maiden name— Bari Serrano. And Charlie was from Utica."

A chill that had nothing to do with the cold shot straight up Nora's spine. "If you believe in coincidence, then that's one huge mindfuck."

"Coincidence? No way. I'm right in line with Jung and synchronicity. There's order in this chaos, Nora. We just have to find it."

Right now, uncovering order in this sort of chaos, much less getting home, seemed, at best, a mirage, fanciful, a childish hope. "So you and Bari were two human test subjects for the insomnia cure, but separated in time by nearly forty years. Is it possible that Mariah's chips have an affinity for each other? Kind of like metal and magnets?"

"Could be. But it gets stranger. In 1970, Mariah was fired from Smith for conducting human trials for her insomnia cure without FDA approval. After that, her bio is sketchy. Some bios say she went to work in the private sector, but the blogs say she went to work for the government. Bottom line? Mariah's cure for insomnia had some intriguing side effects that interested the government."

"What kind of side effects?"

"Some of the blogs claim the chip makes time travel possible."

For long, terrible moments, the only voices she heard were Pham's and her brother's. *Disappeared, poof, gone, Mariah Jones, Travelers . . . black ops unit, they do the disappearances. . . .* She suddenly felt so dizzy and nauseated that she grabbed on to Kincaid's arm. She stumbled back against a car at the curb and he clasped her by the shoulders, holding her up, then wrapped his arms around her, patting her on the back, as though she were a baby who needed to be burped. "It's okay, it's going to be okay, Nora."

No, I don't think so, she thought, and managed to whisper, hoarsely, "They've been disappearing people into the past for decades." *Mom, Jake.* "That's your theory?"

"Yes," he whispered back.

And the horror of it hit felt like a blow to her sternum. She could barely breathe. A vivid mental movie of memories rolled in her head, of that evening so many years ago, Valentine's Day, her mother opening her gifts, and how suddenly and horribly it had changed. The two Freeze officers had burst into the house with weapons drawn, demanding that her mother get up, fast. When her mother had hesitated, when her father had demanded to know what was going on, when neither of them had moved quickly enough to suit the Freeze officers, the female had pointed her weapon at Nora. *Get up now, Mrs. Walrave, or I put a bullet through your daughter's head . . .*

And even her ten-year-old self had recognized that the woman would do exactly what she threatened to do. Her face had been burned into Nora's memory.

"Maybe we're wrong, Nora."

She stepped back, breathing in deeply, exhaling noisily.

"You know we're not." More deep breaths. Her head started to clear, she could think again. "But how has Mariah manipulated all these events?"

"I don't think she has. She just set things in motion and let the human heart and her chips do all the rest."

He grasped her hand once more, their physical connection holding her in the moment, then moved quickly down the street, the dog leading the way. Four cars later, Kincaid jerked on the handle of a VW bus with peace symbols on the door—and it swung open. Nora took the bag of groceries and while Kincaid fiddled around under the dashboard, she and Sunny stood watch nearby. The street was dark, deserted. "Can you do it?" she whispered.

"Yeah, I think so. You two get in the car. As soon as the engine turns over, we're outta here."

Nora slid open the side door, trying to be quiet about it, but it creaked and moaned. The rear seat was gone, the space was filled with blankets, pillows, an empty cooler with the lid up. She coaxed Sunny inside with one of the dog treats the hippie woman had given them, dropped her pack on the floor in front of the passenger seat, set the bag of groceries in the cooler. The air smelled of pot, the seats were torn, a peace symbol hung from the mirror.

The engine finally clicked once, twice, and then turned over. Kincaid scooted out from under the dashboard, shut the door fast, and slammed the old bus into first gear, second, and it chugged noisily up the street. Nora kept looking back, expecting to see lights blazing, people running out and shouting that their van had been stolen. She braced for the wail of sirens.

But nothing happened. They had stolen a VW bus and no one knew about it yet. "Where're we going?" she asked.

"Rummy's. I think we should check Rummy's."

"And if Bari isn't there, then what?"

"Let's play it by ear."

Right. They would wing it. They would figure it out as it

was happening. That was how she and Kincaid always had done things. In the past. The past that was now their future. Or something.

He made a U-turn in the middle of the road and drove on through the darkness. Nora turned her head toward the window, watching the passing landscape, trying to force her mind into a blank, receptive state that might yield information, impressions, some damn thing that made sense. She came up pitifully short in the insight department. A thick fatigue crept through her. Shudders tore up the center of her body. *Disappearing people into the past for decades.* She clutched her arms to her chest and struggled to hold on to her sanity.

By the time Kincaid stopped the bus and announced that they were at Rummy's, she felt like she was parked on the planet Neptune. "I'll wait here," she said, and rested her head against the back of the seat. Minutes passed. She got cold, hungry. She desperately needed to shower, to eat, to sleep. But her mind raced along, hurling up questions. What kind of diseases existed in 1968 for which she hadn't been immunized? Was the food safe to eat, the water safe to drink? Could you get sick when you traveled back in time? Did it screw up your immune system? Your heart? Kidneys? Teeth? *Your mind?*

Maybe they had the time sickness already and it was mental and they really were locked up in a ward somewhere, sharing a massive hallucination, a psychotic episode. Nora threw open the bus door, dropped to her knees, brought her hands to the parking lot pavement. Hard. Cold. Real. She staggered to her feet and stumbled toward the pine trees that lined the back of the lot.

Sunny trotted alongside her, sniffing, eager to explore. When Nora stopped in front of a tall pine, Sunny stopped, too. Nora wrapped her arms around the nearest pine, pressed her cheek against the rough bark, inhaled the scent of it, felt the hard ground beneath her shoes. Real, real, real. All of it. Mentally disturbed people believed their worlds were real— that voices whispered to them, that everyone was out to get them, that aliens were zapping them with invisible rays.

She slipped her arms around Sunny, breathing in the scent of her fur, of woods and winter. "You're real," she whispered, and Sunny drew her tongue up one side of Nora's face, her tail wagging faster.

Tactile evidence might not prove she was sane, but right now her senses were all that she could rely on. She and the dog returned to the bus and a few minutes later, Kincaid got in, shut the door, flexed his fingers against the steering wheel. "She's not there."

"Are we sharing a massive hallucination? Have we lost it?"

"No."

Firm, absolutely firm. She liked that about him.

"Why? Do you think we have?" he asked.

"I was having a bad moment."

He touched the back of her hand. "Did we hallucinate this old bus?"

"Maybe. It could be part of our mutual psychotic break or something."

"Are we hallucinating Sunny?"

"No." Definitely not.

"Okay, then."

"So the dog is our measurement of sanity?"

"Until we come up with something better," he said, and backed out of the parking space. "What now? Got any ideas?"

"We need a phone booth with a phone book. We need to know where Bari Serrano Ovis lives. We can go there."

"She lives in LA. When I saw her, she was visiting her father. I have no idea if she's even here in town. Besides, what the hell will I say to her? I vanished more than a year ago, while she was in the restroom."

"You're here to repay the fifty dollars you owe her. Let's find a phone booth."

Several miles later, he turned onto Genesee Street, which looked like the main drag through downtown. The snow pushed up against the curbs by the plows was several feet high in places. Bad winter here in Utica. Or maybe the winters here were always bad. Kincaid pulled up as close as he could to the curb in front of a head shop, sealed up as tightly as a coffin. Nora retrieved her flashlight, Kincaid handed her some loose change, she swung her legs out. "Be right back."

The front part of the phone book had been ripped out, but everything from K onward was intact. Nora turned to the O's and drew her finger down one page after another, searching for Ovis. There were two: Charles Ovis and B Ovis, same address, different phone numbers. She jotted down the address, worried about how they would find it without a map, without GPS, without any sense at all about the lay of the land.

She dialed B Ovis's number and an operator came on the line. A *real* person. "Please deposit ten cents."

That's it? A dime? She found one from her own time, fed it into the slot, and the phone at the other end rang and rang. No one home. No answering machines. No voice mail. Nothing but a hollow, empty ring.

Next: Charles Ovis. Two rings and a man answered. "Ovis residence."

"Hi. Is, uh, Bari there?"

"No, she's not. Did you try the cottage?"

The cottage? She had no idea if the number she'd called was at the cottage. And the man's voice seemed vaguely familiar to her. "No one answered."

"Then you should try back tomorrow. She may have gone up to Old Forge and as soon as all the roads are cleared, she'll be back."

"Is this her dad?"

"No, it's Rod. Would you like to leave your name?"

Rod. *The* Rod, as in *Rod Serling*? She was talking to Rod Serling? My God, could she track down RFK and MLK and warn them? *Be careful, Martin and Bobby, they're out to get you.* "I'll call back, thanks."

"Would you like to talk to Charlie? He probably knows more than I do about Bari's schedule."

"No, that's okay. Thanks."

She hung up and stood there with her hand on the phone, the cold breeze at her back, and started laughing. She laughed until tears rolled down her cheeks, then paged frantically through the torn book, and looked up the number for the closest state park. The place was open despite all the snow and oh yeah, there were plenty of vacancies and sure, a well-behaved dog was fine at the park and a site with electricity would cost them three bucks a night.

"Well?" Kincaid asked as she got back into the bus.

"Rod said that Bari probably got caught in Old Forge."

"*Rod Serling?* You *talked* to him?"

"Yes." She had recognized his voice; she had watched re-runs of *Twilight Zone* ever since she was old enough to know what a rerun was. It was Rod Serling. "There's a park a few miles from here where we can camp. Dogs are welcome."

"And it's open in March, with all this snow on the ground?"

"Apparently. And it only costs three dollars."

"At this rate, we can go for several days on the fifty bucks. Lead me there, sister."

"Second star to the right and onward straight into morning."

Kincaid looked over at her. "I don't think that's the line, Nora."

"So sue me."

He laughed, put the bus in gear, made a U-turn in the middle of the street, and they headed north toward the campground.

13

Curtis emerged on his knees in the middle of a two-lane road, snow flying around him, the headlights of an approaching car bearing down on him, impaling him like a bug under a microscope. The horn blared, shocking him out of his paralysis, and he dived to the right, skidding through the freshly fallen snow, a human sled, and ended up in a shallow ravine.

Dazed, the side of his face burning, he lay there struggling to catch his breath, the exquisite silence of the snowy darkness closing in around him. His eyes darted here, there, through the thick darkness of the woods that began just a yard in front of him. Brakes screeched, and the glare of the headlights struck a tree three yards in front of him.

Shit, move, get up. But his hands and feet kept sliding in the snow, the pain in his injured foot had shrieked to life. Two men reached him before he could even raise up.

"He's dead, Christ, you hit him," hissed the first man.

"I didn't hit him," the second man insisted. "Where the hell did he come from, anyway? When I came outta that curve, there was just snow blowing across the road and the next thing I know, there he is."

"You didn't hit me," Curtis muttered, and slowly pushed up onto his hands and knees. "I'm okay."

"Your face is bleeding," said the first man.

Curtis ran the back of his hand across his cheek; it came away bloody. *Think fast. Who are you and where did you come from and how did you end up on this road in the middle of nowhere?* "I hitched a ride with this guy and he rolled me and threw me in the woods."

"Greedy bastards," the second man said. "C'mon, we can give you a lift." He and his companion helped Curtis to his feet.

He felt like he'd been trampled by the bulls in Pamplona, by the faithful in St. Peter's Square. His ears rang, his head pounded, his foot throbbed like a diseased heart. He hobbled forward and the first-man said, "We've got a first-aid kit somewhere on *Further*, don't we, Jerry?"

"Somewhere, yeah."

"We'll get you fixed up, man, and get you wherever you're going." Then he stuck out his hand. "Name's Kesey, Ken Kesey. My amigo here is Jerry Garcia."

Curtis's shock was so great he nearly lost his voice. "McMurphy? Nurse Ratched? The Grateful Dead? *That* Ken Kesey and *that* Jerry Garcia?"

"Yeah, but don't tell anyone," Kesey said with a laugh. "We're on vacation."

Curtis climbed into a piece of history—the most famous psychedelic bus of the sixties, home to Kesey's Merry Pranksters. The only pranksters in the bus at the moment were Kesey and Garcia, who apparently had been smoking a lot of pot; the air reeked of it.

"What'd you say your name was again?" Garcia asked, passing a first-aid kit to Curtis, who was in the backseat.

"Ryan Curtis." Garcia really did resemble his photos—all that wild hair, the beard—but he looked so *young*. But then, he *was* young, probably in his midtwenties.

"We're headed to Utica, Ryan," said Kesey. "We can drop

you anywhere en route or you're welcome to ride the whole way with us."

"I'm headed to Utica."

"Good enough," Garcia said. "You have family there?"

"Friends, up in the Adirondacks. How about you two?"

"Jerry's hanging loose until his gig on the fifteenth," Kesey replied. "And right now, we're on a rescue mission. A friend of ours is a scriptwriter and she's been working hard these past few months. We're going to make sure she gets some R and R."

Curtis was beginning to understand why this particular probability had manifested itself. "Another famous member of the Pranksters?"

"An honorary member," Garcia said. "Bari Serrano. She's writing a pilot for Rod Serling and her old man."

"Hey, I've heard of her. She wrote for *Twilight Zone*, right?"

"Yeah, *Twilight Zone, Mission Impossible, I Spy.* . . . She's good people," Kesey said. "But manic about work. Hey, man, help yourself to a beer from the cooler back there."

As Kesey pulled the old bus back onto the road, Garcia lit a joint and passed it back to Curtis, who pretended to toke and handed it forward to Kesey. He didn't need to be any more disoriented than he already was. He opened the first-aid kit and tended to his face, which was just scraped up, then popped a couple of Advil and another antibiotic for his foot. He washed the pills down with a chug of cold beer.

"What's the date, anyway?" Curtis finally asked.

"The date?" Kesey laughed. "Damned if I know. What's the date, Jerry?"

"March something."

Yeah, ask a stoner for the date, Curtis thought.

"Okay, wait a minute, this is important," Kesey said. "We can't be so fucked up we don't even know the date. We left Maine on Friday, right? That was March first."

"That was two days ago," Garcia said. "So it must be March third."

"You sure about that?" Kesey asked.

"Yeah, man, I'm sure," Garcia said. "Ryan, it's March third."

"1968?" Curtis asked.

Both Kesey and Garcia exploded with laughter. "Last time I checked, yeah, it was still 1968," Garcia finally said. "We're a sorry bunch, huh?"

They laughed some more while Curtis sat there, frowning. In several days, Bari Serrano would vanish under circumstances so mysterious that the mystery would endure for nearly forty years. But right here in the psychedelic bus with him were the two people who had been in the photo with Bari and Jake McKee. *Do I dare?*

Dare what? Did it matter at this point what rules were broken, what protocols were violated? Would something change if he brought the future into the past? *Fuck the rules, the protocol, the maybes*. All bets were off.

"Ken, Jerry, do either of you know who this guy is?"

He leaned forward between the bucket seats and handed Garcia the PDA. "Far out," Garcia breathed. "What kinda cool thing is this? Hey, that's me and Ken and Bari and Jake. Goddamn, where'd you get this? Look, Ken."

Kesey glanced at it, then swerved onto the shoulder of the road, stopped, and took the PDA from Garcia. "Incredible, man. Dee has one of these. You know Dee?"

"Dee Runyon?" Curtis asked. "Did she take this picture?"

"Yeah, couple months back, must've been in December. What's this called again?"

"A, uh, PDA."

"Yeah, that's it. That's what she called it. I kept asking Dee where I could get one of these things. So how do you know her?"

"A friend of a friend." He could barely contain his excitement. "Where was the picture taken?"

"Some park in Utica, right before Christmas, I think that was the last time we were at Bari's, right, Jerry?"

"Mid-December," Garcia said, nodding to himself, tapping his fingers to a rhythm only he could hear.

"And how long has Bari been with this guy?"

"Four or five months, since September or October, somewhere around then." Garcia nodded to himself, his wild hair suddenly shot through with light from an approaching car. "Yeah, right around the time she came to Utica to start writing the pilot."

So it seemed that Mariah had brought McKee to the autumn of 1967—or possibly earlier—and somehow had gotten him hooked up with Bari. Had Mariah brought Kat here, too? Would he find her tucked away in some pocket with friends of friends?

"So you know this McKee guy?" Kesey asked.

"I'm actually looking for a woman he was with. Kat Sargent." Curtis described her. "You recall seeing anyone like that?"

"Nope," Kesey said. "So you're like, what, a narc and we're busted?"

"Naw, I'm a time traveler from the future."

They laughed hysterically and Kesey eased the van back onto the road. "Seriously, man, what's the deal with Jake McKee and this woman you're looking for?"

"She's McKee's sister. I was living with her." A half-truth. Curtis was profoundly grateful that the two men were too stoned to realize his story didn't add up. "She took off one day and I haven't seen her since. If anyone knows where she is, McKee will know. I'd heard he was in the Adirondacks, so that's where I'm headed."

"I just love it," Garcia said, lighting another joint. "We nearly hit a dude. He turns out to have a picture of us with Bari and her new guy, and her new guy's sister just happens to be who the dude we nearly hit is looking for."

Huh? Curtis thought.

"I mean," Garcia went on, "is the universe benevolent or what? How much weirder can it possibly get?"

You have no idea, Curtis thought.

An hour later, it was snowing, the wind blowing the stuff in horizontal sheets, visibility reduced to inches. Then they were past it and when Curtis looked again, the psychedelic bus chugged up a Utica street, wipers creating sloppy half-moon arcs against the glass.

They stopped in front of a massive iron gate. Garcia got out and pushed the gate open, then motioned Kesey to drive through. He shut the gate again and when he climbed back into the passenger seat, he was blowing into his hands. "Man, give me California any day."

Give me Florida, Curtis thought. *Give me warmth, sunshine.*

The bus made its way up a very long, curving driveway, past a three-car garage, snow-covered pines, barren trees that stood like naked, orphaned children in the aftermath of a tempest. "An estate," Curtis remarked.

"Fifteen or twenty acres." Kesey pointed off to the left. "The big house is in that direction. You can barely see it, but man, what a house it is. The caretaker cottage, where Bari has been living, is around this next curve. She said if she wasn't home we should just get the key and go on in."

"*Mi casa es tu casa*," Curtis said.

"You got it," Garcia said. "That's her motto exactly."

"Is she out of town?" Curtis asked.

"Yeah, I think she and Jake drove up to her place in Old Forge."

How cozy for McKee, Curtis thought. Like others who survived the shock of being disappeared, he had adapted and adjusted. Even though Mariah apparently had manipulated events to bring McKee and Bari together, she must have known enough about McKee to figure that the odds favored a relationship. Curtis suddenly felt sorry for Nora McKee, who didn't know the half of it and probably never would.

But did this mean that Mariah had done something comparable with Kat? Would she, like McKee, fall into a relationship of convenience? He doubted it. Kat was made of different stuff and their relationship was nothing like the McKee's marriage. Still, the thought nagged at him, a constant reminder that Mariah still held the winning hand.

The cottage stood off to the left—a wooden structure twice the size of his home on the river. Snow drifted across the sidewalk, but here and there, lights glowed like stars, inviting guests up the walkway to the cottage. Another pair of lights glowed from either side of the front door. The overwhelming impression was one of friendliness, Curtis thought, and decided he liked this Bari Serrano. Yet, it was a relief to know that she and McKee weren't here at the moment. He wasn't quite prepared for the confrontation that would entail.

The key was under the welcome mat; no bells went off, no alarms screeched. There was no security system at all, almost inconceivable in his time, where fear was the flag that invariably rallied the masses.

The cottage featured a huge open room with a beautiful wooden floor. Scattered braided rugs floated across it like islands in a flat, dark sea. Wood was set in the fireplace already, with more of it stacked in a bin against the wall, and the furniture, though modest, invited you to sink into it, kick off your shoes, and stay awhile. The kitchen was off to the left, separated from the living room by just an oval-shaped counter. Kesey was already in there, checking out the contents of the refrigerator.

"You gotta love this woman," he said. "Her refrigerator is always full. I'll whip up some chow."

"I'll start the fire," Curtis offered.

"And I'll provide the music," Garcia said, and brought his

guitar from its case, sat down on the couch, and began to strum.

Curtis wasn't an expert on Garcia, but Kat was and because of that, he recognized the pieces that Garcia played. He could almost hear Kat calling out: *That's* "Cream Puff War" *from the Dead's first album, March 1967*. Or: "That's Crystal Envelopment," *from their second album, July 1968*. An album that wouldn't be out for another three months.

After dinner, Kesey and Garcia broke out the liquor and more weed and they all took turns using the only shower. The cottage had four bedrooms and a den and Curtis picked the bedroom closest to the driveway, so that he would see Bari and McKee when they drove up. He brought out the nine millimeter, snapped in a clip, tucked it into the back of his jeans, his sweatshirt covering it.

While Kesey was showering and Garcia was still playing, Curtis slipped into the den and nosed through the piles of paper stacked neatly on either side of a Remington typewriter. A real McCoy, a genuine relic of the stone age. A sheet of paper was rolled into it, with a heading across the top and a list of words and phrases beneath it:

Items to Consider

cell phone	DVD	hybrid cars
PDA	wireless network	Mideast shit
pocket PC	download	USB drive
personal PC	plasma TV	motherboard
Internet	caller ID	Bill Gates
e-mail	mouse	iPod
Google	microwave oven	megabytes & gigabytes

yahoo	CD	scanner
search engines	digital camera	copier
Windows XP	digital photos	oil wars
Windows OS	portable keyboard	blogs
hard drive	global warming	bottled water
browser	memory stick	Starbucks
Apple computers	system recovery	Amazon

Stapled to this sheet were sketches, with handwritten explanatory details. Under the simple sketch of a memory stick, Bari had scribbled: *used to back up data on a hard drive. It comes in various size capacities, from 64 MB to 4 gigabytes. More efficient than storing data on CDs, can carry it with you.*

Next to the sketch of a cell phone was a lengthy explanation of how cell phones worked and how a person's position could be triangulated using cell phone signals. There were dozens of sketches—an iPod, a personal computer, a caller ID, a computer mouse, even a sketch of the Apple computer logo.

Curtis picked up pages from one of the stacks and glanced through them. A script, these were pages from her pilot script for *Connections*.

He was suddenly grateful that he hadn't e-mailed Aiken the photo of Bari Serrano and Jake McKee. If Aiken found it on his own, he would realize where Mariah had disappeared McKee. And *if* he wasn't an ally, then it was likely that Rodriguez and Fenmore or two of their other trusted Travelers would be sent back here, looking for Curtis, figuring he would lead them to Mariah.

Just then, a sensation of extreme strangeness swept over him, a disorientation so powerful that the floor under his feet shifted, slid, and heaved, as if the earth were about to explode through the foundation of the cottage. He thought at first that his body was rejecting his chip—it had happened to him twice in the last three weeks—and he grabbed on to the back of the chair to steady himself.

Then, suddenly, he found himself in what appeared to be a tremendous botanical garden. Groups of tourists wandered through the place. Muted sunlight spilled through a glass dome above him; he could see that snow lay against it.

He had transitioned, abruptly, without warning. Daylight, but where? *And when?* He had emerged by a thick, towering philodendron, didn't think anyone had seen him appear out of thin air, but couldn't be sure. He glanced around quickly, aware that he wore only his jeans and a shirt—no coat, no shoes, just wool socks. He would be conspicuous to anyone who noticed him.

Sure enough, a couple of people in a passing group of tourists glanced his way, and he quickly moved to the far side of the philodendron. *Where am I and why am I here?*

Curtis waited a few moments, then came back around the tree—and a shudder of shock tore through him. A woman strolled in his direction, her nose buried in a brochure, but he would recognize that bouncing braid anywhere. Lydia Fenmore.

Now you know for sure that Joe Aiken is one of them. It was a possibility that Mariah had mentioned.

Slightly behind her was Hank Vachinski, a young, handsome newbie Traveler whom the SPOT rumor mill had pegged as Fenmore's backup favorite to Kat. His dark eyes darted about, restless and alert, his macho swagger a clear signal that he was guarding Fenmore's ass. He was an ambitious young prick who probably would sleep with Fenmore, if that was what she wanted, and the same guy whom Curtis had seen outside his home on the river in the moments before he had transitioned.

He had zero interest in taking on Vachinski, who was at least ten years younger, outweighed him by probably thirty pounds, and was built like an ex-wrestler. As they passed the towering tree, Curtis slipped around the trunk and peered out, watching them.

They were alone in this huge area, Fenmore and Vachinski, the tourists had moved on and there was no group behind them. This had to be Northampton, near or on the Smith College campus. It was the one place where Fenmore, Mariah's first recruit, would look for her—and for him. Curtis could come up with only two reasons why Rodriguez wasn't with Fenmore—his body had rejected the chip or some crisis in SPOT had kept him in 2006.

Fenmore suddenly stopped, glanced down at something hooked on her belt, and whirled around. The object on her belt puzzled Curtis. He was trying to see it more clearly, to determine what it was, and didn't leap behind the tree fast enough. Fenmore and Vachinski spotted Curtis and moved swiftly toward him, splitting apart so that Fenmore approached him from the right, Vachinski from the left. It was a classic move they learned in training, a tactic for dealing with subversives, dissidents, the way dogs sometimes herded sheep and cattle. To see a pro and a newbie executing it against him was almost funny.

Curtis leaped away from the tree, his stockinged feet sliding across the marble floor, and flopped his arms up and down, like wings, taunting her. "Lydia, Lydia," he shouted, his chant echoing in the cavernous room, "Don't be an asshole."

"Mariah intends to shut us down," Fenmore shouted. "She issued ultimatums. We need your help, Ryan."

Sure, you do. "I'll pass. You sided with Simone." His eyes tracked Vachinski, hunkered over and moving with the rapid stealth of a predator, closing the gap between them.

"You know I don't like her any more than you do. Talk to me, Ryan."

The litany of the arbitrator, the peacemaker, the consummate bullshit artist. "Yeah. Go back to your hotel and fuck your young stud and leave me alone," he shouted back.

Blood rushed into Vachinski's handsome face and he broke into a run, galloping toward Curtis with all the verve and passion of a newbie. *You jerks,* he thought, and gathered the details of the cottage den around him—that Remington typewriter, the list of phrases, the chair that he had grabbed onto—and transitioned.

"Shit," Lydia hissed, and unclipped the RFID reader from her belt. The signal for Curtis's spy tag was gone. "He transitioned. We lost him."

Vachinski didn't hear her. He was sprawled on the floor, grasping empty air, and had attracted the attention of a security guard, some old guy who huffed and puffed as he hurried toward them.

"Hey, no running in here," the guard barked. "You need to leave." He glanced down at Vachinski, then looked up at Fenmore. "Both of you."

"Yeah, we're on our way out," Fenmore muttered, and helped Vachinski to his feet. "But the guy you want, my little ole friend, is the one who just vanished under your nose."

They hurried out of Smith College's Lyman Conservatory, past the beds of tulips, daffodils, orchids, water lilies, through room after room, hundreds of square feet under glass, and emerged on Elm Street, one of three roads that bordered the campus. The cold wind whipped up the sidewalk, Lydia's breath hitched in her chest.

"I nearly had him," Vachinski muttered.

"No, you didn't, Hank. You *thought* you nearly had him. Ryan Curtis has years of experience on you." And five hundred years of talent, she thought, but didn't say it. "He knows all the moves, okay? You can't grab him like that. We won't get anywhere if you pull shit like that."

"Hell, you spun around so fast I thought you wanted me to take him."

"Yeah, I know. I should have turned more slowly. But frankly, I was shocked that his tag showed up on the reader."

"But where the hell was the spy tag? He didn't have a backpack or a coat and wasn't even wearing shoes."

"Probably in his jeans."

"You had all his clothes tagged?"

"Everything."

Vachinski didn't look convinced and why should he? The idea that SPOT tagged every article of clothing that a Traveler wore was ludicrous, and Vachinski knew it.

Her reader could pick up any RFID tag within a radius of five square miles. Since each tag had a unique number, the name of the Traveler immediately appeared in the readout. If the Traveler had used an ATM or credit card, the date and location of the purchase was also recorded. But she couldn't tell Vachinski any of this. He would balk, revolt, resign, something.

Or maybe not.

"He came from someplace indoors, Lydia. He's in this time, but not in Northampton. Not yet, anyway."

Maybe there was hope for young Vachinski, after all, she mused, and hooked her arm through his. She sniffed the cold air, like a dog pursuing a scent. "We'll find him. And Mariah. We'll take her out, do him in, but it won't happen today."

He looked over at her, Vachinski with his strong Russian features, his eagerness to please, his ambition to advance through the ranks of an organization that might not exist in their tomorrow. "And so how will we spend the rest of our afternoon and evening, Lydia?"

She laughed, her head thrown back. She felt young and reckless, beautiful and thin. "For starters, I think we'll have dinner at one of those nice restaurants near the campus. We'll ask around. Find out why Mariah isn't on campus." And they would find out why the house where Fenmore knew Mariah had lived way back here and now, was vacant. *And we'll get shitfaced, my handsome friend, and go back to the motel, and fuck our little brains out. Hmm? Is that a plan or what?* "How's that sound?"

"Quite intriguing," he replied, and slipped his arm around her waist and held her close. "But at some point, I'd really like to know the truth about the spy tags, hmm?"

"I don't think you'll like the truth, Hank."

"Is it embedded in the biochip?"

"No."

"But it's embedded somewhere in my body."

"Yes." And within fifteen or twenty years, she thought, it would be embedded in most American citizens.

"Jesus."

He looked genuinely horrified and she quickly took steps to mitigate it. "It's a precaution. If a Traveler gets lost, can't get home for some reason, the spy tag enables us to find him."

"It also enables you to track the person's every movement, every activity, every . . ."

"Not exactly. When you pay cash for something, the RFID tag doesn't record that. But if you buy certain products that are tagged, we know what you buy. Not that anyone sits around all day monitoring this shit. We don't have the time or the staff for that and besides, what would be the point? By the time recruits becomes full-fledged Travelers, they know the stakes."

She didn't add, though, that she had called up Vachinki's log for the last four weeks before she had selected him for this assignment and discovered that he and another newbie Traveler had been spending most of their free time together. They apparently enjoyed expensive pursuits because their ATM withdrawals and credit card purchases were substantial. A new fridge, a new computer, new clothes, new furniture, a trip to Europe.

Their expenses, in fact, indicated that they were preparing to move in together and that they, like Curtis, had bought a place off Cedar Key. A private getaway. Remote. A home they believed that SPOT didn't know about. But SPOT was nearly ubiquitous when it came to the Travelers, in whom untold amounts of money were invested, but only as long as a Traveler remained on his or her timeline in the present. The trouble started when a Traveler went rogue and hid in the past, like Curtis. Then the techie edge was limited.

Limited, she thought, but not entirely without merit. She now knew for sure that Curtis wasn't far away. Sooner or later, he would return to Northampton because only here could either of them pick up a lead to Mariah's whereabouts.

And she and Vachinski would be waiting for him. Ready.

14

The campground was located in a small state park where giant pines swayed rhythmically, in sync, like a line of chorus girls. Nora liked the rustling sounds they made, their susurrous whispering, as if these ancient trees had stories to tell.

The only camping she'd ever done consisted of sleeping in a tent pitched in a neighbor's backyard when she was thirteen. They'd had electric lights, a small TV, music, and had brought out all the food they'd wanted from her friend's kitchen. Weekend after weekend, she and her friend had stayed up till nearly dawn, talking, giggling, freaking each other out. *I heard something, look at that huge shadow, it's Bigfoot, a UFO . . .* And usually they had run, shrieking, into the house.

All of that had ended when Nora's father had remarried and the wicked stepmother had moved in. There were no wicked stepmothers here, but the utter strangeness of their situation was like that tremendous shadow eddying against the wall of the tent, that looming unknown that imagination spun into monsters, aliens, a creature from the Black Lagoon.

The road curved through the walls of trees on either side

of them, where shadows thickened until they were wells of India ink. They passed campsites, most of them deserted. Nora, with the campground map spread open on her lap, kept thinking that anyone their age who was camping here tonight would be, in their time, in their seventies or dead.

The campground store was their first destination, to buy some basic supplies. The guard at the gate had circled its location and that of their campsite on the map.

"We need firewood," Kincaid said. "And food, a pot to cook in, a couple of plates . . ."

"And sleeping bags," Nora added. "Or blankets. The stuff in the back is useable, but we might run the risk of head lice or something. Are you still a vegan?"

"If I'm hungry enough, I'll eat anything."

Good, she thought, because it seemed unlikely that they would find Boca Burgers, tofu, or many soy substitute products in a campground store. It seemed even less likely that it would have an organic fruit and vegetable section. "We're eventually going to need gas, too."

"We can probably fill the tank for a couple of dollars. Gas in this era costs about thirty-five cents a gallon."

No wonder their purchases at the mom-and-pop grocery had cost just under a buck. "What's the price of a house?"

"About sixteen grand."

"And in 2006 it's—what? Over two hundred thousand?"

"Around two eighteen."

"And a car in 1968 costs . . . ?"

"You can get a used Beetle for about eight hundred." He glanced over at her. "Want my complete rundown?"

"You looked it all up after that first time, right?"

He nodded. "God bless the Internet. A loaf of bread costs a quarter, a postage stamp six cents. The median household income in the United States is about seventy-seven hundred a year—compared to nearly fifty grand in our time. The population in the United States is around two hundred million now—compared to three hundred million in our own time. The world population in 1968 is three and a half billion and in our time, it's six and a half billion. Is there a picture emerging here?"

"Yeah. I think living here wouldn't be such a terrible option. If we could figure out how to earn money."

"Well, we've got forty-seven bucks and change. That's a start. And if we run short, we'll just hold up a store or something." He looked quickly at her. "Just kidding."

"Ha. We're already driving a stolen bus."

Kincaid pulled the bus into a parking spot in front of the store, a small wooden building tucked away in the embrace of pines. They wouldn't be alone inside. Two vans, a camper, and a car parked on either side of them probably added up to the sum total of campers in the entire campground.

Kincaid stopped, lowered the windows for Sunny, killed the engine. "Ready, Bonnie?" he asked.

"Let's do it, Clyde."

She counted eleven people inside—an older couple, college kids, a couple of hippies, a family of four. She and Kincaid moved up and down the aisles with their handheld baskets and the calculator in her head clicking with every item she selected. The pickings were slim when it came to food. Since they already had bread, peanut butter, and dog food, they selected a pack of hot dogs, eggs, bacon, a few canned goods, a brick of cheese, coffee, rolls, two thermoses, a six-pack of beer, sodas. She added soap, a bottle of shampoo, a razor, toothbrushes and toothpaste, two towels, a sweatshirt. She looked for bottled water, but didn't find any. Was bottled water even available in this time?

The total came to $11.28, without sales tax, but how much could that be? Two percent? Three? "What next?" she asked, speaking softly.

"A couple of pillows, sleeping bags, some blankets," he replied.

They spent another five minutes adding to their provisions, then got in line behind three college kids, all of them snickering and snorting, their bloodshot eyes vivid road maps to nowhere. Kincaid leaned close to her and whispered, "If it's over forty-seven dollars, be ready to run. I'll cover your ass as we're making our getaway, Bonnie."

"Very funny, Clyde."

The clerk—bald, with a moon face and thick glasses—rang up their purchases. "That's twenty-nine thirty-nine," he said.

Kincaid set two era-specific twenty-dollar bills on the counter, a smart move, she thought, since it would give them smaller bills and change. And they still had almost twenty bucks in reserve. It was a miracle on a par with the division of loaves and fishes.

Outside, Kincaid said, with a touch of glee in his voice, "Things are definitely looking up. Not only do we get to eat, but we sleep in comfort."

Relative comfort. "Optimist."

"If we're not optimists, Nora, then we're fucked."

Good point, she thought.

The site itself was basic, prepped for a tent and warmer weather, but snug and private, embraced by pines. While Kincaid started a fire and prepared to melt snow so they could store water in the thermoses, Nora headed to the restroom and the shower with her new towel, her new shampoo and soap and razor. When she'd left home thirty-eight years away, she knew she'd included these items in her pack. But they apparently had fallen out with her water and other provisions and were probably still in Tyler's storage unit.

The water was plentiful, hot, and it felt wonderful to wash her hair, shave her legs and her underarms, to brush her teeth. Afterward, she drew her 2006 hairbrush through her hair, put on the soft, clean sweatpants from 2006, and the sweatshirt from this time. The rituals went a long way toward minimizing her anxiety.

When she returned, the fire had caught, the wood crackling, spitting smoke and a comforting fragrance. Kincaid was putting hot dogs and bacon on the grill. She hadn't eaten a hot dog since she was in kindergarten and pork hadn't been on her menu for at least fifteen years. But she was so hungry she would eat anything—sand, bark, snow.

"Would you watch dinner while I take a shower?"

"You trust me with hot dogs and bacon?"

Kincaid laughed, no doubt remembering that most of the things she cooked ended up tasting like charred leather. "I'm too beat to give a shit."

He trudged off through the cold and she took over the fire and the cooking and sipped at a cold beer. She fed Sunny and fixed up beds in the back of the VW, making sure there were *two* distinct beds, with *two* distinct pillows and blankets, and room enough for the dog between them. She had liked the kiss back in the cemetery, but didn't intend to sleep with Kincaid. *Been there, done that, no way, not now.* Too complicated.

And in the event she was wrong about all this and was hallucinating in a mental ward somewhere, she brought out her cell and PDA and checked them again for signals. Nothing, still nothing. Did this prove that she wasn't in a straitjacket somewhere? Hardly.

She unzipped Kincaid's pack to check his gizmos for signals—and in a padded side pocket, found three objects that resembled syringes, encased in dry ice. *I injected it up into my sinus cavity. . . .* Was this what he'd been talking about? Why hadn't he mentioned that he had some with him? She removed one of them and carried it over to the fire, where the light was better.

The transparent syringe was as long and slender as a pencil, and appeared to be filled with a blue substance—a liquid or a gel, she couldn't tell for sure—and the tip of it was sealed with a plastic cap. She snapped the cap off with her thumbnail, expecting to see an ordinary needle. Instead, there was a thin plastic extension with a blunt end that had a hole about the size of a point on a ballpoint pen. She depressed the plunger slightly and a small glob of blue stuff touched her palm. It felt cold, thicker than Jell-O, didn't have an odor. After maybe ten or fifteen seconds, it had numbed the spot on her hand. She wiped it off on a rock, poured water over her hand, but the numbness lingered.

Like the lidocaine the dentist used, she thought, and slipped the plastic cap back on. If she injected this thing up her own nostril, would it get her home again? Would it help her to find Jake more quickly? *Do I want to find Jake?*

What was the secret to using this sucker, anyway? It had whisked her and Kincaid nearly forty years into the past, but he didn't seem to understand how or why it worked—other than his theory that because she was touching him and the dog, they had been brought along as well. Suppose it took him elsewhere during the night? She would be stuck here, separated forever from her own time. From him. Nora wrapped the syringe in a T-shirt and zipped it into an inner compartment in her pack to think about later. To use later. *Later when?*

The hot dogs and bacon were overcooked, so she moved them to the edge of the grill. She stabbed one of the hot dogs and bit into it. Fabulous. Did these suckers contain nitrates? Preservatives? Did she care? *Does it matter?*

When Kincaid returned, hair still damp from the shower, they ate close to the fire. Everything tasted shockingly good.

"You know what we are?" he said. "We're displaced people. Time exiles."

"Maybe not. That thing in your nose brought us here, so it can take us back."

"I don't know how it works, Nora. This is *The Accidental Tourist*, okay?"

Was it that random? From the way he had described it earlier, when he had catapulted from his office, the book on hippies seemed to have acted as a catalyst. Maybe the vividness of the photos, the descriptions, had helped bring that era to life or helped to draw it around him. Was that the key? Conjuring mental images of a bygone era?

"How did you put it in?" she asked.

"I told you. I just stuck the syringe up my nose and pressed the plunger."

"How far up your nose?"

"As far as it would go without pain. Those were the directions."

"And then what happened?"

"It's in a cold gel that keeps the biochip dormant and also numbs your sinuses. As the gel warms up, the heat activates the chip and it migrates to some spot in the brain." He paused. "I told you all this."

"What part of the brain?"

"I don't know."

"I think it migrates to the pineal gland."

The flickering firelight cast half of his face into such deep shadow that it was as if it didn't exist at all. The eerie effect struck her as a perfect metaphor for their relationship all those years ago. She'd never had the full picture. For that matter, the metaphor fit her marriage, too.

"Why there?" he asked.

"Because the pineal controls circadian rhythms. I did research on this in graduate school." She tapped her forehead. "The third eye, that's what mystics call the pineal gland. The seat of the soul. That was going to be my thesis. But . . ." She shrugged. "The topic was too esoteric for my advisor."

"Any mention of soul without reference to God or religion would offend the college thought police, Nora. So tell me more about the pineal gland."

The campfire was hot, her stomach was full, the beer had relaxed her. And as she started talking, she felt that she and Kincaid were enacting some ancient, complex ritual—sharing knowledge and wisdom around a fire, with the darkness pressing in against their backs.

"For years, no one understood the gland's function or even how it worked. There were experiments and research, but not much came of it. One experiment in 1917 involved adding crushed pineal glands to water in which tadpoles were swimming. When the tadpoles turned lighter in color, the researchers couldn't explain why."

"Science at its best. So who figured it out?"

"Julius Axelrod. The late fifties. He was interested in neurotransmitter hormones and figured out that the pineal's hormone—melatonin—was actually the neurotransmitter serotonin, chemically converted and stored in nerve terminals, along with norepinephrine, for later release. The conversion explained why the tadpoles got lighter; the melatonin in the water caused the surface pigmentation cells in the tadpoles' skin to contract, lightening it."

"I took melatonin for a while when my insomnia first started. It didn't do much for me."

"I don't know if the stuff you buy over the counter is the same thing, Alex. It wasn't until the early sixties . . . only a few years ago now . . . that Axelrod discovered that when melatonin is released through the central nervous system, it's a powerful neurotransmitter that enables the pineal gland to act as a biological clock. Melatonin is secreted in response to changes in environmental light, which affects reproductive function and circadian rhythms."

"That explains its use as a treatment for insomnia. But how does it make time travel possible?"

She shrugged. "I don't know. Maybe the pineal gland is what allows the mind to reach through time. Maybe it's why DaVinci was sketching airplanes centuries before they existed or explains how Jules Verne was able to write about a submarine twenty-five years before the first one launched or about a spaceship a century before it was created. It wasn't just imagination, but that they mentally *reached* into the future."

"Telepathy?"

"More like precognition, except that they were able to *see* these things they described."

"It still doesn't explain physical time travel."

Nora remembered reading an article on the Internet a few years ago about paracrystalline vesicular grids in the human brain. These grids were so miniscule there were billions of them in the brain, found at the tips of nerve synapses. According to the scientist who had written the article, the fact that these structures existed at all indicated that they followed the laws of quantum physics. So what these grids actually did was to create a physical quantum probability field that interacted with human consciousness to create events. She said all this to Kincaid, then added, "Maybe the chip itself somehow enhances this probability field in the brain and when it's triggered by intense conscious focus, the interaction creates a kind of time machine."

"It sounds like a quantum computer," Kincaid remarked.

Excited now, Nora said, "The first time it happened, you were immersed in that book about hippies. Thinking about how cool it would be to have been a part of all that. Intense desire, right?"

"You think that's the secret to triggering it?"

"It may be part of it. What were you thinking about when you fell?"

He poked a stick in the fire, stirring it up. "I was thinking how badly I wanted to be someplace where I wasn't being pursued or watched."

"Were you thinking specifically of Utica in 1968?"

"I just remember seeing all the blood gushing from my nose and I panicked. But maybe we ended up here because I'd been here before. It could be that the chip has some sort of memory."

"You were panicked about losing the chip?"

"That and the fact that it was *my* blood. I guess when we suddenly moved back in time, my body didn't reject it."

"You've got more chips, though."

This elicited a sharp glance from Kincaid. "I've got a few more, yes. But if your body rejects a chip, your sinus cavity is so torn up that you have to wait until it heals before you can insert another. That can take as long as a week."

"Can't you just inject one into the other nostril?"

"I never tried it. I figured suffering through a week of

sleeplessness was preferable to risking a rejection of another chip and having both my sinus cavities ripped to hell."

"If we mentally draw our own time around us, Alex, I think we can get home again."

"Home to *what*?" He sounded genuinely horrified. "Being pursued by the feds? Being on the run? How long and how far can we run, Nora, before they catch us? That's not going to help us find Jake. Or your mother."

Her mother. Was it possible to find her? She had been thirty-seven when she disappeared. She would be in her early sixties now, unless they could return to the point where she'd been disappeared. Was that possible? *Is she still alive?*

"So what's our plan?" she asked.

"Find Bari. She's our most immediate link to Mariah Jones. And if we don't find her, then I think we should head to Smith. If Mariah was actually teaching there in 1968, it shouldn't be that hard to track her down."

"You always planned well," she observed.

He tossed the stick into the fire and glanced up. "Jake used to say the same thing about you."

"Really?" She disliked the thought of Jake and Kincaid discussing her. "He said this to you? And in what context?"

"I don't remember."

"He's the one who supposedly had all the plans and it turns out he didn't have any plans at all."

"Why do you say it like that?" Kincaid asked.

"Like what?"

"With such . . . *hostility*."

Because she felt hostile—toward Jake for putting her in this position, for sleeping around, and because her marriage had become one more area of her life that lacked closure. "Well, let's see. The guy I was married to for five years was arrested as a terrorist, I was chased, shot at, taken back in time nearly forty years, and now I'm living in a battered VW bus, am basically broke, and I'm trying to figure out what my next step is. On top of it, I had to butcher my hair." *And, oh yeah, I want to divorce him and now I can't even do that and how about if you kiss me again? Huh? How about that? What'd that mean, anyway?* She chomped down on her last bit of hot dog, dropped her own stick in the fire, and stood. "I'm so tired I can barely think straight. I'm going to sleep."

With that, she whistled for Sunny and the two of them crawled into the back of the bus. Nora pulled the heavy blanket over them both and shut her eyes. She dozed and knew she was dreaming, something about being in a car with a naked black man, no one she knew. He was behind the wheel, she was in the passenger seat. She wasn't afraid, just surprised.

Then she came awake suddenly and felt Kincaid wiggle under the blanket beside her—instead of on the other side of the dog. He rolled onto his side and his arm flopped across her waist, so that they lay like old spoons in a drawer. Tarnished spoons, she thought.

"Nora?" he whispered after a few moments. "You awake?"

"Yes."

"I know you feel alone right now, but you're not. We're in this together."

"By default, apparently."

"To me, it feels more like design."

"Mariah's design."

He withdrew his arm. "Mariah didn't make you marry Jake."

Nora sat up. "I married Jake on the rebound, Alex. If you had told me the truth that night in the warehouse, the last five years with Jake wouldn't have happened."

He sat up now, too, drew his legs up against his chest and wrapped his arms around them. "It all happened the way it was supposed to happen. You believed I was capable of things that just aren't in me, and ended up with the one guy who was capable of all of it and then some. You had to go through that before you and I could sit here in an old bus nearly forty years in the past and have a conversation about it."

Her anger surfaced suddenly, vehemently. His condescension. His patronizing tone. Who the hell did he think he was, anyway? But the moment she recognized the anger for what it was—one of her buttons and, therefore, something that had to be scrutinized more closely—her anger vanished as abruptly as it had appeared. She realized that if she was ever to understand her relationship with Kincaid, she had to understand Jake and her marriage. And right then, she remembered that remark he'd made in Wood's Hole.

"In Wood's Hole, you said I didn't know anything about the man I had spent the last five years with. What'd you mean by that?"

He rubbed his hands over his face, his fatigue and anxiety so obvious that she almost wished she hadn't asked. "Nothing."

"You knew he was sleeping around."

"*No bueno por caca*," he muttered. "You know what that means?"

"No good for shit?"

"Yeah. That's how I feel right now, Nora."

"Because you think you're betraying Jake?"

He laughed, but it was a hard, ugly sound. "No. Because you don't have any idea what Jake is and I'm not so sure it's my place to enlighten you."

This sounded like something well beyond infidelity, she thought. "Then who the hell will? Jake?"

He glanced at her, but didn't say anything.

"Forget it," she said brusquely, and slid open the side door and swung her legs out.

She put on her shoes and walked quickly away from the van. Behind her, Sunny barked and then caught up to her, tail wagging as if it were all some wonderful expedition. Nora only went as far as the edge of the trees, where there was still some illumination from the campground lights. She stood with her back against one of the pines, struggling with the complexity of her emotions. She no longer loved Jake, wasn't even sure that she ever had. She didn't even care anymore if they ever found him. But she needed some sort of closure to

her marriage and sensed that whatever Kincaid couldn't
bring himself to tell her would provide it.

Sunny barked and nudged Nora's leg, then trotted back
toward the bus, stopped, and glanced back at her. When Nora
remained where she was, the dog barked again, more insis-
tently, urging her to follow. Nora still didn't move, so Sunny
plopped down, midway between Nora and the bus, where
Kincaid was.

I ain't moving, she seemed to be saying. *Until you do.*

The dog wanted harmony and peace, she thought. *Yeah,
well, don't we all.* She would go back to the bus and sleep in
the front seat. Or outside by the fire. Something. And she
wouldn't press Kincaid again. Ever. This was her issue, not
his. She moved forward. Sunny saw her coming and got up,
wagging her tail, and led the way back to the van.

As they came around the front of it, Nora saw Kincaid
crouched by the fire, adding more logs to it. She backed up
and hurried over to the open door, reached inside her pack
and withdrew the syringe she'd put in there earlier. She carried it over to the fire.

"I'd like to inject myself with a chip," She said, speaking
to his back. "That way, if you're boomeranged back through
time in the middle of the night, I won't be stuck here."

He held his hands out against the warmth of the fire.
"Good idea. I'll get one."

"I already have one. I took it from your pack."

"Thanks for asking," he muttered.

"I was looking for your cell, to see if you had a signal."
Keep it left brain, factual. She sat down on a rock near the
fire, flicked off the syringe's cap. "Do I just tilt my head
back?"

"You need to get away from the fire. If the gel inside
warms up, the warmth will activate the chip. Let's do it in
the van."

They sat in the front seat, Kincaid behind the wheel, Nora
in the passenger seat, and the dog in the back, her head pok-
ing between the seats, watching them. "Okay, you're going

to tilt your head back, so you're comfortable, and insert the syringe up as far into your right nostril as you can, until you feel a slight pressure. Then press the plunger."

"What's the chip look like?"

"It's the size of a grain of salt when it goes in. As it starts to warm up, it expands and then migrates. But when your body rejects it, there's no constriction. It comes out full size, tearing apart your sinuses. Did you ever see that Ewan Mac-Gregor movie, *The Island*?"

"Uh, yeah."

"Remember that scene when . . ."

". . . they put spiders in his eye? *That's* what the chip looks like?"

"When it's fully expanded, it looks more like a bloated tick. And it has, like, spikes or something on its exterior. That's what tears up your sinuses if your body rejects it."

"Gross." But she still tilted her head back and slipped the end of the syringe gently into her nostril. It felt cold, that was all. "Do you ever feel it moving around in your nose?"

"Only if your body rejects it."

She felt a slight pressure now inside her right nostril. She moved the syringe a little higher up, the pressure increased, and she began depressing the plunger, slowly, ever so slowly.

"You need to do it a little faster, Nora. Otherwise the gel will start warming up."

And the tick will expand . . .

She pressed the plunger down completely. Fast. The chill startled her, but the glob itself felt monstrous, spreading through her sinus cavity like a clump of cold mud. She couldn't breathe through that nostril. The numbing quickly spread through her sinuses and up between her eyes and down into the back of her throat and she panicked, snapped upward, and gasped for air. She felt as though she were being smothered.

Kincaid kept telling her to calm down, assuring her the effect would pass in moments. But she couldn't stand it, couldn't breathe, felt like she was dying. She threw open the passenger door and scrambled out, desperate to move, to feel the cold air against her face, to know that she wasn't dying. She stumbled, fell to her knees, and air abruptly rushed into her lungs. She remained on the ground, hands pressed to her thighs, until she could breathe normally again. She felt Kincaid's hand against the back of her neck, then her shoulders. "You okay?" he asked.

"You didn't . . . tell . . . me about that."

"It didn't happen to me. You must've pressed the plunger too fast."

He helped her to her feet and for moments there in the wash of light from inside the bus, his face was just a few inches from hers. Her heart raced and pounded. Then he wrapped his arms around her, holding her close, and she breathed in the familiar scent of his skin and hair, wood smoke, soap, memories. His fingers slid up into her hair—her butchered hair—and her head dropped back and he brought his mouth to hers.

Everything disappeared for her. Only this moment, unanchored and drifting free of time, existed. They stumbled back against the old bus, unwilling to release each other, and fell onto the blankets, the sleeping bag, the nest of bedding. They tore at each other's clothes and as they rolled, Kincaid pulled the blanket over them so they pressed tightly together, caterpillars in the same cocoon.

At first, in her mind, they were in Kincaid's bungalow south of Blue River, swept up in their feverish hunger for each other. But then it moved beyond her memories of what it had been then and became something else entirely, something deeper, beautifully complex, both musical and magical. His every touch scorched her skin and burned new pathways through her brain, her soul. The secret symbols his mouth inscribed on her breasts and belly were ancient, archetypal, Jungian, the language of lovers who have known each other through many lifetimes, in many eras.

They rolled, the old bus creaked, the wind blew through the open door and kept whistling across the nearby trees. They moved as if against a powerful, impossible current, like river creatures struggling to return home. And when it was over, neither let go of the other until the cold air drove them apart.

Kincaid got up and shut the doors and Nora felt the dog settling in just above their heads, the blankets sinking with her weight. And then sleep washed over her, a tidal wave of exhaustion with a rising question mark at the crest of it: what did he know about Jake that he couldn't bring himself to tell her?

15

The sound of a car door woke Curtis instantly. He bolted upward, listening hard, thinking it might be Garcia or Kesey getting something from the bus. Then the soft music of a woman's laughter drifted in with the moonlight that spilled through the blinds.

Curtis sprang off the bed and hurried over to the window. He had left it cracked open for exactly this reason and carefully slid his fingers between the walls and the blinds and moved them so he could see outside. Moonlight exposed the couple like an X-ray—a tall, bearded man with long blond hair and a redhead five or six inches shorter, passionately embracing next to a silver 1963 Sport Roadster. Jake McKee and Bari Serrano.

They looked like models in a car ad, Mr. and Mrs. Good Life America, who were about to hop into their spiffy little car with its Kelsey-Hayes wire wheels and its 300-horse-power 390 engine with two-barrel carbs, and speed off to some exotic destination. Yes siree, Jake McKee had adjusted very well to life in the sixties, Curtis thought.

As they broke apart, Curtis pulled his pack over to the window and brought out his digital camera. Proof, he thought, and adjusted the shutter for light, so the flash wouldn't go off, and snapped several photos of them while McKee was getting their bags out of the car.

Bari gestured toward the psychedelic bus, parked just beyond the cottage, and McKee leaned close to Bari, whispering something, nibbling at her ear. She emitted a soft, intimate laugh and brought her index finger to her mouth, hushing him.

McKee looked so comfortable in his new life that he probably would be content to just stay here. That was fine with Curtis, as long as McKee provided answers about what had happened to him and Kat since Mariah had disappeared them. He moved away from the window, tucked the camera back inside its weatherized case, and quickly changed clothes. He put on heavy socks and his regular shoes. His foot still hurt, but as long as he didn't have to chase McKee, he would be okay. He slipped the nine millimeter into the small of his back, put on his jacket, shrugged on his pack. Now he would be ready for anything.

Ear to the door, he listened. He could hear them at the front of the cottage, talking and laughing quietly. If they woke Kesey and Garcia, things could get a bit dicey. Even though neither of the men seemed to have any idea where McKee was from, Curtis didn't want to risk their finding out. But considering how much the other two men had been drinking and smoking, it probably would take a nuclear explosion to wake them.

He cracked the door just enough to slip into the hallway. His shoes squeaked against the floor, barely more than a whisper beneath the music that now played in the living room. Jazz, Curtis thought. Stan Getz. Or Antonio Carlos Jobim. Sixties stars.

Curtis moved with his back to the wall, the gun now tight in his hand, hoping that just the sight of it—and him—would be enough to convince McKee to cooperate. The clock outside the den read several minutes before four.

He reached the end of the hall, could see the blazing fire-

place, the turntable with a record on it—and McKee and
Bari on the couch. Only the top of her head was visible against
a pillow and McKee, kneeling over her, was pulling his sweater
off over his head.

Curtis stepped out and stopped a yard short of the couch,
so that he was the first thing McKee saw as the sweater came
off. He looked like a thief caught in the act.

"Sorry to barge in like this, McKee." Curtis leveled his
weapon at McKee's chest. "But you've got information that I
need."

"How . . . what . . ."

Bari snapped upward, her head whipping around, her
vivid eyes widening in anger, shock, or both, and grabbed an
afghan off the back of the couch. She wrapped it around herself as she got to her feet. Her hair was short. The color of bur-
nished copper, it set off the beautiful lines of her pale neck.
"Who the hell are you and what're you doing in my house?"

She didn't have to shout or raise her voice to sound authoritative. Curtis admired that quality. "Name's Ryan Curtis. I'm the other part of your script."

"Really." The afghan slipped off her shoulder, exposing
pale skin and a spattering of ginger-colored freckles, just
like those across her cheeks and the bridge of her nose. "And
what part would that be?"

"For chrissakes," McKee snapped. "He's the prick who
arrested me, Bari. Who interrogated me. He's from the
special unit I told you about and he probably knows who
you marry and how many kids you have and when you die
and . . ."

"Shut up, McKee." Curtis stepped closer. To Bari, he
said: "You write the pilot for *Connections,* it airs in 1970 and
for six years and sixty episodes it's at the top of the Nielson
ratings. It's about a special black-ops unit in the government
that disappears dissidents and subversives into the past."

"Ooookaaay." She sounded spooked. "You've got my full
attention." She tugged the afghan closely around her, covering her shoulder. "So you're . . ."

"Don't say another goddamn word," McKee snapped.

"And don't tell me what to do, Jake." Her eyes never left Curtis's. "I, uh, would like to stoop down and get my sweater." She gestured at the floor in front of the couch. "All right?"

Curtis moved to the side of the couch, where he could see the floor. Nothing there that could be used as a weapon. "Go ahead. Start talking, McKee."

"I've got nothing to say to you."

"I do," Bari said, and turned so her back was to Curtis. The afghan slipped away, revealing bare skin, then she pulled her sweater on, and turned. "I'll tell you everything Jake has told me *if* you'll let me pick your brain. Beginning with, why only sixty episodes spread over six seasons?"

All things considered, it wasn't the question he thought she'd ask. "I have no idea."

McKee followed the exchange with narrowed, suspicious eyes, then stared at Bari, aghast. "You're going to help him?"

Bari looked pissed. "Don't you get it, Jake? Mariah manipulated all of us—you, me, your wife, Alex, Dee, even him." She stabbed a thumb toward Curtis. "We've all become her pawns. And for what?"

"She's right, McKee. Now tell me where Kat is."

Silence.

"What happened after Mariah disappeared you?"

More silence.

"Jake, just tell him what he wants to know," Bari snapped, impatient, irritated.

"He fucked up my life. I'm not telling him squat."

"Have it your way." Curtis grabbed his shoulder so fast that McKee didn't have a chance to react.

A heartbeat later, they emerged on a glacier in Antarctica, several hundred years in the past. He and Kat, in the early days of their relationship, had visited this spot—or one like it—to answer a single question: *How long can you survive in temperatures forty degrees below zero, with just a tent, a few provisions and each other?*

There were only three colors here—the utterly perfect blue of the sweeping, unpolluted sky, the blinding white glacier as far as the eye could see, and dark smudges against this white that were thousands upon thousands of seals and penguins. In his own time, the seals would be slaughtered unmercifully, the babies clobbered and shot by hunters, penguins would be a dwindling species, and polar bears in the Arctic would be drowning and cannibalizing each other because of global warming.

Global warming wasn't a factor of life in this time. The ice shelf was thick and deep and stretched for thousands of miles.

Curtis brought out his heavy gloves and an extra jacket from his pack. He pulled on the gloves, draped the jacket over his shoulders.

McKee, on his knees, huddled in on himself, making guttural, animal sounds, and struggled to get up, to stand, to move. But his socks stuck to the ice, his teeth already chattered, his breath came out almost frozen solid. He wore nothing but jeans and a wool sweater.

"OhGodohGodohmyfuckingGod . . ." he stammered.

"This is the land God forgot, McKee. Kat and I used to come here with a tent and a few supplies to see how long we could last without going stark raving mad. Our best record was two days. But we had thermal clothing, food, shelter. You're wearing clothes from Sears, pal, and no shoes, no coat, and the temperature is . . . well, hold on, I'll give you an exact reading." Out came his weather thermometer. "Hmm. About forty-three below zero. I figure you've got about two minutes before hypothermia sets in."

McKee now stumbled around, shuddering, slapping his arms against his body. His teeth chattered so loudly that when he tried to speak, he sounded like a woodpecker. "Why're . . . you . . . do . . . ing . . . th . . . this . . ."

"C'mon, stop bullshitting me. Just tell me what happened when Mariah disappeared you and Kat."

His knees buckled and down he went, bones cracking against ice. He remained silent.

Curtis paced, warming himself. "When hypothermia sets in, McKee, the body tries to protect itself and retain its heat. It does this by vasoconstriction, which halts blood flow to the extremities in order to conserve heat in the critical core area of the body. So when your limbs go numb, you'll know you're on track. You'll go through stages from mild to severe hypothermia. When you reach the severe stage, everything goes critical. Your body temp falls below eighty-eight degrees, your skin goes cold, turns bluish gray, and your eyes dilate. You're so weak that your coordination heads south, you sound and move like a drunk, and you deny there's any problem. Hey, maybe you've been severely hypothermic for some time now. You think?"

McKee doubled over now, breathing hard, his teeth still chattering. Violent shivers racked his body. "We . . . we went from that cell to a . . . a cave somewhere. She was showing off . . . trying to scare me."

Curtis immediately slipped the extra jacket around McKee's shoulders. He was almost too weak to get his arms into the sleeves and once he did, he tried to rub warmth into his frozen feet with his stiff hands.

Enough of this place, Curtis thought, and transitioned to the deserted shores of Lake Maracaibo, circa 1937, about the same time that Standard Oil began its vigorous expansion in the area. But at the moment, they shared the emptiness with just a scattering of oil derricks that rose like monoliths against the flat expanse of blue water. This spot on the western shore of the lake was where he and Kat had thawed out after their two days in Antarctica. McKee lay in the sand, still wrapped up in Curtis's jacket, still shivering, his eyes squeezed shut, the brutal noon sun beating down against him.

Curtis shed his jacket and gloves, shoved them down inside his pack, and crouched next to McKee. The color returned to McKee's face. He groaned, rolled onto his side, and puked. "Keep talking, McKee."

He lifted his head, looked at Curtis, at his surroundings, then reared up and tore off the gloves and jacket and scrambled to his feet like some clumsy clown in a circus act. He lurched down the beach, shrieking, "*Help me, someone help me!*" He tripped, fell to his knees and doubled over, his forehead pressed into the sand, and was weeping when Curtis reached him.

Curtis knelt in the sand next to him, certain now that McKee's stubbornness didn't have much to do with anger at him. "What the hell did Mariah do to you? How'd she threaten you?"

McKee raised up, sand stuck to his forehead and cheeks, where his tears had left wide tracks. "She . . . she took me back to the Neanderthals and dinosaurs and then to some horrid, putrid village in the Middle Ages and promised she would disappear me permanently to one of those places if I ever betrayed her, if I ever told . . . anyone."

He rubbed his feet vigorously, ripped off the wool socks, his wool sweater. His face, now beaded with sweat, had turned the color of beets. Curtis pulled a bottle of water from his pack. It was still mostly frozen from the Antarctic. "Sip. Slowly."

McKee's red, stiff hands wrapped around the bottle. He raised it, shakily, to his mouth, guzzled from it, then rolled the bottle over his face. "She did to me what . . . you're doing . . ."

And suddenly, Curtis saw what he had become in his years with SPOT, a man vested with an incredible power that had blinded him completely. He was no different from Mariah, Rodriguez, Fenmore, White, all the corrupt, ambitious pricks who had governed his life since that first day of training seven years ago. He forced himself to speak; he had to know where Kat was. "Go on," he said, his voice choked.

McKee ran the water bottle across his face again, his

throat, the back of his neck. "She needs us. You, me, Bari, Alex, Nora, Kat . . . we're her soldiers, her troops, her army . . . that's my take on her." He drank more. "For the longest time after she introduced me to Bari, I thought . . . I . . . was stupid enough to believe . . . that I could build a life back here." He dropped the bottle of water in the sand, pressed his hands against his thighs, shook his head. "Now I understand that she's been biding her time, maneuvering us this way and that, positioning events . . . positioning *us* . . .

"You said she took you to a cave, McKee."

"Just to spell out the rules. She had to restrain Kat so . . . so she couldn't leap elsewhere in time. Then . . . then she took us to her home. In Northampton. I knew I could split any time I wanted to, I wasn't restrained, but where would I go? To the cops? They would've locked me up in a psych ward. So I became . . . compliant. I tried to understand Mariah and her plan. But Kat . . . she was . . . she . . ."

He started to weep again and pressed his red, raw fists against his eyes, struggling to contain his emotions. "Mariah kept her handcuffed. In the basement. Like a goddamn animal. Until she . . . could disable Kat's chip. She refused to wait until her chip dissolved or her body rejected it and she wouldn't give her a new chip that would dislodge the old one because . . . then . . . Kat would be able to transition."

He seemed to know quite a bit about the science, Curtis thought. "So what'd she do?"

"She didn't have the surgical knowledge to remove it, tried different things . . . and finally found a way to disable it with a stun gun. Or a taser. I'm not sure which. It caused her body to reject the chip."

A stun gun. Curtis's blood boiled. "And then what?"

"Then Mariah turned her loose. That must've been midsummer, around July. In Northampton."

"Did Mariah give Kat money? Help her to establish an identity? Find a job? A place to stay?"

"Yeah, but Kat said she couldn't stand being in the same town as Mariah. So she left."

"You saw her after Mariah cut her loose?"

"A couple of times. Once, she came by Mariah's place . . ."

"What's the address?"

McKee told him, then continued. "Mariah wasn't home and Kat apologized for what she'd done, for even being a part of something as corrupt as SPOT. The last time I saw her was in Utica, she was on her way elsewhere. That was in September . . . around Labor Day, I think. She . . . refused to tell me where she was going. She was afraid that if she told me, Mariah would get it out of me. She felt strongly that you would look for her, that somehow or another you would piece things together . . . and find her."

McKee frowned and gazed off to his right. The hot, brilliant sunlight glinted against the flat blue waters of the lake, where the crude-oil derricks loomed, dark portents of the future. "Kat said, 'Tell him he shouldn't do a replay of any of this. Our only way to defeat Mariah and SPOT is to move forward along this timeline. Some of the answers he needs are in Mariah's basement. Tell him to look for the hidden wireless connection.'"

The phrase referred to the love letter Kat had left him after their only big blowout, a letter in a hidden file on his computer, in a wireless folder. That was the clue. "McKee, that time Kat came to Mariah's house to see you. Did she ask to go into the basement?"

"Yeah, she said she felt safer talking down there."

"Does Mariah have equipment from our time in the basement?"

McKee let out a sharp, ugly laugh. "Does she ever."

Curtis suddenly was certain that Kat had left him information in a hidden file in a wireless folder on Mariah's twenty-first-century computer. "Was there anything more to Kat's message for me?" Curtis asked.

McKee frowned, rubbed his hands against his thighs, shook his head.

"Did she mention a *special location*?" Like, Woodstock, August 16, 1969. If he transitioned there next, would he find her listening to the Grateful Dead? "Did she use that phrase at all?"

McKee slapped his hands together, brushing off sand, then rubbed his hands through his beard, sand raining from it like flecks of dandruff. "That's the place you people choose in training, so you can transition there effortlessly."

Kat must have been incredibly lonely to divulge that kind of information to McKee. "So? Did she mention that phrase?"

"Yeah. But I need you to tell me something first."

"You're hardly in a position to bargain. You answer my question, then I'll answer yours."

"No deal."

Go fuck yourself. "Have a nice life here on the shores of Lake Maracaibo, 1937." Curtis started walking away from him. "Maybe you can get a job on one of the derricks," he called over his shoulder.

"Wait," McKee said quickly, breathlessly, stumbling along after him. "She said that Mariah might know about her special location, so . . . you shouldn't look for her there until Mariah was out of the picture."

"That's it?"

"Yes. I swear. That's it. Am I going to remain in the sixties? With Bari?"

"That's your question?"

He nodded, his expression like that of some naughty toddler who knew he wasn't entitled to anything but figured he would ask anyway. "Yeah, apparently you do. I found a picture of you on the Internet with Bari, Kesey, and Garcia. You're known as the 'mystery lover,' McKee, the guy who may have been from the future about which Bari will write so convincingly."

He smiled at that, apparently pleased. "What about Nora?"

"What about her?"

"How's she fit into all this?"

"The last I heard, she was on the run. But, no offense, you didn't seem too concerned about her in Bari's living room."

"What the hell was I supposed to do?" He glared at Curtis. "I met Bari when she came to Mariah for her insomnia. The attraction was immediate, mutual, and Nora was nearly forty years in the future."

"C'mon, you're Mariah's puppet, McKee. You said it yourself."

"Hell," he spat. "We're all being manipulated." He sat back on his heels and threw his arms out at the lake, the oil derricks. "*Oil*, Curtis. It somehow comes back to oil and power. According to Mariah, you Travelers can't go back and correct problems in the Mideast because there have been so many problems there, so many points where timelines forked, and you don't understand enough about time to be able to predict which corrections might work in your favor. That's why she gave Alex the design for his car. She hoped it would catch on with consumers, that it would drive us toward independence from foreign oil."

It was news to him that Mariah had given Kincaid the design for his hybrid. "Then she didn't do it soon enough."

"No kidding. Blame Alex. He's a stubborn idiot, has refused all buyouts, he's got ideals, you know? So they snatched me, thinking he would trade the design for me. But if the government gets it, they'll use it as leverage with the oil companies—*give us a cut of your take and we'll make sure your profits keep coming in by killing this design*. Like that. It's what they did with the electric car in the nineties. This won't be any different." He slapped his hands against his thighs and emitted a noise that was supposed to be laughter, but sounded like the dying snorts of a madman. "Just shows how incredibly stupid they are. The only person Alex would trade that design for is my wife."

"*What?*"

McKee looked incredulous. "Jesus, Curtis, you supposedly had me under surveillance for—what? Three months? Six months? A year? And you had no idea Alex and Nora were involved with each other before I met her? You had no idea he's still in love with her? You must be as stupid as the rest of them."

Curtis's dislike of this man suddenly deepened. "I guess we missed the emotional complexities of that relationship because you kept us so busy with your extramarital affairs, McKee."

He drew back, blood rushed into his face, turning it a radish red. "I . . . you . . . you had no right to . . ."

"Save the bullshit for your wife, McKee."

"You violated my rights, habeas corpus is shit in the wind, you spied on me, destroyed my life," McKee shouted, then abruptly sprang to his feet and slammed into Curtis with such astonishing speed and power that it caught Curtis off guard. Air exploded from his lungs and he crashed to the beach. He and McKee rolled across the sand, through the terrible, oppressive heat, McKee punching, biting, kicking, air hissing from between his clenched teeth. Curtis tightened his arms around McKee until they were pressed so tightly together that a bystander wouldn't be able to tell where one man's chest began and the other ended.

Static burst inside his skull, his ears rang, and then he transitioned—and missed the house completely.

He emerged somewhere on the grounds, a ribbon of soft orange light against the eastern horizon. McKee, a dozen yards away, sat back on his hands, looking as surprised as a kid who had fallen off his bike. His shirt and socks were back on the shores of Lake Maracaibo and this time it didn't take him as long to scramble to his feet. He stumbled off toward the cottage, shouting Bari's name.

Yeah, McKee, wake them all up. He could transition to the address McKee had given him, but was reluctant to do so and, quite frankly, didn't know if he could pull it off right now. So many transitions in such a short span of time had worn him out, consumed the sugar in his blood, and left him with a weird travel fatigue, a kind of jet lag. He needed food, a car, maps, sleep.

Bari barreled out of the house, threw her arms around McKee, and helped him into the cottage. Curtis kept moving down the walk, limping now, his foot throbbing. He suddenly couldn't go a step father and sank down to the side-walk, waiting for this strange malaise to pass.

He unzipped his pack, pulled out his jacket, slipped it on. He brought out a pack of peanut butter crackers and his last bottle of water, ice still floating in it. The water and a few crackers helped, but his eyes still begged to close; he still felt weak and depleted. He didn't even know if he could stand. His bones felt like they were filled with yogurt. He wondered if his body was rejecting the chip.

Curtis rested his forehead on his knees and started to doze off when a door slammed. As he raised his head, Bari came out of the cottage and marched over to him, everything about her body language indicating that she was pissed but in control. This was a woman, he thought, who wouldn't lose her composure no matter how angry she was.

In the soft, dawn light, her red hair and pale skin with the Sissy Spacek freckles formed a startling contrast to the soft green of her eyes. "What the hell did you do to him?"

"Scared him worse than Mariah did."

"And you're proud of that?"

"No. But he told me what I needed to know."

"Christ." She shook her head, combed her fingers back through her short hair, then sat on the sidewalk, facing him. She drew her knees to her chest and wrapped her arms around them. "Look, I don't expect you to understand this, but I'm saying it anyway. I know about his affairs, his bull-shit, his inconsistencies. I also know this script has to be written differently then it might have been if I'd never met Jake. It's important in ways that relate to your time—my fu-ture, Mr. Curtis. It has a purpose in the larger scheme of things. My feelings for Jake aside, he's a cocreator of this pilot, like my muse. Without him, this pilot will never be-come a reality."

"I don't want him. I just want to find my partner. And for the record, I'm a rogue agent now." He quickly filled in some of the gaps in her knowledge—Senators Aiken and Lazier, Fenmore, Rodriguez, how Simone White had jammed a pair of manicure scissors up into his foot, his confrontation with Fenmore in the botanical garden in Northampton.

He sensed that Bari absorbed every word he said, that she had some mental filing cabinet where she neatly categorized all this information. She fired questions back at him—about the structure of Freeze, of SPOT, how he had come to be involved in all of it, his relationship with Kat and Fenmore, Rodriguez and the Council. It was as if her questions had grown inside her ever since she'd met McKee and she had refined them, polished them, honed them to glean the maximum amount of information in the least amount of time. Smart, intuitive. Under other circumstances, she would make an ace Traveler.

"Now you've picked my brain," Curtis remarked.

"Oh, honey," she said with a soft laugh. "I haven't even scraped the surface. Did you know that I met Alex Kincaid? That he's also chipped? That he was Mariah's second insomnia test subject?"

"Kincaid?"

She related how they had met at a Utica bar and how Kincaid had disappeared when she was in the restroom. "And he took fifty bucks of mine. And then he turns out to be friends with Jake and Nora McKee's ex-lover. Weird, huh?"

Maybe not so weird, he thought. It had Mariah's fingerprints all over it.

"How can I help you?" Bari asked.

"I need a car. I have to go to Northampton."

"Okay. We've got extra cars. But Mariah doesn't live where she used to." She ticked off a different address than the one McKee had given him. "She got paranoid."

"You knew about her, about what she really is, before McKee came along?"

"No way. She's much too secretive. Brilliant, sly, and probably vengeful, too. But she must've figured that since Jake and I were living together, he eventually would tell me the truth. So one night she called and wanted to know if a woman named Kat had come to the cottage. Mariah described her. Well, yeah, I'd seen Kat the day she came here to talk to Jake. And, shameless voyeur that I am, I eavesdropped on their conversation. And before she left, I talked to her, away from the Jake. But I didn't tell Mariah. Didn't tell Dee, either, and there aren't many secrets that I keep from her. You know, Mr. Curtis, that in exchange for all this information, you have to promise me that you will never permanently disappear Jake."

"You have my word. Besides, I told you, I don't want him."

They were on their feet now, moving away from the cottage, Curtis limping. He still felt bone tired, but for the first time since all of this had started, he knew he'd found an ally. "If I were you," he said, "I wouldn't stay here."

"I don't intend to. We'll be gone in thirty or forty minutes, back to Old Forge, where my dad and I have a place."

There were three cars in the garage—her 1963 Sport Roadster, a black VW Bug, and a Mercedes. "I think the Mercedes is the better choice for you. The Bug is wonderful, but you're more likely to get stopped just on principle. The Mercedes, though, oh . . ." She smiled, nodded to herself, and brushed her fingertips over the trunk of the car. "It's classy."

"I really appreciate this," Curtis said. "Where should I leave it?"

She told him, knew the exact spot, as if she had planned it out already. "It's an apartment I leased after I signed on to Mariah's insomnia program, so I wouldn't have to stay with Dee every time I was in Northampton. It's basic, but comfortable enough and it's got a phone. I can call you if Mariah or someone else shows up." She brought a set of keys from her pocket and handed them to him. "And you can always use the cottage here if you need a place in a pinch. The key's usually in that flowerpot on the porch."

"Are you always so generous with people you don't know?"

"I figure this way you won't refuse me if I ask favors in return."

He found her bluntness refreshing. "Do you own a gun? A rifle?"

"Yes."

"Make sure they work. If nothing else, Lydia Fenmore is innovative."

"The Old Forge place is remote. But we'll be prepared. Just in case." She opened the passenger door. "Let's drive up to the cottage and I'll get you some food and a mug of coffee for your trip."

"That would be great, thanks."

The Mercedes was comfortable enough, with leather seats nearly as soft as pillows, but compared to any Mercedes in his own time, it was basic. Manual windows, a simple dashboard, no CD player, no GPS, no automatic scan for the little radio, no cup holders. He pulled up next to the psychedelic bus, put the Mercedes in park, and Bari got out.

While Curtis waited for her, he rested his head against the back of the seat, shut his eyes, and saw himself back in that botanical garden, at the very moment Lydia Fenmore had suddenly stopped and studied the device clipped to her belt. And then she had spun around . . .

The device. What is it?

RFID? Can she track me?

"Here you go," Bari said, and slid a small cooler into the passenger seat. "It's got snacks and a sandwich that should tide you over." Then she came around to the driver's door, opened it, and passed him a mug of steaming coffee and a sheet of paper. "The paper's for Kat, a note to her from Jerry. She and I immediately connected because of The Grateful Dead. She's an expert on them, on Garcia."

Curtis couldn't help but smile. "That she is. What else did you two talk about?"

"We only had about ten minutes. She was nervous, uneasy, felt that Mariah might have followed her. She told me Garcia passes away on August 9, 1995, from a heart attack in his sleep, and that Kesey goes in 2001. That was really too much information. Details I didn't need to hear. But now that I know, I'm going to change both events. You watch. I will."

And Dead Heads and Kesey fans worldwide would be forever in her debt, Curtis thought, except that they wouldn't know. If she succeeded, would he know? Would Kat? Would either of them have dual sets of memories, as he'd had during the replay to Blue River? No telling. For him, it really was a whole new world.

"One thing, Ryan. I think we know each other well enough now for first names, don't you?" Then, with barely a skipped beat, she asked, "So when do I die?"

"I don't know."

"Does that mean I'm still alive in 2006 or does it mean you really don't know?"

"It means that on March seventh, this year, a house you own in Old Forge burns to the ground and you go missing. The police eventually say you died in that fire, but the Internet conspiracy blogs have you alive and well and living elsewhere. They think you and your mysterious lover faked your own deaths, assumed different identities, and that you wrote all sixty episodes of *Connections*. Your father, by the way, is in an assisted-living facility in California in my time."

"If I help you in your revolution, Ryan—and that's what it's going to be—will you take me to see my dad in your time?"

"But you're here now, and so is he."

"Yeah, but . . . I need to know if this time travel thing is possible for me."

Could he? SPOT had drummed into them that they couldn't travel into the future. He figured that was just one more lie. "You can do it on your own. You've got a chip. It takes intense resolve, need, and emotion. It takes the ability to imagine where you're going. You can find me here." On a piece of scrap paper, he scribbled the date for The Grateful Dead's Woodstock concert and a November 2006 date for Waverunner in Aruba. "Woodstock will be easier for you to get to because it's only a year from now. But finding me could be a challenge among half a million people."

"Woodstock. Jake told me about Woodstock." Bari looked at him, at the paper, shook her head, and rolled her eyes toward the sun. "Shit, and all this time, I was just trying to get some sleep." Then her arms encircled his neck and she hugged him. "Don't wreck my car, Ryan."

She stepped back, he shut the door, and drove on through the open gate.

16

Nora lay as still as a bone, afraid that if she opened her eyes, she would discover that the man next to her was Jake, not Kincaid. Could the chip screw around with reality in that way?

When she opened her eyes, relief swept through her. Moonlight spilled through the windows of the bus and fell across Kincaid's hair, his neck and shoulders, his back. She heard Sunny breathing, sighing, snorting in her sleep. And none of them had gone elsewhere. Good. This was progress. Her right nostril, where she had injected the chip, felt sensitive, but not sore. And apparently her body hadn't rejected the chip; she didn't feel dried blood around her nostril.

The air had turned much colder during the night and she sat up to adjust the covers. The new blanket was against their bodies, with one of the dusty quilts that had been in the bus on top of it, and the sleeping bag beneath them. Sunny was curled up on another quilt.

She laid back against her pillow and stared into the shafts of moonlight. She probably hadn't slept more than—what? Four or five hours?—and had expected her head to feel fuzzy and thick with fatigue when she woke. But her mental clarity astonished her. She felt as if she'd slept ten solid hours, without interruption. Was this part of the chip's effect? She imagined it, this technological marvel, migrating, nomadic, making its journey toward that spot in her gray matter where it would create, as Kincaid had speculated, a kind of quantum field.

Kincaid had used the term quantum computer, but this didn't feel *mechanical*. She already thought of it as some sort of interface between man and machine, something that enhanced the brain's abilities, perhaps kick-starting that 90 percent that supposedly wasn't used. But the moral implications of this kind of technology, the ways it already had been abused, and might be abused in the future . . . it was staggering, with implications so far-reaching and provocative that she suddenly wasn't sure what she and Kincaid were supposed to do with this.

Other than finding Jake, her mother, and getting back to their own time, how could they use this in a beneficial way? Could wars be averted? Could the Holocaust be prevented? Could they prevent AIDS from ever coming into being? Could global warming be stopped? And since the chip made travel into the past possible, could they also go into the future? If so, what were the implications of that?

Cut loose from the constraints of time, it suddenly seemed to her that almost anything was possible.

Kincaid stirred beside her, turned onto his back, and she knew from the shift in his breathing that he had come awake. "You okay?" he whispered, groping for her hand under the covers.

"Better than I've ever been. Alex, the chip affects perceptions, mental clarity, I don't seem to need as much sleep. It's . . ."

"I know." He laced his fingers through hers. "It's . . . a gift. But the greedy bastards who own the technology have perverted it, made it dark, ugly, cruel."

She turned onto her side, lifted up on an elbow, and propped up her head with her hand. "But we aren't like them. With this kind of . . . gift, we can make a difference."

He sat up, turned on the flashlight, and located the thermos of water—melted snow that had been boiled and cooled. He twisted off the cap, offered it to her. She drank, passed it back, and he tilted it to his mouth. Then he added water to Sunny's bowl, twisted the cap back into place. He pulled on his sweatshirt and sat with his back against the wall of the bus.

"Yeah, we can make a difference, Nora. But you need to know about Jake."

Jake, Jake. Jesus God, okay, let's get on with it. "Only if you want to tell me."

At first, she heard a reluctance in his voice, a need to hold back, but as he continued, that reluctance vanished. "Six months ago, Jake and I ran into each other at the gym on campus. We went out to dinner, had too many drinks, and Jake told me he was in debt to the tune of thirty or forty grand. He said you didn't know about it, that his only way out was to either file for bankruptcy or to sell the hybrid I gave the two of you when you got married. He said a dissident group had offered to buy it. His story was plausible. There's a two-year waiting list for the hybrid. My outfit is really small and I can't produce them fast enough to keep up with the demand."

Debt? Bankruptcy? Selling the hybrid? Nora had no idea what he was talking about. She and Jake had had debt, yes, but no more or less than any other married couple she'd known. Several thousand with Visa, a few more thousand on Mastercard, but no mortgage, no car payments. So where was thirty grand in debt? On which cards? She paid most of the bills, she would have seen this—noticed it and balked, ranted, raved.

"The group was offering him twenty grand for the car. Below market value. I kept thinking that if he sold it, you'd be the one riding a bike to work. So I told him I would sell two hybrids if he would take care of the arrangements, and would lend him whatever it took to pay off the debt."

Nora suddenly felt grateful for the dark, that Kincaid couldn't see her face, the way her eyes squeezed shut, the way her mouth tightened.

"I figured I could put whatever was left back into the business. But Jake didn't want to deal with the group. He wanted me to finalize the arrangement. I told him to forget it, I wasn't going on any fucking government watch list."

"Christ," she whispered, rubbing her hands over her face, suddenly understanding what Kincaid had been willing to risk for *her* comfort, *her* convenience. "I'm so sorry he . . ."

"No, don't apologize for him, Nora. He's responsible for this, not you." The coldness that entered Kincaid's voice startled her. "Weeks passed. I didn't hear squat from Jake. And then three days before Jake's arrest, I got the e-mail from peoplesfriend to get out of town. Attached to that e-mail were photos of Jake with a woman, with her name, social security number, some other identifying info. She was the woman he'd been sleeping with, an undercover Freeze operative posing as one of his students. I figure she must have threatened to tip you off about their affair or to get him fired or something worse unless he helped her gather evidence against me."

I'm resigning, Jake had told her that day at the Lighthouse Pub. It all fit now. She pressed the heels of her hands against her eyes, her mouth had gone bone dry, she felt like hurling open the door of the old bus and shrieking like a banshee. But the clarity of her own mind kept her where she was. When she was finally able to speak, she said, "All of this because of the hybrid?"

"I think so. The car I gave you and Jake gets a hundred miles to the gallon. The newer versions, and there aren't many of them yet, get two to three times that. The oil companies are nervous, so that makes the government nervous. I've had multiple offers for buyouts and have refused all of them. The bottom line is that the government wants the design for the car."

"But they have resources, money. They can duplicate it."

"No, they can't." He leaned back on his elbows. "The original blueprint came from Mariah. She filled in everything I didn't know and couldn't figure out. This technology *doesn't exist* in our time. That's why no one can duplicate the design, at least not yet. And frankly, I think they wanted to buy me out so they could kill the whole thing."

"It's just like the biochip, then. The technology for it doesn't exist now, in 1968, so she had to create it from the twenty-first century. But where did she get the technology for the hybrid?"

"I think she got it from our future, beyond 2006. Do you know what zero point energy is?"

"The energy that's contained in a vacuum."

"Well, yeah, that's basically it, but it's a little more complicated than that."

She knew from the tone of his voice that trying to explain the complexities of zero point energy to a psychology professor was the equivalent of delineating the alphabet of the English language to an illiterate from Pluto. But hey, she was a good listener. "So the hybrid taps into this . . . this free energy?"

"Yes, I think so. I can't begin to tell you how it works, but it's why the hybrid gets two to three hundred miles to the gallon instead of seventy or eighty. And it has the potential for hundreds of miles beyond that. That's why they want the design."

Nora sat up, suddenly excited. "How about this for an over-the-top motive? The shadow government wants your design. They have realized you won't sell it or turn it over willingly, so they take your closest friend, Jake, figuring that down the line they'll force you to do an exchange. Your design for Jake."

"No fucking way. The only reason Jake and I were friends

was because he was married to you, Nora. I mean, I knew him before I knew you, but once you and I happened and then you got involved with him and married him . . ." He shrugged, a gesture of resignation. "It was a no-brainer. If I wanted to see you, know what was happening in your life, it meant I would have to be friends with Jake." He paused. "So that's what I did. If the design is what they're after, they should have nabbed you."

Nora pressed her fists into her eyes, struggled to contain her emotions, and failed miserably. She started to cry and put her arms around him, drawing him against her. They dropped back against the sleeping bag and made love again and fell asleep and when she woke, sunlight filtered through the frosted windows.

She remembered everything—details, words, emotions, the entire panoply of Jake's betrayal of her, of Kincaid. Her mind was clearer than it had ever been. And she now had purpose, direction. She dressed and slipped out of the van.

The fire still smoldered and she added some logs and fanned the smoldering embers until they caught. She put on water for coffee, fed Sunny, and went off to shower. When she returned, Kincaid was awake, fixing breakfast. Neither of them said much, she noticed, but what was there to say that hadn't been said already?

Breakfast was pleasant, almost mundane—if she could forget they had less than twenty bucks between them and were trapped nearly forty years in the past. After they'd eaten and packed up the bus, Kincaid suggested they take a walk. He stabbed a thumb over his shoulder, indicating the pines that rimmed the western side of their site, the pines where she had retreated last night. "We'd better learn how to use these chips before we venture any farther. That looks like a private spot."

Kincaid, mind reader. Nora hoisted her pack onto her back, Kincaid did the same, and they followed Sunny into the shadowed fragrance of the green thicket. There was no path to speak of, just an erratic trail beaten down by people who had passed through here before them, many of them lovers who had carved their initials into the trunks of the trees. *KL+JM, 5/16/63, Joe & Stella, 7/4/61, Anne loves Aaron, 2/14/1942.* The oldest carving she noticed dated back thirty years, to 1938.

Nora paused in front of a very large pine, got out her pocketknife, and carved her name and Kincaid's, with a small heart between them, and dated it. *3/4/68.* Beneath this, Kincaid carved his own message: *AK+NM forever,* and dated it. "Now we're officially part of this lovers' lane," he said, and took her hand. "How about if we practice right here? I think we're far enough in the woods so we won't be bothered."

As they settled on the ground nearly forty years in the past, everything about their lives uncertain, unscripted, unknown, she felt absurdly happy. It seemed so simple, this emotion, and so alien to anything she'd felt in the last several years that it shocked her.

Sunny settled between them. "Now what?" she asked. "Do we visualize? Hope? Pray?"

"In Tyler's storage unit, we were all touching." Kincaid held out his hand, Nora clasped it, and she and Kincaid placed their free hands on Sunny's back. "Now we click our heels three times and think of home."

"Right."

"Let's keep it simple. We want this spot, 2006," Kincaid said. "We pull our own time toward us. Or draw it around us. Something like that." He dug out his cell phone, turned it on. "We'll check ourselves with this." He held it up so she could see it. "No signal, no date. If we make it to 2006, we'll have a date even if we don't have a signal."

"Maybe you should turn it off. Our cells were off when we ended up in the cemetery. Time travel might fry the inside of it."

"Off it goes."

They positioned themselves again, so they were all touching. Nora shut her eyes and began to visualize her own time, its grandeur and its pathos, shrinking forests and growing superhighways, technology and triumphs, wars, atrocities and abuses, cities and farms and the unequaled beauty, its people. They sat for a long time, holding hands, touching Sunny, mentally reaching, stretching, struggling. The only thing that happened was that her ass fell asleep and her hands and nose got cold.

Sunny finally moved away from them and Kincaid released her hand, stretched his arms above his head, and stood. "It's not working."

As he reached out to pull Nora to her feet, her eyes fell on the trunk where they had carved their messages. "Alex," she whispered, and pointed. "The carvings look *old*."

He glanced at the trunk, fished his cell from his pocket, turned it on, and they both spun around and tore up the path after Sunny. Not only did the cell have a signal, but it had a date, too, October 30, 2005, nearly a full year before Jake's arrest.

There were fewer trees and the light that spilled through the branches suggested that it was evening. Laughter and voices drifted toward them. They emerged near a concession building festooned with Halloween decorations—pumpkins, plastic skeletons, cutouts of black cats pasted to the windows. A horse-drawn wagon rumbled through the parking lot, past twenty-first-century cars, the gleeful, costumed children inside shouting, "Trick or treat." Beyond the lot, she saw RVs, campers, and way off to the right, tents.

Nora stood there, stunned, paralyzed, frozen, watching the children waving and laughing. The dog sat down in front of them, her tail thumping the ground. Suddenly, the air around them quivered and trembled, like heat above desert sand. The horse-drawn wagon started to fade, the costumed children lost color and definition, the RVs and campers and twenty-first-century cars turned soft, pale, surreal. The old bus they had stolen wavered into view, juxtaposed over the concession building.

"We can't hold on to it," Kincaid said, and dropped to his

knees, pulling Nora down to the ground beside him, and flung his other arm around the dog.

A thick, terrifying pressure built inside her skull, as if the barometer were in a freefall. Static burst inside her ears, her vision went fuzzy, and then her head exploded with an agonizing pain and she shrieked.

Her mouth was still open when the pain began to subside, but no sounds came out. The static was gone, her vision was clear, and she was sprawled on her back, the pack beneath her, elevating her torso. Above her, the towering tips of the pines caught a breeze and swayed like belly dancers. Off to the left, she could see their old bus, solid, real.

Kincaid's fingers tightened on hers; she turned her head to the right, the muscles and tendons in her neck creaking like springs. Kincaid was looking at her already, eyes bright with exhilaration, and Sunny, sitting up between them, looked at them both.

"We made it, Nora. But our aim sucks."

"Practice. That's what we need."

"All of this." His other hand made a sweeping gesture. "I'm glad it's happening with you."

"I can't imagine it happening with anyone *but* you."

"And I don't particularly want to look for Jake. I know how terrible that sounds, but it's the truth."

She wished she could be horrified by how easy it was for them to dismiss Jake, to just write him off. "I don't want to look for Jake, much less find him. But I'd like to find my mother, if that's possible. And I want to blow the lid off this disappearance program."

"Same here. And I've got a few questions for Mariah Jones, Right now, Bari Serrano seems to be the most expedient route to Mariah."

"Then we're on the same page."

"It only took us forty years."

She laughed and they both got up. "Do you know how to shoot a gun?" he asked.

"Sure. I've had so much experience shooting guns."

"I take it that's a no."

He unzipped his pack, dug into an inner compartment, and brought out a handgun. The sight of it struck her viscerally, triggering all the old memories of that Freeze woman decades ago who had stuck a gun in her face and threatened to put a bullet through her head if her mother didn't cooperate. The same acrid taste flooded her mouth, the bile of fear. She shook her head.

"I don't want to carry a gun, Alex."

Kincaid took her hand, pressed the weapon against it, covered it with his other hand. "We have to be able to defend ourselves. I don't intend to die back here, okay? And I sure as hell don't intend to lose you again. So please, take the damn thing."

The muscles in her hand and forearm twitched, tightened, begged to pull away. But she knew Kincaid was right. Their bottom line was survival. It didn't mean she had to kill anyone. She only had to act like she knew how to use the gun so that if she were threatened, the other person would think twice—or concede. If the female Freeze officer hadn't threatened to blow her head off all those years ago, her mother wouldn't have been so eager to cooperate.

"Okay, move your hand," she said, and he did. She clutched the weapon the way she'd seen actors do it in movies, both hands tucked around the handle. "Is it loaded?" she asked.

"No." Kincaid's hand vanished in the pack again and out came a clip. He took the gun from her and snapped the clip into the bottom of the handle. "Now it is. There're thirteen shots. If there's a situation where we have to use guns, always be aware of how many shots you've fired."

"Do you have one of these?" she asked.

He lifted the front of his jacket, revealing an identical weapon tucked into the waistband of his jeans.

"And you got these where, Alex?"

"From a friend."

"When?"

"When I became convinced I was under surveillance. It's possible that our time displacement screwed up the firing mechanism. I don't have any idea how time travel affects anything. But since our cell phones and my PDA worked for the few minutes we were in 2005, I'm assuming the gun will work, too."

He explained the basics. They definitely weren't in an area for target practice, but Nora hoped that if they were in a position where she had to pull the weapon, the intimidation factor would count more than her aim. "So did you go to a firing range or something to learn how to shoot this sucker?" she asked.

"A firing range?" He snickered. "You've got to show ID and proof of ownership at a range. I learned in the woods behind the warehouse where we run the hybrid business."

That was a part of Kincaid's life about which she knew exactly nothing. "And if you were being followed and watched, how did you do that?"

"I went about my life," he said. "And that was pretty boring to the bozos who were watching."

Nora slipped the gun in her jacket pocket, but its weight felt as strange and alien to her as those few moments they had stood in 2005. A couple of kids ran into the woods and they hurried back toward the campground.

Twenty minutes later they were in the bus. Nora still felt that wonderful mental clarity and hoped it was permanent. She spread the map open on her lap, brought out Jake's compass to take a reading. But the needle still spun wildly and the inscription from her on the back of it disgusted her. She rolled down the window and tossed the compass out.

"I thought you had a lousy sense of direction," Kincaid remarked.

"Not anymore. Take the next left."

"Shit," Kincaid murmured. "Look in your side mirror."

Two or three lengths back, a cruiser followed them. It didn't speed up, no lights flashed, no siren sounded. But it was there, tailing them, watching. "If we're pulled over . . ."

"I spread ash across the license plate, so even if the bus matches a stolen vehicle description, he might not stop us."

Nora reached for her seat belt, then realized there wasn't one. They weren't standard items on cars yet. She nervously watched the cruiser in the mirror. It didn't come any closer, but it didn't turn off or go away, either. "Bari's street is coming up."

"I wish that prick would pass us," Kincaid grumbled about the cop.

But he didn't. When Kincaid slowed and put on the blinker, the cruiser's blinker came on, too. It turned as they turned, slowed when they slowed to check numbers on the mailboxes. If he suddenly decided to pull them over, they would have to take off. Not only was the van stolen, but they didn't have proper ID and were armed. They wouldn't be able to outrun him in this old bus, probably wouldn't have much luck losing him in daylight, and they were still pretty much in the dark about how to use the chips. So they might have to shoot at him.

Please don't stop us.

Kincaid drove slowly past number 63, a sprawling two-story mansion half hidden behind an iron fence and towering pines. The fence ran, unbroken, down the remainder of the block, which meant the estate was enormous.

"The driveway gate is open," Kincaid said. "I'm turning in. The cop's right on our ass. If he calls to us, we pretend we don't hear him and just get out, like we belong here." Kincaid turned into the driveway, stopped behind a dark Cadillac, and the cop car pulled alongside the curb.

As Nora climbed out, she checked the side mirror; the cop had his radio mike to his mouth. She slid open the side door, and Sunny bounded out, wagging her tail. "Just leave the bags, hon," Nora called, loudly enough so that the cop would hear. "We can get them later."

We belong here. We're visitors. We've done nothing wrong.
The dog bounded across the yard as though she were

home, nose to the ground, tail whipping back and forth. Nora and Kincaid followed, his arm tight around her shoulder again. She loved how it felt. "Is he watching us?" Kincaid whispered.

"I don't know," she whispered back. "Don't look around."

As they neared the front porch, the door opened and a tall man jogged out, his thick hair the same soft shade of gray as his running clothes. He didn't seem surprised to see them. In fact, he acted as if strangers on his front lawn were a common occurrence.

"Morning," Nora called cheerfully. "I called last night. Is Bari back yet?"

"Did you check the cottage?" he asked, jogging in place.

"We weren't sure how to get there," Kincaid said.

"Bari told us to check the main house first," she added, and extended her hand. "I'm Nora, this is Alex. Are you Bari's dad?"

He stopped jogging, grasped her hand. "Charlie Ovis." He tilted his head toward Sunny. "Gorgeous dog."

"Her name's Sunny," Kincaid said.

"Morning, Mr. Ovis," called a voice behind them.

Even before Nora glanced back, she knew it was the cop. Sure enough, he stood just outside the gate, hands jammed in the pockets of his jacket, his small round face ruddy from the cold. Ovis waved.

"Morning, Ben."

"Wasn't sure you were home, sir. I saw the old bus pulling in and I felt I'd better check."

"Not a problem."

"You have a great day, sir."

"You, too, Ben." Ovis waved. "Thanks again."

With that, the cop got back into his cruiser and drove off.

"We've had some robberies on the street recently," Ovis explained. "Ben's the nervous type, always keeping an eye out."

A zealous cop, Nora thought. There were plenty of them in her time.

"So did you two work with Bari in California?" Ovis asked.

"No, we met her through Ken," Kincaid said quickly.

"Ah." Ovis nodded. "So you're writers."

"Not published yet," Nora said. "But hopeful. Anyway, we were supposed to meet her and Kesey and the gang here sometime today."

"I don't know if Ken and Jerry made it and who knows about Bari? Maybe they've all been here and left." He shrugged. "With that group, you can never be sure. I'll walk you down to the cottage."

"Hey, Charlie, hold on."

A tall, dark-haired man in identical sweats jogged toward them across the yard, Sunny loping alongside him. Decked out for a run, he was smoking a cigarette, and as he neared, Nora experienced a kind of groupie stupor. The man was Rod Serling.

In person, his dark eyes held that same intensity that they did on the *Twilight Zone*, but he looked taller, leaner, and had a quick, engaging smile. "I've been adopted," he said with a laugh, stabbing his thumb toward Sunny.

Ovis introduced them as Bari's friends and Nora, starstruck by Serling's presence, suddenly felt like English was her second language. In the two years following her mother's disappearance, reruns of *Twilight Zone* and *Night Gallery* had saved her by opening her young, impressionable mind to other explanations for her mother's disappearance. The explanations changed with each episode—that her mother had been imprisoned in a painting, trapped in another dimension, abducted by aliens, shrunken to the size of an ant by mysterious and unknown forces.

Gushy greetings sped up her tongue. She bit all of them back and managed a polite, "It's wonderful to meet you, Mr. Serling." *But hey, no smoking while you run. And if you don't quit, your heart gives up the fight in the summer of 1975.* "Sorry to interrupt your run like this."

"Aw, hell, the run is Charlie's idea." He inhaled deeply on

the last of his cigarette, the smoke curling in fancily through his nostrils, then flicked the butt off into the yard. "He thinks I'll quit smoking if I take up running."

"A guy can hope," Ovis muttered. "I'm going to take them over to the cottage to find Bari."

"She got home?"

"Don't know," Ovis replied.

They headed through the trees, past small rises of snow, an empty fountain with a gargoyle face nearly covered by dead leaves, and pines that leaned inward. Birds, hidden in the shadows, sang as though their hearts were breaking. Kincaid walked with Ovis, and she, Serling, and the dog kept pace just behind them.

Serling talked about dogs, books, movies, TV shows, a steady stream of consciousness that followed the slopes and rises of the landscape and the rhythms of her mood. Nora suddenly wondered, again, if she was locked up in that mental ward she often thought she would find at the end of this journey.

After all, here she was, with the man who had written about what she and Kincaid were now living. In one memorable episode, "Walking Distance," a guy named Martin Sloan was driving across country to the town where he'd grown up—and time traveled into his own childhood. Granted, this wasn't the time or place of her childhood, but she was with one of those rare creative geniuses whose insights might provide her with answers.

"True story, okay?" Nora said. "In the early part of the twentieth century . . . this century," she corrected herself, "two women went for a walk in a famous, ancient garden somewhere in Europe and encountered all kinds of strange anomalies. Only when they left the garden did they realize they had walked back in time." She had read that story at Kincaid's place way back in the early days of their relationship. "How could such a thing be possible? I mean, scientifically?"

The way Serling suddenly regarded her, the intensity of

his gaze, unnerved her. It was as if, at some level, he understood that Nora and Kincaid were that garden she'd mentioned, that *they* were the anomalies. Not that he would express it. His imagination, though, would seize on these feelings, weave tales from them.

"I'm not so sure about science, but I think if you can imagine it, it can happen. Suppose we surround ourselves with things from a particular era in the past—furniture, buildings, clothes, the culture—and lived in that environment long enough to *un*condition our minds. Then we put ourselves into an altered state and engage our imaginations to reach out to that past. I think we could walk right back into it, like your women in the garden. Science just hasn't caught up to the imagination."

Was this what had happened to them back at the campground?

Serling pulled another cigarette from a pack tucked into his jacket pocket, offered her one, and she shook her head. *Can I change this?* A tantalizing possibility. Did he have to die at the age of fifty-one, from complications of a coronary bypass? Or was that just one of his possible appointments with death? Was that how it worked? Were you born with several possible times to die that depended on the choices you made as you lived? Was life, like death, a traffic circle with many roads shooting away from it? Choose one and you lived and died according to that probability. Choose another and a different probability opened up.

When they reached the cottage, Ovis looked around. "No psychedelic bus. And I don't see her car." He reached into a large, round ceramic pot that held dirt but nothing else, and plucked out a key. "She's still gone. Otherwise the key wouldn't be here."

The inside of the cottage was chaotic—beer and wine bottles spilling from the garbage, dirty dishes stacked in the sink, towels crumpled on the couch, everything suggesting a hasty departure. The air smelled of pot, but Ovis either didn't notice or didn't care. He went over to the fridge, removed a note from the door, and read, "'Dad, I'll be back in a couple of days or I'll call. Am taking script with me." He frowned. "She might still be in Old Forge. But it's odd. We always tell each other where we'll be."

"She's got a guy now," Serling remarked. "That changes things."

I am standing here in 1968, in a cottage in Utica, New York, listening to a conversation between Rod Serling and his business buddy about the buddy's daughter's new boyfriend. Yeah, lock me up. Nora felt weird, shaky, uncertain, as if all the strangeness had permanently debilitated her. She moved closer to the counter and leaned against it.

"Well, at this point in the script, there're only two places she'd be. Old Forge for silence and privacy or in Northampton, visiting Dee." He glanced at the clock on the kitchen wall. "I'm guessing Northampton." He picked up the receiver of the old dial phone, and dialed. Listened. Shook his head. "No one's answering. It's too early. But I'll give you the numbers." Ovis flipped the note over, sketched a map on the back of it and scribbled directions. "The place in Old Forge is difficult to find. Just follow the map. I jotted Dee's address on here." He handed the paper to Nora. "And when you see Bari, please tell her I don't appreciate her taking off without letting me know how to get in touch with her. Remind her we've got a deadline on this script."

"The script for the *Connections* pilot?" Kincaid asked.

Ovis and Serling both looked surprised. "She finally has a title?" Serling exclaimed.

"That's what she called it, right, Nora?" Kincaid glanced over at her, his eyes signaling that he needed help.

"Uh, yeah." A framed photo on the bookshelf had distracted her. "I think it's just a working title, but it's got a great ring to it."

"Connections, connections," Serling repeated softly, nodding, his smile widening. "I like it, Charlie."

"Me, too." Ovis slapped his hand against his thigh and laughed. "I really think this pilot is going to happen, Rod.

Didn't I tell you this new guy was having a positive effect on her?"

Nora didn't hear the rest of what they said. She now stood at the bookcase, where she could see the photo. Her ears rang; she felt as if she were perched on her toes at the very end of the world's highest diving board, and knew that if she stepped off, the pool wouldn't be deep enough to keep her from hitting bottom. Her arm reached, an entity independent of her, of her body, and her fingers closed around the frame.

The picture had been taken in some rustic spot, the background trees bursting with autumn colors, a river just visible off to the left with sunlight glinting against it. The couple in the photo looked so deliriously happy, so completely into each other, that Nora couldn't quite wrap her mind around them as separate people. The woman was lovely—short, copper-colored hair, eyes like a cat's, her smile as genuine and wide as the Grand Canyon. And the man, dear God, the man was Jake.

Her Jake.

Her ex-Jake.

Her disappeared Jake.

Impossible.

Kincaid was suddenly at her side, staring at the photo. She felt his body tense up, felt his incredulity as though it were an extension of her own emotional fabric. "Wonderful picture of Bari," Kincaid remarked, his voice smooth, betraying none of his surprise. "Is this the guy she's been telling us about?"

"That's him," Ovis said. "Jake McKee. Have you two met him?"

Kincaid said, "Bari has talked a lot about him. We feel like we know him."

Nora marveled at the effortless way he kept the conversation flowing while she floundered in some vast sea of unknowns. After that, everything came to her in a dramatically altered perspective, as if she had injected herself with some powerful drug. She heard herself thanking Ovis and saying they better get going. But her consciousness had taken flight. *Get me outta here.*

Then she was free of the cottage, Kincaid making a U-turn in the driveway and Ovis and Serling on the lawn, waving like fathers sending their kids off to college. And she didn't know what the hell she felt.

"You first," Kincaid said finally.

She hesitated, floundered, void of direction. When she found her voice, it sounded choked, ugly, raw. "There're only two explanations, Alex. Curtis and his partner disappeared Jake to Utica and he just *happened* to meet Serrano, they hit it off, and hooked up or . . ."

". . . Mariah disappeared him," he finished.

"And that's the only explanation that makes any kind of sense."

Since the beginning, so much of this had smacked of manipulation, design, an intricate puppetry. Nora now understood just how complex those manipulations had been, but still wasn't sure of Mariah's motive. If she was working against Curtis and his people, which seemed likely now, then one way to do that would be to shatter the secrecy surrounding the time-travel program. Maybe she hoped to accomplish that through Bari's TV series, with Jake feeding Bari information that would make her script authentic. But in Nora's time, that series had peaked decades ago, was still in reruns, and hadn't prevented the time-travel program. In her time, all of this had happened already.

Or had it? Was it even the same series? How odd that she—who had been such an avid fan of Serling's work—couldn't recall much about *Connections*. She'd seen some of the reruns, but her memory of the specifics was vague. Something about humans from the twenty-second century who travel back to 1968 to interbreed because most people in that century were sterile and humanity was dying out.

"Did you ever see *Connections*?" she asked.

"Yeah. It was nothing like what's happening to us."

Definitive. Absolute. Again. "Maybe it will be now."

Kincaid rubbed his jaw. "It's impossible to second-guess all this shit. I've tried it. Your head starts splitting apart. We just have to keep moving forward, following the leads we find."

"Here's my theory, for what it's worth. I think Mariah has declared war on the time-travel unit her invention helped create. She can't wage battle all by herself, so she's made us victims of the system, figuring that when the time comes, we'll join her revolution. And Bari's script is integral to her plot."

"Okay, so she's Che Guevara and we're the peasants and when we rise up and topple the evil system, she appoints herself the leader and it starts all over again?"

"Yeah, something like that."

"Hey, I'm all for toppling the system, but I don't do well with bosses, gurus, or dictators."

"Then we need to make a concerted effort to learn how to control these chips so they don't control us."

"Let's get out of Utica first," he said, and drove faster.

17

Curtis drove for a long time with his mind racing, calculating, puzzling, until he finally settled into a kind of highway trance. Half an hour outside of Northampton, he pulled into a gas station, parked near the restrooms, and rested his head against the seat. Eyes shut, he struggled to sort through what he knew and did not know and needed to know before he could continue.

Jake McKee had told him that Mariah had released Kat around July 1967 and that he had last seen her during the Labor Day weekend, when she was on her way elsewhere. He claimed Mariah had helped Kat establish an identity, so that would entail a birth certificate or a driver's license or both. With either one, she could obtain a passport and with a passport, she could travel.

He was confident that Kat would attempt to get him a message as soon as possible after Mariah had cut her loose. The best way to do that was for her to fly to Aruba and leave him a message at Waverunner, the place where they had stayed during previous trips together in their own time.

But Waverunner didn't exist until 1987, when a pair of avid windsurfers—an Aruban and an Antillean from Curaçao—bought the property they were renting for their wind-surfing business. Back then, it was a coconut plantation—Plantage Tromp—frequently visited by Holland's queen when she was on the island and the site for parties and treasure hunts for kids. Still, it was the most obvious place Kat would go and he needed to check it out before he reached Northampton.

Curtis got out of the Mercedes, his pack slung over his shoulder. Even though he wasn't quite up to par yet and desperately needed sleep, he had eaten the food Bari had provided for his drive and felt somewhat stronger now. He could do this. Had to do it. His target would be Aruba in mid-September 1967, time enough for Kat to have gotten here.

And if your body rejects the chip? He refused to think about it.

He went into the men's room, turned on the light, locked the door. It was hardly a great spot for a transition, but he would be hidden here. He sat on the floor, legs stretched out in front of him, his back against the door. *Aruba*, he thought.

In their two years together, he and Kat had visited the island six times, always in their own time. Vacation. Leave. A weekend respite. They took different flights, from different cities, circuitous routes that made it nearly impossible for Rodriguez and Fenmore to track them, if they were so inclined. Quinta 22 was their home at Waverunner, a one-bedroom apartment on the second floor that faced the swimming pool. The wide porch where they usually sat in the evenings was shrouded by bougainvilleas, palms, ivy with leaves as large as microwave ovens. During the day, they windsurfed, kite sailed, scuba dived. Occasionally, they rode horses to the other side of the island, shopped in downtown Orangestad, and did real tourist stuff, like visit the wild donkey refuge or the butterfly farm.

At night, they often hit several of the eleven or twelve casinos on the island. Neither of them was a true gambler, but they went for the challenge, to test who they were, the same reason they had gone to Antarctica for two days. Gambling was a tremendous temptation for a Traveler—transition back a few minutes in time and the jackpot was yours. But they played fair and to Curtis's astonishment usually won several hundred bucks, money that went into an account on the island.

But mostly during these vacations, they kept to themselves—barbecuing fresh fish from the market, watching DVDs from Waverunner's collection, using the wireless connection to collect e-mail and news, and making love. They did a lot of that. So even though Aruba lacked the exotic third-world flavor of some of the other Caribbean hotspots, his memories of the island were bright, vivid, positive, and it was easy to conjure the details.

In his time, this tiny island—seventy-seven miles square in size, less than twenty miles long and six miles wide at its widest point—was a popular tourist destination with Europeans and Americans. Dutch and Papiamento—a native dialect—were the official languages, but English and Spanish were spoken as well. The Marriot and other chain hotels now occupied its beaches, amd celebrities frequented its nightclubs and casinos. But in the late sixties, tourism was in its infancy, none of the American hotel chains had arrived, and the big deal on the island was Standard Oil's refinery, where more than eight thousand people were employed.

So he focused on the island's physical qualities—the heat, the perpetual sound of the wind, the cactuses, the colorful buildings in Orangestad, the coconut palms and dividivi trees, the lighthouse at the far tip of the island, the startling blue of the Caribbean. He *reached* and *reached,* but nothing happened.

Scraping empty. Curtis pressed the heels of his hands against his eyes. The damp stink of the restroom assaulted his senses. *You will do this.*

He *reached* again, his need overpowering everything else. He suddenly felt like the rubber in a slingshot, his muscles stretching, elongating, becoming painfully taut. He kept thinking, *Aruba, Waverunner, mid-September 1967.* And then everything let loose, the stone flew out of the slingshot, and he abruptly found himself in the midst of a thicket of trees, the intense heat almost unbearable.

His knees gave out and he sank to the ground, breathing hard, his face sheathed in sweat. He shrugged off his pack, unzipped it, grabbed the remains of his last bottled water, and forced himself to only sip at it. He tore off his jacket and sweater, his shoes and socks, and stuffed everything down inside his pack. He rocked back onto his heels, getting his bearings.

He was definitely in Aruba. The divi-divi trees were an island hallmark, odd-looking things that leaned perpetually in the direction the trade winds blew, toward the west. As far as he knew, they didn't grow anywhere else—people had tried but the divi-divi seemed to prefer Aruba. He got up and started walking west, in the same direction the divi-divi trees leaned. A *kododo blauw*—a luminous blue lizard—scurried across the white sand in front of him.

Within a few minutes, the divi-divi trees gave way to coconut palms, curving gracefully upward from the hot sand, fronds shaking and clacking in the wind. The palms thinned and he reached a small concrete-block house, its exterior a soft, faded yellow. Twenty years or so from now, this structure would become Quinta 7 at Waverunner.

No cars or people in sight. The pale blue wooden shutters were closed. "Hello," he shouted. "Anyone home?"

His voice echoed, parrots lifted from the trees, squawking at his intrusion. Eventually, the windsurfers who would build Waverunner would add on to this structure until there were more than twenty separate apartments, a swimming pool, a small windsurfing shop and lobby, a parking lot. Years later, the Marriot would rise up across the street.

Curtis reached the porch and noticed the welcome mat, the wooden swing, the hammock strung up between two posts. He rapped at the door but it was just a formality, he didn't think anyone was inside. After a few moments, he turned the knob and the door creaked open.

Sunlight slanted through a nearby window, exposing dust motes that floated in the still, hot, dank air. Empty bookshelves, a coffee table, even the few pieces of remaining furniture had gathered dust. No one had been inside this building for weeks. He stepped back onto the welcome mat. It looked like a license plate and read: ARUBA—ONE HAPPY ISLAND. For him it definitely was that.

Curtis stepped to the side, off the mat, then stooped down and turned its edge over. There, resting against the tired wood, was an unmarked legal-size envelope. He snatched it up, noting its weight and the way it bulged at one side. Curtis tore it open and a small round watch face slipped out— the digital watch that Kat wore around her neck during every transition. She used it to orient herself and to check the accuracy of their target. Unlike a cell phone or PDA, which depended on external signals to relay dates and times, the watch—once it was set—was self-contained and gave a readout regardless of where the wearer happened to be in time. He knew Kat had left it so that he would immediately know the date and time. *September 16, 1967, 4:03 pm.*

He removed the sheet of paper and eagerly unfolded it.

Ryan, I took a flight from Boston to Miami, hung around there for a few days, just to make sure I wasn't being followed, then flew from Miami to Aruba. I've been here a day already and haven't seen anyone who seems suspicious. Right about now, I'd welcome the sight of any familiar face—except Mariah's.

I feel pretty confident that Aruba is the first place you'll look. It's safe to leave notes here. The house is uninhabited.

Mariah kept me chained in her basement in Northampton for weeks, until she figured out a way to disable my chip. She finally used a stun gun, causing my body to reject it. Before that, she tried to remove it surgically and I nearly bled to death. I think she felt guilty afterward and told me she was going to take me back, but when she attempted a transition, she went and I didn't. She thinks that her botched surgery screwed up something inside me, so that I can't be transitioned by anyone else. I begged her to chip me and let me go on my own, but she refused.

I know you have a spare syringe on you. But according to Mariah, all the chips SPOT has been using for the last year are defective. She sabotaged them somehow. The only chips that might work for me are the ones she produces. So, in the freezer of Mariah's house there are several hundred of them. These are advanced suckers, Ryan, capable of doing things SPOT hasn't even imagined. I need one of those chips. Otherwise I'm stuck in this time for good. No Traveler will be able to transition me. Not even you.

She initially took me because she seems to think that your search for me and whatever you experience will force you to see SPOT for what it is and then you'll join her. She introduced McKee to Bari Serrano so that Bari's TV series will now be about what happened to us—you, me, the McKees, SPOT, everything. She believes the series will alter the existence of SPOT. Or will create a new timeline in which SPOT as we know it won't exist. Or that you and I will join her in her fight against "the forces of evil." Apparently no one has ever informed her that she's the very face of evil.

Look for Jake McKee at Bari Serrano's home in Utica. Her address, Mariah's, and useful phone numbers are attached. Bari will help you any way she can. I love you, Ryan, and I know we'll find each other.

> Kat
> September 15, 1967
> 11:01 AM, LMT

Curtis sank down against the porch steps and read her note again and again, his heart seizing up with so many conflicting emotions that it was moments before he could think clearly. And when he could, he glanced at the date and time on the watch again, then at the date and time beneath Kat's signature.

Yesterday. She was here yesterday. She had included the date so that he would know where to find her when he had a syringe.

Fuck the syringe. He would go back there now. Immediately.

Curtis tucked her note in his wallet, refreshed himself with a sip of water and a snack, then *reached* for September 15, 1967, any time between eight and eleven a.m. He might not be able to target it exactly, but he would be close enough.

Nothing happened.

He *reached* again and again and failed. He was aware that it didn't have anything to do with low blood sugar or too many transitions in a short period of time. This was the result of a spiritual and emotional despair, a tearing away of his heart and soul. He didn't possess the skills to handle this sort of loss. It wasn't something you were taught in training. It wasn't even mentioned. But Mariah must have known that Curtis, with his partner gone, would feel as if a part of his own soul had been ripped away from him. She'd known it would diminish his ability to transition, that he would tire more easily, that his aim wouldn't be as precise, that he would reach points—like now—where transitioning was impossible.

After all, in a world where you could go anywhere in time, at just about any time you wanted, intimate relationships kept you grounded and focused. It was why SPOT linked male and female Travelers and encouraged Travelers to live together, to marry, to have families. There was an element of blackmail to all of it, too. When you had roots, you were less likely to go rogue, break the rules, buck the system. This way, SPOT's substantial investment in Travelers was protected.

And at the moment, the absence of his partner and the possibility that he might not even get back to the Mercedes, much less transition to yesterday, terrified him. It meant both he and Kat would be stuck, with Curtis always living just a day ahead of her in time.

A strange noise startled him, his head snapped up. A small group of wild donkeys made their way slowly through the divi-divi trees, a clutch of photographers at a respectable distance behind them. They were all headed this way—toward the house, toward him.

Shit. He hastily pulled on his socks and shoes, grabbed his pack, shot to his feet. He vaulted over the porch railing and sprinted along the side of the house, Kat's watch clutched in his fist. One of the men in the group shouted, "Hey, you, hold on. Hey, *Bon dia, Kiko ta kiko . . .*"

The photographer apparently had mistaken Curtis for a native, shouting out words and expressions in Papiamento. *Good, day, what's up . . .*

What's up, pal, is that I need to get outta here.

He loped toward the thicker palms off to his right, suddenly stumbled, and couldn't catch himself. He sprawled in the hot sand, his body sinking down against it, into it. *Get up, fast . . .*

He reared up on his knees, listening hard, his breathing ragged. He no longer heard the donkeys or the photographer shouting tortured phrases in Papiamento. Didn't hear anything except his own breathing and the wind. *What the hell.* He opened the fingers of his right hand and looked at Kat's watch. It was 10:27, September 15, 1967. *I did it.* In less than half an hour, Kat would arrive and slip her envelope under the welcome mat on the porch of the old house.

Move, screamed an impatient inner voice, and he pushed to his feet. Elated that he had beaten the odds, that his will had been stronger than his despair, that he had done what Mariah probably hadn't foreseen, Curtis practically ran back toward the house. When he finally stumbled inside and sank down onto the dusty couch, it was 10:57. Four minutes.

The door stood open, he could see outside—the welcome mat, the porch, the palms, the divi-divi trees. He could hear the wind. *Dear God, dear God.*

The first two minutes passed with excruciating slowness. During the third minute, he felt as if time had stopped altogether. His head ached, his eyes dried up, his mouth tasted of desert sand and wind. The door slammed shut, startling him from the torpor that had claimed his body. Curtis stared at the weathered wooden door, willing it to open, and finally sat forward, pressed his hands against the cushion, and stood. He weaved to the door, threw it open.

Kat, kneeling in front of the welcome mat, shot to her feet, her dark hair wild, eyes wide with astonishment, and threw her arms out. "Ryan," she whispered, and they lurched toward each other like drunks.

She slammed into him, her arms encircling him, his arms clutching at her, and they fell back into the chair, and there they stayed, embracing, hugging, his face buried in the curve of her neck. Her skin, her scent, the taste of her sweat: it was her, Kat, here, now, impossible.

They tore at each other's clothes, her mouth found his, and they made love in the chair before they ever uttered a word to each other. For the longest time afterward, neither of them moved and the only sound was their collective, labored breathing. Then Kat lifted her head from the curve of his shoulder and his hands came up to her beautiful face, his fingers slipped into her hair. Tears rolled down her cheeks. "I . . ."

"I'll get the syringe," he said, his voice hoarse, soft. "I'll get every goddamn syringe in her freezer so this never happens to us again."

A frown furrowed down between her eyes, she pulled back slightly. "You went rogue, didn't you."

It wasn't a question. She somehow knew. "I had to." And it all spilled out, everything that had happened since Mariah had disappeared her and McKee.

When Kat spoke of her experiences, her voice grew hesitant, often choked, as if she didn't want to dwell on the months in Mariah's basement. At some point, they made love again and then showered in the small bathroom at the back of the house, using the soap and towel that Curtis carried in his pack. Afterward, they left the old plantation and walked across the road to the beach and caught a cab into Orangestad, where Kat was staying.

He was in dire need of a real meal, so they ate on the outdoor balcony of a restaurant that overlooked the harbor where the tourist ships docked. And it was here that they planned the specifics of what would happen once Curtis had the syringes. They set up two times and locations here on the island in 1967, separated by a day, with their fallback as Woodstock, Jerry Garcia's concert, in 1969. As soon as Woodstock was mentioned, Curtis remembered the note Bari had given him for Kat. He dug it out of his pack and handed it to her.

"From Jerry Garcia, courtesy of Bari."

"No way," she said, incredulous.

"Read it."

"You didn't peek?"

"It's to you, not me."

She quickly unfolded it and read aloud: "Hi Kat. Consider this an invitation to be my guest at Woodstock on August 16, 1969. I have no idea what Woodstock is, but Bari assures me that I will. Peace and see you then. Jerry Garcia.'" She raised her eyes. "I'm going to frame it. When this is all over and we have a life together somewhere, it's going to hang on a wall as a reminder of all this . . . this weirdness."

Curtis knew he wouldn't need a reminder.

"This is going to work, isn't it, Ryan?" She looked to be on the verge of tears.

"It'll work." He said it with more conviction than he felt. "But I need for you to describe Mariah's house—the layout, whether there's a security system, is there an attic, where's the door to the cellar, if . . ."

"I remember the drill, Ryan." She spoke softly. "In

here . . ." She tapped her temple. "It's only been several months, you know." With that point clarified, she slipped a notepad from her bag and proceeded to sketch the floor plan of Mariah's house. "There's no security system that I know of. But the outside doors, the door to the bathroom at the rear of the house, and the basement door are electronically controlled. The windows may be, too, I'm not sure. The circuit breaker is in the carport, hidden behind shelves. Even if you cut the power, though, she's got a shitload of locks on the front and back doors." She turned the sketch so he could see it, pointed with the pencil. "Right here. The rear bathroom window. I think it's the best way to get inside. Just break the glass." Her pencil moved up the paper, away from the bathroom. "This hallway takes you into the kitchen. The fridge is next to the pantry. Be sure you get the syringes on ice as soon as you can. This generation of chips apparently thaws out more quickly."

"Where's the door to the basement?" he asked.

"Inside the pantry. It looks like a wall of shelves—the back wall. If the power's off, you just have to push it inward. Are you going to take her computer equipment?"

"At the very least," he promised. "What's her class schedule like? When isn't she there?"

"I don't know what her teaching schedule is like this fall. But last spring, she used to get home by three or so and then always left right around dusk, after dinner. Maybe that's when she wreaks her havoc."

"The time displacement thing in the holding area, Kat. How's she do that?"

"It's the new chip. The ones in her freezer. SPOT would love to know about that feature. If she catches you in the house and pulls that shit, you won't be able to transition even if she doesn't restrain you. I discovered that when she took McKee and me to some cave at the dawn of time."

Curtis folded the sketch and put it in a zippered pocket in his jeans. "I guess the thing that puzzles me most is that if she can do all this—pause time, transition like none of us has ever done, interfere in replays so that the present and future are changed . . . why the hell doesn't she just go after SPOT on her own?"

Kat sat forward, fingers laced together, her expression as inscrutable as a fortune cookie. "Ryan, that's exactly what she's doing. Through us. We're her slave army. I mean, think about it. She has left me stranded. If I want to get home, I need one of her new chips to do it. *You do this for me, Kat, and I'll give you one of the new chips so you can get out of here.* With McKee, she can threaten to return him to his mess of a life in Blue River or disappear him to some horrid spot in history if he doesn't cooperate with her agenda. And with you, she promises to tell you where I am if you'll play the game her way. She has all of us over a barrel, Ryan."

Bad enough that he had spent seven years of indentured servitude to SPOT as Rodriguez's loyal foot soldier. He had no intention of signing up with Mariah Jones. "She won't when I'm done with her."

"Then there's Rodriguez. And Fenmore. And the senators. Mariah threatened to release information to every media outlet on the planet unless they shut down SPOT. She actually bragged about it to me."

"I figured as much when I ran into Fenmore and Vachinski in that botanical garden in Northampton. I think they were sent back to eliminate me and Mariah."

"That makes sense. As long as either of you are alive, you're a threat to them."

"I don't give a shit what happens to SPOT. I'm ashamed that I was ever a part of something that helps a corrupt elite stay in power, makes the rich even richer, uses torture, shreds the Constitution, and tears apart families and lovers just because some schmuck files bogus charges. And then there's the Council, five assholes on what amounts to a tribunal, who have the supreme power to decide guilt or innocence, to make and break laws as they see fit, and to sentence people anywhere in time. And as far as I know, no one has ever been judged to be innocent." His blood pressure had shot up and now his foot ached, as if to remind him just how corrupt all of it was. Loathing welled up inside of him, nearly choking off his air. "Jesus, Kat. I've got to try to make things right."

She reached across the table and covered his hand with her own. "We can do that, Ryan. We can try to bring back the people we've disappeared. We can try to undo the damage we've done. But let's deal with Mariah first."

She paused, seemed to take a deep breath, and he sensed there was more she hadn't told him. "What?" he asked. "What is it?"

She went on in a soft, halting, terrified voice. "Mariah . . . showed us the future, Ryan. Me and McKee. The stuff they taught us . . . about not being able to travel into the future, it's bullshit. You can do it. Not with the generation of chips we've been using but definitely with the ones she has. It . . . was just a glimpse, but Jesus, Ryan, it's bad. Worldwide drought, the Amazon has practically dried up, more intense hurricanes farther north because the oceans are so warm, massive flooding along the coasts because the ice at the poles is nearly gone . . . shortages of food, gas, medicines, millions of displaced people, war . . ."

"Okay," he said softly. "I get the picture."

"And it's the *near* future." She looked utterly terrified. "When we get all this straightened out, maybe we can do something constructive, do something that will . . . will make a difference, to mitigate or prevent . . . what she showed us."

Maybes and what ifs: His life always seemed to come back to that.

Shortly afterward, they left the restaurant and walked through the downtown, past duty-free shops that sold mostly imports from Holland. In a grocery store, he stocked up on supplies—and also bought three cans of lighter fluid, half a dozen dish towels, and a box of kitchen matches. Kat eyed the items, looked at him, but didn't ask. Didn't have to ask. She knew.

When they were on the street again, Curtis handed her a

wad of cash, most of his sixties stash. "Take this. So you won't be short of money. And look, it's possible that Mariah just pretended to try to transition you. I'd like to try."

"Then aim for where you left Bari's Mercedes. Because if you can do it, I'm going with you. I've got a score to settle with this bitch." She stopped, slipped her arms around his neck. "And if it doesn't work, Ryan, we know where and when to meet."

She kissed him. Curtis inhaled the sweet scent of her and *reached* for the dirty restroom in the gas station in 1968 where he had parked the Mercedes, *reached* with his love and need for Kat, *reached* with her as bright as a goddess in his mind.

And when he transitioned, he felt Kat fall away from him like an article of clothing, and emerged in the filthy restroom as alone and lonely as a refugee.

18

The brick apartment building on Green Street looked dirty, tired, and weary of winter. But then, that was how most of the brick buildings in downtown Northampton appeared to Lydia.

In its favor, though, was a courtyard through which she and Vachinski now walked. Birds swept back and forth between a feeder that hung from one of the bare trees to an empty fountain, twittering and singing and adding a touch of beauty to an otherwise oppressive atmosphere. Also in its favor was accessibility. Anyone could walk through the building's front door and into the narrow front hallway without encountering a security guard, a need for keys, or a coded card. And here in the hallways were the stairs and elevator, intercoms and mailboxes. Six mailboxes, each one labeled.

Runyon, D, Mariah's buddy, lived in apartment five.

Lydia pressed the intercom button several times, but no one answered. Same story with the intercom for apartment six. Everyone had left for school or work already. "We're clear," she said softly, and nodded toward the elevator. The emptier the third floor, the easier their job.

The elevator, a claustrophobic box no larger than her

closet, made a lot of racket as it ascended at a snail's pace and she suddenly wished they had taken the stairs. Vachinski, in typical newbie fashion, unzipped the fanny pack hanging from his belt and examined his tools with a surgeon's precision. He looked eagerly primed for action. It sort of spooked her.

He was competent enough, but more than once since their arrival early yesterday afternoon, she found herself wishing that Rodriguez were here. She preferred to travel with an experienced partner, someone who understood the delicate balance between planning and action. When she was in the mood, though, Vachinski was amusing, they enjoyed each other in bed, and so far, he still acknowledged that she was in charge.

The elevator doors opened—on the second floor rather than the third—and two teenage boys stood there, book bags slung over their shoulders, their uniforms suggesting that they attended private school. "Hey, you're hogging the elevator," said the tallest boy.

"Take the goddamn stairs," Vachinski sneered. "Lose some of that flab." He stabbed the button for the third floor and the doors clanked shut. "Little shits," he muttered.

"We could disappear them, take them someplace where they'd learn some manners," she said.

"Really?" His eyes brightened and he grinned.

"I'm joking, Hank."

"Oh." He sounded disappointed, his smile shrank, and he turned his attention back to his tools.

The temptation to use the biochip for personal gain and amusement always existed and most Travelers indulged at some point. But Vachinski had a wild, cruel edge that worried her. He would get a kick out of disappearing the two teens simply because they were smartasses.

The only time she and Rodriguez had done anything even remotely similar was in New York years back, when three young men, gang scum, had tried to roll them. They had disappeared the three to a gladiator ring in ancient Rome.

Within minutes, two of them were dead and the third was nearly trampled. When they deposited the survivor back in a New York alley, he'd run off, screaming for help and salvation and no doubt was still in a psych unit somewhere. But that was hardly the same thing as disappearing a couple of preppie teens just because they had attitudes.

The elevator doors clattered open on the empty third floor, where light spilled through the windows at either end of the hallway. Vachinski pressed the button to keep the doors open and snickered. "Now they'll *have* to take the stairs."

"Just get us into the apartment, Hank."

He picked the lock without damaging it, the door swung open, and he winked and swept his arm grandly before him. "Madam," he said. "After you."

Corny, but what the hell. She kind of liked being called madam.

The apartment, though small by twenty-first-century standards, had large, wonderful windows that admitted a lot of light, and made the place seem larger than it actually was. The hardwood floors throughout all five rooms infused the place with warmth. The scrupulous organization and tidiness was a bit anal for Lydia's taste, but it made her and Vachinski's job much easier.

"You take the bedrooms," she said.

"I was thinking we could both take the master bedroom."

"I'm flattered, Hank, but let's stay on task here."

"Yeah, yeah, whatever," he muttered, and headed down the hall toward the bedrooms.

Lydia lingered in the den, a place of imaginary sounds: the radiator hissed, the oak desk called to her, the crowded bookcases and the photos of Dee Runyon and the people in her life whispered, *Check me out.* She studied the photos, grateful that Dee or her daughter had tagged each picture with names and the dates the photos were taken. *Mom & me in Grand Cayman. Bari, Ken, & me, Jerry Garcia concert. Mariah, Mom, & me in Salem.*

Bari, Lydia thought. That would be Bari Serrano, Dee Runyon's buddy, Mariah's first human subject besides herself, and the creator of *Connections.*

She pulled out the leather chair, sat down, and started searching the drawers. The first two yielded absolutely nothing of interest. But the third drawer was locked, always a hopeful sign. Lydia jimmied it with a tool from her own supply of twenty-first-century wonders, slid it open—and instantly felt an insidious, shuddering horror. Hidden under an address book and a small paper bag filled with pot were a PDA and a cell phone.

In 1968.

She picked up the cell, turned it on. The background photo was of Bari Serrano—and Jake McKee.

Fuck. This is bad. It has to be bad. It's definitely bad. She clicked through the menus and felt like puking. Every number listed in the phone book was one that she recognized— her home and cell, Rodriguez's cell, and multiple phone numbers for every member of the Council, every mentor, Traveler, and recruit.

On the PDA, she found more photos—of McKee and Bari, of Mariah with Bari, of Mariah with Dee Runyon and her teenage daughter, Kim. The address book listed home addresses for everyone who was anyone in SPOT, and included e-mail addresses and phone numbers for Alex Kincaid, the McKees, Senators Aiken and Lazier, and URLs for the major news outlets and political blogs in the twenty-first century.

Shaken, Lydia put the PDA and the cell in her bag, shut the drawers, and pressed the heels of her hands against her eyes. *What's this mean?* Mariah hadn't done this randomly, she obviously had a plan. But what?

Think, think.

She sat back, smoothed her hands over her jeans, struggled to calm down, to reason it out. Despite the apparent madness of Mariah's schemes, Lydia knew there was always a cool, calculating mind behind everything she did, every decision she made. Or at least there used to be.

Bari, what had Mariah told her about Bari? Lydia recalled that shortly after Mariah had recruited her for SPOT in 1974, she'd told her how the chip had cured Bari's insomnia. Lydia had suggested that she recruit Bari for SPOT, since she was chipped already, but Mariah explained she wouldn't make a good candidate. She was too focused on her writing, too close to her old man, and had gotten married two years earlier to one of the producers on *Connections*. She never knew about the side effects of the chip.

But she disappears McKee and Kat, brings him here, in-troduces him to screenwriter Bari . . . Why? Why would Mariah do that that? Did it mean Bari wouldn't marry the producer?

She and Mariah had watched *Connections* during its fifth season, she remembered, because it was a time-travel adventure. In fact, Mariah had made it mandatory for all the early recruits. And later on, Lydia had watched it in reruns in the late 1980s with her youngest daughter. She never had understood its popularity.

Yet, intuitively, she felt that Bari and her TV series were key to all this.

She quickly retrieved the cell and the PDA and went through them more carefully, looking for Bari Serrano's ad-dress or phone number. Two addresses were listed—in Utica, New York, and in LA—and four phone numbers. She picked up the receiver of the old-fashioned black dial phone, dialed one of the Utica numbers. Caller ID hadn't been in-vented yet, so she didn't have to worry about Bari knowing where she was calling from.

Three rings, then: "Charles Ovis."

"Hi, is Bari there?"

"No, she's out of town."

"This is a friend of hers from LA, Mr. Ovis. I'm going to be in town and really wanted to see her. Is there another number where I can reach her?"

"Try one of these," he said, and reeled off two numbers.

Lydia jotted them down, thanked him, and hung up before he could ask her name.

The first number matched Dee Runyon's and the other matched one of the three listed for Bari, in a different area code. Lydia dialed the operator and reached a live person almost immediately. "Operator," the woman said.

"I have a number for which I need an address."

"The number, ma'am?"

Lydia ticked it off.

"I'm checking, just a moment, please." Then, finally: "The only address listed for this number is Rural Road Two, Old Forge, New York."

"Thanks. That'll do."

How beautifully simple some things were in this time, she thought, and began searching the Word files on the PDA from her time. A file labeled *grades* was exactly what the name implied. *Roster 205* was a list of Mariah's registered students for a sophomore botany class. And on it went through a dozen files until she clicked on one labeled *Numbers*. Here, she found summaries of all sixty episodes of *Connections*, with an asterisk next to episodes 4, 13, 25, 37, 48, and 59.

Why? Why those episodes? What's it mean?

The *Connections* pilot she remembered involved a group of time travelers from the distant future—2151 or something—who traveled back to the Sixties to interbreed with the locals because nearly all humans on their timeline were sterile and humanity was dying out. But the pilot summary she read on the PDA didn't have the faintest resemblance to her memory. *When Jim Danforth is arrested for crimes he didn't commit and subsequently disappears, his wife, Eva, is plunged into a search that leads her into the heart of a shadow government that holds the secret of time travel.*

Lydia clicked on the summary for the second episode, the third, fourth, fifth and with each one, her despair deepened and the pieces of Mariah's brilliant scheme, her grand design, fell into place. She suspected that if she had Internet access right now, she could look up this series and discover that even these episodes would be changing as rapidly as events in real time changed. Mariah had gone back to the source year, 1968, when her first human experimentation was already underway, when Bari Serrano was working on her pilot, and had introduced Jake McKee into the equation. And that, Lydia thought, had changed everything.

It had sent Bari's series in a new direction, describing the events that had begun on October 27, 2006, and continued right now. It had ripped Kat away from Curtis, turning him into a rogue agent; had sent Nora McKee and Kincaid on the run; brought the senators to the Cedar Key facility; and even changed her relationship with Rodriguez. After all, if none of this had happened, she and Vachinski wouldn't be here and she never would have slept with him.

Bile surged in her throat, she pressed her knuckles into her eyes, and struggled to contain her mounting panic. In essence, Mariah had created a new timeline, something Lydia hadn't believe possible, at least not in a tangible, verifiable way.

And in doing so, Mariah had practically assured the destruction of SPOT, the very organization her invention had helped to create.

Vachinski suddenly appeared, practically skidding into the den. "Lydia. Someone's at the front door," he hissed. "I heard the jingle of keys."

"Jesus, what impeccable timing." Lydia dropped the cell and PDA back into her bag and shot to her feet.

They made a beeline for the living room. Vachinski stood to the left of the front door, so he could shut and lock it as soon as the person entered, and Lydia ducked behind the door in the kitchen, where the only other entrance to the apartment was located.

Through the crack, she saw the front door open. A willowy teenage girl entered. Kim Runyon. Lydia recognized her from the photos. She moved with quick, impatient determination, making it clear that she had places to go, people to see, things to do. A typical self-absorbed teen. A book bag hung from her shoulder, she had a bag of groceries in her arms. In person, she looked even more exotic than her photos—her light chocolate skin testimony to mixed parentage. Right behind her hurried mom, a Caribbean beauty who wore lots of flashy jewelry and carried two more bags of groceries.

"Kim, honey, can you put that bag on the kitchen table?"

"That's where I'm headed, Mom."

She hastened into the kitchen, her mother moving along in her slipstream, asking all the usual single-parent questions. How many exams did she have tomorrow and was she prepared for them and where did she want to go for spring break? And then Lydia stepped out and said, "Sit down and shut up. If either of you makes a sound, I'll shoot the other."

Mother and daughter whipped around, eyes wide, terrified. Dee dropped her bags of groceries. The bottoms split open and pieces of fruit rolled across the floor, a package of spaghetti popped open, a jar shattered, spewing sauce the color of blood across the floor. "What . . . who . . ." she stammered.

"You heard her, Ms. Runyon." Vachinski, standing in the kitchen doorway, spoke in a low, menacing voice, his weapon trained on Kim. "Sit the fuck down. You, too, kid."

Kim looked helplessly at her mother, who stammered, "Just . . . just do what they say, honey." Dee, sitting down now, pushed her purse across the table. "The money's in there. Just take it. Please don't hurt us."

"This isn't about money, Ms. Runyon, and no one's going to get hurt as long as you answer our questions." Lydia brought out the cell phone and PDA and set them on the table. "Where did you get these?"

"I . . . you had no right to . . . ."

"Answer the goddamn question." Vachinski moved across the room at the speed of light and pressed the muzzle of his nine millimeter into Kim's cheek. "It would be tragic, Ms. Runyon, to blow apart your daughter's beautiful face."

"Please," she whispered, her voice anguished. "I'll tell you whatever you want to know. Just don't hurt her."

"Then let's try again," Lydia continued smoothly. "Where did you get these items?"

"From Mariah. Mariah Jones. Kim is taking an advanced class with her. I . . . she . . . asked me . . . to keep them for her."

"Do you know what they are?"

"A cell phone and a . . . a PDA."

"And what else do you know about them?"

Tears now rolled down her cheeks; her mascara was smudging. Kim reached across the table and grasped her mother's hand. Dee blinked, said, "That in 1968, they haven't been invented yet."

"For chrissakes," Vachinski barked impatiently, and flung his arm around Kim's neck and brought the muzzle of his gun against her throat. "Get to the bottom line."

Shudders tore through the kid as she sobbed. Dee begged, "My God, please . . . please . . ."

"Talk fast," Vachinski said, softly, cocking his head to one side, eyes widening, as if he were making fun of Dee's fear.

"I know . . . about the chip . . ." Stammering now, stumbling over her own words, her dark eyes flicked from Kim to Vachinski to Lydia. "I know what . . . what it does. Who Mariah is. About your time travel unit. . . . That's who you are. With that unit in the twenty-first century, the one Mariah helped to create. Is that . . . that what you want to hear?"

"Now we're making progress," Lydia said, and touched Vachinski's shoulder. "Back off, Hank. She's getting the idea now."

But Vachinski, ignoring Lydia, leaned forward, over the girl, and ran his mouth slowly over the top of her head, as though he were tasting and smelling her hair. Then his mouth moved down the curve of her neck, and across her right cheek, every caress languid, deliberate, revolting.

Lydia suddenly felt as if she were peering into the darkest pockets of Vachinski's soul. *This is who I really am*, his small, secret smile whispered as he stepped back. *I like young girls.*

Her disgust at herself for having slept with this pervert, for having betrayed Rodriguez in this way, was nearly too great to bear. She just wanted to get out of here, stand under a long, hot shower, and then disappear Vachinski to some very distant era. But she didn't even have that option because he was chipped.

Kim pressed her head into her folded arms and fought back her sobs. Dee looked homicidal.

"And where is Mariah now?" Lydia finally asked.

Dee glared accusingly at Lydia, making it abundantly clear that she had seen Lydia's disgust and that her complicit silence now made her just as guilty of perversion as Vachinski. Dee swallowed hard, forced herself to breathe through her anger, as if she had been trained in such techniques, and managed to exert enough control to say, "Out of town."

"Out of town or elsewhere in time?"

"Gone, she's gone, I don't know where the hell she went, she doesn't tell me everything, she just asked me to hold on to those devices and . . . and to . . . to advise her classes that they were supposed to work on their independent study projects. That's all I know, I swear, that's all I know." She swiped her hand across her cheek and leaned toward her daughter, running her hand over Kim's bowed head.

"When will she be back? Why'd she leave?"

"I don't know. She didn't say."

Vachinski moved toward the girl again and Dee shrieked, *"I don't know and that's the goddamn truth. Keep that monster away from my daughter."*

Lydia grabbed Vachinski's arm, jerking him back, and his head snapped toward her, eyes narrowed, poisoned, enraged. Then, just as quickly, the rage and poison vanished, and he said, "Okay, okay, calm down, Lydia." As though she were the one approaching meltdown.

She went over to Dee and struck her across the face,

cracking open her lip. "Don't scream like that again." She whipped a dish towel off the rack and tossed it at her. "You're bleeding. One more thing. What's Mariah's address here in town?"

Dee held the towel to her lip, her eyes filled with pain, regret, contempt, rage. "And I suppose once I tell you where she lives, you'll shoot us."

"And we'll start right here," Vachinski said, and pressed his gun against the top of Kim's head. "The address, Ms. Runyon."

"It's . . ."

"Don't tell them, Mom," Kim sobbed. "Don't . . ."

"Shut up." Vachinski rapped his knuckles against Kim's temple, then shoved her head forward, into her arms. "And keep your goddamn head down."

Dee spat out the address and while Vachinski kept his weapon pressed up against the back of Kim's head, Lydia scribbled the address on a notepad. Then she scooped up the cell, the PDA, shoved them into her pack, and brought out a roll of duct tape and several pairs of handcuffs.

"It's a mistake to leave them here," Vachinski said. "We need to disappear them."

"We're not here for that." The sharpness in her voice, the don't-fuck-with-me edge, shut him up. She tore off several lengths of duct tape, pressed the ends to the edge of the table. "Do you know who I am, Ms. Runyon?"

"You're a . . . fucking monster," she hissed. "Just like him."

Yes, I am, she thought. *But not quite as bad as Vachinski.* "Do you know have any idea what Mariah has gotten you involved in?"

"You're . . . you're Lydia Fenmore. Mariah's first recruit for the time travel program."

"Wow, I'm impressed. Really. It's good to know that Mariah felt the need to confide in someone. It makes her, well, more human. And do you know that Mariah has threatened our programs with extinction? Did she tell you that?"

"She never tells anyone everything. She just drops hints, bits and pieces, here and there."

Lydia gestured for Kim to get up, to go over to the fridge, and sit on the floor. "Sounds just like her. I had a certain fondness and respect for Mariah up until she screwed things up by disappearing Kat Sargent and Jake McKee. I already know that you've met McKee, I saw the pictures on the cell, the PDA. But did you meet Kat?"

Dee shook her head. She seemed incapable of speech now, the cords in her neck standing out as she watched her daughter negotiating the spilled tomato sauce, food, and fruit. Kim, struggling to control her sobs, sat on the floor, back to the fridge.

"Is that a yes or a no?" Lydia asked.

"No," Dee whispered. "I never met her."

"Where did you think McKee came from?"

"I . . . he . . . was one of her insomnia subjects, that's what I thought."

"Tell me about Bari's home in Old Forge. How do I get there?"

"I've . . . never been there. I just know it's on a rural road north of town . . . on a river."

Lydia pressed a length of tape across Kim's mouth, then pulled her arms behind her and wrapped her wrists in tape and cuffed them, too, for good measure. She finally wrapped duct tape around Kim's ankles. The girl hiccupped, her sobs ebbing, horror pooled in her eyes, eyes that begged her mother to do something, to help her. Lydia sympathized, she really did. As a mother herself, she understood that the connection never left you—not at eighteen, not at twenty-one, not at any age.

"How did McKee meet Bari?" Lydia secured each of Dee's legs to the legs of the chair in which she sat, then pulled her arms behind the chair and cuffed them. "Do you know?"

"Bari . . . got chipped. For her insomnia. She met Jake . . . at Mariah's."

"Ah, Mariah, matchmaker." But always with a plan in mind,

a grand design, a scheme. "And tell me about Bari's script, Dee. Tell me about *Connections*."

"She doesn't talk about . . . about what she's writing. She's never mentioned a title . . . I . . ."

"C'mon, you're telling me you never looked at the files on the PDA?"

"She asked me to hold on to those things. I don't have a clue about how to use them."

"Right." Vachinski laughed. "And if you believe *that*, Lydia, I've got property to sell you in ancient Greece."

She ignored Vachinski and pressed the last piece of tape across Dee's mouth, then leaned in close to her face. "When you see Mariah again, please give her my regards. And if I were you, I wouldn't do her any more favors. You're in deep shit as it is, Dee. While I feel pretty confident that a friend or coworker will find you two before you starve or die of thirst, we can never be entirely sure, can we?" She patted her cheek lightly, a matronly pat, then straightened up and glanced at Vachinski. "We're done here, Hank."

"Too bad," he murmured, and glanced at Kim with a certain longing that opened a hole a mile wide in Lydia's stomach.

Before they left, Vachinski locked the kitchen door, scooped up one of the fallen apples from the floor, rubbed it against his shirt, and bit into it. Neither of them spoke until they were in the elevator, on their way down.

"So how long have you had this lust for young girls, Hank?"

He made a face and looked at her as if she were nuts. "What're you talking about?"

"That disgusting display with the kid."

He laughed and shook his head. "C'mon, that was for effect."

"Really. For effect. It sure seemed that you were having a whale of a good time, licking her neck and shit."

"I didn't lick her goddamn neck."

"And sniffing her skin."

"You're nuts," he muttered.

"I know what I saw." *And you, pervert, are now out of this game.* At the same moment that she pressed the elevator's STOP button, she slammed her left elbow upward, into Vachinski's throat, and he stumbled back, into the wall of the elevator, gasping for air, eyes wide with shock. She grabbed his arm and *reached* for the medical building on Cedar Key, in her own time, *reached* with such a deep need and desire that the transition was quick, smooth, flawless. It happened so fast that Vachinski was still clutching his throat, struggling to breathe when they emerged in an examining room in SPOT's clinic.

Lydia spun around and kneed Vachinski in the balls, swung her pack at his head, and he sank to the floor, wheezing, gasping, moaning. Seconds, she knew she had only seconds before he tried to transition, so she cuffed him to the leg of the examining table, a stainless-steel structure soldered to the floor. It would be impossible for him to escape from the cuffs, and therefore impossible for him to transition.

Lydia backed away from him, breathing hard, tendons in her shoulders shrieking, the years of her inactivity now glaringly apparent. She groped behind her for the knob, turned it, backed into the hall, shut the door, and threw the dead bolt.

She had tricks he didn't know about. Pervert.

You're a monster, like him.

Was she?

"Hey, excuse me," someone shouted. "You're not allowed to be in here."

Lydia turned, the nurse who had shouted recognized her. "Oh, Ms. Fenmore. I'm sorry, I didn't . . ."

"Get Dr. Berlin. Fast."

"I'm not sure he's on duty right . . ."

"Find him. Tell him it's urgent. And no one goes into that examining room until he gets here. Dr. Berlin needs to bring a sedative. Understood?"

"Uh, yes, ma'am. Of course."

As the nurse went to a wall phone to page Berlin, Lydia felt as if she held a crushing weight against her shoulders and collapsed into the nearest chair. She shed her heavy jacket and sweater and ripped off her shoes and socks. She was still sitting there ten minutes later when Berlin hastened up the hall.

"Lydia, are you okay?" he asked anxiously.

"The problem is in there." She stabbed a thumb toward the closed door. "It's Vachinski. You need to remove his chip. As of right now, he's out of the program. Once you've removed his chip, call security and have him taken to Snake Island. What day is it, Doc?"

"October thirtieth, just before eight a.m."

Forty hours left until Mariah's deadline, she thought. "Have they shut down Snake Island yet?"

"I'm not in that loop, Lydia. I've been so busy around here trying to pack stuff and make medical look like it's shut down that I don't know what's going on in the other departments. Also, there was a security breach early this morning and that sped up everything."

"Who was it?"

"I don't know. Like I said, I'm not in that loop. You'll have to ask Ian."

She pushed to her feet, touched Berlin's arm. "How many chips can you spare?" She was going to need help, a lot of it. A small army. "Or do you even have any to spare?"

His eyes, usually so unnaturally wide because of his contacts, now narrowed and focused at something over her shoulder. He seemed to be avoiding looking at her. *Like he's guilty of something.* She was too worn out at the moment to puzzle through it.

"I've got two boxes here on site. The rest were shipped to a secure location."

"Two boxes. That's twelve?"

"Right."

"I'd like them all."

"They're all defective, Lydia. We still haven't figured out the problem."

"I want them."

He nodded. "Okay. As soon as I've got Vachinski's chip out, I'll give you a call and you can pick up the boxes. And, Lydia, Ian had left instructions that I was to call him if you showed up. So I went ahead and did so. He said he'd meet you out front. He's on his way over."

"Thanks, I appreciate it."

As soon as she left the medical building and stepped into the warm morning light, a strange, sudden panic seized her. It was as if she were watching a car speeding up behind her at a stoplight, knew that it wouldn't brake in time, and that she couldn't move far enough to the left or right to avoid a collision. She wanted to bolt, flee, transition back to Northampton immediately. She knew where Mariah lived, where Bari lived, she was armed, she could finish this job herself. But in her heart, she knew that she couldn't. Alone, she was no match for Mariah.

And then a dark SUV pulled up, Rodriguez got out, and the decision was made for her. He hurried over, eyes anxious, face eaten up with worry, and hugged her hello. He pulled back, and ran his thumbs over either side of her face, his eyes searching hers. "How bad?" he asked.

"Worse than we imagined."

"Here, too. Aiken and Lazier have taken over, a committee has been appointed."

A takeover was inevitable, she thought, and looked past Rodriguez's shoulder, to the SUV. Aiken was in the passenger seat, his plump face glistening in the morning light, and Lazier sat behind the wheel. Her loathing of these two men surged. "Berlin said there was a security breach yesterday morning. Was it Mariah?"

"I'll tell you about it later. What did you find out?"

"That we need to go back with between six to twelve people. You, me, and four to ten officers from Freeze. There will be two different locations—Northampton and Old Forge. It's the only way to prevent the damage she's going to do."

"You won't have a tough time selling them on the idea."

"And Ian, we need all the episodes of *Connections*. And if we can't get all of them, we need episodes four, thirteen, twenty-five, thirty-seven, forty-nine, and fifty-nine. And we need them yesterday."

His expression just then was unreadable, something that hadn't happened much in their long history. "Joe Aiken got them. But how did you . . ."

"Those episodes are . . ." What? What were they? Clues? But to what? Her head ached, the sun hurt her eyes, the heat reminded her of open fields and lazy summer days. She still wanted to flee, to grasp Rodriguez's shoulder and transition. And then right brain grabbed left and the two merged and she grasped it, the truth—as ephemeral as a dream. "Those episodes are where we can change the outcome."

Horror flooded his eyes. "I think things are changing already. The intruders were Nora McKee and Alex Kincaid."

She opened her mouth—to speak, exclaim, scream, she didn't know—and blood streamed down over her lips and into her mouth. Her body was rejecting the chip. An image exploded in her head of that hideous bloated tick thing, floating in the toilet while Rodriguez bled and retched and she suddenly clawed at her nose and shrieked, *"Get it out, Ian, get it out,"* and her eyes rolled back in her head and blackness claimed her.

The Longest Distance

Time is the longest distance between two places.
—Tennessee Williams

There ain't no answer.
There ain't gonna be any answer.
There never has been an answer.
That's the answer.
—Gertrude Stein

19

Once they crossed the Massachusetts state line, Nora dozed off, only to be jarred awake some time later when the bus slammed into a pothole. They had left the highway and were bouncing through a wooded area where leafless trees rose on either side of them, their branches varying shades of gray and brown, a patchwork quilt devoid of color. Dry brush scratched like hungry mice against the sides of the old bus.

"Bathroom stop?" she asked.

"Theory stop. It won't take long."

Sunny, anticipating a chance to romp, stuck her head between the seats and barked, as if asking how much farther, anyway? Half a mile later, Kincaid stopped the bus and they all got out. Sunny trotted off, nose to the ground, and Nora and Kincaid stood there, watching her like parents keeping an eye on a rambunctious child.

"So what's the theory?" she asked.

"Suppose Sunny is chipped?"

"Why would you think that?"

"Partly because of the way you found her. Or that she found you. But also because I remember reading on one of the conspiracy blogs that the government used the chip in animal experiments."

"That theory's pretty far-fetched. It means she would be . . . what? Thirty or forty years old?" Nora shook her head. "I can't buy it."

"You don't have to." Kincaid paced now, hands jammed in the pockets of his jacket, his voice thick with excitement. "Just bear with me, okay? Back at the campground, you and I were off our target by a year. Sunny didn't have any say in where we went. She was just along for the ride. But suppose we engage her? Suppose we let her target the time and place?"

Nora thought he was joking and laughed. "C'mon, Alex. She's a *dog*. She doesn't understand much of what we say."

"Oh, I think she understands most of what we say and I'd bet the farm that she understands *home*."

As in, *ET call home*? "Whatever. Let's try it." She whistled for Sunny and the retriever did a one-eighty and loped back toward them. Nora handed her a treat, praising her for being such a good dog, then she and Kincaid pulled their packs on and sat in the open side doorway. Sunny jumped up between them, tail wagging.

"With a little luck and some help from our friend here," Kincaid said, stroking Sunny, "maybe we can make some headway."

Jake had once said that he believed each person was born with a certain quota of luck, like a cat with nine lives, and when you used up the quota, that was it. You were in for dark times. It had struck her then, as now, as morbidly fatalistic, but if true, she figured she and Kincaid had used up the equivalent of eight lives of luck.

They clasped each other's hands and rested their free hands on Sunny's back. "Home, Sunny," Kincaid said softly. "Take us home."

Sunny's head snapped up, her ears twitched, the fur on her back stood up. She looked at Kincaid, then at Nora, who said, "You know that word, Sunny? *Home*?"

Her tail thumped against the floor, she barked, and she

nudged Nora and then Kincaid with her nose. But nothing happened. They were still sitting in the open doorway.

"Maybe we need to help by silently repeating *home* to ourselves," Kincaid said.

"But we'll be thinking of our version of home."

"True." He thought a moment. "What are we, Nora? What have we become?"

"What?"

His index finger made a circle in the air in front of his face, then picked up more and more speed until it was just a blur. "Watch my finger and imagine the circle it makes as a spinning light—blue collapsing into red, then into green, yellow . . ."

Like a ride at Disney World, she thought, and suddenly snapped her fingers. "We're light chasers."

"Exactly." He laughed. "We're chasing the light of other times. And that's how we have to imagine this. We don't *empty* our minds when we attempt to move back in time. We *fill* our minds with this image, the blurring, spinning river of light."

Light also meant illumination, making the invisible visible. With light, there could be no shadows, no darkness, nothing hidden. She equated light with truth. Yes, this image worked for her. They sat, still and silent, filling their minds with the spinning light, for what seemed like a very long time. The longer she sat there, the more she felt like a kid who wished she could fly and believed that hoping would make it so. And just when she was about ready to pack it in and suggest they get back on the road, she felt an unbearable pressure in her skull, as if a giant had seized the sides of her head and squeezed with shocking strength to pop her brain out through her crown, like pus from a pimple.

The pressure surged and then spread, a fire that shot up through her nose, raced across her forehead, sped down the back of her skull, dug into her neck and shoulders, and ate the flesh from her cheeks. She gasped, her eyes snapped open into blackness, every muscle in her body shrieked for her to leap up, to run. But a paralysis gripped her, she was blind, deaf, lost. Then the excruciating pressure blew off the top of her head, freeing her, releasing her, and the next thing she knew, she was on her hands and knees, wheezing like an asthmatic.

It was dark, a cool breeze caressed her face, she smelled ocean. But this wasn't the air of Blue River or even of Massachusetts, of that much she was certain. Her hands and knees were pressed against asphalt that still held the heat of the day, the air was too warm for her heavy jacket and wool socks. *Kincaid's theory is right.* But where was she? And where were the dog and Kincaid?

When Nora rocked back onto her heels and looked around, a ripple of shock shuddered through her. An airstrip. She was on an airstrip lined with pale blue landing lights and buildings rising on either side of it; windows here and there were lit up.

She heard shoes slapping pavement and glanced around. Kincaid and the dog loped toward her through the starlight, the dog in the lead. Nora stood, her legs shaky, as if she'd been pedaling a bike for hours, and started toward them. The dog shot past her and Kincaid, barely slowing down, just grabbed her hand, jerking her to her feet, and pulling her after him. "Someone's coming," he hissed urgently.

Off to her left, headlights bobbed through the darkness like luminous moths, but she didn't hear an engine. Had they been seen?

They crashed through some low brush, following Sunny, who seemed to know where she was going and what she was doing. Nora's pack felt heavy against her back, her knees ached, her heart hammered so hard she was sure it could be heard in the quiet. They stumbled up a beach dune, through a field of sea oats, then slid down the other side and dived for the ground.

Flattened out against cool sand as white as spun sugar, cheeks sinking into it, she and Kincaid looked at each other, his face only inches from hers. "You think this is Sunny's home?" she whispered.

"It's sure not ours."

Nora turned her head, lifted up slightly. Sunny was flattened out just in front of her, peering through the sea oats, growling softly. "Ssshh." Nora slid her fingers into the dog's fur.

The headlights belonged to an electric cart, the kind she imagined that old guys on golf courses drove. Four people inside. They were too far away and there wasn't enough light for her to see their faces. The cart turned toward one of the buildings on the dune side of the airstrip and parked on the front sidewalk. All four passengers got out, two men and two women. Sunny started growling again, not loudly enough for the others to hear her, but enough to communicate her distress.

The group went inside the building and Nora and Kincaid remained still for another few minutes, waiting to see if they would come back out. She finally sat up, shrugged off her pack, brought out her cell phone. Kincaid also brought out his PDA. Both devices had signals—and dates—*October 30, 2006, 1:02 A.M.*

A thrill swept through her, followed instantly by incredulity, and then rage. This technology had existed for decades, folded in secrecy, buried in black-ops budgets, a dark force that disappeared people who disagreed with the official government version of reality. It enabled the powerful to retain their power, the rich got richer, and so what if it ripped families apart and forever scarred them. They were collateral damage, nothing more.

"I'm going to get the GPS on this thing working," Kincaid whispered. "So we'll know where we are. Call Tyler."

"Can you download the *Connection* episode summaries, too?"

"I'm on it."

She quickly punched in the secure number Tyler had

given her. It rang half a dozen times before he picked up, his voice thick with sleep. "Yes? Hello?"

"Tyler, it's me."

"Nora. My God. Where the hell are you? What happened? Are you okay?"

"It's so good to hear you," she whispered, her voice thick with emotion. "Are you and Di okay?"

"We're good, we're fine, we're in North Carolina, we were forced to head south. But what happened? Where're you and Alex? The two of you and the dog just . . . disappeared."

She had to explain this in fifty words or less. "We went back in time. That's what the whole thing's about. A special unit in Freeze that disappears people into the past."

"*Time travel?* That thing in Alex's nose?"

"Yes."

"Holy crap, Nora. Does that mean that Mom . . ."

"I think so. Look, I don't know where we are, but as soon as I do, I'll call you back. We're going to take these bastards down."

Kincaid interrupted her. "We're on Cedar Key, Florida's west coast, maybe fifty miles from Gainesville, on the Gulf of Mexico. Tell him that."

She passed on the information to Tyler. "We'll send you the image from the GPS so you can find out what's here. We're on an airstrip. I'll call you back as soon as we know more."

"Stay safe," her brother said.

Kincaid e-mailed the image to Tyler and started the download of episode summaries for *Connections*. Sunny growled softly again and Nora crawled up next to her and peered out through the sea oats. The electric cart was on the move once more, headed away from the building, back up the airstrip. She, Kincaid, and the dog crawled farther down the beach and when the cart was out of sight, they stood and hurried forward, hunkered over, along the edge of the water.

The tall sea oats formed an effective barrier between them and the runway, yet they were fully exposed to the marina and the water beyond it. But the marina looked deserted—just a single light burned at the end of the pier and no one seemed to be around. She didn't see any boats, either.

Nora removed her jacket and sweatshirt and tied them around her waist. Sunny kept her nose to the ground, following a scent, perhaps sniffing her way through memories. They reached the end of the airstrip. Sunny hesitated, then suddenly loped ahead, toward the far side of the runway.

The buildings were wooden, old, most of them with wide porches, and looked like they had once been two-story homes. They followed the dog around to the back, where moonlight glinted off a large body of water, the Gulf, she thought. Behind the second house, Sunny stopped, raised her head, sniffed at the air. Lost? Getting her bearings? Then she kept on trotting forward. Behind the third house, she growled again and moved warily up the steps of a long, wide porch. Adirondack chairs in various pastel shades lined the wall on both sides of the double doors.

No lights back here, just the milky cast of the stars. It was so quiet that their footfalls on the wooden porch sounded preternaturally loud. The door and windows were locked, but Kincaid had his handy pick and went to work. In sixty seconds, the lock clicked, the door swung open.

"You're going to have to teach me how to do that," she whispered.

"Add it to the list."

"Of . . . ?"

"Things we'll do together."

She loved the sound of that.

They followed Sunny through the door. Flashlights aimed at the floor, they made their way through what looked like an office lobby and now Sunny dropped back, hugging Kincaid's side. She kept growling. Along the hall on the other side were several nicely decorated offices that looked like they should be inhabited by well-heeled attorneys or stockbrokers. They ducked into two of them, looking for a computer or something else that would identify what kind of work was done here. But there were no PCs, not a laptop in sight. She guessed the employees took their wireless laptops home at night.

The largest office had what they were looking for—a PC. "I'll check it out," Kincaid whispered. "See what else is in here."

Sunny waited in the doorway, their sentry.

"Alex, did you feel that excruciating pressure in your head?"

"Yeah. So that'll be our warning. If one of us feels it, we immediately go look for each other. And for Sunny."

Nora went over to the small fridge first, opened it. Bottled water. Definitely her home time. "Alex, catch," she said softly, and tossed a bottle to him. His arm shot up, he caught it, turned back to the computer.

She stuffed six bottles and a couple of apples into her pack, then moved along one wall of books, her fingers trailing across the spines. Many of the books appeared to be history tomes that covered specific eras: the culture of Elizabethan England, a day in the life of the ancient Anasazi, the Roaring Twenties, weapons in the Civil War, the Vietnam War, a timeline of World War II, life in ancient Greece, the Salem witch trials. Those were just the ones that leaped out at her.

The third wall was a visual gallery of many different eras, sketches, paintings, even photographs of historical details—weapons, fashion, cars, hairstyles, soda cans, money, animal and plant life. There were even some grainy photos of people from various eras—women in hats and long dresses on a Manhattan street in what looked like the 1800s, men hanging from the sides of a San Francisco trolley, probably around 1900, and a very strange picture of a rocky road lined with wooden crosses, several with bodies on them. No date on that one, but the closer Nora looked, the creepier she felt. It looked like an actual photo from around the time of Christ.

When there were no cameras.

When a photographic image wasn't even an idea in anyone's head.

She lifted the photo off the wall to study it more closely—and exposed a small, round disk that resembled a doorbell. Security? Or something else? Why would a security button be located here? She believed this fell into the *something else* category and pressed it.

The bookcase closest to her began to move, to open inward, like something from an outdated movie. It was so hokey she nearly laughed aloud. But when she shone her flashlight through the wide open door, her amusement died. She walked into a huge room crowded with so much clothing and *stuff* that she couldn't see the opposite wall. She felt for a light switch, flicked it—and a pall of unreality seized her.

Rack after rack of period clothing filled one side of the room; the other side held dozens of shelves filled with what could only be described as the props equivalent of Pham's Market, ant farms to zit zappers for more historical eras than she knew existed. Nora dug out her digital camera and started taking photos.

Whoever was in charge of this room was admirably organized, with each section labeled by millennium, century, half century, quarter century, and then further categorized by geographic location. She marveled at robes from Jerusalem in 35 A.D., at a woman's corset and petticoats from England in the time of Jack the Ripper, at a box of Havana cigars from Cuba, circa 1944, at a car radio from 1951. It was as if she had stumbled into the paragon of make-believe, the holodeck on the Starship *Enterprise*.

She took half a dozen photos of the immediate area, then stopped in front of a handsome mahogany dresser with several dozen drawers, each labeled by decade. She opened *1940s*. Inside, she found a wad of cash and some loose change from the era, costume jewelry, hairpins, combs, brushes, makeup, writing utensils, paper, the accoutrements of daily life. She ran her fingers over the items, wondering who they had belonged to, how they had come to be here, what their histories were.

Nora slid out the drawer labeled *1960s*, plucked out the cash, rolled off the rubber band. Mostly small bills, ones, fives, with tens and twenties tossed in. It amounted to $92, a windfall. Nora stuck the bills in the pockets of her jeans and opened the drawers labeled *1940s* and *1950s* and took the cash from these, too. Anything before 1968, she thought, was probably legit.

Larger items were stored back here, each with an explanatory note fixed to it. The high-wheeled bicycle from 1870 was the first metal bike and during the 1890s it was the newest trend among young men with money. To Nora, it looked like something that would be used in a circus act. The sewing machine from 1925 was invented by a French tailor and used only a single thread and a hooked needle. A GE toaster from 1909 had just one heating element and had to be turned by hand. The refrigerator from 1925 was the first that was hermetically sealed. And on and on, one item and description after another.

She could just imagine the time travelers in training traipsing through here, being coached on a particular era. Were there experts among them, people who specialized in one decade or period of history? And how much did all this cost? *Your tax dollars at work.*

As she took more photos, Kincaid and Sunny came in. He stopped, his face the color of old bread, eyes darting around, taking it all in. "Holy shit," he breathed. "The props and costume department."

"It's . . ." She couldn't find the right adjective for whatever this place was. Shocking? Astonishing? Shameful? Wasteful? What? She finally just shook her head. "You think every building along the airstrip has a room like this?"

"Probably. This place is definitely their headquarters, Nora. I got great info from the computer and sent a text to Tyler, telling him to get his butt down here. I even found him a hotel downtown. " He wagged a memory stick. "Here's a partial inventory of what props and costumes went where and with whom for the last thirty years."

Before she could say anything, an alarm cried. She and Kincaid looked at each other, neither of them moving, then both of them moving at once, lurching for the door. Sunny shot past them at the speed of light.

Nora skidded into the hallway, headed for the porch door. The window that faced the airstrip suddenly blazed like high noon, the brilliant light spilled across the floor. Apparently the alarm had triggered every security light on every building along the airstrip.

As they crashed through the porch door, two men raced around the corner of the building, shouting, *"Stop where you are!"*

And when they didn't stop, the men opened fire.

They zigzagged toward the moonstruck water, the men right behind them, and raced into a clump of gnarled trees that leaned in the direction the wind usually blew. Kincaid pulled out his weapon and when the men came into view, he started firing. One of them went down; the other dived for the ground. Kincaid motioned for her to keep running. "Head into those mangroves."

"Leaving you here? Not a chance." She brought out the gun he'd given her, slammed in a clip, and when the bastard on the ground started firing again, she and Kincaid retaliated. She emptied her clip, popped in another, and she and Kincaid raced for the mangroves, the dog leagues ahead of them.

The searchlights of an approaching chopper swept across the trees and the beach in undulating waves that exposed everything in glaring relief. She didn't see anything that could save them—no boat, car, electric cart, horse, no marvelous trick of the chip that Kincaid had pulled in Wood's Hole. Time didn't screech into slow motion. If anything, it seemed to speed up, everything around her pulsating, pounding like a heart clogged with cholesterol.

They raced into the mangroves, splashing through water that rose to their knees, then their thighs. The tightly braided branches snagged in Nora's hair, clawed at the back of her shirt, caught on her sweatshirt. She tried to jerk it free and when it held fast, she tore it off her waist and kept moving.

Sirens shrieked, the chopper came around again, hovering over the mangroves, the blazing lights searing through the braided branches. Then the trees ended and there was nowhere else to run except onto the beach on the other side, where they would be completely exposed. Their luck had just run out. Nine lives, used up.

The sirens were on top of them, shouts rang out, and they huddled there, arms around each other and the dog, and struggled to do what they had done before. "The bus, we need to get to the bus, the same day and around the same time we left," Kincaid murmured.

"Down there, in the mangroves," voices shouted.

Shit, she thought, and then the crippling pressure seized her head again and she went blind, deaf, and numb.

20

Then she was on her side, one arm thrown across Sunny, her wet, cold feet pressed against Kincaid's spine, the gun digging into the small of her back, her pack as heavy as a corpse. Nora rolled onto her hands and knees and promptly threw up. Beside her, Kincaid was retching and now Sunny was on her feet, weaving back and forth between them, whimpering, barking, apparently not feeling very well herself.

Kincaid finally got up, swaying as though he were on the deck of a ship in rough seas, and let out a whoop of triumph. "Nora, we did it. The theory worked. But I feel like I got run down by a semi." Then he promptly dropped to his knees, doubled over, and vomited again.

"Ditto," she muttered.

After a few minutes, he weaved toward her, helped her to her feet, and they lurched the five hundred yards to the old bus. They both reeked of puke; their shoes and jeans were soaked. They climbed into the back of the bus, helped Sunny inside, and the three of them collapsed.

When they woke a while later, light carved broad swaths across the ground, like bolts of colorful fabric, and held the slender shadows of the trees. Nora guessed it was late afternoon. Both of them were hungry and filthy and since the nearest shower was hours back in a Utica campground, she and Kincaid took sponge baths, using some of the bottled water she'd taken from the building on Cedar Key. They changed into clean clothes, fixed sandwiches, fed Sunny, and just before dusk, pulled back onto the highway.

While Kincaid drove, Nora plugged her laptop into the lighter, grateful that the bus had a lighter at all, and transferred everything from Kincaid's memory stick to her computer. Then she connected Kincaid's PDA to her laptop and copied the episode summaries of *Connections* that he had downloaded.

Episode summaries first, she thought, and clicked on the file from the Internet Movie Database. In the pilot for *Connections*, Eva Danforth's husband was arrested for crimes he didn't commit, subsequently disappeared, and her search for him led her into the heart of a shadow government that held the secret of time travel.

> She discovers that dissidents and "undesirables" are disappeared into the past by a unit of specially trained Travelers and that the shadow government uses this ability for its own nefarious agenda. On the run for her life, she must figure out where in time her husband has been taken and how to get him back.

It was basically correct in terms of what she'd experienced except that it sounded as if Eva would do anything to find her husband because he was such an upstanding, loveable guy. Because they had such a perfect marriage. Because their lives had been torn apart by his arrest, for something he didn't do. There was no hint that in the moments before his arrest, his wife had told him she wanted a divorce. Nothing here about his infidelities, his betrayal of his close friend, that the student he'd been sleeping with was an undercover Freeze operative.

She read it aloud to Kincaid, who just shook his head. "It's Jake's typical spin."

Nora noted that there was no rancor in his voice, no bitterness or anger. It seemed that Kincaid had reached a kind of Zen state where Jake was concerned. When she said as much, he glanced over at her, that magnificent face momentarily visible in the lights of another car. "His path, as screwed up as it is, brought us together. How can I be angry about that?"

She suddenly realized there were many parts of Kincaid that she had yet to discover and that the discovery was integral to this strange journey.

"So go on," Kincaid said. "What about the second episode?"

She read aloud: "Eva, with the help of her brother, George, meets up with her husband's close friend, Kevin . . .' That's you, Alex . . . 'who is also on the run from the shadow gov. They're ambushed by a guy named Sanchez, the head of the time-travel unit, and some of his men. A time distortion occurs that catapults them into the past, where they become separated from Kevin. Meanwhile, Sanchez has another big problem—his best time traveler has gone rogue, threatening the existence of the unit.'"

"Wait a minute," Kincaid said. "This sounds like you, Tyler and I go back in time and I get separated from you and Tyler. I don't like that."

"We already changed it."

"Yeah, we did, didn't we?" Kincaid looked pleased. "And who's the time traveler that went rogue? Ryan Curtis? If so, that means that Bari either took creative license with whatever Jake told her or Jake lied. Or both."

The summary downloads ended in the middle of episode 57, but she figured that in real life, they were up to episode 37. This was the point where Eva and her brother discover that her husband and a female time traveler had been disappeared to 1968 by the mysterious woman who had created the biochip and was attempting to topple the time travel unit. Husband and best buddy met up with a writer—Bari?—and buddy and writer become lovers. The trio set out for Boston rather than Northampton to find the creator of the chip.

Was *that* accurate? Had Mariah Jones been the one who disappeared Jake? It seemed likely. What seemed just as likely was that these episodes concerned only one possible version of events in which she, her brother, and Kincaid had been catapulted back in time. She and Tyler were separated from Kincaid, who found his way to Bari and became her lover. In reality, this version had been changed in Tyler's storage unit.

She went into the props file she'd copied from Kincaid's memory stick and scrolled through it, frowning, trying to make sense of it. The entries were by date, followed by a T with four numbers after it, then a list of items—specific articles of clothing, amount of money, toiletries, and so on, each tagged with a code that probably identified the era or specific year to which someone was disappeared. The T numbers identified the Traveler who had done the disappearance. Like T6747 for Ryan Curtis, she thought.

The first person had been disappeared on January 4, 1975, by T1101, and had been provided with eight items from the properties department. Her eyes ran down page after page, looking for February 14, 1983, the day her mother had been arrested. There was nothing listed for that date, but three days later, T1101 and T1102 were provided with era appropriate clothing, shoes, under garments, and $100 in "local money" for their accused, #8002. In addition, #8002 was given two bars of soap, a comb and brush, a box of Tampax, a pair of prescription glasses, and a year's supply of soft contact lenses.

Her mother had worn soft contact lenses in 1983, the first year they were available. But did that prove this entry was for her mother? Intuitively, she felt that it was. Nora stared at the entry, at the paltry list of items. She imagined her mother deposited on a lonely road in some hideous and violent era, with a hundred bucks of local currency and a few essentials. *Here we are, Mrs. Walrave. Good luck and adios.*

Within the space of a few moments, her emotions spanned the spectrum from depression, sadness, confusion, rage, and—strangely enough—elation. All of it, she suspected, was symptomatic of bipolar disorder, the tidy, sanitized term for schizophrenia—*you are wacko, beyond repair, a complete fuckup.*

Except. It was easy to escape into her neat and organized psychological compartments, the main wall of defense between her and the rest of the world and the very reason that she hadn't done well at intimate relationships. But when the defining event in your childhood was your mother's arrest and disappearance, it did irreparable damage to the foundation of who you were. How could you trust anyone or anything from then on? If you relied too much on stability, that stability would be snatched from you. If you loved too deeply, that love would become tarnished and twisted by events over which you had no control.

There it was, Nora McKee's psyche, such as it was. She threw it into a mental fire and watched it burn—hot, fast, like money.

She, who had never camped in her life, shot a gun, or considered time travel as even remotely possible, had experienced all three and then some. It had changed her. But had it changed her in ways that counted? In ways that would make a difference? Or had it left her as more of who she already was? She had no idea.

Thirty minutes later, the sun had set, the wind had picked up, the temperature had dropped, and Nora stood in a phone booth in downtown Northampton, a genuine phone booth, the kind Clark Kent used to become his other persona, the thing that cell phones would make obsolete. She went through the phone book, looking for a listing for Jones, Mariah. There were lots of Joneses, even a couple of entries for

Jones, M, but no Mariah. She called both numbers for Jones, M, but neither had a Mariah living there.

She had better luck with Runyon. There was only one. Nora jotted down the address and hurried back across the street, to the park where Kincaid and Sunny waited.

"Forty-one Green Street," Nora said.

"Practically on campus. It's maybe four blocks from here. Let's walk."

"We don't have a leash for Sunny."

"They probably don't have leash laws. And we know she won't bolt."

They grabbed their packs and started walking. Just about everyone in 1968 seemed to smoke—on the streets, on campus, in restaurants and bars and coffeehouses. Here and there, she caught whiffs of pot, and heard strains of sixties music.

Sunny seemed oblivious to all of it. She trotted along, block after block, nose to the ground, tail wagging as if she were in her home territory. Nora couldn't imagine how that could be, since she had found Sunny miles and decades from this spot. But she no longer needed to know how something was possible to accept what her senses told her. Since it now seemed likely that the dog had been chipped, perhaps Sunny had been bouncing around in time for decades. She might have dozens of spots she thought of as *home*.

Forty-one Green Street was a small apartment building with a courtyard in the front that buffered it from pedestrian and vehicle traffic. Sunny didn't just trot through the gate— she raced, barking with excitement, and shot across the courtyard and up to the front door. Nora and Kincaid loped after her, he opened the door, and Sunny darted in and headed for the stairs.

"She acts like she's been here," Nora whispered.

Kincaid, checking out the names on the mailboxes, nodded. "Then her memories of this place are vastly more positive than her memories of Cedar Key. Runyon is in apartment five. I'm guessing the third floor."

"Lead the way, Sunny," Nora said.

The dog raced up the stairs and Nora and Kincaid followed, glancing at each other now and then, both of them spooked by the Sunny's behavior. Sure enough, she stopped in front of apartment five, barked, pawed at the door, barked again. "Quiet," Nora scolded, afraid that the people in the apartment across the hall would come out to see what was going on.

Nora rang the bell, knocked, rang again. Sunny suddenly darted up the hall and vanished around the corner. They found her at the apartment's back door, whimpering and pawing as though she intended to dig her way in. Kincaid knocked, waited, knocked again. From inside, muffled sounds, then something crashed to the floor.

Sunny went nuts and when Nora tried to pull her back, she growled. "Okay, back off, Sunny," Kincaid said. "You win. We're going in."

He started to pick the lock, frowned, and said, "This lock's been picked already." He turned the knob and Sunny exploded through the door and ran over to the teenage girl tied up on the floor, a toppled chair to one side of her, and a woman tied to another fallen chair on her right. Dee and Kim Runyon screamed into the duct tape that sealed their mouths and Sunny scrambled frantically from one to the other, crisscrossing the scattered fruit and vegetables and the long-dried tomato sauce on the floor. The air stank of urine. They had been like this for a long time.

"We'll get you loose." Nora dropped to her knees in front of the girl and peeled the duct tape off her mouth.

Kim gulped at the air, as if surfacing from a long time underwater, and gasped, "Thank you, thank you . . . my mom, get her free . . . they . . . the woman . . . hit her . . ."

Kincaid was already at Dee's side. He had righted her chair and now peeled back the duct tape on her mouth. When she spoke, her voice was as dry as dead leaves. "I'm . . . okay, Kim. I'm . . . is it possible to get . . . the cuff off?"

"We'll do it," Kincaid assured her. "Let me get your legs free first. We need scissors."

"In the drawer," Kim said. "Far left."

Sunny butted in, licking Kim's legs, arms, and then her face, and Kim rubbed her face against the dog's fur. "Your dog . . . is beautiful."

Uh-oh, this isn't as simple as it looks. "She obviously likes you. In fact, when we came into the building, she acted like she'd been here before. I thought she was your dog."

"She pretty much led us to your apartment," Kincaid said, returning to Dee, the scissors clutched in his hand. "She knew there was a back door."

"She's the dog that . . . I mean, who the hell *are* you people?" Dee asked.

"I'm Nora McKee. He's Alex Kincaid."

Dee's eyes bulged, a pulse hammered at her temple. "Aw, shit. Don't tell me." She shook her head, blinked hard several times. "Do you know Jake?"

"I was married to him." As soon as she said it, she realized she'd spoken in the past tense.

"This . . . this isn't supposed to happen. It's not possible." She shook her head vehemently. "Mariah assured me . . ."

"Mariah *lied*," Kim burst out. "She *used* you, Mom. Used both of us. Used Bari. That's pretty obvious now."

Snip, snip, went the scissors in Kincaid's hand. *Snip, snip, snip.*

"Let's get you two free and then discuss Mariah," Nora said. "What were you going to say about the dog?"

"We get her in the early seventies," Dee said, the bracelets on her arm jangling. "We keep her for Mariah whenever she's out of town. She . . . the dog . . . is the first experimental animal for Mariah and her goddamn chip."

Nora and Kincaid exchanged a glance. "Who did this to you, Ms. Runyon?"

"Lydia Fenmore."

"And her perverted companion," Kim spat. "Some guy named Hank."

"Fenmore," Nora repeated. "I don't know that name." She

took the scissors that Kincaid passed to her and snipped away at the tape around Kim's hands. "Who is she?"

"The number-two person in SPOT."

"SPOT? What's that stand for?"

"How can you be *here* and not know *that*?" Dee blurted.

"I'm here by accident. I'm here because . . ."

"Because Mariah Jones treated me for insomnia," Kincaid said.

"Jesus God," Dee murmured. "You're her *other* human guinea pig?"

"Nearly forty years in your future. And I didn't know about the chip's side effects."

Dee seemed to be struggling with the ramifications of all this. "This is so royally screwed up."

You got that right, Nora thought, and cut away the last of the duct tape on Kim's hands.

The teen groaned softly as she brought her arms around to the front of her body. She rubbed her wrists, flexed her stiff fingers, started to stand, but her legs refused to cooperate. "I've got to use the bathroom," she mumbled, and Nora helped her to stand.

"Go with her, Sunny," Nora said.

The dog needed no encouragement. As the two left the room, Dee was more forthcoming and spoke in a hushed, hoarse voice. "Lydia Fenmore is now the number-two person in the unit Mariah helped to create—Special Project Operation Temporal. From this time . . . *my* time . . . she'll be Mariah's first recruit around 1974. She . . ."

"Is the number-one person a man with a Hispanic name?" Kincaid asked.

Nora knew he was thinking of Bari's script, of the man she named *Sanchez.* She knew because she'd been thinking the same thing.

"Ian Rodriguez," Dee replied. "I believe he's Cuban."

Bingo. "Who disappeared Jake?" Nora asked.

"Mariah. At the same time, she also disappeared a Trav-

eler named Kat Sargent. Her lover, Ryan Curtis, another
Traveler, has gone AWOL or whatever the hell they call it,
and he's looking for her."

She felt fairly certain now that Curtis—T6747—was the
"best agent," the rogue agent, to whom Bari referred in her
script.

"Look, I've known Mariah for a couple of years, ever
since Kim got into Smith on a full scholarship. But she
doesn't tell me much. Some of what I'm telling you is what
I've pieced together. I just want you to know that."

As Kincaid went to work on the cuff that held Dee's ankle
to the leg of the table, more of the story tumbled out, the cell
phone and PDA that Fenmore found, that she didn't know
where Mariah had gone, the way Fenmore's partner had
treated Kim. "I'm done with Mariah's bullshit, her manipulations. She put Kim at risk."

"If it's any consolation," Kincaid said, "your daughter
wins a Nobel in botany while she's teaching and doing research at Harvard. She credits Mariah for her passion for
botany and her mother for believing in her."

Dee's eyes brimmed with tears. "Mariah never let on. She
refused to tell me much of anything about our futures. But
she did tell me about the dog."

Kincaid finally freed her and Dee exhaled loudly, rubbed
her wrists and ankles, removed her large hoop earrings, and
gripped the edge of the table and pulled herself up from her
chair. "Bottom line—that's what they say in your time,
right?" she added with a slight, ironic smile. "Well, the bottom line is that Mariah figured the human heart all wrong. I
think in some version of these events, you"—she looked at
Kincaid—"were slated for Bari. You met her at Rummy's
Bar and Grill, right?"

"Uh, yeah," Kincaid said. "Months ago."

"Regardless. That would have changed Bari's script, too.
That you and Nora are together . . . and I'm assuming that's
what this is . . . I don't think Mariah even considered that
possibility. That's going to change Bari's script in a vastly

different way. Second bottom line . . . Lydia Fenmore forced me to give her Mariah's address and the address to Bari's hideout in Old Forge. My first call will be to Bari. But you two need to get to Mariah's to do whatever needs to be done to stop her or get rid of her to end this travesty." She spat out the address, as though it were something distasteful she'd bitten into. "But Fenmore and her buddy were here hours ago, this morning, so it may be too late already."

"What are you going to do?" Kincaid asked.

"Get the hell out of here. Go someplace where Mariah will never find us."

"Mom?" Kim stood in the kitchen doorway, Sunny at her side.

"Go pack a bag, hon. We're leaving."

"But what about the dog?"

"She isn't ours."

Not yet, Nora thought. *And now, maybe never.*

Sunny seemed to understand what was going on. She looked at Kim, whose fingers were climbing through her fur, and then looked at Nora and Kincaid. She finally flopped down on her side and rolled onto her back, legs in the air. *Can't do it,* her body language screamed. *Don't make me decide, don't make me choose.*

"Kim, we need Sunny right now," Nora said gently. "She knows stuff that we don't. May we borrow her a while longer?"

"Uh, yeah, sure. But if you keep her, can I at least visit her?"

"Absolutely." Nora turned her attention to Dee again. "Could you call Bari now? I'd like to speak to Jake."

"Let me just clean up a little," Dee said, and wobbled and swayed her way across the kitchen and to the bathroom.

While Nora went to work cleaning up the floor, Kincaid fixed grilled cheese sandwiches with sides of sliced fruit and a bowl of delectable turkey for Sunny. When Dee returned, she called Bari's number in Old Forge and got through.

"Hey, it's me . . . Yeah? Weird shit? It's about to get a lot weirder. Could you put Jake on? . . . I don't give a damn if he's napping. Wake him up . . . yeah, it's really important, Bari." She handed the receiver to Nora.

"Dee," Jake said, his voice hoarse from sleep. "What's up?"

What's up? So casual, so cool, so goddamn hip that Nora nearly vomited. "What's up, Jake, is that it's Nora, and you two need to get out of that place. Pretty soon, it's going to be surrounded by bastards with guns, okay?"

"Nora?" He nearly choked when he said her name. "What . . ."

"I'm with Alex. Long story short, we're taking these fucks down. I'm not sure how or when, but we're going to do it. In the meantime, Bari needs to finish that script. Tell her everything. Tell her the truth. Tell her that before you were hauled off, I told you I wanted a divorce. That's got to be in the script. If Bari's series is going to be the wakeup call, Jake, it has to be the unvarnished truth."

"I . . . you . . ." And he broke down, babbling about a council and electroshock and what Ryan Curtis had done to him and how Mariah had disappeared him and . . . dear God, he hadn't meant to hurt her and what the hell was going on, anyway?

"Just get out of there," Nora said. "Fake your deaths. Flee to Canada."

"Nora, I'm so sorry for . . ."

"I don't want your apology, Jake. Just don't screw up your relationship with Bari because there's more at stake than just the two of you."

Silence, then: "Could you put Alex on the phone?"

And she did. They, too, had a score to settle. At least now, with Jake, she had a form of closure—not face-to-face, nothing quite that satisfying, but the phone conversation would do for now. Things were definitely looking up.

Kincaid was on the phone for maybe four minutes, hardly spoke, then passed the receiver to Nora, his expression closed, tight. She couldn't read what he felt just then. "Bari wants to speak to you."

Oh. Bari. Soon to be very famous scriptwriter. Bari, her husband's lover, the woman who would write the definitive script of all this weirdness. Bari Serrano, daughter of Charlie Ovis, buddy of Rod Serling, who had gotten her through the darkest times of her life. What the hell, why not?

"It's Nora."

"Okay, this is, like, hallucinogenic weird. I get most of the picture. And you need to know that Ryan Curtis is on our side. I talked to him, spent time with him, he gave me info for the script. All he wants is to find Kat. His partner."

The woman who punched Jake, Nora thought. "Bari, it's really important that you tell the truth in your screenplay. Remind Jake of that when he's feeding you information. Remind him that our marriage sucked, all right? Episodes four, thirteen, twenty-five, thirty-seven, forty-nine, and fifty-nine are critical."

"Okay. Got it. Can you tell me why?"

"Mariah earmarked them, I don't have any idea why. We know SPOT's headquarters are on Cedar Key, Florida. Did Curtis tell you that?"

"Yes. He explained the structure of SPOT, how they've managed to keep it all so secret . . . stuff I can use in the script. But I'll need to know how . . . how it ends, Nora."

"We'll be in touch." *Somehow.* "I think there may be more than sixty episodes."

"Right now, I've got half a pilot."

"That'll change fast. Look, since you're chipped, we may need your help. Did Curtis tell you how to use it?"

"He said it takes intense resolve, need, and emotion. It takes the ability to imagine where you're going."

"That's it?"

"Apparently the chip does the rest. Curtis is already in Northampton. I have an apartment there. That's where he's staying." She gave Nora the address. "And if you need help from us, here're a couple of numbers."

More scribbling. "Do you have any idea where Mariah is?" Nora asked.

"No. Don't want to know, either."

"By the way, your dad said to tell you he isn't happy that you left without telling him where you'd be," Nora said.

"I'll remedy that. And remind Alex that he owes me fifty bucks."

Nora smiled at that. "It got us this far, that fifty. I'm going to hand the phone back to Dee."

She passed the receiver to Dee, then tucked the sheet of paper where she'd jotted phone numbers and addresses into her wallet. She sat down at the table with Kincaid and the girl, a pall of unreality settling around her, and ate the food he had fixed. Anything that smacked of normalcy was welcome.

"What do you know about me?" Kim asked.

The question was directed to both of them, but Kincaid answered. "You mean, your future self?"

"Yeah, like, what do I become? Who am I in 2006?"

"A famous professor at Harvard," Kincaid replied.

Her eyes widened. "Harvard? Really? Wow, that's so cool. Professor of what?"

"Botany," he said. "You do some very original research for which you're recognized."

"Yeah?" Her eyes shone like wet streets. "What kind of recognition?"

"Big time," Kincaid assured her.

Dee came back to the table with an ice pack against her swollen lip. "Kim, honey, can you get that wooden box off my dresser?"

"Sure. Hey, Mom, I'm going to be famous!"

She ran off and Dee said, "Bari asked how you two are fixed for money."

"We've got a hundred plus," Kincaid replied.

"We're good," Nora said.

"That's not enough."

"We're fine for now," Kincaid insisted.

Kim returned with the wooden box, set it on the table in

front of her mother. Dee dropped her ice pack on the table, slid open the ornately carved top, brought out a thick wad of cash. "Please take this. It's Bari's money. She's been incredibly generous with us."

"Look, we're fine. Really. But down the road, we may need help."

"I'll be glad to help when Mariah is dead. Please take the money. It's ten grand. Now, there're a couple things you should know about Mariah's house," Dee went on, and described the neighborhood, the street, the layout of the house, and that it would be extremely difficult to break in. "The place is like a fortress."

"Is there a basement?" Kincaid asked.

"Yes, but the windows are sealed or something. It's impossible to get in."

"What about an alarm system?"

"She has one, but it's not tied in to a police department or anything like that. It's something she rigged up herself. I don't know how it works."

"We'll get in," Kincaid said.

"Like I said, that Fenmore woman was here twelve hours ago. You may find that Mariah's house has been broken into already."

"They probably didn't have to break in to get in," he said. "We'll go by Bari's apartment first to see if Curtis is there."

A few minutes later, Dee and Kim hugged them good-bye and Kim threw her arms around Sunny. For moments, the dog hesitated, glancing between Nora and Kincaid and the family she would have—or might have—several years from now. Then she followed Nora and Kincaid through the door.

On their way to the park, where they'd left the bus, their respective conversations with Jake loomed between them, a continent of tension and division. "Okay, so what'd Jake say to you?" she finally asked.

"He's an asshole."

So much for Zen. "That's what he said?"

"Actually, in a roundabout way, he called me an asshole. He said if I'd just made the arrangements for the sale of the hybrids, none of us would be in this situation."

"Right. You'd be the one who was disappeared elsewhere. So he basically blames you for everything that's happened."

"That about sums it up."

"Well, I'm eternally grateful that it turned out like it did."

He looked over at her, his eyes dark, quiet, inscrutable. "No regrets?"

"None. You?"

"Not a chance," he replied, and tightened his grasp on her hand as if he intended to hold on to it forever.

21

Flashlight in hand, Ryan Curtis unlatched the front gate of Mariah's square brick house, cut across the front yard, and ducked into the empty carport. He already knew no one was home. He had spent the afternoon watching the place—from inside the Mercedes, on foot through the neighborhood, and, later, pretending to be a jogger. No one had entered or left. With just a single street lamp midway up the road, the end of the block was as black as the far side of the moon. The darkness and the wall around her property would keep him well hidden.

The carport was large enough for a single car, with space along one wall for shelves that held a few gardening tools, some empty ceramic pots, bags of mulch and potting soil, and half a dozen empty boxes. Just like Kat had described. He set the flashlight upright on the hot water heater and began moving the boxes and potting tools to the side until he exposed the circuit breaker. It was padlocked, but the puny thing was meant only to deter—not prevent—entry, and he picked it easily. He opened the circuit box door and threw the master switch, shutting down the power.

It surprised him that Mariah was so careless with the circuit breaker. He immediately wondered if there was a security system that Kat didn't know about or some hidden trap inside the house.

He grabbed his flashlight and shone it at the door that led into the house. It was metal, with a heavy-duty dead bolt. He probably could pick the lock, but getting the bolt out of the jamb would require tools he didn't have in his pack. He turned the beam of light on the ceiling, looking for an attic door. The ceiling was as flat and seamless as a sheet of paper. So, he thought, the rear bathroom window would be his entry point, just as Kat had recommended.

Curtis withdrew a device from his pack that would detect an alarm system, if there was one, and moved slowly along the side of the house. The flashlight's beam revealed that the basement windows were rectangular slits of milky glass, much too small for an adult to squeeze through even if the glass was broken. Quite effective for keeping prisoners inside and intruders out.

His device continued to indicate that there wasn't any security system engaged in the house. Apparently her only security was the electronically controlled doors. Again, that struck him as sloppy and, given how careful she'd been about other details, somewhat odd.

At the rear of the house, he stopped in front of a metal door identical to the one in the carport. To either side of it was a large window. According to Kat's sketch, the window on the left was where he should enter. Curtis set his pack on the ground and brought out a glass cutter, a Toyo "Tap Wheel" that cut through thick glass with the ease of a knife through melon. Available at your favorite Internet store. He removed four sections of glass, slipped the cutter back into his pack, then wrapped a towel around his hand and knocked out the rest of it. The glass tinkled as it hit the floor inside. He made sure that no jagged edges remained in the frame, then grabbed his pack again and climbed through it.

The bathroom door was shut and had no knob or handle. This was the first electronic door. But with the power off,

Curtis simply had to lean into it and slide it to the right to open it. He stepped into a hallway where faint residues of mysterious fragrances lingered in the air—soaps, perfumes, oils, incense. The hallway walls were bare; the living room was sparsely furnished and unlived in. It was as if Mariah had never sat on the couch, turned on the radio or TV, or had a snack at the coffee table. The kitchen was a bit more personal, with a couple of stained-glass mobiles hanging in front of the window, a bronze peace sign on one wall, a dream catcher on the other.

He opened the freezer door and there, just as Kat had said, were hundreds of syringes, stacked neatly between ice trays and frozen foods, from the floor to the top. From a side pocket in his pack, Curtis withdrew a freezer-sized Baggie filled with identical baggies, one of the most useful items he carried for any transition. He started loading the syringes into the Baggies, twenty-five to a bag. He wrapped clothing around the bags to insulate and protect them before putting them into his pack.

When the freezer was empty, he grinned wickedly to himself. The bitch could produce more chips, of course, more gel and syringes, but it would take time and he hoped she would run out of time before she had any new chips. Little by little, he would even the score until she was forced to come after him. Then he would disappear her so far into the past that she would never find her way back.

He hoisted his pack over his shoulder and opened the door to the pantry, a huge room packed with enough canned goods to sustain a family for months. Kat had told him the back wall was actually the basement door and if the power was off, all he had to do was lean against the shelves and the door would swing inward. So he did and the entire wall started to move, creaking and groaning, the hinges squeaking.

Curtis slipped inside, the flashlight's beam probing the inky darkness. Steep stairs, but that was all he could see from here. He decided to leave the door ajar. It made him too uneasy to shut himself in a room that, according to Kat, had no other exit. Yes, he could transition if he had to, but the repeated transitions with McKee and to and from Aruba had seriously depleted his reserves. He didn't want to transition unless he absolutely had to. He left the pantry door ajar enough so that he would hear Mariah if she suddenly returned.

On the wall just inside the door was a security panel—turned to the Off position. He guessed it had prevented McKee and Kat from escaping when Mariah had kept them here. Curtis moved cautiously down the stairs, alert for a trap of some kind. A trip wire, a hidden alarm, no telling. But he reached the bottom of the stairs without incident. It all seemed much too easy.

He began exploring, looking behind bamboo room dividers and curtains of hanging beads that hid a couch and a small TV, a makeshift bedroom, even a rudimentary kitchen. Had this been Jake McKee's little apartment? And where had Mariah kept Kat?

Handcuffed.

Behind one bamboo divider, he found Mariah's office, and what a high-tech marvel it was—PC, flat-screen monitor, laptop, several laser printers, a PDA, digital cameras, memory sticks, and several cell phones. Since the phones didn't work in this time, she apparently kept them for her journeys to his time. They were the disposable variety, basically untraceable as long as you used a phony e-mail address to activate them.

He set his flashlight on end and turned on the laptop. Since it was plugged in, the battery would be powered up. Just a quick look, he thought, to determine if he should take it and the PC.

While the system booted, he turned on the digital camera and clicked through the photos stored on the camera's compact flash card. He found photos of himself, Kat, the McKees, Kincaid, Fenmore and Rodriguez, even of the Council members. Another cluster of pictures focused on the Cedar Key facility and even included photos of the interior of the holding area on Snake Key. The dates on them ranged from the spring of last year to a week before McKee's arrest. She had been thorough, he thought, and put all three cameras into his pack, then turned his attention to the laptop.

He no longer had to look for the hidden wireless connection. He was searching for something that probably was even more elusive—a blueprint of her overall plan, her bigger picture, and some indication of where her safe haven was located. He was sure that Mariah had set up havens in several eras, places to which she could transition if things fell apart here. But there were so many folders and files that it would take hours to click through them all. And the longer he sat here, the more uncomfortable he felt. Best to transition somewhere safe with all her equipment and then return to even the score a little more.

But where would be safe? The safe spots he'd had in his own time—his condo, his old Florida house—weren't secure anymore. Bari's apartment here in Northampton was out; he was afraid that Fenmore and Rodriguez knew about it. It had to be a place he had been to before, in the chip's memory, so the transition wouldn't exhaust him completely and he could return here to finish the job. *Shit, think, c'mon.*

He slid her laptop and PDA into his pack, disconnected the cables and wires from the PC, the monitor, the printer. He set the monitor on top of the PC tower, lifted it. Yes, he could carry these easily enough.

But to where?

Bari's cottage, a couple of hours ago. Fenmore and her lapdog Vachinski might be there already, but he sensed he faced a greater risk from them here. He had seen them in Northampton and knew they were here for the same reason he was—to find Mariah. Could he transition? Moments ago, he'd been worrying about whether he had the physical reserves to do this. He thought a moment, weighing the pros and cons, then reached into his pack, opened the top Baggie, and removed one of Mariah's syringes.

These are advanced suckers, Kat had said. And if he

chipped himself with one of these, it should cause his body to reject his other chip, one of the many Mariah supposedly had sabotaged.

He flicked off the cap, tilted his head back against the chair, inserted the end of the syringe into his right nostril, and depressed the plunger. The gel was thicker and colder than he was accustomed to and numbed the inside of his sinuses in a flash. He kept his head tilted back for a full two minutes, felt a stab of pain as the chip began to thaw and to migrate. But otherwise, it wasn't much different than anything he'd experienced before.

How long did it take for the chip to become functional? Five minutes? Thirty? Oddly, he didn't know, had never asked, and had never been told. Dr. Berlin, who probably knew as much about the chips as Mariah, usually kept him in recovery for fifteen to thirty minutes, time he didn't have right now. He figured the recovery period was just a formality, one more insidious attempt by those in charge to make Travelers believe they were basically helpless without all the rules, regulations, protocols. After all, if you could chip yourself in an emergency in the field, who needed the doc?

He put on his pack, picked up the PC tower and monitor, and created a blazingly vivid mental image of Bari's cottage, then *reached* for it. He felt his body struggling to transition, but it was as if his weight, his mass, couldn't quite make the journey. Everything seemed sluggish, slow, weighted down. He *reached* again, *reached* with the same intensity of desire that had gotten him to Aruba, and his skull started throbbing, his heart pounded, sweat streamed from his pores. The excruciating pressure in his head became unbearable, sucking at his eyeballs, sending hot flashes of pain into his ears. And then it blew off the top of his skull.

The next thing he knew, he was on his knees, sweat rolling into his eyes, the contents of his stomach surging in his throat. He heard the rush of his own blood through veins and arteries, his bones felt like they had turned into Swiss cheese, his head spun. He sat back on his heels, saw that he was outside Bari's cottage, on the walkway where the two of them had spoken after he had returned McKee.

The sun was just slipping away, a chilly breeze blew across the grounds, and the air tasted of impending snow. The computer lay on its side in front of him, the monitor was on its back on the hard ground to his left. Had he dropped them? He didn't know. He didn't know if he had the strength to get up, either, so he sat there a while longer, struggling not to puke, waiting for the pressure in his ears to equalize.

Maybe he had overdone it.

He finally got to his feet, picked up the tower and the monitor, and staggered over to the front door of the cottage. *There's always a key under the flowerpot*, Bari had told him. *If you need it.* He needed it.

And it was there, just as she'd said.

The inside of the cottage looked like the scene of a raucous party that had been disbanded quickly—garbage overflowing, clothes left where they'd fallen, dirty dishes abandoned on the kitchen table, the counter, and filling the sink. He set the tower on the counter and relieved himself of his pack as well. He always hesitated about divesting himself of the backpack, something drummed into them during training, the equivalent of a crab abandoning its shell. The pack, after all, held not only personal items, but everything that gave him an edge in whatever era he visited. He just didn't have the energy to carry the weight.

And right now, the pack held syringes that needed to be kept chilled. He unloaded all the Baggies and put them in the freezer. He packed one Baggie in ice to take with him when he left. Twenty-five syringes, for emergencies.

Curtis fixed a peanut butter and jelly sandwich and wolfed it down with a glass of iced tea. He realized he hadn't eaten for hours. No wonder he was so messed up.

He thought about where he should hide Mariah's computer tower, monitor, cameras, and cell phones. From his stay here with Garcia and Kesey, he knew all the nooks and crannies in the cottage and decided the most secure spot would be the attic. The stairs to it were in the cedar linen closet in the hallway. When he opened the closet door, the fragrance of cedar washed over him, saddening him, then angering him. Kat's cedar chest sat at the foot of their bed in the old Florida house.

Curtis pulled on the cord, the hinged stairs unfolded, and he climbed them, turned on the attic light, and returned to the kitchen to get everything. He had a difficult time getting back up the attic stairs, trying to balance the objects in the crook of one arm while holding on to the railing with his other hand. By the time he finally hid everything, he was so wasted he could barely climb back down. As he weaved up the hall toward the kitchen, something red struck the floor in front of him. Then another splotch appeared. *Blood, Jesus, here it comes.* His body was rejecting the old chip.

Curtis rushed into the closest bathroom, looked at himself in the mirror, and thought he might pass out. Blood poured from his left nostril, where his old chip had gone in three weeks ago. He grabbed a towel off the rack, ran it under cold water, held it to his nose, and tilted his head back. But this forced the blood to stream down the back of his throat and nearly gagged him.

He dropped to his knees in front of the toilet and let the blood gush out. He kept his eyes shut. He had heard the stories, listened to the descriptions, had no desire whatsoever to *see* it. After a few minutes, the stream began to diminish and something plopped noisily into the toilet bowl. He didn't look; he just flushed it away. Then he showered and stood for a long time under the hot, unforgiving spray. He made sure the bleeding had stopped before he put on clean clothes. His torn-up sinus passages ached. His life was beginning to feel like an endless, painful flight from Armageddon.

Back in the kitchen, he was shocked to see that it was now the same time as when he'd left Mariah's. He'd used up whatever advantage those hours might have given him. Well, so be it. He retrieved his bag of syringes from the freezer and rearranged the frozen foods and ice trays so that the other Baggies were better hidden.

Time to go. But when he tried to transition, he couldn't do it. He couldn't *reach* far enough, his imagination seemed to be mired in wet concrete, and he panicked. His lungs refused to work, his stomach heaved.

He suddenly heard voices outside, male voices, and he shot to his feet, gulping at air, his pack over his shoulder, and hurried into the hall, to the linen closet again, shut the door. Breathing hard, he pulled down the attic ladder, and scrambled up. He raised it up up after him and moved quickly to the window that faced the driveway.

The glass was filthy, the light was gone, but he saw a truck parked out in front of the cottage, the lettering on the side visible in the glow of the porch light: LENNY'S CLEANING SERVICE.

Go away, Lenny. Please.

And then Lenny and his crew were inside the cottage and Curtis was huddled in a corner of the attic, struggling to transition, and couldn't do it.

Fuck, how'd this happen? Mariah's newer and supposedly improved chip wasn't doing squat. *Which does things we can't even imagine,* Kat had told him. Like slow down time. Like get you to where you waned to go at the speed of light. Yeah? So why couldn't he transition? Why wasn't time slowing?

He kept *reaching* for that basement, *conjuring* it in his head, *imagining* it. And then the desire to escape shut down, he stopped visualizing, he was resigned to wait it out here, in a corner of the attic. And just that fast, he found himself in the makeshift bedroom in Mariah's basement, as if the release of his need and desire had catapulted him to exactly where he wanted to be. In other words, by doing the complete opposite of what he'd been taught, he had arrived at his target.

The hippie beads clicked together, as if his arrival had

stirred up the air. He was spent, scraping empty, and would be lucky if he had the energy to climb out of here the way he had climbed in and to walk the half mile to the market parking lot where he'd left the Mercedes. But he'd made it.

From his pack, Curtis withdrew the dish towels, the lighter fluid, and box of matches that he'd bought in Aruba. He put some of the matches in his jacket pocket, then twisted the top on the can of lighter fluid, and started squirting the stuff—across the bed, into the linens, the towels, the pillows, the throw rug. He grabbed a fresh towel from the wall rack, saturated it, and spread it out like a throw rug between the bedroom and the crude kitchen.

In the kitchen, he soaked the dish towels with lighter fluid and squirted the stuff across the top of the stove, the refrigerator, the chairs. Every stream of fluid connected to every other stream, a network of miniature pools and creeks and rivers. He backed into her office, paused in the doorway and turned. He took immense pleasure in covering her office with lighter fluid—desk, chair, printer, cell phones. He emptied the can, opened another, backed out of her office, and headed up the stairs.

At the top of the staircase, he bunched up the last of the dishcloths, set it on the step just below him, opened the third can of lighter fluid, and soaked the bundle. He lit a match, held the flame to it, and smiled as it burst into flames. The stream of lighter fluid quickly caught fire and raced down the steps and then out in every direction, a web of fire.

You think you're a god, bitch? Think again.

Now get out fast. Curtis shut the door, hastened out of the pantry, and backed his way through the kitchen, leaving a new stream of lighter fluid that would lead right to the front door. He wanted very much to circle around to the back of the house, soaking everything in sight, but he already smelled smoke from the basement. He needed to get the hell out before that gas line in the basement kitchen blew.

He unlocked the front door, slipped out, struck a kitchen match on the jamb, and held it to the lighter fluid. The flames raced through the stream of lighter fluid behind him. "Fuck you, Mariah." He left the door ajar and raced for the gate.

Before he reached it, the air around him rippled and quivered, like heat above asphalt on a blistering summer day, then tore wide open, light spilling over him, revealing the unthinkable. Six Freeze officers, Rodriguez, and Fenmore quickly formed a half-moon around him. All of them were armed—rifles with lights mounted on them, trank guns, no telling what else.

How'd they find me?

"Hello, Ryan." Rodriguez spoke pleasantly, as if they had been standing here for sometime having a normal, civilized conversation. "We got an e-mail saying you'd be here."

Mariah set me up? But how? "Mariah's your enemy, Ian, not me."

"We have differing opinions on that point," Rodriguez said, and his arm snapped up and he fired a weapon Curtis hadn't seen.

A bright, sharp pain lit up his thigh. Curtis knew immediately what it was—a metal claw attached to a narrow steel cable that would prevent him from transitioning. His thigh burned and throbbed where the claw had gone in. Blood oozed down the inside of his leg and seeped into the fabric of his jeans.

"This has gone far enough, son," Rodriguez said.

I'm not your goddamn son.

"You've created so much havoc," Fenmore said. "And it's so silly, really. We can find you nearly anywhere."

He thought, again, of that device she'd carried in the museum, how she had glanced at it and spun around. *Fuck you.* "So did your little fling with Vachinski get boring, Lydia? It must have, since you're here with Ian. I don't suppose your open relationship is quite open enough to discuss your other lovers, though, right?"

Rodriguez looked shocked, then enraged, and jerked hard on the cable, as if fighting a fish he'd hooked, and it caused the claw buried in Curtis's thigh to rip at the tissue, the skin.

He grimaced and pulled back, refusing to make it easier for the son of a bitch to touch him, transition him. They would shoot tranqs only as a last resort because he had to be conscious for a transition to take place.

"Oh, for chrissakes," Fenmore snapped impatiently. "Let's get on with it. A car's coming up the road."

She wrenched hard on the cable, yanking Curtis forward like some stubborn, disobedient dog. She lunged to grab him and he yanked back so hard on the cable that Fenmore stumbled and tripped over her own feet. Before she had a chance to react, the front windows of the house blew out.

Shards of glass shot everywhere, flames whipped outward and upward, waves of intense heat rolled through the yard, black, greasy clouds of smoke closed around him. Free now and hidden by the smoke, Curtis stumbled back, coughing, his eyes streaming with tears as the smoke bit at his eyes. He ran for the wall, the weapon banging against the ground behind him, the claw still embedded in his thigh.

As he vaulted over the wall, three rapid explosions roared thunderously through the darkness, deafening staccato blasts that shot orange tongues of fire and flaming debris into the sky. Then flaming debris rained down into the street and neighboring yards, igniting dried bushes and trees. Up and down the block, people poured out of their homes, shouting, frantic. Curtis jerked the weapon toward him, jammed it and part of the cable into his pocket, and loped out into the street, waving his arms at the approaching vehicle. A van, it was an old van. Its headlights impaled him, the driver slammed on the brakes, and Curtis zigzagged toward the open side door and threw himself inside.

The van took off, rattling like a bag of old, dry bones, and Curtis lay there on his back, gasping for air, blood running thick and warm down his leg, his thigh throbbing. The piercing shriek of sirens shredded the air, followed by two more explosions.

"We need to ditch the bus," the driver shouted. "You got wheels?"

"Hang the first left. My car's in the market lot. Thank you for saving my ass." He raised up on his elbows and felt the cold, hard pressure of a gun at the back of his skull.

"We're not saving *your* ass, Mr. Curtis. You're going to save *ours*."

Aw, shit.

And the person moved to his side. "Remember me?"

It was Nora McKee.

22

In the seconds before the windows blew out, Lydia Fenmore thought she smelled smoke. Then there was no more time to think because the flying glass struck the three Freeze officers who were closest to the front of the house and they went down like sitting ducks in a shooting gallery, one right after another. As soon as Lydia reached them, she knew they were dead. Since it was impossible to transition a dead person, she swept up the men's weapons, removed their ID and cell phones, shoved everything into her shoulder bag, and shot to her feet. And then the house went up like a rocket to the moon.

The blast of fire and heat stole her breath and she dived, instinctively, for the ground, where the smoke was thinner, the heat less intense. As she scrambled forward on her hands and knees, eyes tearing from the smoke, she suddenly understood that Curtis hadn't been at Mariah's to capture or to kill her, but to seek revenge for her having disappeared Kat. This was *his* fault. But who sent the e-mail telling them where he would be? Mariah?

She shouted for Rodriguez, her voice swallowed by the *whoosh*ing noise of the fire, the wind that fueled it. He wasn't chipped and couldn't transition unless she was touching him. "*Ian*," she shouted again.

A second explosion rocked the darkness and hurled dark plumes of smoke and burning debris a hundred feet into the air. Lydia threw herself against the ground and covered her head with her arms as burning wreckage from the house showered down on the front yard. Dry, brittle branches caught fire and the flames quickly leaped to another tree and then another and another until the entire yard was burning, a biblical purge by fire.

Lydia stumbled to her feet, shouting for Rodriguez again and again, and finally heard him calling back. Nearly blind from the smoke, she followed the sound of his voice and found him crouched next to a pair of fallen Freeze officers, unconscious and bleeding profusely from head and chest wounds.

"We can't take them," she shouted above the roar of the fire. "Get their weapons." She quickly took the men's IDs and cell phones, hoping that she hadn't overlooked something that would tip off the local authorities that they were unusual in any way. With luck, the fire's ferocious appetite would consume enough of them so that any attempt at identification would be impossible.

"Where's Curtis?" Rodriguez yelled, shoving weapons in his bag.

"I don't know. He escaped." And probably transitioned.

Just as she grabbed his arm to transition, a third explosion blew the rest of the house to smithereens. Rodriguez threw open the gate and they staggered out onto the sidewalk, the piercing shriek of sirens close now, almost on top of them. Lydia heard the squeal of brakes, blinked her eyes clear, and saw Curtis hurling himself through the open side door of an old VW bus. And then she threw her arms around Rodriguez and transitioned them to her safe location, that tranquil spot by a lake in upstate New York where she had vacationed with her family as a kid.

They emerged flat on their backs in soft grass, by the

shore of the lake in what felt like high summer, in an unknown year. Geese winged across the cerulean blue dome of the sky, the tops of the tall pine trees swayed in a warm breeze, even the air smelled green. She just wanted to remain where she was, stretched out in the grass, and drift in the fragrances, the warmth, and forget the fiasco at Mariah's. But she was sweating under her jacket, stank of smoke, and her feet screamed to be free of socks and shoes.

Lydia raised up on her elbows, located her bag in the grass on her right, saw Rodriguez hauling himself up onto his hands and knees off to her left. The weapons they had collected from the dead officers were scattered around them, flotsam from everything that had gone wrong at Mariah's.

A thick, dense wall of pines rose around them, a forest primeval that ended just short of the lake. When she used to come here before her parents got divorced, family cabins dotted the lake. Since she didn't see any structures along the shores of the lake, she guessed they were somewhere in the 1940s. Not that it mattered. They wouldn't be here any longer than it took for her to recharge her reserves.

She struggled out of her jacket, tore off her shoes, her socks, her sweater, removed the memory stick that hung around her neck and set it carefully in the nest of her discarded clothes. Now: jeans rolled up. Perfect. She weaved through the tall grass toward the cool, inviting water. She knew now that she and Rodriguez were alone, he would grill her about Vachinski. She'd seen the rage on his face when Curtis had taunted her. *Is it true? You slept with him? With that goddamn ape? Why?* She could pretty much predict the script and, quite frankly, didn't have the energy for this argument. Not now. Maybe never.

The cool water felt so good against her tired feet that she stripped off the rest of her clothes and waded into the water until it was waist deep. Her nipples tightened, goose bumps exploded along her arms, the mud at the bottom oozed up between her toes. She waded out farther, ducked under the water completely, then burst through the surface, refreshed, revived, nearly clean again.

When she turned, Rodriguez stood on the prayer rug of a beach in his bare feet, shirt, and jeans rolled to his knees. He looked like some farmer from the Midwest, hands shading his eyes against the bright light.

"The water's great, Ian," she called.

He shed the rest of his clothes, put his memory stick on top of them, and strode quickly toward the lake, his tall, thin body a milk white where his clothes usually covered him and tan where they did not. A patchwork of dark and light, she thought, just like their long and convoluted relationship.

He stopped when the water reached his chest. "Go under," she said. "It's refreshing."

"The only thing that's going to refresh me right now, Lydia, is knowing why you slept with an asshole like Vachinski."

Here we go. "He's not an asshole, Ian. He's a creep. A pervert."

"Then why did you sleep with him?'

"Because I was traveling for the first time in years and I felt thin and beautiful, reckless, adventurous, and at the time I didn't know he was a pervert. Besides, you weren't around."

He looked as if he had been punched in the gut—eyes bulging with horror and incredulity, his face shiny with sweat. "Because I *wasn't around*? What the hell kind of answer is that?"

She started to tell him it was an honest answer, but stopped herself. Why grind salt into the wound? The bottom line was that ever since Mariah had recruited her thirty-two years ago, she had learned that the only way to survive time travel was to compartmentalize your emotions. The feelings that counted were those that you felt *in the moment*. You had no past, no history that held you back, no emotion that caused you to think twice. And so, although she loved Rodriguez and he had been a part of her life for the last two decades plus, he had nothing to do with her sleeping with Vachinski. Rodriguez belonged to her life in the present, Vachinski had become part of her life in the past. Nothing connected the two men, the two events, the two times.

"It didn't mean anything, Ian. And . . . when I realized he has a fondness for teenage girls, I was so . . . so thoroughly disgusted that I brought him back."

"And still smelled of him," Rodriguez spat. "And . . . and acted like he had come unhinged when it was *you,* Lydia, *you* were the one who had come unhinged."

"I didn't come 'unhinged.' I just saw him for what he was, a guy who never should have been recruited."

"How convenient," he muttered, and cut his way through the water until he was standing less than a foot away from her, glaring, his eyes contemptuous, hateful.

Something inside of her snapped. "Don't you dare look at me like that," she shouted. "Like you're guiltless. You *chose* to marry someone other than me way back when. You *chose* to make her your partner. I would've given it all up if you'd said the word. But you never said the word. You were too busy climbing your way through the hierarchy and keeping your wife pregnant. And keeping your little fuck chicks handy. I know what went on, Ian. You and Jake McKee are cut from the same cloth. So don't give me any holier than thou looks, okay?"

"Jesus, Lydia. And since we've been together, how many have there been? *How many?"*

Good God, what was wrong with him, anyway? Hadn't he heard anything she'd just said? *"It didn't mean anything.* How many times do you want me to say it?" With that, she flopped back against the water, arms thrust out at her sides, and kicked her feet slightly, just enough to keep her body afloat.

But suddenly he grabbed her by the ankles and jerked her down, down, and under, and held her there, his hands tight against her shoulders. Her arms flailed, air escaped from her lungs. In the strange, underwater light she could see with as-

tonishing clarity—the bubbles that hissed from her mouth
and rose slowly to the surface, like clusters of fish eggs. She
could see her own body lunge forward, toward him, nails
scraping down his arms. But because it all occurred in such
a weird, terrifying slow motion, she knew that he didn't feel
it, that it didn't deter him, that it wasn't enough for her to
transition.

And then he seized the sides of her head and squeezed as
though he intended to crush her skull. More bubbles escaped
her mouth, she needed air, fast, dear God, she was seconds
from passing out. If she passed out, she would drown, she
would die, that would be it, an absurd death in an unknown
era.

She dug her nails into his forearms, slammed her knee
into his balls. The impact wasn't as hard as it would have
been in the open air, but it did the trick. The pressure on her
skull ebbed. She wrenched free of his grasp and surfaced
abruptly, gulping at the air, her feet seeking purchase against
the muddy bottom, the rocky shoals, the beach.

Then she was out of the water, racing naked up the beach,
arms tucked in at her sides, bare feet slapping the wet sand,
running as she had never run in her life. But in the end, it
didn't matter. Rodriguez tackled her, they both crashed to
the sand and rolled. He was on top of her, screaming unin-
telligibly, his face bright red, his fingers knotted in her hair,
slamming her head again and again against the sand. *Bitch,
bitch, you compromised me, humiliated me* . . .

She bit into his shoulder and tasted the hot, awful salt of
it, and he reared up, away from her, and she tore her arm free
and slammed the knuckles of her free hand into his esopha-
gus. Rodriguez gasped and fell back, his hands flying to his
throat. Lydia rolled free of him, across the sand, into the soft
grass. And for seconds, she thought she saw two figures near
the pines, watching them. Then Rodriguez shrieked and shot
upward and lunged for her.

Lydia scrambled to her feet, spun around, and kicked him
in the groin. He stumbled back, eyes wide with astonishment

and pain, and she threw herself at him and they crashed to the ground. Floodgates flew open, adrenaline poured into her, and Lydia, blind with rage, grabbed his hair and slammed his head against the ground again and again until he finally, mercifully, went still.

She collapsed against him, sobbing, sand covering her naked body like a second skin, sand in her hair, her mouth, her nostrils. Her fingers caressed his forehead, his nose, his beautiful mouth, his hair. "Ian, Ian," she whispered. "We can't do this to each other." She turned her head, cheek against his chest, and shut her eyes, her reserves so depleted that she despaired of ever transitioning out of here.

The warm sun beat down against her back. She lay against him for what seemed like a very long time and then raised up, frowning slightly, horror clawing through her, and stared into the dark blankness of his eyes, into his dilated pupils.

"Ian?"

No response.

"Ian?"

Nothing.

"Dear God," she whispered, and slipped her hands under his head. She felt the warm stickiness of blood. It covered her hands like wet, shimmering gloves. Frantic now, she brought her fingers to the side of his neck. She couldn't find a pulse. She pressed her ear to his chest.

Silence.

Huge, ugly sobs exploded from her mouth, echoing across the lake, through the trees. She pounded on his chest, screaming at his heart to start, to beat, and then she tipped his bloody head back and struggled to resuscitate him. She pounded some more, resuscitated again, felt desperately for a pulse, but there was nothing, nothing, just silence.

Lydia pressed her bloody fists against her eyes, her staccato sobs like hiccups, and doubled over, her forehead pressed against his knees.

He tried to kill me, was holding me underwater, trying to drown me, to . . . to . . .

Lydia leaped up, ran toward the lake, and dived into the cool, cleansing water. *Get it off, wash the blood off, oh God, dear God, what the fuck have I done?* She swam like a woman possessed, swam until her muscles screamed and her limbs ached and her heart hammered. And when her body refused to go any farther, she drifted on her back beneath the blue sky, kicking her feet or moving her arms now and then, working her way back toward shore, her mind a merciful blank.

When she finally crawled onto the beach, she was no longer sobbing, her body had been washed clean of his blood, a crisp clarity had seized her. He had tried to drown her and she had defended herself. She wasn't guilty of anything more than that. And to everyone else, he died in the explosion at Mariah's.

And with him dead, I'm now director. It really was just that simple. A strange calmness claimed her. *Director.*

Lydia weaved across the beach to his clothes, scooped up the memory stick he had put there, and set it down on top of her own clothes. She returned to his body, took hold of his ankles, and dragged him across the rocks, the grass, toward the lake, his head bumping along, leaving a trail of blood. It didn't matter. There wouldn't be anyone around here for years. By the time the first trees were razed, the first summer cabin was built, the first family arrived, his body would be long gone, bones mired in mud at the bottom of the lake. And who would ever know?

None of what had happened here was in the episodes of *Connections*. Why not? Because Jake McKee didn't know about it? Because no one but her knew? Was that it? Yes, of course, that had to be it. *No one knows but me.*

When she reached the beach, exhaustion seeped through her. She kept pulling and dragging his body, backing into the water until it supported his weight. Then she shoved him away from shore and watched his body float away, as though she were enacting some ancient, sacred ritual. She didn't feel regret, sadness or even shock now. If she felt anything at all, it was relief. Twenty-six years of angst and uncertainty were over.

Lydia slipped the cords of both memory sticks over her head. They rested between her breasts, glinting in the light. Information was power and right now, she had two-thirds of all the information about disappearances—names, locations, eras, supplies doled out, who did the disappearances, how the accused and guilty reacted. The list Mariah threatened to release to the press consisted of just partial names and dates. The sum total of SPOT's records were kept only on memory sticks. Hers, Rodriguez's, Simone's. So let Miriah release her fifty thousand names. Let her stir up controversy and chaos. In the end, what could be proven?

She rolled up her filthy, smoky clothes, and carried them over to where Rodriguez's clothes lay. She searched his ~~ckets, removed his ID, cell, PDA, everything from their ~~ She put these items in her own pack, then dug out ~~ clothes and got dressed. She left her shoes and socks because the grass felt so luscious and soft against her feet, swept up the soiled clothes and carried them into the pines, where she thought she had seen two figures. She obviously had been hallucinating. She was quite alone here. Lydia left his clothes under a full, thick, blossoming bush.

It was cool and blissfully fragrant in the pines and she stood there for a few moments, breathing it all in, listening to the songs of birds that were hidden in the branches, flitting through the shadows. *It's going to be okay, it'll be fine, you did what you had to do.* And she believed it until she walked out of the pines and saw Mariah standing where Rodriguez had fallen.

Mariah. Here.

She stood with her arms crossed, her legs planted slightly apart, and she didn't look a day older than when Lydia had seen her last more than a decade ago. Same gorgeous skin as smooth as dark chocolate, same penetrating eyes, arrogant mouth. She wore jeans, a loose cotton shirt, lightweight shoes, and was shaking her head. "Lydia. What a goddamn disaster. You kill Ian, you were supposed to nab Curtis and my house blows up instead. Good God, what're you going to do for an encore?"

Too stunned to think, much less reply, Lydia struggled to transition, to escape, but couldn't. Her exhaustion was too extreme, she needed to raise her blood sugar, to rest, to . . .

"Fatigue, low blood sugar, fucked-up intentions . . ." Mariah clicked her tongue against her teeth. "The basics, Lydia, how quickly you forget the basics." Mariah smiled, her arms dropped to her sides and she swept one arm back toward the lake, where Rodriguez's body still floated. "I think we should undo what's been done here. It just doesn't fit into my plans."

"That's . . . that's impossible," Lydia stammered, stepping back. "He's dead. Even *you* can't undo a death. And if you had identified yourself in that e-mail, if you'd given me an earlier time, then we could've gotten Curtis when he was still inside your house."

"Oh, but he's clever, that one. He never acts the way I expect him to. I can keep tabs on only so many probabilities, you know. Curtis has become a huge problem. And so have you."

"What do you want from me, Mariah? From us? What do you *really* want? To take SPOT back and make it yours?"

"I told you people what I want. And what will happen if you don't meet my demands."

Lydia lifted her arms and shook her hands. "Wow, your threats terrify me. So what if you release your stupid SPOT timeline and your list of names and dates? The only people who'll notice are the conspiracy bloggers. You obviously haven't been paying attention to the mainstream media in the last fifteen years. They're more interested in entertainment—you know, how Celebrity A runs off with Celebrity B's husband or wife. No one does investigative reporting anymore. There's no market for it. *The viewing audience doesn't give a shit.*"

"Then why is everyone on Cedar Key scrambling around, trying to make the place look like it's been shut down, Lydia? Why are all of you acting like you're complying with my demands?"

"That order came from the senators, not from me."

Mariah flung her arms out toward the lake. "And not from Ian. He won't be issuing any orders from here on in. As far as what I want . . . it's happening. SPOT is collapsing. And it'll continue to collapse until anyone who can disappears into the past to avoid investigation and prosecution. And even if you and your mentally deranged Council members, arrogant senators, and a handful of pathetic Travelers and mentors try to put Humpty Dumpty back together again, it won't work. Not with defective chips. And you know why those chips are defective, Lydia?" She rocked toward Lydia, her eyes bright with madness, her voice quiet yet sharp. "Because I sabotaged them."

"That's not . . . possible. Only Doc Berlin has . . ."

"Exactly," Mariah said softly, her smile sharp, brilliant, triumphant. "When you treat your employees like crap, when you treat them like servants, like soldiers in your private little army, they rebel. Berlin rebelled. He's helping me. He's the gatekeeper of the technology. So here's the deal, Lydia. If you and your people want SPOT to continue, you'll have to get your chips from me. From Berlin and me. Why should everyone but me cash in on my invention, Lydia? A business decision. That's the bottom line."

Mariah stepped closer to Lydia and she moved back. "You pretend to be omniscient, but you didn't know that Curtis was going to torch your house. You don't know how any of this is going to end. All you do is meddle, make empty threats, and create chaos."

Mariah folded her arms across her chest and just shook her head, her expression that of the wise crone who regarded her younger sister as a hopeless imbecile. "Lydia, Lydia," she said softly. "I never pretended to be omniscient. I'm just smarter than the lot of you and know more about how the chip works. In fact, my chip is capable of things your people won't match for decades, if at all. On second thought, though, if I were so smart, I wouldn't have recruited you in the first place."

"You started all this bullshit when you meddled by disappearing Kat and McKee." She kept moving back, determined not to let Mariah touch her, transition her. "You're to blame for everything that's happened, not me."

"But we're not talking about *everything*, Lydia. Right now, we're just talking about what happened to Ian. In your devious little mind, I'm sure you've justified this as self-defense. So just to set the record straight, let's take a little stroll down memory lane, shall we? And I'll show you what my chips can do."

Lydia spun and ran, her bare feet slapping the grass. She made it into the trees, but Mariah brought her down like a wolf with its prey and they slammed to the ground, rolled through pine needles, light and shadows. The air went strange, bright yet milky, like it had been in those moments when Rodriguez had held her underwater.

She must have blacked out for a few moments because now she was pressed back against the pines, Mariah holding tightly to her arm, forcing her to watch herself and Rodriguez as they struggled.

The two figures I saw. They were myself and Mariah, here and now.

"I don't want to see it," she whispered, and wrenched her arm free of Mariah's grasp. But she couldn't move quickly, could barely move at all. The air around her felt as thick as overcooked oatmeal. *This is what happened in Wood's Hole, in Jake McKee's cell, time slowing, stopping.*

Mariah grabbed her by the neck, squeezing tightly. "Watch closely, Lydia," she hissed. "See what you've become."

Now she—the other Lydia—was on top of Rodriguez, fingers tangled in his hair as she slammed his head repeatedly against the rocks, screaming, *"Die, die, die, die."*

She heard the sickening crunch of bone against rock as

his skull shattered, and yet the other Lydia kept screaming and pounding his head against the rock.

"You killed him," Mariah whispered. "You killed the man you supposedly loved."

Mariah let go of her neck and Lydia's knees buckled and she sank to the ground, weeping, her heart breaking.

She didn't know what happened after that. When she raised her head again, the air was normal, Mariah was nowhere in sight. She was in the cool pine forest, terrified of stepping out of it, into the open. She crawled over to a bush and peered out into the clearing, at the beach. There, in the distance, she saw Rodriguez's floating body. But no one else.

I hallucinated Mariah.

She stood and slipped cautiously away from the protection of the pines, the shadows, her gaze sweeping from one end of the clearing and the beach to the other. No Mariah. Lydia hurriedly gathered up the weapons, then went over to get a PowerBar from her pack, something that would raise her blood sugar levels quickly. Stuck to it was a purple Post-it:

> *Let me know when you & your pals*
>
> *are ready to do business with me.*
>
> *& because of our past relationship,*
>
> *Lydia, I'd even cut you in on a*
>
> *share of the profits. See you soon.*
>
> *—MJ*

Lydia tore the Post-it into tiny pieces and hurled them into the air. A breeze caught them and carried them away.

23

Even the man who had catapulted Nora's life into chaos didn't argue with a gun to his head. She found a measure of satisfaction in that. He sank back to the floor of the bus, on his side, legs drawn slightly toward his chest, like a babe in the womb. He didn't look like much of a threat at the moment. His breathing was labored and a cable protruded from his thigh like some weird device in *Matrix*.

"My weapon is in my bag, Mrs. McKee. I'm injured and I can't transition. You don't need the gun."

What gall. She had the upper hand and he was telling her what she didn't need. "Unlike the last time we met, Mr. Curtis, you're hardly in a position to tell *me* what to do."

He didn't have any response to that.

"*Transition*," she went on. "That's a peculiar word. Is that what you people call it when you people leap from one era to another?"

"Yes."

"Okay, Mr. Curtis. Sit up, back against the door. And take off your pack."

He rose up with obvious effort, shrugged off his pack, and set it between them. Nora pulled the pack next to her. It felt like it was filled with bricks, indicating that he was much stronger than he looked. She quickly patted down his jacket pockets, then his shirt pockets, and felt something in the right pocket. She dug her fingers inside and brought out the face of a watch. To her surprise, it registered the correct date.

"It's self-contained, not dependent on any external signals. And it's not digital," he explained. "That's why it registers the date."

"I'll remember that." Nora dropped it back into his shirt pocket. Then she unzipped his pack with one hand and dug around inside, her other hand keeping the weapon pressed up against his side. She found his gun, brought it out, dropped it inside her own pack, then pulled out something bulky with a shirt wrapped around it. She unfolded the fabric.

"Wow, Mr. Curtis. Syringes. From Mariah's freezer? How many of these do you have?"

"Twenty-five here, several hundred in Bari's freezer in Utica."

"That would be Bari Serrano?"

Curtis nodded. Sunny, watching him warily from the passenger seat, growled softly, making it abundantly clear that if he made any sudden moves, she—one of the most gentle breed of dogs—would tear his throat out.

"Okay, I'm turning," Kincaid called. "How far down is the market where you're parked?"

"Three blocks, on the right. My car is parked in the back."

"That's Alex Kincaid," she said. "In case you hadn't guessed."

"*Kincaid?*" Curtis exclaimed. "How . . . how can you two be chipped?"

"Long story short," Kincaid said, "Mariah treated me for insomnia. I had some extra syringes and Nora chipped herself."

"Right now, we're more interested in what you're doing," Nora replied. "Did you torch Mariah's house?"

"Just getting even."

"For?"

"She disappeared my partner."

"Ah, right. Kat, the woman who punched Jake when he was arrested. Disappeared with Jake by Mariah, we understand. And Mariah made sure that Jake met Bari Serrano. We know all that, Mr. Curtis. Tell us something new."

"Look, I'm profoundly sorry for what we did to you and your husband. I'd like to say we were just doing our jobs, but that doesn't excuse anything and frankly, the organization we worked for is corrupt and our jobs were rotten to the core."

"Sounds like you've been enlightened," Kincaid said. "What's Mariah's grand design here?"

"I don't know."

"And just for the record," Nora went on. "The day you arrested Jake, I had just told him I wanted a divorce. So stop calling me Mrs. McKee. The name's Nora."

Behind them, around them, the sirens grew in pitch and intensity—cops, fire trucks, ambulances. Kincaid careened into a turn. "What kind of car am I looking for, Curtis?"

"A black Mercedes." He turned and looked out the window, searching the dimly lit parking lot. "There it is, third car on the left."

"I need your keys," Kincaid said.

"They're in my pocket." To Nora, he said: "I'm going to get them, okay?"

"Then give them to me."

Out came the keys, he handed them to Nora, and she passed them to Kincaid. Moments later, he nosed into a parking space next to the Mercedes. While Kincaid transferred their bags and coolers into the trunk, Nora helped Curtis out of the bus and into the back of the Mercedes. Sunny had climbed into the passenger seat and although she no longer growled, she continued to eye Curtis with suspicion.

Nora set their packs on the floor and Curtis leaned back against the seat with undisguised relief, hand supporting the cable connected to whatever was in his thigh.

"What's that thing in your leg?"

"A metal claw. If you're chipped and restrained in any way, you can't transition."

"But you're not restrained now. Why can't you transition?"

"I'm injured, wasted . . . fuck, I'm burned out." He paused. "The gun the cable is connected to is in my pocket. I'd like to remove it and eject the cable."

"Go ahead."

Her weapon was just a formality now. She sensed that Curtis was telling the truth. He wasn't in any shape to transition or drive and he knew that she and Kincaid were his ticket out of here. Just the same, she kept her weapon trained on him while he withdrew the cable gun from his pocket. He pressed something on the inside of the grip and the cable dropped to his lap. He passed the gun to Nora, who set it on the floor. "How deeply is the claw embedded?"

"I don't know. It feels like it's in there deep."

"You're bleeding a lot."

"It'll bleed even more if I pull it out. I'm hoping this is the generation of claw that you can slip out after fifteen or twenty minutes with minimal damage to tissue."

"Why would fifteen or twenty minutes make any difference?"

"Body heat. It may cause the claws to straighten out."

"Body heat. Like the chip."

He looked surprised. "You seem pretty well versed in the chip."

"Not really. Alex is my expert. But next to you, we're in preschool."

"Well, if you've got Mariah's chip and have attempted to target a time and location, you have to release need and desire, the opposite of what I was taught. That's how this generation of chip seems to work best."

Kincaid started the car. "Bottom line, Curtis. If you can't do your thing right now, do you know of any safe houses?"

"You two are chipped, so you can transition us somewhere."

"At the moment, I think it's safest to, uh, opt for more traditional modes of travel," Kincaid said. "We're still learning."

"Bari Serrano's cottage in Utica should be safe. For now. For tonight. Beyond that, I don't know."

"How do you know Bari?" Nora asked.

"This is her Mercedes."

Which didn't answer her question, but made her feel as if they had slipped down the rabbit's hole.

As they pulled out onto the road, another fire truck sped past, siren wailing, two cop cars racing behind it. Nora slid down in the seat until her knees were pressed against the back of Kincaid's seat, and noticed that Curtis did the same. "Your dog keeps watching me," he muttered.

"She was Mariah's dog. And in a few years, she'll be Dee Runyon's dog. She's chipped. Because of her, we were able to transition to your facility on Cedar Key."

In the uneven glow of passing streetlights, his face looked older, worn out, his eyes sad. "Just so we're on the same page, it's not *my* facility. I'm now considered a rogue agent."

"Just like in *Connections*."

"You two seem to be better informed than I am."

"Only about some things."

They settled into an uneasy silence and pretty soon, there was only the soft whisper of tires against the pavement, music playing softly on the radio. "We're out of town," Kincaid announced. "I think it's safe to sit up."

Nora leaned forward and rubbed the back of Kincaid's neck. "If you get tired of driving, just holler." He reached for her hand, brought it to his mouth, and kissed the back of it.

"Did you transfer the cooler from the bus?" she asked.

"It's in front of Sunny's seat. I'll take anything wet," Kincaid said.

"Coming right up." Nora reached over the seat, past Sunny, and plucked out three bottles of Coke and the last of the peanut butter sandwiches she had made earlier. "How about you, Mr. Curtis?"

"Whatever you've got."

She dispersed bottles of Coke and the sandwiches. She had so many questions for this guy she didn't know where to start. But she figured that conversation would flow more easily once they broke bread together. "When we ended up on Cedar Key, we made it into the props department and got data off the computer. I discovered that Travelers 1101 and 1102 are the likeliest ones to have disappeared my mother in 1983. Who do those numbers belong to?"

Curtis sipped at the Coke, shook his head. "There are forty of us. I don't know everyone's number. And in 1983, the program was only eight years old and had maybe a dozen Travelers. But if I had to take an educated guess, I'm betting those numbers belonged to Lydia Fenmore and her husband. She's been around since the beginning. She's the assistant director now. In fact, she and Ian Rodriguez, the director and her partner, were back there in Mariah's yard, with half a dozen Freeze officers."

In the moments before they had sped up the block, Nora had seen a man and a woman lumber through the gate. So close, she thought.

"Would this Fenmore woman know where Nora's mother was disappeared to?" Kincaid asked.

"I don't know. In the years she's been with SPOT, she probably has disappeared thousands of people. I don't know if she would remember your mother or not. Then again, because it's your mother, maybe she would."

"Thousands?" Kincaid burst out. "How the hell many people in all have been disappeared?"

"I don't know the exact figure. But SPOT has been in existence for thirty years, so it's probably safe to say there are *many* thousands."

Thousands of parents and grandparents, sisters and brothers, spouses and children, lovers, cousins, friends.

Softened, perhaps, by the food, a sense of temporary security, and company, Curtis rested his head against the back of the seat, shut his eyes, and just talked. His voice was quiet, the stream of his words constant, as if he had a deep need to confess. He covered the gamut of events that had occurred since he and Kat had brought Jake to Cedar Key. Nora noticed that Kincaid had turned off the radio, so he could hear everything Curtis was saying. Neither of them interrupted him.

Nora was repulsed by his description of Jake being shocked, but fascinated by how Mariah had interfered in the replay of Jake's arrest, thus changing the past—and the present—in a tangible way. Curtis ended with his transition to Aruba, which explained why he had stolen the biochips from Mariah's freezer.

If she were listening to him as a psychologist, then his story branded him as delusional and probably bipolar as well. Then again, if he was delusional and bipolar, so were she and Kincaid. But since they were, at this very moment, nearly forty years in the past and deeply mired in the machinations of the shadow government, she was profoundly grateful for his honesty.

"How did Jake react when he found himself on an iceberg?" Kincaid asked.

Curtis described it, Jake shrieking, belligerent, freaking, and Kincaid murmured, "Couldn't happen to a nicer guy."

"Could you put the syringes in the cooler?" Curtis asked.

"You bet." She transferred the Baggie to the cooler. "Do you think it's possible that Mariah's chips have an affinity for each other? You know, like metal and magnets?"

"I don't know. But it makes a kind of sense. It would explain why Alex met Bari the first time he found himself in Utica and why you all ended up in Utica and maybe even why you and the dog found each other."

"How did you know where and when Kat would be in Aruba?" Kincaid asked.

Maybe it was the way Kincaid asked it, out of sequence, unrelated to what they'd been talking about seconds earlier.

Or perhaps it was the fact that the question was personal. But he sounded hostile when he snapped, "That's none of your business."

"Hey, we're your allies, Curtis," Kincaid barked. "We're just trying to understand what the fuck happened to our lives."

He scrutinized them both with such undisguised suspicion that she felt like disappearing into the seat. And then he shocked her by saying, "I'm trying to figure out the same thing."

"Good, so we're all on the same team," Kincaid said. "How'd you know where to look for her?"

His story filled in some of the missing pieces—how Jake said he'd seen Kat for the last time around Labor Day 1967 and Curtis's certainty that she would try to leave him a message in Aruba, where they had spent vacations together. It all somehow melted into his theft of Mariah's computers and why he really had set fire to her house—as much to lure her out as to get even with her.

"And if you lure her out of hiding, what then?" Nora asked.

"I disappear her very far back."

"And what's that do, exactly?"

"Allows me to sleep through the night."

"Beyond that," she persisted. "Beyond sleeping at night and finding your partner. Once you've done all that, what then?" *What're your plans? Are you on our side?* "You can't return to SPOT."

"I don't want to go back to that life. I'd like to . . . to return some of the people I disappeared. People I knew were innocent, but whom I disappeared anyway. And . . . I'd like to explore the future."

"The future?" Kincaid exclaimed. "Is that possible?"

"Kat said Mariah took her and McKee into the future, for a glimpse. It was pretty awful. Maybe if I could see what she saw, I would know what back here can be corrected or changed so that we don't annihilate ourselves."

A resourceful man, this Ryan Curtis. And she and Kincaid needed him to be at full capacity, so she brought the first-aid kit from her bag. "I've got some EMT training, Mr. Curtis. How about if I take a look at your leg?"

"I can do it," he said. "Do you have scissors?"

She passed him scissors and turned on the flashlight, holding it so that he could see what he was doing. He cut a large hole in his jeans, exposing the spot where the claw had entered his upper thigh. The cable that protruded looked like a thin, dark, and very dead snake. Blood continue to ooze around the cable and Nora dabbed it away with Betadine-soaked cotton balls. He cut off his jeans to just above the injury, moved the cable to the right, then left, "I don't feel any resistance. I'm going to ease it out. Do you, uh, know how to take stitches?"

"I even have the right kind of needle. And bandages. And antibiotics."

"I'm already taking antibiotics." He began to pull gently on the cable. The ooze of the blood became thicker, she dabbed it away, he kept inching it upward and grimaced several times. Millimeter by millimeter, the cable emerged, thin and bloody. Air now hissed through his teeth, his hands shook, but the end of the cable appeared and dangling from it was a cylindrical object about half an inch thick, with three pronged legs, but no claws, no hooks.

"Looks like you have the newer generation," she said.

Blood streamed from the hole in his thigh and Nora quickly thrust the flashlight at Curtis, blotted the hole with a sterile gauze pad, squirted Betadine into it. Then she applied pressure with fresh pads. His face had gone completely white and he leaned his head back, but watched everything she did.

"How's it look?" Kincaid asked.

"Deep," she said. "But I think he can get away without stitches." Nora removed the gauze. "The blood flow is less." She cleaned it with more Betadine, applied antibiotic salve with a Q-tip, and dressed it with a bandage and medical tape, which would continue to apply pressure. "You'll live," she said.

He didn't say anything and when she looked over at him, she saw that his eyes had closed, his head rested against the window, and he snored softly. The flashlight had slipped out of his hand and lay on the seat between them. She picked it up, leaned forward, and whispered to Kincaid: "He fell asleep. I'm going through his bag."

Kincaid flashed her a thumbs-up. "We've got a good hour to Utica."

Nora sat back and dug through clothing, shoes, tools of all shapes and sizes, several digital cameras, and brought out two laptops. She set them on the seat between her and Curtis. Which one belonged to Mariah? She put his pack on the floor again, turned on the top computer, slipped it over onto her lap.

Dozens of icons lined up across the desktop screen. She clicked *My Computer,* the C drive, then *documents and settings* and *Mariah's documents*.

Hello, bitch.

Nora got out of her memory stick, copied the documents folder, then began clicking through the files, each one more astonishing than the one before it. She found the strange and disturbing history of Special Projects Operation Temporal, what Curtis and Dee Runyon had referred to as SPOT, with names of all its previous directors, assistant directors, and Council members. She discovered phone numbers, e-mail addresses, and addresses for both senators involved in this organization, for every Traveler, mentor, Council member, and for Lydia Fenmore and Ian Rodriguez. There were photos of the Cedar Key facility, blueprints of its buildings, even photos of the holding area on Snake Key. And there were photos of her and Jake, of Kincaid and Tyler, Diana, and of Jake's most recent lover.

She felt violated, soiled, as though her private life had been raped. But she kept clicking and came across a lengthy file on the biochip. Much of it was too technical for her to grasp, but it appeared to be a recipe for making the chips. One entry explained why there was a stun gun in Curtis's pack. Apparently Mariah had used a stun gun on Kat Sargent to force her body to reject the chip. *A taser will do the same thing, but could injure the subject. My preference is the Talon Mini 80,000 volts stun gun, applied to the side of the neck.*

Nora reached into Curtis's pack for the stun gun and slipped it into her own pack along with two sets of hand-cuffs, then continued reading. The most revealing section of the file read: *Once they realize their current batch of chips is defective, the law of supply and demand kicks in. Berlin has produced 1000 chips that we can sell immediately, for the bargain price of $5 million. Joe Aiken won't like that, but if he wants SPOT to continue in any form, he'll have to coop-erate. There's some wiggle room in that price for bargaining.*

Profit? *That* was her bottom-line motive? And who was Berlin? Excited, Nora clicked another file, a letter to Senator Joe Aiken from *peoplesfriend*, the name Mariah had used in her e-mail correspondence with Kincaid. In it, she de-manded that SPOT be shut down by midnight on Halloween 2006. *If you haven't shut it down, then I will do it for you by releasing the attached information to every media and Inter-net source.*

Nora clicked the Word file: Names & Dates for 50,000 of the Disappeared.

"Jesus God," she whispered. *Fifty thousand?* Curtis had said "thousands," not *fifty* thousand. That was the population of Blue River. And the way the heading was worded indi-cated the figure was fifty thousand of a larger number of dis-appeared individuals. *How much larger? How many people can you disappear in thirty years? Seventy-five thousand? A hundred thousand?* Families ruined, lives ripped apart, plun-dered.

She pressed her fists into her eyes and struggled to catch her breath, to contain her rage. *Keep reading. Get as much as you can before he wakes up.* Her hands dropped to her thighs, fingers tightening against her jeans. *C'mon, Nora, scroll. Pay attention.*

The names were arranged by the dates of disappearances, beginning on April 15, 1975, with a seventeen-year-old boy. No other information was provided—not *where* they took him or *who* took him or the *charge* against him. But if he were alive, he would be forty-seven now.

She kept scrolling, horror mounting, eyes burning. Finally, on February 17, 1983, she found it. *Elizabeth Walrave, 37.*

For a long time, her body seemed to be frozen, paralyzed, like the screen, like time. Nothing existed except her mother's name, the date, and her memory's sequence of events on that night twenty-three years ago, unfurling slowly, vividly, in brilliant detail and color. *I can find her.*

She might be dead. She might not want to be found.

But I need to know.

At least now she knew for sure that her mother really was among the disappeared, that Travelers 1101 and 1102 had truncated her young life by taking her somewhere. Lydia Fenmore might be able to provide the *where and when.* But if Mariah Jones made good on her threat to release the information about SPOT and the fifty thousand on Halloween, Nora doubted that she would ever find out where and when her mother had been taken. Lydia Fenmore and whoever else knew would flee and the closure Nora had sought so desperately for her entire life would elude her. Again. Forever.

She suddenly understood how to beat the opposition and knew she couldn't depend on anyone but herself and Kincaid.

Nora took all of the syringes from the Baggie in the cooler and put them in chunks of ice rolled up in one of her shirts. Now Curtis would have to help them before he could help Kat. Nora felt guilty about it, but did it anyway. She wasn't sure what the temp had to be before the chips warmed and expanded, but hoped she would be able to stash them in a freezer or use them before they reached that point.

Next, she slipped her fingers very carefully into Curtis's shirt and withdrew the watch face. She put it inside a zippered pocket in her jeans.

"You're awfully quiet back there," Kincaid said.

Nora leaned forward again, slipped her arm around his neck, and pressed her cheek to his. She inhaled the scent of him, a comforting, familiar male smell. "It's all about the chip," she whispered, and told him what she'd found in the files. "Hide Mariah's laptop somewhere at Bari's. I'm going after information on my mother."

"Without me?"

"Curtis thinks it's just his fight. I want him out of the way for a while. Get him to Bari's, make copies of all the files on the laptop, and hide it. Then you two transition to October thirtieth, around seven p.m, somewhere in downtown Cedar Key, and call me. Or e-mail me. And bring Sunny. She'll find me."

"Are you sure, Nora?" He turned in his seat, slid his hands up along the sides of her face, forcing her to look at him, to answer honestly.

"I'm sure."

He kissed her then, kissed her despite the fact they he was driving, one of those kisses you got once in a lifetime if you're incredibly lucky, she thought, and her left hand dropped to her pack, fingers tightening around the straps. And she *reached* for Cedar Key, *reached* for what her and Kincaid's life might be without the burden of politics and bullshit, *reached* because she didn't know what else to do. Then, following Curtis's advice, she released all desire and need.

Her senses quickened; she had a brief sensation of unbearable speed, as though she were on a spinning carnival ride that increased the G-forces until her skin felt as if it were peeling away. And then she transitioned.

24

Nora suddenly found herself on a street corner, in the twilight, with an electric cart filled with teenagers headed toward her, pedestrians in front of her, and an approaching car to her right. The teens were gawking at her, so she was pretty sure they'd seen her appear.

She quickly turned away from them and moved up the block, struggling to get her bearings. The air smelled right, of salt and sand and fish. Many of the buildings were small and funky, and looked as if they'd been slapped together from weathered driftwood. She felt certain she was on an island, but didn't know for sure which island until she passed a shop called Cedar Key Arts & Crafts.

Several yards later, she ducked into the mouth of an alley that ran behind a restaurant. Pack and jacket off. She stuffed the jacket down inside the pack, unzipped a side compartment, brought out her cell. Signal, date, time: October 30, 6:03 P.M.

She called Tyler's cell. He hadn't heard from her since one this morning, when she and Kincaid had transitioned to the airstrip and he sounded eaten up with anxiety and worry.

"Nora, I've been thinking the worst. Are you here? In Cedar Key?"

"On a corner downtown, on what looks like the main street. Where . . ."

"We're at the Cedar Key Island Hotel. Head east. It's on the left, midway down the main road. I'll meet you in the lobby."

"I'll be there in a jiffy."

Nora turned back toward the corner where she had emerged, looked up and down the road, turned left, and practically ran the several blocks to the inn. Like the other buildings in town, it looked old, battered by the elements, but the lobby was small and intimate, with beautiful hardwood floors. It even boasted a piano near the French doors, which were open to a courtyard. A wedding reception was in progress out there, music, voices, and laughter drifting through the open doors and windows. The sounds of ordinary life.

Her brother came hurrying past the reception desk, but if she weren't looking for him, she wouldn't recognize him. He was growing a beard, had lightened his hair, and wore glasses and clothes that made him look like a professor on sabbatical. He hugged her hard, relieved her of her pack, and slung his arm over her shoulder, hurrying her into a stairwell, his body shielding her from the desk clerk.

"Your and Alex's photos are everywhere," he whispered. "The clerk told me that some Freeze officers have been handing them out this morning."

"Their security cams out on the airstrip must've picked us up. Any photos of you two?"

"Not around here. Not yet. Only on the Internet."

"How'd you pay for the room?"

"A credit card that belongs to Di's grandmother. Different last name. She left right before you called to get us some take-out food. But I called her, told her you were here. She's on her way back."

As they made their way up the stairs and to Tyler's room,

Nora filled him in, her hushed tone a tribute to what she had learned in three days—plus nearly forty years—on the lam. Tyler didn't interrupt until Nora brought out the syringes, handed him one, and put the rest in the tiny freezer of the pint-sized refrigerator. Then he bombarded her with questions. She answered them as well as she could, describing what she had experienced and what she'd learned from Curtis and from Mariah's notes about the chip and how to transition.

Tyler ran his fingers over the syringe, as if testing it against some inner measurement for high strangeness. "It's pretty obvious that none of us can return to our lives as they were before all of this started. But how're we going to establish lives in the past? What do we do for money? How do we rent apartments, buy homes, cars, establish identities? We need a base of some kind. Or are we going to live even farther back? Horse and buggies, caves . . ."

"I haven't thought that far ahead. For the time being, I think we have a temporary base in the sixties, with Bari Serrano."

"And Jake," he added.

"If he's part of the package, fine. I don't care one way or another right now." She brought out her memory stick, Tyler plugged it into his laptop, and copied Mariah's files onto it. "I'm going to find out where they took Mom and one way or another, we'll bring her back."

"Back to what?"

"Back to . . . to wherever we end up. And then I intend to find as many of the disappeared as I can."

"Goddamn, Nora. It's taken them thirty years to disappear fifty thousand plus. How can four of us even make a dent?"

Four of us. "We might have five, if Curtis joins us, possibly six if he can bring Kat back. But we can do it without them."

"If Curtis took all her electronics, maybe she no longer has a list of the fifty thousand to release to anyone."

"I think Mariah has backups of backups, Tyler."

"Then how're you going to prevent the release of this information?"

"We're not. We're going to release it first, tonight, on the conspiracy boards, as just a list of disappearances and without all the explanatory information about SPOT. That way, when she releases it to the mainstream media, it'll look like the work of some crackpot. There'll be an e-mail address with our release so that anyone who has a missing family member can get in touch with us and we'll do what we can to get these people back."

"So they become straight disappearances, like a central source compiled from public records?" he asked.

"Exactly."

"Sounds ambitious but doable. I can set up a Web site. What else?"

"I've compiled a folder on information relevant to this program. It, minus Mariah's threats to shut down SPOT, should be e-mailed to every member of the Senate Intelligence Committee, to the attorney general, and to a federal prosecutor of your choice. You copied it onto your laptop. It's under a file called *sunnydog*. But don't do it till you get another call from me. I'm going to use that as leverage to get info on Mom."

He rubbed his hands together. "Okay, where do I start?"

"With the chips. And then pack bags with everything essential for you and Diana and as soon as she's back and you're both chipped, drive to a hotel in Gainesville that has wireless access. Work from there."

He went online, clicked around. "And how will we meet up with you?"

"When I'm finished here, I'll call you."

"Comfort Inn." He ticked off the address. "And who're you going to approach about getting information on Mom?"

"Senator Joe Aiken."

Tyler whistled softly. "Okay, let's get this show on the road." He breathed deeply, held up the syringe, flicked off the top that covered the needle, tilted his head back. He didn't hesitate, didn't ask more questions, just slid it up into his right nostril. It took him all of sixty seconds and he had no reaction whatsoever, none of the suffocating sensations that she'd experienced. "I don't feel any different," he announced.

"Just in case your body rejects it, I'll leave you some extras."

As Nora helped him pack, Diana burst into the room with bags of take-out food, shut the door, locked it, leaned against it. "The town's crawling with Freeze. I mean, they are *everywhere*. Like they're preparing for an invasion or something. And the road to the airport is blocked off. There's talk that they may block off the road onto the island."

"You two need to get out of here now," Nora said urgently. "Get your bags packed . . ."

"We never unpacked," Tyler said.

"Where's your car parked?"

"The alley out back." Tyler peered through the blinds. "There're a lot of tourists out and about now. And it's dark. We'll be fine. Nora, we rented an electric cart." He motioned her over to the window and pointed out the cart, the third in a lineup of six parked at the curb.

"Here's the key," Diana said, and slapped it into her hand. "But wear this." Diana thrust a light jacket with a hood at Nora, then hugged her. "Hello, good-bye, I miss you, we've been worried sick, Tyler will fill me in, please, please be careful."

Nora hugged her back, Diana zipped up her suitcase. "C'mon, Tyler, we need to split."

"Wait." He removed the Baggie of syringes from the freezer, selected three, passed the Baggie to Nora. "The Comfort Inn," he reminded her. "Love you." And then they were gone.

Nora waited for a few minutes, watching the street. She put on the lightweight jacket that Diana had given her, hurried down the stairs, paused at the lobby door. She started to flip the hood over her head, but decided it might attract more attention than if she just hurried through with her head bowed. It wasn't cold enough to warrant a hood.

But when she walked out into the lobby, she saw a pair of Freeze officers at the front desk. Nora made an abrupt turn that took her straight through the open French doors and into the courtyard. The wedding reception was now in full swing, the band loud, people dancing, laughter ringing out, the bride and groom radiant as they moved from table to table, talking to guests seated at the tables.

Nora, so inappropriately dressed, was as obvious as a heart attack. She already drew curious glances from service personnel behind the long table that served as a bar. Worse, the only exit out of the courtyard—a tall, wooden gate—was shut and blocked by that long table. She glanced back into the lobby, where the Freeze officers had turned away from the desk and were staring right at her. She spun around and raced across the courtyard, bumping into people on the dance floor, stumbling past tables and chairs, trying to lose herself in the crowd. Just before she reached the bar, the band suddenly went silent, shouts rang out behind her, the crowd parted, and for a single breathless moment, the officers had a clear shot at her.

Before either of them could fire, Nora dived under the table, jerking hard on the white cloth that covered it, and bottles crashed to the floor—gin, rum, scotch, soda, wine, water. Chaos erupted in the courtyard as everyone tried to get out of the way at once and Nora shot to her feet, hit the latch on the gate, and exploded through it.

She ran over to the third electric cart at the curb, tossed her pack in the passenger seat, jammed the key into the ignition, and pulled away from the curb. As she made a U-turn in the middle of the road, the Freeze officers raced through the gate and opened fire. Nora, her mouth flashing dry with mounting panic, threw herself forward, over the steering wheel, to make herself a more difficult target, and veered haphazardly from one side of the road to another. But they kept firing. She didn't trust herself to shoot back while she was driving the cart.

One shot tore across the canopy roof. Another whistled past her head. In the side mirror, Nora saw one of the men chasing her on foot while the other loped toward a car across the street from the hotel. The cart did about ten miles an hour, hardly fast enough to outrun a bicycle, much less anything else. She looked frantically around for a side street, an alley. But the only alternative was an unfenced yard. She swerved into it and the cart bounced across grass, flattened a bed of freshly planted flowers, sliced a path through a garden at the side of the house, and slammed down into an alley behind the house.

Sirens sundered the air. The Freeze boys had called for backup and they were closing in. Nora drove until the alley ended, then stopped, grabbed her pack, and ran across a deserted road that paralleled small, wooden buildings lining the water. She plunged into a thicket of vegetation to the right of the buildings and dropped to her knees to catch her breath, to orient herself.

But she had no idea where she was in relation to anything on this island. She brought out her PDA, was relieved to see that she had a wireless signal, and went online. She got the address for the Old Fenimore Mill, where Curtis said Senator Aiken was staying, and activated the GPS. Once she had a fix on her own location, she entered the address for the Fenimore. A second blinking light appeared, less than a quarter of a mile from her, the route laid out.

Even though the sirens were still loud and close, she peeked out of the bushes, didn't see any cars, and took off. Within a minute, she reached the grounds of a condo, cut through its parking lot, and hugged a line of trees that curved down into a dry gully and up again between what looked like a saltwater marsh and a curving line of four-story buildings. According to the GPS, she had reached Old Fenimore Mill. Now she had to locate building C.

All the buildings were raised up on tall concrete pilings, a safety precaution in the event of flooding, with plenty of dimly lit parking space beneath them. Nora darted to the front of the closest structure: building B. She hurried on to building C. Second floor, apartment three, she thought.

Curtis had said that Senators Aiken and Lazier were here alone, without security people. She hoped that was still true. Since Aiken was the first of the private investors in SPOT, she thought it was safest to assume that he was chipped and knew enough about how it worked to get himself out of a bind. So she tucked the weapon Kincaid had given her in her jacket pocket, clutched the stun gun in her right hand, and started up the stairs.

The cool October wind blew off the salt marsh, thick with a rich meld of scents—of salt and water and wildlife. The tide was out and now that it was dark, stars popped into view against the vast, black skin of the sky, their light glistening against the wet islands that had appeared as the water receded. The cacophony of frogs, a loud, alien sound, traveled in the wind.

She stopped in front of apartment three, rapped three times, quickly, loudly, and stood to one side of the peephole in the door. She brought out her weapon.

From inside, a male voice: "Hold on, I'm coming, Rick."

Rick. That would be Richard Lazier, the junior senator from somewhere out west. She couldn't recall exactly which state or what he stood for and at the moment, didn't care. The door opened and Aiken stood there, a fat man in a bathrobe who took in everything in at once—who she was, that she was armed.

"Mrs. McKee." He sounded breathless, as if he had only enough air in his lungs to utter her name.

"Senator. It's time for us to talk."

She stepped forward, gesturing with the weapon for him to move back into the apartment. When she was just inside the door, she kicked it shut, and, without taking her eyes off of him, turned the lock. Her other hand snapped up and she pressed the stun gun to his neck.

Aiken's eyes bulged and rolled back in their sockets, his knees crumpled, and down he went. *I have just committed a federal offense.* He twitched and drooled as if he were having a seizure, but his nose didn't bleed. He apparently wasn't chipped. Odd.

Nora hurriedly checked out the rest of the condo. He was quite alone here. The TV was on, tuned to CNN, live shots of the strife in the Mideast, a frozen dinner steaming on the coffee table, the porch doors open to the cool wind off the marsh. She snatched his cell and keys off the coffee table, pocketed them, then went into his bedroom and pulled clothes and a jacket off hangers.

When she returned to him, his twitching was subsiding. Nora dropped the clothes on the floor in front of him and backed up to the wall, the nine millimeter aimed at his chest, waiting for him to open his eyes.

He wheezed, raised up on his left elbow, glared at her. "The stun gun wasn't necessary, Mrs. McKee."

"If you were chipped, it was very necessary. Get dressed."

"I don't know what you're talking about."

Right. "C'mon, put the clothes on." He was somewhat modest, turning away from her as he dropped the bathrobe. "And why aren't you chipped? As the first investor, I expected you to be."

"Like I said . . ."

"Cut the horseshit. I had quite an interesting chat with Ryan Curtis. I know the current biochips are defective. That's why you're aren't chipped. Your body already rejected it. And I'm betting that quite a few members of your organization are in the same state."

"You astonish me, Mrs. McKee." He turned, fully clothed now, and sat on the floor to put on his shoes and socks, his jacket. "I've read your file. I knew you were bright, but I never saw you as *this* resourceful. We would love to recruit you."

Smooth, this Aiken, and a good psychologist. She would give him that much. Here he was, a fat man with a gun in his face and no apparent escape route, yet he was trying to make a deal like this was some sort of reality TV show where the ending was stacked in his favor.

"Recruit me for SPOT?" she laughed.

"A vastly changed SPOT."

"Since I didn't even know this outfit existed until three days ago, I don't know what that means."

"No more random disappearances, no more disappearances because someone's got a gripe or an ax to grind. There'll be an oversight committee, we'll be serving the people in the way they should be served."

She didn't know whether to laugh, cry, or flee. "And exactly how are the people served by an ultrasecretive organization that disappears their family members and loved ones, and keeps a certain group powerful and rich? How are people served by living in an atmosphere of suspicion and terror? Why not use the chip to promote peace? Or to end hunger and poverty? You know, to foster all the stuff that's sadly lacking?"

His smile reeked of condescension, as though he were royalty and she was some lowly peon who just didn't get it. "I admire your idealism, as naive as it is. But that's not how world affairs work."

"Only because people like you benefit from being powerful. Maybe you need a few years in AIDS-ridden Africa."

His smile shrank. When he spoke again, his voice was low, menacing, ugly. "You really have overstepped your bounds, Mrs. McKee. Do you really think this organization has been allowed to exist for thirty years just because of me? There are so many other players involved, at so many different levels of government, both nationally and internationally, that even if your group gets rid of me and all the others you think are in charge, SPOT will continue in some form. It has to."

Jake's shadow government, she thought, the cabal. That was what Aiken was talking about. "With defective biochips, there won't be any SPOT at all. Mariah hopes to profit from that by selling you her chips. The new, improved version that can stop time, reverse time, who the hell knows what its limits are."

"That's old news, Mrs. McKee. We're meeting with her at nine to discuss her business proposals."

"Meeting her where?"

He rolled his lips and didn't say anything.

Nora cocked the gun. "Where?" she repeated.

More silence.

She adjusted her aim slightly and fired just to the right of Aiken's head. His body jerked, the blood drained from his face, he blurted, "At the . . . Bones and Nails . . . a . . . a bar twenty miles from Cedar Key."

Nora quickly punched out Kincaid's number and, without saying his name, left him a detailed message.

"That was a mistake," Aiken said when she disconnected from her call. "You shouldn't bring anyone else into this situation. It's tricky enough as it is. And since you're obviously here because you want something, what do you have to offer me in return?"

His arrogance snapped the last of her patience and she grabbed his fat chin and leaned in close to his face. "I think you're supposed to ask what *I want,* not what I *can offer you.* And what I want is the date and location where my mother was disappeared. Elizabeth Walrave, February 17, 1983."

Aiken didn't flinch, didn't seem to be scared, didn't react in any of the ways she expected him to. He just shrugged, like none of it was a big deal. Then it dawned on her that he didn't know she was chipped. Didn't have a clue.

"I don't have that information."

"Really. Then let's jog your memory, senator."

And she grasped Aiken's arm and *reached* for Marconi Beach in the early eighties, a place of fond family memories, in a time before her mother had disappeared, before her childhood had turned to shit. She *reached,* her need and desire grappling for that time, struggling to reach it. Then she abruptly withdrew the energy, and suddenly she and Aiken were surrounded by sand. Waves crashed at their feet, a cold, bitter wind bit into her skin.

Aiken, on his hands and knees, looked around wildly, snorting like an enraged bull. "Jesus God, what the . . ." He heaved his heaping mass of flesh upward and staggered away from her, from the water, his body illuminated by a thin ribbon of pearl-colored light ebbing along the horizon.

Nora didn't know whether it was dawn or sunset, whether she had reached Marconi Beach or not. But wherever she was, the beach where Aiken stumbled along, screaming for help, was deserted. Nora stared after him, thinking of Curtis's description of how Jake had acted when he'd found himself on an ice floe and then on the shores of Lake Maracaibo. *Clones from the same psychological mold, these two.*

She pressed her fists against her eyes, wishing that she were still a psychology professor at Blue River, oblivious and stupid, blind and deaf. Then she remembered the watch face and unzipped her jean pocket and brought it out. *February 7, 1981, 6:38 a.m.* Two years and ten days before her mother would be disappeared.

She slipped the watch back into her pocket and went after Aiken. Her shoes slapped the sand, the waves slammed against the beach, receded, rose up and slammed again. He could have made this so much easier by just by telling her what she wanted to know when they were back in the living room.

When she reached him, he was on his knees, dimpled hands pressed to his thighs, his face frozen with horror, his jacket flapping in the cold wind. She sank to the sand in front of him. "Joe, who's the greater enemy? Me or Mariah?"

He struggled to compose himself, to deal with what was. He sniffled, wiped his hand across his nose, his mouth, his eyes. He glanced out at the rapidly darkening ocean, then looked back at her, "Mariah." He paused, hiccupped, went on in a soft, choked voice. "Right now, SPOT's medical facility is jammed with Travelers whose bodies are rejecting the chips. Other Travelers are stranded in the past. . . . SPOT is collapsing, Mariah has us by the balls and she knows it. She . . . she wants five million for a thousand chips. *Five fucking million.*"

Exactly what she had read on Mariah's laptop. "C'mon, that's loose change for you. So the issue isn't money, it's her power over you."

He rubbed his hands against his thighs, blew into them, warming them. In a small, halting voice, he said, "You don't understand. The biochip is our country's greatest hope. With the chip, we can end nuclear proliferation, end the crisis in the Mideast, and . . ."

". . . and you haven't done any of that in thirty years. But with a new improved chip, you can dominate the world once and for all by disappearing everyone who gets in your way. I understand completely, senator. You'll be doing more of what you've been doing for the last thirty years, but expanding your territory. North Korea, China, Russia, Syria, Iraq, Iran . . . disappear all the troublesome fuckers. Yeah, I get it."

"No, no, it won't be like that. You've got it all wrong."

"I don't think so. But guess what, Joe? I've got the recipe for the new, improved chip. Got it off Mariah's laptop. And I have enough chips for every Traveler and all your investors and then some that will last until more can be produced."

"*You* have it? The *new* one?" His eyes burned brightly, as if with fever. "You were chipped with it?"

"Yes."

"And that's what you're offering in return for information about your mother?"

"It's what I'm offering in return for all the records." *And the only thing you'll be getting out of it is a prison cell.*

"But why do you need all the records?"

"The question here is why don't you have all the records?"

He brought his pudgy fists to his thighs, exhaled noisily. "The bylaws are written so that the entire detailed records about disappearances are divided among the director, assistant director, and the senior Council member. That's Ian Rodriguez, Lydia Fenmore, and Simone White. They're . . . supposed to give copies of those records to us. They're supposed to give us that information tonight. All these years, we've gotten only partials. That's just one . . . of the problems we're trying to rectify. But Ian's dead, so I . . . I guess just Lydia and Simone have that information now."

"When did Ian die?"

"In the explosion at Mariah's house."

Really? How interesting. She had seen him and Fenmore running away from the house. "So with him dead, Lydia is director?"

He nodded and the picture suddenly got much clearer for Nora.

"Are you . . . going to disappear me here permanently?"

That would make me as bad as you. "It depends on how cooperative you are."

"I'll do whatever you . . . want. Anything."

"Good." She unzipped her pack, set a bottle of water and an apple in the sand. "I'd like you to wait right here. I'll be back shortly."

"But . . . but . . . You just said . . ."

"I know exactly where you are. Don't worry, I won't do to you what you people did to my mother and Jake and—what? Fifty thousand others? I'll be back. I just need you out of the way right now."

And before he could move or say another word, she *reached*—and *released*.

25

Curtis, Kincaid, and the dog emerged in the middle of the Fenimore complex, near the pool. Fortunately, it was dark and too cool to swim so the pool area was deserted. A brisk wind blew off the salt marsh, rattling the palm fronds like maracas in some mariachi band and carrying the shriek of sirens, close but not on top of them. Curtis figured they were coming from somewhere along the main street.

"It's just past eight," Kincaid said, "and Nora left a message five minutes ago. You'd better listen to this." He held out the cell. "Press one."

Curtis was pissed off enough already that Nora had taken Kat's watch and the entire Baggie of syringes. Without at least one syringe, he couldn't bring Kat back. But Nora had known that, of course, and it was why she'd done it. *If you help us first, then you'll get the syringe you need to rescue Kat.*

Well, not exactly. He could transition back to Bari's and get another syringe. Unless Nora had done that already and taken all the syringes in the freezer. Quite possible. He believed she might be one of those rare people who had a natural talent for traveling, someone who took to it like a proverbial fish to water, as though traveling were her true element. Still, he was pissed. She had used all the information he'd spilled during that time in the backseat to meddle in what was *his* battle, not *hers*. So when he hesitated and didn't take the cell immediately, Kincaid snapped, "Get over it, man. You fucked with our lives first. She had every right to do what she did."

He couldn't dispute that. Nonetheless, Curtis snatched the cell out of Kincaid's hand, pressed one, and listened to Nora's hushed, urgent message. For moments afterward, he felt numb. And then a kind of elemental horror claimed him. *Profit and greed?* That's what all this had been about? Mariah selling her new, improved chip to SPOT for some millions? And Aiken, that bastard, was going to *negotiate* with her? He and Rodriguez, Fenmore, and all the other big honchos were going to sit around a table at a biker bar and discuss this as though it were a *legitimate business deal*?

And then he started laughing. He laughed until his ribs ached, until Kincaid grabbed the phone out of his hand and took off, racing after Sunny. The dog loped across the grass, past hedges, headed for building C. Curtis realized that Sunny had picked up Nora's scent and ran after her and Kincaid.

He was vaguely aware that the sirens sounded closer, that blue lights spun like strobes, that he heard the roaring engine of a very large vehicle. A marine engine? Headlights suddenly impaled them and they all froze—Sunny, Kincaid slightly behind her, and Curtis—as a Hummer tore across the gravel driveway, aimed straight at them. Before he could move, before he could even think about moving, the Hummer screeched to a stop and Nora leaned out the driver's window, shouting, *"Fast, the cops are right back there!"*

She threw open the driver's door and scooted into the passenger seat. Kincaid scrambled behind the wheel, and Curtis and the dog leaped into the back. Kincaid hit the accelerator and the Hummer shot forward before Curtis had even shut his door. Wind whistled through the Hummer. Curtis twisted around and saw two unmarked Freeze cars right behind them, tearing across the grass and flowerbeds, but in opposite directions, to cut them off.

"Head up the main street until I tell you to turn," he shouted.

His door slammed shut. He got out his weapon, lowered his window, aimed at the closest unmarked car, and started firing. But he needed a better shot at them.

"Put down the rear window," he yelled, and Kincaid did and he scrambled into the rear well and opened fire again. This time, he hit a tire on the front vehicle, the driver lost control, and the car crashed through the sliding glass doors of the complex office.

The other cruiser raced toward them from the right, trying to cut them off, and Kincaid swerved the Hummer toward it, a maneuver so smooth and flawless that Curtis forgot how pissed off he was. Kincaid drove this sucker like he'd been driving tanks all his life. Metal shrieked against metal, the car dropped back, and the Hummer shot up the main street.

Either Nora or Kincaid had activated the GPS and the mechanical voice announced that a turn was imminent. Curtis climbed into the backseat again, where the dog sat at attention, panting, unsettled, and leaned forward. "Take the next right turn. It's Highway Twenty-four and it'll take us off the island. It's only two lanes, there could be roadblocks if either driver called for backup. It's the only way to get to Bones and Nails. And where's Aiken?"

"Marconi Beach, February 7, 1981," Nora replied. "I wanted him out of the way. But when I transitioned back to his condo, Senator Lazier and a couple of Freeze guys had broken into the place. They saw me when I made a dash for Aiken's Hummer."

"He rented this gas-hungry monster!" Curtis exclaimed. Aiken, who had talked about severing America's dependence on foreign oil? And, worse, Curtis had bought into his rhetoric.

"And one other thing," Nora said. "Ian Rodriguez supposedly died in that explosion at Mariah's."

Curtis barely had time to process that information before Kincaid hung a fast right onto Highway 24 and raced forward, hands gripping the steering wheel.

"I'm calling Tyler and telling him to release everything in twenty minutes," Nora said.

"Release what?" Curtis asked. "And where's your brother?"

"He and my friend Di are chipped and they're releasing Mariah's files to the press, the Senate Intelligence Committee, the attorney general, a federal prosecutor of Tyler's choice, and all the major blogs and newspapers. But the information is going out strictly as a disappearance program. These bastards are done."

Jesus. Who the hell did she think she was? She and Kincaid had slammed into his world with all the subtlety of a pair two-ton gorillas and acted like they were calling all the shots. Yet, Curtis felt a sneaking admiration for both of them.

They crossed two bridges before the first roadblock appeared—half a dozen state police cars, lights spinning, with cops lining the either side of the road. "Here comes the ultimate game of chicken," Kincaid warned, and barreled straight toward them.

As the Hummer bore down on the roadblock, Curtis told Kincaid to open the sunroof and shut the rear window. He did both and Curtis popped up through the sunroof, Nora joined him, and when they were within a hundred yards of the roadblock, they both opened fire. Nora handled the weapon like a pro, a fact as surprising to Curtis as the way Kincaid drove the Hummer.

In fact, he didn't slow down, hesitate, or falter for a second. Kincaid simply aimed the Hummer straight at the cars in the roadblock so that it locked onto the barricade of glass and metal like a missile on a target. Two cruisers suddenly sped out of the way, opening a narrow passage through which the Hummer raced in a volley of gunfire.

They discovered that the windows of the Hummer were bulletproof, the first indication that the vehicle wasn't Aiken's rental car, but probably his private vehicle, driven down here by some well-paid lackey. A mile past the roadblock, the cops reconnoitered and within moments, a line of cruisers raced after them, lights flashing, sirens wailing. "You are twelve minutes from your destination," the GPS announced.

Twelve minutes too long, Curtis thought. The dog was huddled on the floor. Their chances of arriving quietly at the Bones & Nail were less than zero. That meant that Mariah and the rest of them would be long gone before they ever arrived and it would all be for nothing. "I don't know about you two," Curtis said. "But I've had enough of this bullshit. Let's go in *our* way."

"Transition out of a moving fuel tank at hundred miles an hour?" Kincaid balked. "Bad idea."

"You've been to this bar?" Nora asked.

"Yeah. Let me do the transition."

"Alex?" she asked.

"Let me stop the Hummer."

Curtis dropped one hand to Sunny's head, put his other hand on Kincaid's shoulder. The Hummer began to slow and Nora pressed her right hand over Curtis's. "Okay, we're on the shoulder," Kincaid announced.

The tires kicked up gravel, sand, brush. The speedometer needle fell to fifty, thirty-nine, fifteen. The cruisers were nearly on top of them. "Seat belts off," Curtis said, struggling to keep his voice quiet, calm, and Kincaid tapped the brakes.

Curtis *reached* for the Bones & Nails, *reached* and *released* and then the Hummer was gone and the four of them emerged in a restroom, music pounding against the walls, the stink of cigarette smoke and booze permeating the air. A biker guy standing at a urinal looked stupefied by their appearance out of thin air, and stammered, "What the fu . . ."

Nora zapped the biker with the stun gun and as he fell back, Curtis and Kincaid caught him and laid him gently on he floor. Kincaid moved fast to the door, locked it, and Nora worked the biker's arms out of his jacket. She already wore his cap low on her head.

"I'm the least recognizable of the three of us," she said. "And as far as we know, Mariah has never laid eyes on me. I'll go out to the bar and see what's what and text you if they're all there."

"And then what?" Kincaid asked.

"Mariah will be chipped for sure," Curtis said. "Sunny and I will take care of her first. Can you two transition Fenmore and White? To Marconi Beach? I can meet you there. Then we'll decide what to do with the lot of them."

"I don't want anyone permanently disappeared," Nora said.

Here it was again, Curtis thought, Nora acting like she was in charge. "You don't have to permanently disappear anyone, Nora."

Her dark eyes darted to his face. "I mean, I don't want any of us to permanently disappear anyone."

"No, what you mean is that you don't want me to disappear anyone permanently," he shot back. "I'm going to do what I think is best and you do the same."

"For chrissakes," she whispered urgently, straightening up. "We've got to agree on how we're going to handle this."

"We *do* agree," Kincaid snapped. "Ryan takes care of Mariah, we take care of the others. What he wants to do with her, Nora, is *his* business, not ours."

Curtis knew from the expression on her face that it wasn't what she wanted to hear from Kincaid. She started to argue the point, but apparently thought better of it. "Whatever." She slung her pack over her shoulder. "I'll text you."

"Let's get this guy into a stall," Curtis said to Kincaid.

They pulled the biker into the last stall, handcuffed him, wrapped his ankles in duct tape, and sealed his mouth with a strip of tape. When they hurried out of the stall, Nora was gone and the door to the restroom was whispering shut.

While Kincaid locked the door, Curtis slipped a silencer on his weapon.

* * *

Nora made a beeline to the crowded bar and squeezed in
at the end, where she could see the entire room in the wall
mirror. The booths against the far wall and most of the tables
in the middle of the room were filled. Off to the left, two
men played pool while half a dozen people looked on. The
jukebox volume was turned up so high that the walls seemed
to tremble and shake. How could anyone conduct any kind
of meeting in here?

"What can I get you, ma'am?" The bartender, an aging
hippie biker type with a thinning gray ponytail, leaned forward on his elbows so that he could hear her.

"I'm supposed to meet Lydia Fenmore here. Has she arrived yet?"

"Yeah, through there." He pointed a long, bony finger off
to the right. "See that exit sign? Go that way and hang a
quick left."

"Thanks. Do you know if everyone else has arrived already?"

"Half a dozen suits, the bitchy biker chick, the senator
who sold out Florida, some of his security people, and a
bunch of Freeze. Does that just about cover it?"

"Is a tall black woman with them?"

"Yeah, she got here a while ago. Listen, you tell Lydia I
don't want no trouble back there. I'm allergic to Freeze, you
know what I'm saying? And I'm pissed she brought them.
You tell her that, too. Those pricks are standing guard outside the room and no one can get in there without an ID
check. And this is *my* goddamn bar."

"I've got the same allergy. In fact, is there any other way
into that room? I'd rather not have any dealings with Freeze
at all. But I do need to talk to Lydia."

"Sure thing. Take the hallway that leads away from the
restrooms. It curves around into the kitchen. Just inside, on
the wall, are the aprons the kitchen help wear when they're
serving back there. Put on one of those. Freeze won't stop

you and if anyone in the kitchen bothers you, tell them Adam Bradley sent you in to help serve."

"Thanks so much, Mr. Bradley. I really appreciate this." As she turned away from the bar, she sent a text message to Kincaid.

Nora hastened back through the crowd and when she ducked into the hallway, Kincaid, Curtis, and Sunny were waiting. She shed the biker's jacket, hung it on the doorknob of the men's room, and they made their way up the hall, the dog's claws clicking against the tile floor as she strained at the leash snapped to her collar. She wondered where the leash had come from.

The inside of the kitchen reminded her of Pham's Market, high energy, focused, everyone scurrying around, doing his or her job. The only obvious difference was that country western music played from a radio somewhere. One guy in an apron told them the kitchen was off limits and dogs weren't allowed.

"Bradley sent us in to help serve," Nora said.

"Yeah? The dog, too?" He rolled his eyes. "Whatever. This place is getting nuttier by the second. Aprons are over there . . ." His tattooed left arm shot out and he pointed at the wall. "And then take those platters of chicken wings in there." His right arm shot out and he pointed at all the platters of food lined up on two serving carts.

"Got it," Nora replied.

They donned the full aprons with the bar's logo blazing across the front—crossbones made of nails. Curtis, who had been peering through the square window in the door to check the situation in the adjoining room, now strode over, pushing two serving carts in front of him, both of them draped with tablecloths and filled with platters of food.

"They're all in there, at a large table under the window— Fenmore, the entire Council, six or seven guys who're probably investors, and there must be another half dozen feds—probably Freeze—and the senator's own security personnel. Mariah's right in the middle." He pushed one cart over to Nora, lifted the tablecloth on his, and whistled softly for Sunny. "C'mon, girl. You're going to hide here."

Sunny didn't hesitate. She stepped onto the lower section of the cart and crouched down like she'd been doing this sort of shit all her life and Curtis unsnapped her leash. "When did you two become such close buddies?" Nora asked, still pissed at Curtis for not agreeing to her agenda concerning permanent disappearances.

"When the dog realized we're on the same side," Curtis replied. He set his pack next to her, dropped the cloth back into place, then raised the metal cover on one of the platters, revealing a dozen pieces of steaming corn on the cob, and pushed it aside. In its place, he set a weapon fitted with a silencer and covered it with the metal top.

Nora and Kincaid exchanged a look. "The gun's a bad idea, man," said Kincaid.

"Like you told Nora, Alex. What *I* choose to do is *my* business. Mariah is *my* problem and I want as many options as possible. You can bet that everyone in there is armed. I suggest you be prepared to defend yourselves." He gestured at Nora's biker cap. "May I?" he asked.

"Sure." She handed it to him, he pulled it down low over his eyes, and turned away from them, pushing the cart along in front of him, and disappeared through the swinging doors.

"I think we're going to be too vulnerable without some chaos in there," Nora said, watching Curtis thought the window in the door.

"I was just thinking the same thing," Kincaid agreed, and set his pack on the lower shelf of the cart. "Let me go in next, and as soon as it looks like Curtis is closing in on Mariah, hit the fire alarm. That'll throw the feds off."

Nora caught his hand and squeezed it. "Be careful, Alex."

He kissed her quickly, then moved on through the doors. She watched him through the window, his body hunched forward, head bowed, the back of her throat dry with dread.

* * *

"Here's to a successful negotiation that's satisfactory to everyone involved," Mariah said, holding up her glass of Perrier, then clicking the edge of Lazier's glass.

Up and down the table, glasses clicked together, beginning what Lydia hoped would be a quick, neat deal. She felt uneasy with so many people around. In addition to the fifteen at their table, there were half a dozen Freeze personnel in here, three of the preppie senator's security people, and the bar employees who came and went with drinks and appetizers.

And yet, everything so far had gone smoothly. Never mind that Aiken hadn't shown up or that Mariah acted like an empress holding court. The preppie senator and his investors were fascinated by everything she said. Even the members of the Council were taken with her. All of them except Simone White had known her only as the inventor of the chip and SPOT's first director. Her legend had preceded her. Now they saw her as a god.

The investors and Lazier kept up a steady stream of questions that Mariah answered with quick wit or an astonishing knowledge of science and quantum physics. The preppie senator with the doctorate in quantum physics looked utterly spellbound. It made Lydia want to vomit.

On one level, the whole thing was a charade because Mariah was responsible for the fact that SPOT, at least in its former incarnation, had collapsed and not a single person in this room was chipped—except for Mariah. Everyone at this table was the equivalent of an abused spouse, she thought, who nonetheless continued to sleep with the enemy because of what the enemy offered.

And for Lydia, who had arranged this meeting, the offer was seductive. She was to get a quarter of whatever Mariah's buyers—government or private investors or a combination of both—agreed to pay for the first thousand chips, with Dr. Berlin getting another quarter. She, as Mariah's official liaison, would be the most powerful individual in SPOT, with a guaranteed seat on the oversight committee that Aiken and

Lazier were putting together. In many ways, it all felt like the resolution of some long, strange war where both sides held the same ideology, but simply had different methods of implementing it.

The kitchen doors swung open again and more servers appeared, pushing carts filled with chicken wings and corn on the cob, baked beans and potato salad, piping hot bread, all the specialties of the house. Another server appeared to remove the now-empty salad plates and soup bowls. Mariah leaned toward Lydia and asked, "Any word from Joe yet?"

"Nothing. I'll try him again. His driver was supposed to bring him. Maybe they had car trouble."

"It's not like him," Mariah said. "The . . ."

And suddenly she snapped back against the chair, eyes wide, shocked, mouth falling open. A red rose of blood bloomed on the shoulder of her blouse and another burst against the front of her blouse. She gasped and fell forward, arms flopping across the table like fish out of water. Simone screamed, *"She's been shot, Mariah has been shot."*

Even as Lazier and his investors leaped up, a fire alarm shrieked, the ceiling sprinklers spun to life, spraying water everywhere, and pandemonium erupted around her. Everyone was shouting, scrambling to escape or diving for cover. Just as Lydia shot to her feet, one of the servers slammed his cart into the table, jarring Lydia to the bone, knocking her back, and trapping her between the wall and the edge of the table. The server lunged for Mariah, a reddish-gold dog at his side, and Lydia realized it was Curtis, my God, Curtis, here, now, with the golden retriever that had been their one and only experiment on dogs. Then Curtis, Mariah, and the dog vanished.

That's not happening to me, she thought, and shoved the table away from her and looked frantically around for the best way out. But someone had thrown open the door to the front of the bar and people poured in like an army of ants, hungry for the excitement, the uncertainty, the chaos. The lights flashed off and on, then off completely, plunging the room into darkness. Screams erupted, furniture crashed to the floor, water from the sprinklers poured over her. She knew she would be trampled in seconds if she moved. Then the safety light winked on, a single bright beam where the spinning water glistened like handfuls of diamonds.

Near panic now, certain that Curtis hadn't been alone, Lydia weaved through the frenzied crowd, shoving her way toward the emergency door, her clothes drenched, the din pounding, hammering, pummeling her senses. Her car, where had she left her car? Front or back? Jesus, she couldn't remember. And getting to the emergency exit was impossible, the crowd was converging on it, cops were pushing their way in.

A volley of shots rang out, people shrieked, shoved harder, and someone behind Lydia stumbled, screaming for help, and grabbed onto her leg. She stumbled, kicked savagely, freed herself, and shoved forward, sideways, locked in a full-blown panic. She constantly swiped at the water that rolled into her eyes, began to slip and slide in the puddles that covered the floor, staggered toward the kitchen doors, past cops who were shouting and trying to herd people one way or another.

And then someone grabbed her shoulder and Lydia jerked free, and spun, her right arm swinging, hand fisted. But arms tightened around her neck and she gasped, she couldn't get free, couldn't breathe, and suddenly she was sinking into sand, in a cold, silent moonlight, a bitter wind biting into her face, chilling her through her wet clothes.

Whether it was the chill or her terror, her mind snapped abruptly into clarity and she knew that whoever had grabbed her around the neck had transitioned her. And done it well, smoothly, professionally. There was only one Traveler she knew who could do it like that—Curtis.

But when she raised her head, Nora McKee and Alex Kincaid were crouched in front of her, the moonlight painting their features in a surreal way, so their faces looked waxen, not quite real. To Kincaid's right, Simone White was struggling to push up from the sand, but couldn't find purchase, as her hands kept sinking into it. And just to Lydia's right was Joe Aiken, on his knees in the sand, as though he'd been praying, his pudgy hands flat against his sandy thighs. Shock rendered her mute. Her mouth opened, shut, then opened again.

"Sweet Christ," she whispered. "Joe . . . what . . ."

"Just give them the goddamn information," he barked.

"*What* information?"

Nora McKee leaned in so close to Lydia she could feel the warmth of her breath. In a voice as sharp as glass, she said, "February 14, 1983. You stuck in a gun in my face and threatened to blow my head off if Elizabeth Walrave didn't cooperate with you. Are you remembering now, T1101?"

Oh shit. "I . . . I don't know what you're talking about."

Nora grabbed the cords that held the memory sticks and yanked them off Lydia's neck. "Two memory sticks. And one of them belonged to Ian Rodriguez and you took it when you killed him. He was alive after the explosion at Mariah's. I saw him when we picked up Curtis. He was running just as fast as you were. You disappeared him somewhere and then *killed* him so you could become director." She yanked at the cord around Simone's neck. "And here's the rest of the information I want." Nora stepped away from her, from Simone, from Joe, the memory sticks clutched in her hand. "We're outta here," she said, and grasped Kincaid's hand.

Something else happened after that, but Lydia Fenmore didn't know what it was. Her brain went south, her body failed her, she collapsed against the wet sand and surrendered to her enormous fatigue. Her eyes shut, she wanted to sleep and wake up in her safe spot, but before she and Rodriguez had transitioned to Mariah's, before she had gone back with Vachinski, before McKee had been arrested, before, before, before, way back to the day she had met Rodriguez, tai chi master of the Santa Barbara Fitness Club.

I want to offer you a job, she'd said to him after his class, and he turned his head and smiled in a way that lit up her insides.

Curtis emerged on an empty, grassy hill, the light as smooth and pale as pearls, with Mariah Jones in his arms, the dog at his side. He had no idea where or when in time he had leaped, but it didn't matter. He knew from the ragged sound of Mariah's breathing that she was dying. Her nose was bleeding, too, so her body had rejected the chip and she couldn't transition, couldn't escape him. Not this time.

He set her down in the long, velvet grass. The lake below them was as round as a coin, untouched, pristine, and caught the perfect sweep of brilliant blue sky. Her eyes fluttered open, brimming with pain, anger, and other emotions he couldn't read. Her fingers closed around Curtis's wrist and Sunny, crouched beside him, growled softly, a warning.

"You . . . didn't have to shoot me," she said hoarsely.

"It was the only way to end this insanity."

"I knew . . . this was one possibility, but Curtis, I didn't think you had it in you to get this far. And I totally . . . miscalculated Nora McKee. And the dog." She laughed, but it collapsed into a fit of coughing. Blood oozed from a corner of her mouth. "And Kincaid, that bastard, after everything I gave him . . . the design for the hybrid, the biochips . . . but you won't find Berlin. He's *my* guarantee."

Dr. Berlin? Curtis's thoughts flew around, worker bees in search of the hive, and began piecing it altogether. Berlin. Of course. He wasn't just in charge of medical, but of the production of the biochips. He started to grill her about Berlin, but realized he didn't give a shit. Berlin couldn't hurt him. Not now.

Not yet.

Mariah coughed again and Curtis lifted her head to make it easier for her to breathe. "So what will you . . . do now?" she asked, her voice a ragged whisper.

"Bring Kat back and then start returning as many of the disappeared as possible."

"You . . . can't go back to the day of the disappearance. It's . . . a sealed door. I don't . . . know why."

"And you're probably lying." Another fit of coughing seized her and he kept her head elevated until it passed. When he set her head down again, her grasp on his wrist loosened. "How can Sunny still be alive?" he asked.

"The same way . . . I'm still alive. Born in . . . 1913 . . . went back and chipped my younger self . . . Sunny's aging slowed . . . when she . . . was chipped."

Mariah extended her fingers toward the dog. It wasn't clear to Curtis whether the gesture was intended as a peace offering or a taunt, but to the dog, it didn't matter. Sunny bared her teeth, a low, menacing growl deep in her throat, and snapped at the air close to Mariah's hand.

"Even your dog turned against you," he said. "Sunny, Dee and Kim Runyon, Lydia, Aiken . . ."

"If she doesn't remain . . . chipped all her life, she'll age like this." She tried to snap her fingers. "All of my lab animals . . . died when their chips were removed. And that's the clincher, Curtis. You and the others will have to . . . remain chipped all your lives. The joke's . . . on you."

And she started to laugh, coughed, then started to choke, and Curtis stood and backed away from her, trying to understand the implications of what she'd said. *The joke's on you. Liar.*

But even as he stood there, struggling with unanswerable questions, something happened to her body. Her hands turned knotted, crippled, arthritic, and the skin burst with age spots, wrinkles, shriveling like something in a horror movie. Then the aging sped up her arms and down into her legs and up across her throat and into her face. In a flash, her hair went white, her gums began to bleed, her teeth loosened, she cried out in agony.

"Shoot me," she pleaded. "Fast." She tried to raise up on

her elbows, but her bones were now too brittle and her forearm snapped in two and the skin peeled away like tissue paper, bits of it lifting into the breeze along with strands of her white hair. She shrieked, a high-pitched sound that echoed endlessly across this empty place, and then her broken forearm simply disintegrated. The breeze lifted the dust away.

It happened so fast and his horror was so extreme, that he couldn't move, didn't breathe, just stared in abject terror at what was happening to her, fully aware that one day it might be his destiny as well.

Her feet crumbled next. She shrieked again. And then the decay swept up her legs and he couldn't stand the sounds she made, the sight of it, and he lurched forward and shot her through the head. Sixty seconds later, all that remained of her was a pile of clothes and a pair of shoes.

Curtis spun around and ran, ran across the emptiness as if he could escape his own future, and the dog raced alongside him, barking, whining, howling. And when he couldn't run another step, he fell to his knees in the soft grass, flung his arms around Sunny, and they transitioned.

Nora stared at Fenmore, stiff and still in the sands on Marconi Beach, the dawn light hesitant, playful, playing hide and seek with clouds. *This is the woman who fucked your life at age ten. Walk away. And walk away from the corrupt senator who now staggers to his feet shouting, "Wait, you gave me your word . . ." And walk away very fast so you and Kincaid can find a haven for yourselves and never look back.*

But she couldn't do it. The psychologist in her recognized that Lydia Fenmore was sliding into a catatonia from which she might never recover, that something in what Nora had said had snapped the final bit of sanity that held her together. So Nora went over to her and gathered Lydia in her arms and thought, *Take me to where she needs to go to understand what she needs to understand.* And she *reached* and *released* and . . .

. . . found herself in a mirrored aerobic room in who knew where or when. Half a dozen people were doing tai chi and all of them saw her in the mirror, stopped, turned, stared. The instructor—a tall, thin man whose body was all sinew and muscle—looked as stunned as everyone else, but recovered enough to say, "Who . . . are you?"

"Mr. Rodriguez?" Nora asked.

"Uh, yes . . ."

Nora set Lydia carefully on the floor and repeated words from a Jimi Hendrix song: *"When the power of love overcomes the love of power, then the world will know peace."* And even though Nora didn't love Lydia, even though she was the person who had threatened to kill her if her mother didn't cooperate, who had left her with such a desperate need for closure, she could now forgive and forget and move on.

"Lydia needs your help now," Nora said, and backed away from Lydia, from Rodriguez, and *reached* and *released*, as Rodriguez and his students stared at her, at Lydia, stunned, aghast, and *reached* and *released* and grasped Kincaid's outstretched hand on Marconi Beach.

Then everything became strange, chopped up, as though events were slammed and stuck in fast-forward. One moment she and Kincaid were in the lobby of the FBI building where they left Simone White and Senator Aiken, and in the next moment, she was on the run in Blue River, then in that Utica cemetery with Kincaid, then in Northampton, Cedar Key, and back on Marconi Beach. Everything raced past her, through her, offering her at every turn a choice, a voice, a decision.

And when time slowed down again, she was in her own time, in the living room of an apartment in Aruba, sitting on a couch with Kincaid. Curtis and Kat sat on the opposite couch, her brother and Di were sprawled on cushions on the floor, Sunny stretched between them. They were watching a DVD of *Connections,* their story told through the lens of Hollywood.

"They dissed the depth of my trauma," Kat grumbled when the DVD ended. "They really glossed over what the hell I went through in that basement."

"Bari didn't know about your trauma," Curtis said. "We never told her that part of it."

"I told her," Nora said. "It got edited out. You two were reunited, true love won out, welcome to Hollywood. And we still don't know what happened to Mariah." She looked pointedly at Curtis, but he said nothing. He had never revealed what had happened to Mariah, whether she was alive or dead, where he had taken her. She knew he would take that secret to the grave.

"She got eighty episodes," Curtis said. "I think that was important to her."

"Will the series ever be revived?" Di asked.

"I think it depends on how we live it from here on in," Kincaid replied, and glanced over at Nora. "What time do you want to leave tomorrow?"

"Ten?"

"Ridiculous," he balked. "By ten, the trade winds will be blowing furiously, it'll be hotter than hell, and you'll be melting, Nora. I say dawn."

Dawn, noon, sunset, did it really matter? Nora wondered. They would be going back to Blue River in the winter of 1695, around the time when the town's infamous witch trials and executions had begun, a period so dark, violent, and cruel it had rivaled the barbarism in Salem in 1692. Her mother had been deposited on the road leading into Blue River, left there with her clothes and currency for that era, with Tampax and soft contact lenses to last her a year, left there because a rival caterer in 1983 had pointed the finger at her and called her a subversive.

And she was only the first in a very long list of hits on Tyler's Web site about the disappeared.

Please help me, read one e-mail. *My fiancée disappeared in the fall of 1987 . . .*

My brother vanished in . . .

My cousin has been missing since . . .

My daughter, son, dad, mother, grandfather, grandmother, uncle, aunt, friend, lover . . .

Help me, please.

Their work was cut out for them.

But right now, at this moment in time, Kincaid stood and said, "How about a walk?"

Sunny heard that word, *walk,* and beat Kincaid to the door.

The three of them stepped outside, onto the porch where the wind blew, shaking the palms and strumming the divi-divi trees. They headed out through the old trees of what had once been a coconut palm plantation. For now, it was the place they called home.

In the fall of 2008,
Pinnacle Books
will be delighted to present
a terrifying new thriller
from
T. J. MacGregor.
Please turn the page for a preview.

Aruba, March 15, 2007, 3:33 a.m.
Alex Kincaid bolted upright, listening hard for the noise that had awakened him. But all he heard was the island's music, that strange, rhythmic beat that played here 24/7—wind shaking the trees like tambourines, then strumming the branches as though they were the strings of Jimi Hendrix's guitar.

His fingers twisted around a corner of the damp sheet and he swung his legs over the side of the bed. Even though the window was open, the air conditioner was also on, his and Nora's concession to his need for fresh air and her insistence on comfort at night. The apartment's AC unit hummed and clattered and he had to concentrate to find the noises beneath and behind this sound and that of the wind. The soft cries of the parched earth, the sad and lonely howl of a stray dog, the crash of waves against the nearby beach, the squeal of tires against the road: business as usual.

Any messages or codes preserved within nature's under-currents were apparently meant for senses more sharply honed than his. The wind ruled, end of story. Just as he started to stretch again, the dog growled, low menacing growls that signaled danger. And it was close.

Kincaid quickly joined Sunny at the window. The golden retriever's paws rested on the sill, her ears twitched, she kept growling. He ran his fingers through her fur, which stood straight up along the length of her spine. "What is it, girl?" he whispered.

She whimpered and licked his hand and kept staring out into the moonlit field one story below. The misshapen branches of the divi-divi trees swayed in the wind like hula dancers. Off to the right stood an abandoned school bus, windows busted out, the front squashed in like an accordion. Beyond the field lay the road that looped around the island. On the other side of the road rose the first of the resort hotels, grand, sprawling places, most of them American, that were the heart of the island's economy.

At this hour of the night, there wasn't even a car in sight.

He started to turn away, but Sunny barked, an event rare enough so that he glanced back, frowning. "It would be so great if you could learn to speak English," he said.

She dropped her paws to the floor and trotted over to the bed, waking Nora, Sunny's version of a dog snub. Who needed English?

"You have to go out, Sunny?" Nora murmured sleepily.

"I'll take her out," Kincaid said, even though he doubted this was about a need to pee.

Whimpers, another bark, then the dog seemed to be staring at something in the hall and suddenly shot through the bedroom doorway.

Now he was spooked. Kincaid peered through the window again, and *saw* what Sunny had sensed, several figures making their way through the moonlight, toward the old bus.

Kids? Not at this hour.

Thieves? Possibly. But thieves would target lone houses in neighborhoods, not a cluster of apartments that catered to windsurfers.

"What is it?" Nora whispered.

"I'm not . . ."

Something shot through the open window, eclipsing the rest of his sentence. "Grab Sunny," he shouted. "They've found us!"

Nora vaulted out of bed and sprinted through the bedroom door. Kincaid lunged toward the dresser, snatched up his and Nora's packs, and raced after her, one hand covering his mouth and nose as a canister rolled across the floor, spraying tear gas everywhere. He kicked the door shut, ducked into the bathroom and snapped towels off the rack, then pressed them up against the crack under the door.

It might buy them a few moments.

Already, the tear gas seeped into the towels and in minutes the front door probably would burst open. Fortunately, they were in the process of moving out of Waverunner, the apartment complex where they had been living these past months, and most of their belongings were in the new place they had rented in Santa Cruz, thirty minutes inland. They also had cleared all the syringes out of the freezer and taken them inland as well. So whoever had shot the tear gas canister, he thought, was welcome to whatever remained in the apartment.

The glow of the night-light plugged into the wall under the living room window provided enough illumination for him to see Nora checking the dead bolt and chain on the front door, her cell pressed to her ear. She spoke in a hushed, urgent tone, warning the others, telling them to get out of their apartments now. Sunny had found her Frisbee and carried it in her mouth as she moved closer to Nora. She knew the drill. They all did.

Kincaid swept Sunny's leash off the coffee table and paused long enough to part the blinds with his fingers and peer outside. From here, he could see the moonlit parking lot, the lush vegetation that surrounded the swimming pool off to the left, and the row of hedges that ran along the wall on the right, marking Waverunner's property line. The figures came from that direction, materializing from the shadows with the stealth of the assassins they were.

He counted half a dozen of them, all wearing dark clothes. No telling what agency they were from, which country, which rogue group. It didn't matter. They ran, hunkered over, through the moonlight, crossing the parking lot and vanishing into the trees around the pool.

"Here they come," he said, and hurried over to Nora and Sunny, both of them crouched now against the far wall. He passed Nora her pack, she slung it over her head, then adjusted it so the pack rested against her hip.

"We'll meet them at the house three hours ago," she whispered, and wrapped one arm across Sunny's back.

The front window shattered. The explosion of glass tinkled like wind chimes when it struck the tile. Three tear gas canisters rolled across the living room floor. The stuff spread so quickly that within seconds, Kincaid's eyes watered, his lungs burned, the dog wheezed, and Nora stifled a violent spasm of coughing. A heartbeat later, a fourth canister slammed into the wall behind the couch, spewing tear gas that spread quickly through the air pouring out of the AC vents.

Kincaid grasped Nora's hand and flung his other arm across the dog's back. "We're outta here."

ROCKET MAN

Jan L. Coates

Red Deer Press

Published in Canada by Red Deer Press, 195 Allstate Parkway, Markham, ON, L3R 4T8
www.reddeerpress.com

Published in the U.S. by Red Deer Press, 311 Washington Street, Brighton, Massachusetts 02135

Edited for the Press by Peter Carver
Text and cover design by Daniel Choi
Cover image courtesy of iStockphoto

We acknowledge with thanks the Canada Council for the Arts, and the Ontario Arts Council for their support of our publishing program. We acknowledge the financial support of the Government of Canada through the Canada Book Fund (CBF) for our publishing activities.

 Canada Council for the Arts   Conseil des Arts du Canada    ONTARIO ARTS COUNCIL CONSEIL DES ARTS DE L'ONTARIO
50 YEARS OF ONTARIO GOVERNMENT SUPPORT OF THE ARTS
50 ANS DE SOUTIEN DU GOUVERNEMENT DE L'ONTARIO AUX ARTS

Library and Archives Canada Cataloguing in Publication
Coates, Jan, 1960-, author
    Rocket man / Jan L. Coates.
Issued in print and electronic formats.
ISBN 978-0-88995-494-6 (pbk.).--ISBN 978-1-55244-327-9 (epub).--
ISBN 978-1-55244-328-6 (pdf)
    I. Title.
PS8605.O238R62 2014   jC813.6   C2014-902102-X
                                            C2014-902103-

Publisher Cataloging-in-Publication Data (U.S.)
Coates, Jan L.
    Rocket man / Jan L. Coates
[120] pages : col. ill. ; cm.

Summary: Thirteen-year-old Bob has a lot of challenges to face: the school bully, the feeling that he would be better off invisible, and above all, the reality that his father is suffering from inoperable brain cancer. But Bob's keen desire to play basketball – and help his father – transforms his life.
ISBN-13: 978-0-88995-494-6 (pbk.)
1. Coming of age – Juvenile fiction. 2. Bullying – Juvenile fiction. 3. Father and son – Juvenile fiction. I. Title
[Fic] dc23   PZ7.C6384Ro 2014

10 9 8 7 6 5 4 3 2 1
Printed and bound in Canada

MIX
Paper from
responsible sources
FSC
www.fsc.org   FSC® C016245

For Liam,
and for basketball fans,
players, and benchwarmers,
and for families learning to live with cancer

*A hero is an ordinary individual
who finds the strength to persevere and endure
in spite of overwhelming obstacles.*

– Christopher Reeve (Superman)